I0628722

THE SECRET KEEPER LETS GO

(THE SECRET KEEPER SERIES BOOK 5)

BREA BROWN

Copyright © 2019 by Wayzgoose Press. (Note: An earlier, slightly modified edition of this novel, with the same title, was originally published in 2013, ISBN 978-1983005480.)

All rights reserved.

No part of this book may be reproduced in any form or by any electronic or mechanical means, including information storage and retrieval systems, without written permission from the publisher, except for the use of brief quotations in a book review.

Cover design by Keri Knutson at alchemybookcovers.com

Second edition ISBN: 978-1-938757-66-2

CONTENTS

For the vast community of women's fiction writers. We are a force with which to be reckoned.

HERE WE GO AGAIN!

"*H*oly, Holy, Holy, Holy—"

Shit! I think my water just broke. Either that, or that extra glass of orange juice I drank with breakfast was a mistake for my poor, crowded, kicked-on bladder. No way. That's not pee. I'm not feeling any sense of relief, only wetness. Oh, great. Just great.

It would figure that I'd go into labor the day before my scheduled induction, and in such a public place, too. Not only am I at church, but it's inexplicably packed today. As in, it might as well be Christmas Eve or Easter, that's how many people are here today. Not sure what that's about, except that the weather is exceptionally mild. Maybe people were going stir crazy and didn't have anything better to do than go to church? Nah...

Back to the problem at hand—or bottom. Okay. Positive things: this water-breaking thing is more like a trickle than a gush; I'm wearing black; our three other children are in the nursery, so I'm not wrestling with any of them; it's almost time to go up to Communion (which is also a negative, but I'm viewing as a positive, as it's a chance for me to get Brice's attention to let him know what's happening); when

Communion's over, the service will be basically over; and last but not least...

I'm about to no longer be pregnant!!!

Oh, and...

We finally get to meet our new daughter!

Or son.

Whatever. I mean, God's will and all that. Healthy baby is Priority Number One, of course. Blah, blah, blah. It better be a girl!

I try to remain calm while Brice delivers the Words of Institution before inviting everyone to the Lord's table. I distract myself by scanning the crowd for my doctor, Dave Klein. There he is, way over on the north side of the sanctuary, which means he'll be one of the last people to take Communion, unfortunately.

Oh, well. What's a few more minutes? It'll be fine.

I think.

While I stand in line, waiting for my turn at the rail, I attempt to ignore the growing damp in my pants. I'm sure nobody can tell, and I'll simply slip from the sanctuary after Communion, rather than go back to my seat, where I'd have to sit in a puddle.

I chuckle at myself, observing how calm I am, like this is no biggie. Like I'm not going into labor in the middle of church. Like I'm not about to have a baby. Is this what it's come to? When going into labor is as ho-hum as standing in line at the post office, one has been pregnant too many times. Noted.

Please make it a girl, Lord, I pray, pushing aside the thoughts I'm supposed to be having before Communion— you know, about repentance and my salvation. I do that every week. I'm sure God will be okay with my thinking about something else just this once. These are extenuating circumstances.

Finally, I kneel at the rail, take my Communion wafer from Assistant Pastor Wes Anthony, and focus for ten seconds on the task at hand.

Brice comes by with the cup, but before he places it against my lips, I look up at him and whisper, "My water broke. Or is breaking. Dripping, sort of."

His initial response, "Take drink— What?" gets the attention of the communicants on either side of me.

I widen my eyes at him in an effort to convey, *Play it cool, Rev.*

He swallows loudly but resumes his delivery of my blessing before whispering back, "Go tell Dave. I'll, uh, finish up here and—"

"Relax."

Now I'm regretting telling him, but I was too excited to keep it to my—

Ow. That contraction meant business!

He takes in the grimace on my face. "Go in peace, and go find Dave."

He moves to the next person, his speech faster with each drink. "Take drink; this is the blood of Christ, shed for you for the forgiveness of your sins.

"TakedrinkthisisthebloodofChrist,shedforyoufortheforgivenessofyoursins.Takedrink.Takedrink."

I rise from the rail as soon as the contraction ends, but I'm not even to the back of the sanctuary when the next one starts building. I stutter-step and clutch at my back, but I keep moving, feeling Brice's eyes on me. By the time I get halfway to Dr. Klein, the sweat's popping on my brow, and I'm not feeling as calm and confident as when I first felt my wet panties.

A glance toward the front of the church confirms for me that Brice is still staring at me. After we make eye contact during my latest pause for breath, he turns to Pastor Anthony and whispers something.

Wes's head rises sharply, but his serene expression doesn't change. Not many things rattle the assistant pastor. I seem to be the one most capable of delivering the things that do, though. And I feel like I'm about to deliver a baby in the nearest pew.

Instead, I grip the back of it, concentrating on breathing deeply and riding out the contraction while the worshipers sing the distribution hymn around me, as if nothing's out of the ordinary. At the apex of the pain, while my eyes are squeezed shut, I feel a hand fall on my shoulder.

Dr. Klein's familiar voice whispers near my ear, "Hey. This kid in a hurry, or something?"

I smile weakly, grateful that I didn't have to walk all the way to him. "I think so."

"Then I think we better get you to the hospital."

The cramp fades, so I stand straight, instantly forgetting the urgency with the absence of the discomfort. "Oh. Well, I'm a little worried about my drippy pants."

"Your water broke?"

I nod. "But other than that, when I'm not having contractions, I'm okay."

He laughs. "Yeah. I'm sure. That's usually how it works. But they're only going to keep coming, faster and harder, until this baby's born. You know the drill."

"I don't want to be a bother," I state. "I'm sure you have other plans today. Our scheduled induction is tomorrow."

After shooting me an amused look, he pats my back, "I think you're worse off than I originally thought. Let's go."

"My purse. And my kids," I suddenly remember.

As if by magic, Mitzi and Jared appear at my side. My best friend murmurs, "It must be a girl. Maximum drama and urgency."

I repeat my worries about my purse in the pew and the boys in the nursery.

She rolls her eyes. "Don't worry. Jared and I will take care of everything. Let me go get your purse. Then we'll get Brice's keys from him so we have a way to get your kids home."

I nod. "Thanks. Are you guys available to babysit?"

"We'll squeeze you into our schedule," she replies. "Now, go have a baby."

Jared's releasing me from his bone-crushing hug when I see Marianne and Clark over his shoulder.

"We saw you guys back here when we were headed to our seats after Communion," Marianne explains.

I look up and, chagrined, see that a *lot* of people have noticed us on their way back to their seats. Most people are turned, looking at us. The organist continues to play the hymn, because she's above us in the loft and can't see us, but not many people are singing.

"Oh, hell," I mutter. "Everyone needs to stop staring at me."

"Well, let's go, then," Dr. Klein suggests. "The way those contractions are hitting you, we don't have much time before you'll have the urge to push."

"Really? I thought we'd have at least a few hours."

"This guy—or gal—is ready. And your body knows what to do, with or without your help."

As Dr. Klein helps me into the backseat of his car (which he's covered with a plastic grocery bag to protect it from my soggy ass... classy), Brice catches up to us with my purse, which doesn't match his shoes at all, I notice wryly. Smoothing his hair, he ducks into the backseat with me.

"You two thinking of leaving without me?" he asks, nerves making his voice shake.

"If need be," Dr. Klein says. "We need to get to the hospital right now."

"Yeah, this hurts," I say through gritted teeth. "I need my drugs."

Dr. Klein laughs as he looks over his shoulder to reverse from the parking space. "That's probably not happening."

"What?"

"I don't mean to scare you, but let's just put it this way: if you feel the need to bear down, tell me right away so I can pull over and help you birth that baby."

"In the car?" Brice and I cry together.

"It happens," Dr. Klein says with a shrug in his voice. "Or so I've heard. I've never helped deliver a baby outside of the hospital. Well, there was that one time in one of the exam rooms at my office. That lady didn't even know she was pregnant, though. Talk about a wild day."

Brice squeezes my hand. "It'll be okay. Just breathe… and stuff."

Speeding through the streets toward the hospital, Dr. Klein turns on his hands-free mobile device and uses voice activation to call the ER. As he explains the situation to the person on the other end of the line, he pauses every once in a while to get information from me.

"She's been having contractions for…"

"Well, since yesterday morning, I guess. But they were—"

"Twenty-four hours," Dr. Klein says toward the phone's speaker.

"Since yesterday? You never said—" Brice begins.

"And her water broke."

Ignoring Brice's incredulity, I concentrate on answering the doctor's questions. "At church. Like, fifteen minutes ago. But it's a slow leak, not—"

"Fifteen minutes. I've observed three contractions— strong, long ones—since then. I need a delivery suite prepped for me now, in the ER. I don't have time to get her upstairs. This is her third—rather, fourth—pregnancy. We're close to delivery time."

Suddenly unable to hold back my hysterical giggles, I look over at Brice, but he's not laughing. He's pale. And sweaty. And his eyes are fluttering, like he's having a hard time staying awake.

"Are you okay?" I ask between chortles. "This is crazy, isn't it?"

He grimaces. "Yeah. Uh, insane." His right hand fumbles with the window controls on the door next to him. "Just need some air. Feeling sorta carsick."

"Don't puke on me," I demand.

Leaning away, lifting his face toward the cool, fresh air streaming through the two-inch crack at the top of the window, he replies, "I won't. Don't worry about me."

The next contraction is already building, so I don't have a choice about what will be getting my attention for the next minute or so. The queasy man in the backseat with me is going to have to get a grip.

I can see, off in the distance, the tallest tower of the hospital, so I focus on it while I breathe through the discomfort and try my hardest not to think about pushing a baby from my hoo-hah with no epidural.

She's going to be beautiful and worth it, no matter how much it hurts, I tell myself. *And it will be over soon. Very soon, if Dr. Klein is right. Holy mother shitdamnballs, this hurts!!!*

I stomp my foot, bite my lip, and utter a "Mmmmph!" that catches Dr. Klein's attention.

"Another one already?" he asks, accelerating through a yellow light.

Assuming his question is mostly rhetorical, I merely sit forward and rest my forehead against the back of his headrest. Focusing on the hospital tower isn't as helpful as I'd hoped it would be.

"Pastor, you okay back there?"

Brice mutters a lackluster, "Yeah. I don't like riding in backseats, that's all."

"We're almost there, folks. I'm going to drop you at the ER entrance, where they're supposed to be waiting for you. I'll meet back up with you after I scrub."

"Whatever!" I say, grinding my teeth.

Ohmigosh, why do men insist on talking nonstop when there's a laboring woman present? It's like they think they can remain in control as long as they're talking. But really, it just makes the pregnant woman homicidal. I want to yank this baby from between my legs, cut the cord, and throw the placenta at the talking person's head!

Finally, the bands around my abdomen begin to loosen, little by little. The pressure in my head lessens, the sharp jabbing between my legs goes on hiatus, and I feel like a normal person again.

I take a deep, steadying breath and laugh. "Whoa. That was a bad one." I pant for a while, then smile in Brice's direction. "This is awful, but it'll be over soon, right? You still look like you're about to be sick. Are you okay? I— Oh, crap. Here comes another one."

Dr. Klein pulls into the circle driveway in front of the ER doors, where a stout guy in scrubs waits with a wheelchair. Unfortunately, I'm not moving from this car while feeling like this. I resume my death grip on the driver's seat.

When the car stops, Brice leans closer to me, "Honey, we're here."

I swat blindly in the general direction of his face, perversely glad when I make decent enough contact that I hear a slap.

"Ow. It's okay," he simultaneously flinches and forgives.

"Not sorry," I growl. "Back off!"

"Oh. Okay. I'll, uh, come around that side of the car and—"

"I don't need an effing play-by-play, Brice! Just... shhhhh!"

Too soon, he's opening my door from the outside, offering his hand to me. "Come on, now. The wheelchair's right here. You need to scoot a few—"

"Fuck off!" I growl, not caring that I'm saying it to someone in a clerical collar in front of a complete stranger.

The guy "driving" the wheelchair offers quietly, "Give her a few seconds, Father. She'll get out when she's ready. Or you and I can lift her."

"Don't touch me!" I say in a voice scarily reminiscent of a beefy, bald Batman villain.

Dr. Klein rolls down his window and tells the nurse, "He's not a priest, he's *the* father. Who happens to be a pastor."

"Oh. Sorry about that. I forget that a lot of you guys wear those... things," the nurse says, patting his throat.

"No problem," Brice replies. "I'm used to being mistaken for—"

"You guys really need to shut up!" I beg, close to tears.

Fortunately, they comply without question. As soon as the tide of pain wanes to manageable levels, I abandon my damp perch, barely noticing and definitely not caring when the plastic bag sticks to my butt.

I shoot both my husband and the be-scrubbed stranger a contrite look and sincerely say while transferring myself to the wheelchair, "Gosh, guys. I'm so sorry! It's just— It's seriously the worst thing I've felt in my life!" I punctuate this with a laugh, like it's also the funniest thing I've ever experienced.

"We get it," the nurse assures me. "Hang on, now. I'm going to wheel you as quickly as possible where you need to be so you can get undressed and in bed before the next one." To Brice, he directs, "Keep up with me, dude."

2

OH, BABY!

*T*hirty minutes and surprisingly few curse words later, we have a baby.

"It's a boy!" Dr. Klein crows, as if he had anything to do with it. (And before *that* rumor starts, he didn't, by the way.)

Nearly delirious from a level of pain I didn't even realize was possible to survive, I crane my sweaty neck and say, "Oh, she's so cute! Look at her! Wait. She has a penis." I grab Brice's forearm and pull, bringing his face closer to mine. "She has a penis," I repeat. "Why does she have a penis?"

He smiles sheepishly. "I think it's because *she's* a *he*. Just an educated guess."

"But— No. She can't be a he. She has to be a *she*."

Suddenly, the squalling, red-faced, ding-dong-possessing baby is plunked onto my chest by someone who thinks I'm physically capable of holding an infant right now.

"Look, Mama!" the clueless nurse says in one of those grating Southern accents that my Yankee brain can rarely understand. "You've got yourself a brand new baby boy who'll probably worship the ground you walk on!"

I instinctively bring my arms up to hold the squirming, squalling, naked baby, but my eyes remain locked with Brice's, which are reddening and filling with tears. Mine follow suit, but probably not for the same reasons.

He cups his hand over the back of the baby's head but leans closer to my ear and says, "It's okay to be disappointed, but no despair allowed."

I blink and nod while he brushes his lips against my cheek.

"He's beautiful," he whispers, "just like his mom."

The tears flow freely now, but I study the baby for the first time, as if to verify my husband's claim. I don't know about the comparison to me—he looks remarkably like the other three, who are clones of their father—but he *is* cute. At least, I'm sure he will be when he stops screaming and peeing all over everything and everyone.

"Oh, now," I cluck at him. "It's not so bad. Your brothers have done most of the hard work training us, so you're in good hands."

Brice rubs a knuckle along the newborn's cheek before Dr. Klein summons him for the ceremonial cord cutting. (What is the deal with that tradition, anyway? If I were a dad, I'd want no part of that. Gross!) As soon as the disgusting deed is done, the nurses take the baby "for just a second" to get his "specs," as Brice calls them.

Dr. Klein requests that I give him one more push to birth the placenta. Then I'm allowed to fall back against the damp pillow behind me and rest as much as I can with my uterus still contracting like it hasn't received the memo that the baby has vacated its premises. I've decided I didn't miss anything with the other three deliveries, and I never want to do this spontaneous, drug-free birth thing again.

I turn my head to watch the two nurses measure, weigh, and swaddle my son. The nameless child.

Oh, gosh. What are we going to name him? Foolishly, I've only thought of girls' names for the past nine months. I was so sure he was a girl, even though all the older ladies at church said I was carrying like it was a boy. I summarily ignored them and went about my fantasy-filled gestation. I even bought a baptismal gown for her. Him. Whatever.

They bring him back to us, but I defer to Brice, who I know is dying to hold him. I ask one of the nurses to get a picture of the three of us. She takes several shots, even a few of Brice by himself, and I do my best to pretend this is normal. Like I'm as happy as I was with the other three. Like I'm as happy as I'd be if he were a girl.

Because I *am* happy. A little *less* happy than I thought I'd be, but still happy.

I'm sure I'll snap out of it as soon as I spend some time alone with the little guy. And figure out what to call him. And return that dress. Crap. It was outrageously expensive, but I impulsively splurged on it, because it was for my only baby girl.

Brice interrupts my suddenly urgent attempts to recall the online boutique's return policy by asking, "You want to hold him now that it's quieter in here?"

Sure enough, the room has emptied. Brice is holding a bottle to the baby's lips, but the infant doesn't seem that interested.

I imagine he's thinking, *What the heck is happening? There I was, minding my own business, floating around, and it's like someone pulled the plug! I started feeling heavier and heavier; then I was being squeezed through a tunnel into this cold, bright place, and all these people are manhandling me and staring at me, and now they want me to eat? Not likely!*

Exhausted, I nevertheless nod and hold open my arms.

"He's a little one," I say, finally feeling that familiar, maternal tug. "What did the nurse say? Six-nine?"

Brice nods. "I think." He checks the card on the rolling bassinet. "Yep. Six pounds, nine ounces, eighteen inches. Compact guy. Not much bigger than each of the twins."

The "compact guy" squints at me through the gel on his eyes.

"Hi," I say. "You decided to calm down and take stock of your surroundings?"

He blinks and yawns.

Brice laughs. "I don't think he's impressed."

"I don't blame him."

We stare at him for a while longer, trying to figure out which of the boys he looks most like, comparing eye, nose, and brow shapes.

Suddenly, Brice says, "I'm sorry I didn't tell you."

Thinking we're still talking about our newest child's physical characteristics, I drop my jaw, lost. "Huh?"

"I thought it would be better for you to find out on delivery day, like you planned."

I catch up to the fact that he's talking about *him* being a *her*, but I'm still confused. "What do you mean, you thought it would be better? You *knew*?"

He blinks at me, as if I've lost my mind, not the other way around. "Yes. Of course I knew."

"What? How? You saw it on the ultrasound?"

With wary patience, he says, "Nooo, I *saw* him, remember?" When I continue to look blankly at him, hoping he doesn't try to tell me the Pastor Kit now includes X-ray vision, he sighs. "At the urologist's office. I *saw* that we were going to have another boy, but—"

"*That's* what you saw? And you didn't tell me?"

"I knew you'd be disappointed then, but I was working off your theory about being too happy when he arrived to be disappointed, so I thought it was better not to tell you."

I blink rapidly.

"You *said* you didn't want to know!" he reminds me.

"But *you* knew!"

"Well, yes. You knew that, though. At least, I thought you knew that I knew."

"How would I know you knew?"

"Because I told you I saw it."

After pausing to count to ten and recite the Serenity Prayer (*this is supposed to be a happy day, damn it!*), I point out, "But you never told me exactly what you saw, just that whatever it was made you go back on your promise to do what needed to be done to make sure I never again have to almost have a baby in the back of someone's car. With no drugs!"

"You don't believe I saw anything that day, anyway, so if I'd told you, would you have believed me?" he asks gently.

"Maybe!"

I can tell he's not buying it, but he sounds sincere enough when he says, "Then I'm sorry."

"You're sorry."

"Yes, I'm sorry. I should have told you. Or I should have at least asked if you wanted to know, but I assumed I knew that you didn't want to know. Because you told me as much."

"That's when we *both* didn't know."

"I didn't realize it made a difference."

"But you never said a *word*. You never let on at all! You — How did you keep it a secret?"

He shrugs. "I dunno. It was only for the past couple of months."

While I swallow back tears, he hurries ahead. "But, hon. Trust me. This is okay."

"I know it is! It's more than okay! I love this baby!"

I sound like I'm trying to convince myself more than anyone else, but so what? I'm not the one who withheld such important information.

"How could you let me get my hopes up like that?" I ask, still thinking about that beautiful, intricate baptismal gown hanging in the closet of the more-feminine-than-masculine unisex nursery at home.

Oh. My. Gosh. The nursery! He insisted we go with the turquoise-and-brown motif, even though I thought yellow was cheerier (and more girly). But he wouldn't back down. At the time, I thought he had taken a sudden, unexpected interest in interior design. Now I know he simply thought yellow was too fey for his latest Y-chromosome-carrying kid. Sexist jerk.

Before he can defend himself, a veritable team of nurses enters the room.

"All right, then," the Southern one in charge says. "We need to take the little one to the nursery for a while so y'all can get situated in a private room upstairs."

I readily hand over the baby and move to get out of the bed. I wish I could tell Brice to stay down here.

Placing a hand on my knee to hold me in place, the nurse drawls, "Sit tight, Sugar. You get to ride in style. We'll wheel you through the halls in your bed, lickety split."

Oh. Simply fabulous. Would it be weird if I hid under the covers?

～

Aidan Brannigan Northam is blissfully unaware of the cold war his penis has started between his parents.

When you have four children under the age of three, however, you can't very well *not* talk to your spouse, no matter how justified the silent treatment may be. It's impossible. But I'm only deigning to talk to Brice for the sake of the children. If it were just the two of us in our house, there'd be no talking whatsoever. Of course, if it were just the two of us, we wouldn't be in this quasi-argument to begin with.

He's trying to get back in my good graces, but he should know by now that it's not going to be as easy as "letting" me name our newest son one of my "Leprechaun" names. He didn't have much choice there, anyway, because I refused to name him anything Brice came up with during the two months he *knew* we were going to have a son but *assumed* I wouldn't want to know.

Anyway, Aidan and his male member are assimilating well into our household. That is, he's adding quite nicely to the chaos as he trains us to tend to his every whim. He also has his older brothers—except Brooks—wrapped around his tiniest finger.

Brooks isn't giving up the "Baby" title without a fight. A big fight. I have to keep a close eye on the fifteen-month-old when he's around his new sibling. His murder weapon of choice seems to be anything he can fit up the newborn's nose. Fortunately, it's a tiny orifice, so Brooks has been unable to find anything small enough for the job. I know it's only a matter of time before he moves on to other, possibly more effective strategies, though.

Suddenly, Max's new and mostly annoying position as family tattletale is coming in handy. If only we could get through to him that telling us everything repeatedly, even after we've acknowledged his statements, is unnecessary, it would be slightly *less* annoying when he's informing us about something potentially life-saving regarding his younger brothers. But Max prefers to drive the point home, whether he's telling us that the twins aren't praying at the dinner table or that Brooks is trying to murder Aidan or that he, himself, requires a diaper change.

Which reminds me... What were we thinking when we decided it would be okay to listen to the "experts" and let a three-year-old decide when he was ready to potty train? No. Experts, you are wrong. When one is ready to pop out Baby #4, the oldest child doesn't get a choice about ditching the diapers. He can bitch about me to his therapist and blame all of his adult problems on me, but I'm not wiping four asses multiple times a day. Unfortunately, I only did the math *after* I brought home the fourth ass.

Therefore, we're force-toilet-training Max now that we have a newborn in the house. And by that, I mean, we'd be as successful trying to use The Force as we have been with our slap-dash method of "Do you have to go? No? Okay. You already went in your diaper, didn't you?" and, "You're not getting off that potty until you go. Oh, all right! If you'll stop screaming, you can get down."

Like I said before, the adults aren't doing a lick of training in this house.

The only kid who's not being intentionally difficult (because let's face it, newborns choose to be a pain, and nobody can convince me otherwise) is Harris. Like his twin, Brooks, though, he's fifteen months old. That, in itself, makes him higher-maintenance than I need him to be right now. The funny thing is, he's showing more interest in potty training than Max is. The *un*funny thing is that he shows it by undressing himself, taking off his diaper, and peeing and pooping wherever he happens to be, which is never in the bathroom.

Aidan is only a week old, and I'm already exhausted. One or more of us isn't going to make it through his first year alive. Or sane.

Which is why it's nearly impossible for me to hold a grudge against Brice. At this point, I've almost forgotten what was so bad about what he did. I know it was bad, because every time I think about it, my eyeballs jiggle in their sockets from the spike in my blood pressure, but I can't put my finger on *why* I'm still so mad at him.

I *didn't* want to know the baby's sex beforehand. The whole point was for me not to worry or fret or bemoan what now seems the inevitability that I will forever be outnumbered in this family of phalluses. I wanted to be blissfully unaware. I wanted to believe, even if only for thirty-something weeks, that there was the possibility I'd be holding a sweet, pink, penis-less baby girl on delivery day. I would have been furious with Brice if he'd tried to burst my bubble, especially based on his ridiculous pre-vasectomy, valium-induced vision, which we both know was a cop-out so he wouldn't have to get snipped that day.

Okay, that's not true. We don't *both* know it. He believes what he saw, whatever it was. I now know part of it was that our unborn child at the time was a boy. Big whoop. He had a fifty-fifty chance of getting that right.

What I don't know is what else he saw that made him hop down from that operating table. It had to be more than just, "We're having another boy." If anything, that news would make him more determined to stop the reproduction train. No, he must have seen *more* than Aidan. But that means...

Uh-uh. He's out of his vision-seeing gourd if he thinks I'm having any more babies. No way, José, Mary, and Jesus. Nope. If he ever wants to put his special friend anywhere near my now-defunct baby chute, he's having that procedure. His little don't-ask-don't-tell stunt about Aidan's gender identity sealed that deal.

Oh, who am I kidding? He said "three years." When he backed out of that vasectomy, he asked me to wait three years before taking permanent birth control methods. Three years. I can't abstain that long. We'll have to trust other methods—and God—until then. Not a problem for the pastor, obviously, but I'm scared to death.

Three years of living in fear and celebrating every one of my next thirty-six periods seems like forever, but it will be over in a sleep-deprived flash. Or fog.

Max is proof of that. While it seems he's always been a part of our lives, it also feels like only yesterday that we brought him home, both of us amazed and terrified and overwhelmed by the new responsibility in our lives. *That* was nearly three years ago.

Before we know it, Aidan will be talking non-stop, tattling on everything from his brothers to the dust bunnies under the coffee table, and thwarting our efforts to potty train him.

Brice won't want to start all over again with another baby at that time. He'll be forty. We'll both be seeing the beautiful, diaper-free light at the end of the tunnel. He'll conquer his fear of the vasectomy and do the right thing, accepting God's answer and giving up this silly "vision" nonsense, seeing it for what it was: not faith, but a hallucination.

That will be a hard thing for him to accept, though. I'll have to be here for him. My heart preemptively hurts for him when I think about it. I must be getting soft in my older age. Or, possibly, lack-of-sleep is hindering my better grudgement.

Whatever it is, with every cup of half-caff coffee he sets on the bathroom counter for me while I'm in the shower, with every midnight feeding he assumes, with every outing he takes with the other boys so that my ears can stop ringing, and with every kiss he places on the back of my neck when he thinks I'm dead asleep, my ice-encased heart is melting, bit-by-bit.

Why am I mad at him, again?

3

MITZI'S NEWS

*T*here's a distinct benefit to never having been a decent hostess: when you have a new baby, and people come over to visit you, they expect even less than usual from you, which is good, because I'm too tired to even offer my guests a glass of water. It's only Mitzi, Jared, Clark, and Marianne, anyway.

Plus what's wrong with Brice? Last time I checked, he had two working legs, so if it's that important to be hospitable, he can play bartender.

Yes, I'm mad at him again. I think my ambivalence directly correlates to fluctuations in hormone levels and the amount of sleep I've managed to steal in the past twenty-four hour period. At this moment, the Hormone Level is "Threat," and the Sleep Tally is "Zero," so he's pretty much shit out of luck.

Honestly, I'm just trying to get through this social visit without crying, cursing, springing a leak in one or both boobs, or falling asleep in the middle of the conversation.

Mitzi guarantees the latter won't happen when she murmurs while holding Aidan and stroking his head, "I guess I'd better get a lot of practice with this guy, since Jared and I are going to have one of our own in a few months."

She exchanges a knowing look with Marianne, who scrunches her shoulders around her ears and grins.

My heart skips several beats. "Oh my gosh! Really? You're pregnant?"

Mitzi nods, fanning her face with her free hand. Blushing, she says, "Oh, sheesh. I cry about everything! Don't mind me."

"Congratulations, guys!" Brice booms.

I shoot him a dirty look for being so loud while the older boys are napping, but he doesn't see me, because his back's turned to me as he hugs Jared, then leans down to give Mitzi a kiss on the cheek.

"You guys are going to be such great parents!" he gushes. "When's the due date?"

I'm not thrilled with the volume of his voice, but I'm glad he's doing the talking for both of us, because I'm too speechless and overcome with emotion to ask any of the dozens of questions I have.

"End of August," Mitzi answers, still beaming from ear-to-ear through her happy tears.

I glance at her belly and realize with dismay that *I* look more pregnant than she does, even though—pause to do the math—she's in her second trimester already!

"Good planning," Brice says to Jared. "Slow time in the church year. Peyton and I don't seem capable of having babies outside of the Lenten, Advent, Easter, or Christmas seasons." He winks at me. "We need to work on that, hon."

I chuckle weakly. *Work on it yourself with your new wife, your hand.*

The next thing I notice is that Marianne doesn't have to

ask any questions, because it's obvious she already knows all this. Before me.

Clearing my throat, I try to inject sunshine into my tone when I ask, "Does Jen know?"

Mitzi beams. "Oh, yeah! She's super-stoked."

"I see." Icicles dangle from the two short words. I thrust my chin at Marianne. "And *you* know."

She nods warily.

"Well, that's nice. So, I'm the last to know."

Jared jumps in, pushing his glasses higher on his nose. "That wasn't by design, though. We, uh, wanted to wait until we were sure everything was... okay. And by then, you were in the hospital, having this guy. We didn't want to steal your thunder."

I suck my left cheek through my teeth and bite on it while I hold back the tears. I keep my eyes pinned to my lap. Finally, composed, I look up and smile.

"Of course. That was so thoughtful. And I'm happy for you two. I'm so damn happy." To my horror, I dissolve into wet, messy, square-mouthed crying. "I'm sorry!" I sputter. "Excuse me."

I rush to the powder room, close the door, and collapse onto the toilet.

And nearly fall in, because *someone* didn't put the lid down the last time they used it. Catching myself before I hit the water requires muscles I either haven't used in a while or that are still tender or swollen from childbirth.

"Mother fudgemaker," I hiss, almost as annoyed that I denied myself the release of saying the real word as I am at the need to use it. I've been married to Reverend Bleep-Machine for too long.

Using the small pedestal sink for leverage, I pull myself from the toilet and softly lower the lid. Gingerly, I sit, acknowledging that it was probably a blessing the lid was up, because if I'd plopped onto the closed toilet as hard as I'd intended, I most surely would have busted my tender vittles.

I don't want to see anything positive about this, though. I'm crying in the half-bath, while a roomful of adults sits on the other side of the door, wondering what the hell is wrong with me and how they should deal with me.

Apparently, Brice lost the rock-paper-scissors match (on our wedding day) to determine who would come check on me, but I answer his timid knock with, "I'm fine! I'll be out in a minute. Talk amongst yourselves."

A few seconds later, the door inches open, but instead of Brice's face through the crack, it's Mitzi's button nose I see.

"Can I come in?" she asks sweetly.

I want to tell her no, but I feel like I've used up all my "horrible" on her for the day. Instead of saying yes, I say nothing and simply wait for her to enter.

I regret my decision when she closes the door behind her and turns to me with that sympathetic face I know so well.

"Don't," I tell her. "Don't pity me or be understanding or... whatever. I don't deserve it. I'm being inexcusably rude. And I'm embarrassing the hell out of myself in the process. I'm such a mess right now."

She wraps her arms around me. "You're not the boss of me. I'll do whatever I want. I'm about to be a mom, you know."

I snort against her abdomen. "Yes. A good one, too. And you and Jared are going to have the cutest baby. Or babies."

"It's only one. That we know of."

"Oh. Yeah. I was talking about future ones, too."

She laughs. "I think I'd like to make it through this one first, before I think about future ones."

I pull away from her and look into her face. "Are you sick all the time?"

"I was. It's getting better."

"I missed it," I lament, on the verge of tears once more. "Not that I wanted to witness you suffering, but you know what I mean. I wasn't there for you. You had to go it alone."

"I do have a husband," she reminds me. "He's good with a washcloth. And he can open a sleeve of crackers in record time. Same with a two-liter of ginger ale. Quick on the draw."

I smile at the image of Jared wearing a holster, a sleeve of crackers in one side and a jug of soda in the other.

"I'm sure he's been great. And Marianne, too."

"You're hurt I told her before you."

When I shrug, not only because I feel petty admitting it, but also because I can't answer without crying, she sighs.

"She guessed. A long time ago. I couldn't lie. But I made her promise not to tell you before I had a chance. This is the first time it's felt right to tell you. And even now, I know it wasn't. I should have waited until you and I were alone."

"Waited even *longer*?"

"Maybe. That's just it; I couldn't wait another minute, even if it meant telling you in front of other people. It's my fault you got so upset." She puddles up.

I sniff and pull two tissues from the box on the back of the toilet. "Oh, Lord. Now we're both going," I say, handing one of the tissues to her and dabbing under my eyes and nose. "No more crying, okay? Let's go out there and pretend like nothing happened. I do it all the time."

She laughs wetly. "Yeah, Jared's told me a few stories. Which *you* never told me, by the way."

"They're mortifying."

"All the more reason to tell your best friend," she presses, offering me a hand up.

When we're both composed, she turns to me before opening the door. "I do have a question I've been too embarrassed to ask anyone else, even my doctor."

Before I can wonder what that could possibly be, she continues, "Is it normal to be so..." She lowers her voice to a whisper. "...*horny*? Like, all the time? I remember Brice saying something about that at a game night a while ago, but..." She blushes. "Jared can hardly keep up with me."

I bite my bottom lip to keep from laughing in her face. "You're fine," I say, when I have things under control. "It's all about hormones."

"But Marianne said—"

"Maybe *she's* the weird one. Ever think about that?"

Mitzi giggles. "Yeah, maybe."

"Enjoy it while you can without interruptions. And without weighing your horniness against your tiredness."

She looks worried. "Yeah. See, you and Brice look *really* tired right now. Like you'll never have the energy to have sex ever again."

"Maybe that's for the best." When she shoots me a questioning look, I smile shakily and wave a dismissive hand at her. "Just kidding. We better get back out there."

It's been a week since my humiliating performance during our friends' visit. I've been trying to be less crazy, but it's been disturbingly difficult. I'm starting to think something's seriously wrong with me. For real this time. Not because of anything I've looked up on WebDoctor, either.

Okay, I did look up "postpartum depression" to see if I

was a threat to myself or my children, but for once, the app ruled out a condition for me. I'm not *that* far gone. Yet.

It still shouldn't be this much of an effort to feel okay and behave normally. I'm more tired at night from putting on my happy act than I am from chasing around three toddlers and taking care of a newborn. That's not right.

My hope, though, is that it will cease to be an act eventually. Eventually, I'll be genuinely content again. Until then, I'm going to have to fake it.

Brice has turned off his light for the night, and I'm on my side, facing away from him, forcing myself to relax so I can get some sleep, when he leans across my body to look at my face in the semi-darkness.

I pretend to laugh at him, but I'm a little creeped out by his behavior.

"Since when is *this* a thing for us?" I ask.

"It's not. I'm checking on you," he says, as if it's the most logical response in the world.

"Checking my nostrils for lice?"

"Do you feel all right?"

I want to tell him the truth, but I'm too afraid of it.

Before I can even come up with a decent lie, though, he asks, "When was the last time we went on vacation?"

"Our honeymoon," I quickly supply.

"No way."

"Yes way."

"That's not acceptable."

I roll onto my back so he's no longer crushing my sternum. "It's your fault. You can never get away."

"Do you want to go on vacation with me?"

"Just the two of us?" I dab at the drool collecting in the corners of my mouth at the prospect.

He nods. "Yeah."

Reality hits me at the same time as the knowledge that I desperately need his proposed fantasy to come true.

Emotions clog my throat. "That would be so great. But what about the kids? They're so much work. I can't imagine anyone agreeing to stay with them while we took off for a week."

"Aw, come on. We have good kids! They're good for other people, anyway. And everyone loves them. I bet we could find some willing victims," he wheedles. "And we don't have to go right away. As a matter of fact, I think we should wait a few months, to give us time to make arrangements and save some money. But maybe this summer?"

I shake my head. "It's hopeless. And stupid to even dream about it. I'd feel bad, leaving the kids."

He sighs, seems to be thinking, opens his mouth, closes it, then says, "Do you feel good right now?"

The way he's looking at me, searching my eyes, I'm powerless to do anything but cry and shake my head.

He tilts his head as he swipes my tears from my face with his thumbs. "Oh, hon. You need a vacation."

"Why, though? What's wrong with me?"

"Nothing! Except you're tired."

"But lots of women do what I do. Lots of them do it with a lot more kids. And they're not on the verge of a mental breakdown. They don't need to leave their babies with someone so they can escape for a few days. Why am I so weak? Why can't I do this? Why?"

He presses his lips to my forehead. "Shhh. C'mon, now. Calm down."

I try to do what he says, but I'm releasing about a month of pent-up emotion that doesn't want to be suppressed anymore.

Over my crying, he says, "Everyone's built differently.

You do a lot of things that other women—and men—aren't able to handle. When you're working, you juggle being a mom and a wife with a job outside the home, and it always amazes me how well you balance it all."

"It's because I'll do anything to get away from here for a few hours."

"Okay, but you're making a valuable contribution to our family's finances, so I'm glad it's something you enjoy and look forward to doing every day."

"It's an excuse to not be a mom."

"So what?"

"That's wrong! I shouldn't want to get away from them."

"I guess I'm wrong, then."

"What do you mean? You're always happy when you're around them."

"How many hours a day is that?"

I think about it. "Well, only one or two on weekdays, but all day on your weekends."

"Not by myself. You're here with me Friday mornings and all day Saturday. I'm rarely alone with them."

"You take them out—the three oldest ones—by yourself all the time."

"I choose to do that, yes. And when I'm not in the mood, I don't." I simply stare at him until he says, "You see what I'm gettin' at here?"

"Not really."

He squishes my face between his hands. "You're alone with them a lot. And it's tiring. I'm tired after feeding them and getting them ready for bed on weeknights. And you're even here for part of that time." Letting go of my face, he rolls onto his back, grabs my hand, and stares at the ceiling. "Anyway, that's when things are normal. For the past month, you've been with all four of them non-stop. You need a break, whether we take a vacation or not."

"I guess I could get a facial or a pedicure or something during their naps this Saturday."

"Is that the best you can do?" He sounds amused.

I turn my head to look at him. His teeth glint in the darkness.

"What do you mean? It would be relaxing!"

"It would be a couple of hours, tops. I'm talking about something bigger."

"Like a whole day?"

"Like a whole weekend. My weekend, anyway. Friday and Saturday. Maybe a trip to Vegas with Mitzi or Jen or Marianne. Or all three. Or alone, even, if that's what you'd rather do. Away from here. Away from the kids. Away from me."

"You're sick of me."

He groans. "No. But tonight, I watched you sing ten verses of 'The Wheels on the Bus' while staring at a speck on the rug, long after Max, Harris, and Brooks had wandered off and stopped singing with you. It was terrifying."

"I did that?"

"Yes."

"Creepy."

"Totally. I wanted to tell you to stop, but I was too scared."

I laugh and wipe the last of the drying tears from my face. "No, I mean it's creepy that you were watching me."

He laughs, too. "Oh, that. Well, it was mesmerizing. I had no idea that song even had that many verses."

"Max and I made up some of our own," I divulge.

"Sometimes we can keep the twins entertained and still—and fully clothed—for up to twenty minutes by singing it."

"You'll have to teach me the extended version before you go on your fun weekend."

That brings me back to real life. "Oh. Yeah. About that. I can't do that."

"Why not?"

"That's not fair to you, to leave you with all four kids for two days. And I'd have to pump so much breast milk. Ugh. I hate pumping. It's been nice not having to do it this time around."

He lets go of my hand and rolls onto his stomach, wrapping his arms around his pillow. "Then wean him before you go. But you're going. And we're going on vacation this summer, you and me. Alone. To the beach. Maybe we'll fly to Florida and drop in on Vince. I'll handle everything."

"Brice, I—"

"I'm putting my foot down."

I can tell by the set of his jaw and the gleam in his eyes that he's not kidding. And he's not giving in.

I swallow. "Okay."

"Okay?"

"Yes." My heart flutters with something that feels suspiciously like hope. If I'm remembering that feeling correctly.

"Good." He rises on his elbows, leans over, and kisses my lips. "I love you. Goodnight."

"Love you, too. Goodnight," I say in a trance, already imagining what I'm going to do with my free time.

4

GIRLS' WEEKEND

*I*t's not Vegas, but I'm not much of a gambler, anyway, so a simple weekend in Kansas City with Mitzi and Marianne, doing girlie things, is fine with me. It's far enough away (about three hours) that I feel like we're actually away from home, but it's not so far that I feel like I've abandoned my family. It also helps that Brice's mom is there to give him a hand, if he needs it. Not that I expect him to.

When we were planning our trip a couple of weeks ago, two days seemed like forever to the three of us. Now that we're here, it looks as if we're not going to be able to do everything on our list. The one thing that will *not* be denied, though, is eating at the restaurant owned by television chef Lidia Bastianich. Our reservation is set for the minute we arrive in the city. It's Priority Number One.

Well, almost. My first priority after being stuck in the car for three hours and drinking a giant coffee this morning is to use the restroom. Mitzi accompanies me, but Marianne "Iron Bladder" Pryce opts to wait in the bar area and take in the atmosphere of the restaurant. My eyeballs are too busy floating to do any sightseeing.

Once Mitzi and I rejoin Marianne, the hostess leads us through the dining area, toward a grouping of tables in the large, airy room. She stops next to a table that seems to be occupied already by a woman with long, blonde hair. The hostess says something to her and gestures to the three of us. Before I can wonder too long about what's going on, the woman turns, and I see that it's Jen.

I come to a halt in the middle of the restaurant and stare at her grinning face. Mitzi and Marianne continue toward her, and both give her gentle, ladylike hugs when they arrive at the table. When they see I'm not with them, they turn and laugh at my reaction.

"Told you she'd be surprised," Jen says to the other two women.

I will not cry. I won't do it. The hormones will not *win this time.*

It's all I can do not to run the final distance to my best and oldest friend in the world, but I don't hold back with the massive hug I give her when I finally arrive in front of her.

She grunts with the force of the squeeze. "Geez, P. I'm glad I haven't eaten anything yet, or you'd make me barf."

"What are you doing here?" I cry, pulling away from her and dabbing at the persistent tears gathering in the corners of my eyes.

She sits, so we follow suit. Before she has a chance to answer my question, our waiter approaches us, rattles off a list of main courses, and takes our drink orders. He leaves us with menus, which we promptly ignore while Jen finally replies, "Someone told me that you three were having a fun weekend without boys and thinking of not including *me*."

"I told you about it, and you said you had stuff going on this weekend!" I say.

"Yeah! Flying here and hanging out with you guys. Plus, I need to meet my new quasi-nephew in person. *And...* Well, it would be nice to go on a real date with Wes, instead of falling asleep talking to him on Skype."

"His voice puts me to sleep, too," I mutter.

She pushes on my shoulder, but she's blushing when she picks up her menu to pretend to consider her options.

"I'm so glad you're here," I say more seriously, also using my menu as a distraction from my emotions.

Jen's presence is a pleasant surprise, so I don't let myself dwell on the fact that, once again, Marianne knew something before I did. Jen's participation in this weekend is obviously a gift, of sorts, to me, so it would be petty for me to focus on my paranoid feelings about being edged out of the group.

Plus, that's not what's happening, surely. Right?

Anyway, what matters is that we're all here together this weekend, and it's going to be more fun than I've had in... years.

As soon as our waiter returns with a basket of bread and several metal pots of various flavored butters, he takes our orders and directs us to the *antipasti* table, which bears an eye-popping amount of salad, fresh fruit, and cured meats. We return to our table and dig in to our appetizers, practically moaning with each new food we try.

"Holy crap," Jen says after a few minutes. "I could make a meal from this stuff. I have to stop eating now, so I'll have room for my pasta."

I nod my agreement and push my plate away. "I know. And did you see those desserts on the other table up there? I saw some tiramisu that I'll be disappointed to have to pass up if I'm too full."

"There's a second stomach for dessert. Isn't that what Brice always says?" Mitzi chimes in.

I roll my eyes. "Brice would love this place."

"They serve food; of course, he would," says Jen. "Anyway, let's not talk about guys yet. I mean, later, maybe. But we can make it through a meal without talking about men or kids, can't we?"

Marianne holds up a hand, as if volunteering for a challenge. "I can. I love my husband *and* my daughter, but I've never been so glad to get away for a couple of days. I'm in a rut."

Mitzi's eyes shift to the tablecloth, and she plays with her fork when she says, "I guess I'm in a rut, too, although I'm not stressed out, or anything. Mostly kind of bored. It'll be nice to do some different things the next two days."

Jen nods. "Yes! Work is stressing me out," she says, referring to her job as a corporate web designer. "It will all be waiting for me when I get back, but I'm not going to even think about that."

We discuss what we're going to do next (shop on the Plaza) and for the rest of the day (check into the hotel, eat somewhere else fabulous, shop some more) and tomorrow (spa time, walk the Bohemian neighborhood near the hotel, and yet more shopping before heading home). Our main courses arrive, so we forgo talking in favor of eating and moaning, then *be*moaning the fact that we're full too soon.

Brice is right, though; there *is* a separate stomach for dessert, so we take some of everything from what the restaurant calls the *dolci* table and waddle back to our seats. After voting for our favorites (Mitzi, the crostata; Jen and me, the tiramisu; and Marianne, the torte), we pay our bills, sip coffee, and chat about nothing of consequence. I feel my shoulders slowly relax and my back teeth unclench.

This is going to be good.

~

We've already had facials and massages; now we've moved onto the mani/pedi phase of our pampering. Our nail techs have walked away for the moment, giving our feet time to soften for our pedicures. (Oh, gross!)

"Can we talk about guys and kids now?" Mitzi asks as we sit in a row of raised chairs with our feet soaking in hot water.

Marianne groans playfully, then says, "Before we go there, what was the deal with the couple in the hotel room next door to us this morning?"

Jen and Mitzi stare blankly at her.

I laugh. "You guys didn't hear them?"

Marianne mutters, "Unbelievable."

"You people with kids are light sleepers, apparently," Jen says in a sort of defense of her coma-like sleep state.

"I was out of it," Mitzi says. "What were they doing?"

Jen levels her with one of her classic "dumbass" looks. "What do you think they were doing, Mitz?"

"Oh." She giggles. "Nope. Didn't hear that."

When I woke up, it was still dark outside. I'd forgotten how loud a real city is, compared to the relative silence of Springfield. At home, the garbage truck on Friday is about the only thing—other than our children—that disturbs the early morning silence. Sometimes birds chirp too enthusiastically for my taste in the tree outside our bedroom window. And that sums up the noisemakers in our neighborhood.

This morning, though, a jackhammer was clanging in the distance; car horns were honking; emergency vehicles were blaring their sirens. Oh, and the couple next door was having loud, vigorous morning sex. When I lay there with my eyes closed, I could almost trick myself into thinking I was back in my apartment in Chicago, when I was still single.

Even when I opened my eyes and appeared to be lying next to a curly, snoring Dolly Parton wig, it felt like waking up after one of our single girls' sleepovers.

Except my boobs never hurt that bad when I was single. Not even when I was pregnant with Secret.

Lying there, I told myself I wasn't going to get any more sleep, no matter how early it was, and that I should get up and express some milk under the hot water in the shower to relieve my discomfort. But I didn't want to move. Frankly, unlike Marianne, I was enjoying listening to the sexual performance of our amorous neighbors.

As I knew would be the case, by the end of my six-week recovery period, I was ready to resume sexual intimacy. So when Brice and I got the green light from Dr. Klein last week, I was excited, but I approached our return to love-making with the usual postpartum nerves. I always worry—for whatever reason—that my physical parts down there aren't going to work the way they always have. Like something may not have been put back together correctly. Hey, I've heard of it happening, so it's not the craziest fear.

Turns out, I should have been less worried about the basement level and more worried about the penthouse suite.

I knew I should have pumped first, but I hate pumping, and I didn't want to get off my nursing schedule. Plus, there's nothing like pumping breastmilk to make you feel as un-sexy as possible. Like a cow attached to a milking machine.

I thought, *It'll be fine. It hasn't been* that *long since Aidan last ate. And they really do look better when they're inflated. Plus, I've nursed how many babies now? Nothing unsavory has ever happened during sex.*

But this time around, it's like my mammary glands have kicked it into overdrive.

Anyway, Brice is a boob guy, what can I say? Even now, when they resemble a pair of insecure, wandering eyes and never seem to be "looking" in the same direction, he enjoys them, and he makes me feel like they're beautiful. And he knows they're still my most sensitive erogenous zone, so he pays attention to "the girls," especially when I seem hesitant or nervous.

His ministrations during our reunion were working, too. I was much more focused on what his hands were doing than about any worries regarding Aidan's nursing schedule or if I was still going to be tender where it mattered. For the most part, I was enjoying myself, in the moment, glad our sexual sabbatical was ending.

My brain and other parts were, anyway. Unfortunately, my boobs got the message that it was chow time. Right when Brice was eye-to-"eye" with good ol' primed-and-rarin'-to-go Righty. Apparently, he squeezed and tugged just so, and she got him good, before I could even register that things were starting to feel heavy and achy and tingly in that area in a non-sexual way.

He immediately let go of my love handle and pressed his palm to his left eye. The feeding sequence launched, milk then poured freely from me, trickling in a semi-transparent river down the slope of my breast, pooling at my side.

"Oh, no!" I gasped, not sure which problem to address first. I chose to tend to my husband, who was wincing and blinking and rubbing at his irritated peeper. Anyway, with no further "stimulation," I was pretty sure my bazooka would eventually get the hint and slow its flow without further intercession from me.

Before I could ask if he was okay, Brice started laughing and said, "Ouch! If you didn't want me to do that, all you had to do was say something."

"I didn't do it on purpose," I said, around my own giggles.

"Sure. Oh, wow. That burns like crazy."

"Lemme see." I pushed him onto his back and looked down on him.

"You're dripping on me," he said flatly, while he squinted and blinked to try to clear the foreign liquid with his own tears.

"Consider it payback."

"Touché."

Finally, after another minute or so, he was able to keep his eye open long enough for me to take a look.

"Yeah, it's red," I stated unnecessarily.

"Ya think?"

"I'm sorry."

"It's not your fault."

"Well, not technically, I guess, but I still feel bad." I rested my weight on top of him and kissed his streaming eye. The pressure against my chest kept the milk a-flowing.

"We're making a mess," he said with a chuckle.

"I don't mind. Do you?"

"No. I guess not." He gave his eye a final swipe with the back of his hand and smiled up at me. "Well, look at us. Still experiencing firsts in the bedroom."

Once we accepted the fact that we'd be a little soggier— and stickier—than usual that go-round, everything else went fine.

"Hello! Earth to Peyton!" Jen trumpets through her

cupped hands. "You're about to put someone's eye out over there."

I blush and pull the front of my shirt away from my erect nipples.

"Leave her alone," Marianne says, albeit through her laughter. "Nursing does a number on your body. You have no control over those two things while you're breastfeeding."

"I guess not!" Jen says with a snicker. "And it doesn't seem like Peyton minded what our neighbors were up to."

I narrow my eyes at Jen. "I'd think it would be of more interest to *you* than me. Maybe I should have woken you up. I don't need to live vicariously through other couples."

She pokes her tongue into her right cheek. "Low blow there, P."

"Interesting word choice."

Mitzi clears her throat. "Ladies! I have an important announcement to make, if we're finished discussing S-E-X."

This quiets most of us, although Jen mutters, "Actually…"

Mitzi ignores her and plows on, "Jared and I found out last week that we're having…"

We hold our collective breaths.

"…a girl!"

Marianne and Jen squeal and whoop. I grin and laugh more at their reactions than at the news. I'm too busy letting jealousy and happiness duke it out, waiting to see which one wins. Jealousy has the advantage at the moment.

Fortunately, Marianne is monopolizing Mitzi's attention with talk about clothes she still has from when Jessica was a newborn and how much fun baby girls are, so my silence isn't too conspicuous.

When things quiet, however, and our nail techs return to proceed with our foot treatments, Jen prods, "Isn't that great, Peyton? A quasi-niece for us to spoil rotten! Better than having one of your own, because you won't have to deal with her angsty, drama-queen behavior when she's a teenager."

"It's awesome," I lean forward to look down the row at Mitzi. "Congratulations, Sweetie. You're going to be a great mom, possibly the greatest of all time, and I can't wait to meet this lucky little person."

Emotionally, she replies, "Thanks, P. You know, Jared's driving me insane. He hovers all the time! It was nice to get away for a couple of days. But I miss him."

"He'll lighten up. Brice barely let me carry my own purse when I was pregnant with Max." I smile, feeling a tiny pang of nostalgia when I remember. "You only get one first time." *Well, some of us get more than one, but I don't wish that on my friends.* I glance nervously at Jen at the thought, but she's focused on what the pedicurist is doing to her toenails. "It's their way of being involved."

Marianne says, "That novelty didn't last long for Clark. He went from 'Don't lift that bag of flour' to, 'You've got those groceries yourself, right?' in a matter of weeks."

We laugh at the expense of lovable yet clueless Clark.

"Yeah. Milk it for all its worth," I say. "Once he sees you give birth, the jig is up. That's when they realize, 'Holy shit. She could probably kick *my* ass if she can do that.'"

"I don't know if Jared's going to be able to handle being in the delivery room," Mitzi says, sounding worried.

Turning her attention to her phone and examining a text, most likely from Wes, Jen wrinkles her nose. "For real? He needs to get a grip."

"It's not for the faint-of-heart," I say in defense of Mitzi's sweet-natured, nervous husband.

"Clark refused to look down there. He stayed close to my

head and asked them to take the mirror away. I felt bad for him! But when you think about it, nobody should see their wife like that."

"It's a perfectly natural thing, people!" Jen surprises me by saying. She, of all people, has always struck me as a likely proponent for fathers' waiting rooms and freshening up before receiving visitors.

"If you ask Brice, I'm sure he'd tell you he'd rather see a vaginal birth than another C-section any day. He still gets pale when he talks about Max's delivery. I was passed out, so I have to take his word that it was not a pretty sight."

"Being passed out sounds a-okay with me," Mitzi says. "I'm so afraid of the pain. Is it really as bad as they say?"

"Yes," Marianne and I answer together, then laugh.

"Seriously, I thought my va-jay-jay was going to rip apart with Aidan."

"Sheesh! Don't sugarcoat it for the poor girl," Jen grumbles.

"What's the point in lying?" I snap. "The moral of the story is, get to the hospital early and get an epidural."

"Amen!" Marianne interjects. "Even if you're not that uncomfortable, make them think you're dying. Don't be proud. The anesthesiologists only move quickly for the whiners."

I nod solemnly. "It's true. And whatever you do, don't go to Communion or otherwise dick around after your water has broken. Call an ambulance."

"I'm telling Brice you called going to Communion 'dicking around.' You're gonna be in so much trouble," Jen says.

With a snort, I dismiss her threat. "Whatever. He was *not* amused that I didn't act with more urgency at the time. Epidurals are good for dads, too, you know."

"Anyway," Marianne says cheerfully, "I think we should change the subject. Mama-to-be looks a little peaky over here."

"Sorry!" I call down the row. "Um, yeah. Baby girl. So happy for you and Jared! And everything's going to be great!"

I'm sure it's true, too. And I'm relieved to realize that I truly *am* happy for my friend. And I mostly mean every word I've said.

5
JEALOUSY

*J*en's staying with Mitzi and Jared during her visit ("It's a little crowded at your house, P."), so after I drop off everyone else, I have a ten-minute solo drive to get myself in the right mental state to return home.

Most moms would be missing their babies so badly that they couldn't wait to get back. And they'd have called home several times during their days away, to check on things and hear their little ones breathe into the phone.

Not I. I'm not ready to go home. And my dialing finger never even got itchy or twitchy during our two days in Kansas City.

I picture all sorts of mayhem waiting for me at the house: half-naked babies covered in food and their own bodily waste; Mary and Brice, exhausted, flopped on the couches, letting the kids do whatever they want, possibly even putting their sticky, slimy hands on the walls, the glass door, and the TV screen.

It's okay, I tell myself. *Because I got a facial and a massage and a mani/pedi, and I ate wonderful food at Lidia's and got five straight hours of sleep. I've got this.*

What I'm not prepared to face is an empty house. An empty, clean, peaceful house. My room-to-room exploration proves I am, indeed, alone, so I unpack.

I'm holding my dirty clothes over the empty hamper in the laundry room (I haven't seen the bottom of that thing since... ever) when the garage door buzzes open, and I hear minivan doors slamming and sliding and little voices echoing against the concrete floor, followed by staccato footfalls and a chorus of "Mommy's home!"

I smile quietly at their unbridled, gleeful tones. So they *do* like me. I'm not just that dirty-haired lady who feeds them, changes their diapers, and tells them "no" all day.

After the excitement dies down and everyone but Harris has moved on to other activities that are much more entertaining than hanging onto my legs, Brice kisses my lips and says, "Sorry we weren't home when you got back. We went out to dinner, and it took longer than I thought it would."

"You went out to dinner? With *all* the kids? Like, at a sit-down place?" We haven't been out to dinner as a family in more than a year.

"Yeah. I know, it's expensive, but—"

"I don't care about that."

I just spent a bunch of money in Kansas City. Like I'm going to begrudge him one meal?

He shrugs. "It's just..." He looks embarrassed when he says sotto voce, "...I had to get out of the house for a while."

"And you decided taking three toddlers and a newborn to a sit-down restaurant would be good for your nerves?"

"They did great!" His ashamed expression morphs into pride. "Max and Brooks even remembered to wait to pray after they brought our food." He nods toward Harris. "This guy was already digging in, but you know, that's to be expected."

Mary comes back from the living room and takes Aidan from Brice's arms. "I'll get him bathed and ready for bed."

"Does he need to eat?" I ask hopefully. As usual lately, I feel as if I'm about to pop a button on my shirt.

Brice and Mary exchange a regretful look, but Mary's the one brave enough to break it to me that, "Well, kid, he ate at the restaurant, but maybe he'll need topping off before bed?"

I look at the clock on the microwave. In two hours, I will have toppled over and won't be able to get up without a crane hooked to the back belt loop of my jeans.

I shoot them a cheerful smile, though, and say, "No problem. He still has bottles in the fridge, right? I'll figure something out."

Brice's shoulders relax.

Mary smiles and leaves with Aidan.

Harris stumbles after her, yelling, "Gammy! 'old *me*!"

Alone in the kitchen, Brice and I look at each other like we've never had a one-on-one conversation before. My mouth twitches.

He finally asks, "You had a good time?"

I nod eagerly. "Yes. Excellent. And guess who showed up? Jen! Please, tell me you didn't know she was going to be there."

He widens his eyes and laughs. "No clue. Wow. That's fun!" He looks behind me, as if she may be hiding there. "Where is she?"

"At Jared and Mitzi's. Probably staying in the pink-and-purple nursery," I can't help but mutter at the end.

He winces. "Oh. Mitzi told you, huh?"

While I think of at least seven ways I can murder him with things readily available in the kitchen, he rushes to explain, "I haven't known long. Jared told me last night. He came over for a beer, after the kids were in bed."

I study his face, trying to decide if I believe him.

"Ask my mom. She was there."

That's when I realize how wrong it is to doubt him. "Sorry. You know, I—" I stop, not sure I want to go into it. "Never mind. Yeah. She told us. This morning."

"It stinks, doesn't it?" he surprises me by saying.

Now's my chance to be the bigger person, to have a more selfless reaction to something than he does. So what do I say?

"Yeah, it does! Why do *they* get to have a girl? Because Jared's stupid sperm had the right sex chromosome? And why is your girl sperm so slow?" I turn on him.

He blinks. "Um, I don't think sperm has a gender, but—"

"You know what I mean."

"We have the kids we're supposed to have."

"I know that. Blah, blah, blah! It's still not fair." I plop onto one of the stools at the breakfast bar and sigh. "Plus, Marianne and Mitzi knew that Jen was going to be in Kansas City, but *I* didn't. Nobody tells me anything anymore."

He rolls with the abrupt subject change. "Don't you think Jen wanted to surprise you? To make you happy?"

"Whatever. You know what would make me happy? If they'd stop excluding me from shit. That would be super."

He comes around the island and pulls me from the barstool. In the midst of a warm, gentle hug, he says, "I'm sorry."

"Yeah, well, anyway. Enough of my complaining." With

no further wallowing, I say lightly against his chest, "The house looks nice. Better than nice. Fabulous."

"Mom's quite the whip-cracker. I wasn't allowed to rest unless I was sleeping. I faked sleeping a lot."

I laugh at the mental image of him pretending to be asleep while his mother stood over him. "What do you mean?" I lean back to look into his face.

He glances over his shoulder toward the living room, turns back to me, and wrinkles his nose. "It didn't matter if the kids were napping, or whatever. She always had something more for me to do. Laundry, dishes, making dinner. Dusting. She made me *dust*. I'll be glad to go to work tomorrow. So I can relax. And tomorrow's Palm Sunday, if that tells you how crazy it was *here*."

I'm somewhat perplexed by her described behavior, until he continues, "She said, 'Peyton doesn't sit on her duff when the boys are napping; she does housework.'"

I cover my mouth and giggle.

"I missed a great soccer match on TV, because I was cleaning the upstairs bathrooms—ninja-style, since I wasn't allowed to make any noise. It took forever." Again, he looks toward the kitchen doorway, making sure we're still alone. "Stay in here with me for a while, or she'll put me back to work."

"Sounds like you already did everything."

"No, she noticed some things around the house that need fixing—"

"Oh, yeah. The faucet in the half-bath is dripping."

"It is?" He looks dismayed. "Oh, son of a Bit-o-Honey. That wasn't one of the things *she* noticed. But she's obsessed with the burned-out light in the foyer."

"Oh, gosh. That's so high! And it's been burnt out for

months. It would probably seem too bright in there now if you replaced it."

"I know. I told her my desk lamp was good enough—"

"Brice!" we hear from the other room.

He hugs me more tightly and whispers, "Distract her while I slip out to my woodshop." Abruptly letting me go, he steps into the dining room, returning with one of the chairs. "Tell her I'm fixing the wobbly leg on this, which she insisted on using last night at dinner, even though there were four other chairs available."

"Are you really going to fix it?"

"Eventually. It might take me a few days to figure out how, though, if you get my drift."

I roll my eyes at him. "I can't believe I'm going to lie for you, because you don't know how to tell your mom no."

He shoos me toward the living room and opens the garage door to make his escape. "You're not ly—"

Mary appears in the kitchen doorway. Brice practically dives down the garage steps, the dining chair under one arm. The garage door bangs after him as he yanks it shut with his free hand.

I turn to Mary with an innocent smile. "You just missed him. He's going to try to figure out how to fix that loose chair leg you discovered." Holding my smile, I blink and offer, "Tea?"

6

MARY'S MOVE

I'm already in bed when Brice sneaks into our bedroom. And I'm not exaggerating when I say "sneaks." He's definitely tiptoeing and slinking and making a point not to make any noise when he closes our bedroom door.

"She's been in bed for hours," I say.

His face relaxes, and his muscles slacken.

"What's your deal, anyway?" I ask as he undresses for bed.

He mumbles while taking off his clothes and tossing them in the hamper, "I dunno. It's my mom. She's been all up in my business this weekend."

"She's worried one of her grandchildren is going to kill another one on your watch," I report succinctly.

"I *knew* she couldn't wait to tell you about that. It wasn't that big a deal."

"It was to her."

"Aidan was never in any danger."

"I believe you."

"*She* doesn't."

"Oh, I know *she* doesn't."

Over tea, I listened to her for nearly twenty minutes as she griped about Brice's addiction to his phone and described what could have been a horrific situation involving Brooks, Aidan, and a fireplace poker. I reassured her that the fireplace tools would go in a locked closet from now on (we rarely use them, anyway), but it sounded like Brice had learned his lesson about keeping a closer eye on the boys. I could tell by the set of her mouth that she wasn't convinced.

Brice puts on a pair of flannel pajama pants and ties the drawstring at the waist. From his dresser, he selects a gray t-shirt that says "Got Jesus?" across the chest and tugs it over his head. "I agree that I should watch them better some-times, but I have things under control. I'm not going to let anything bad happen to any of them."

"Sometimes it's not about 'letting' things happen, though. Things just happen. In the blink of an eye."

He flounces into bed, going through his usual gyrations to prop himself against the headboard for reading. "Are you going to start in now, too?"

When he slides his brand new reading glasses onto his nose, I have to turn away from him to hide my smile and subsequent laughter.

"Cut it out over there," he demands mildly.

I turn my head toward him once more. "I think they're cute."

"They're a necessity, thanks to spending all day, every day in front of screens," he grouses.

"Ah, yes. Screens. Oh, and you're getting older, too."

"It has nothing to do with my age."

"Of course not."

With suddenly close attention to his book, he drops,

"What's *your* excuse? You've been a four-eyed nerd since you were a kid."

"Bad genes. And I'm peeing in your perfect gene pool, too, so be prepared for our kids to have weak vision, like me." Ultra-casually, I say, "Your mom's right; you're a spoiled snob."

"Excuse me? When'd she say that?"

I struggle to control my amusement. "Well, she didn't call you a snob. That's my word. But she said you were spoiled."

Actually, what she said related to my fears that I'm not doing as much for Aidan (namely, nursing him as long) as I did for the other three and that he'll somehow know this or sense it and feel slighted, less loved. Mary immediately blamed Brice for my worries.

"He got everything, because not only was he an only child, but he was a late-in-life child, the baby we thought we were never going to have. He never had to share his toys or wear hand-me-down clothes or be compared to any siblings when it came to athletic ability or grades or anything! If he thinks that's how it's going to be for all of his kids, he has another think coming."

I summarize what she said, using a tongue-in-cheek delivery. Unfortunately, he doesn't catch on that I'm kidding.

"I'm not the one who thinks everything has to be fairsy-waresy!" he cries. "That's *your* issue!"

"I know! And I told her that, okay? Chill out!"

"I didn't *ask* to be an only child. As a matter of fact, I begged for a younger brother or sister."

"Oh, but why would they have more children, when they already had perfection?"

"You have a point there. As for the other thing…" With affected nonchalance, he returns his eyes to his book as he asks, "Are you worried about leaving the kids alone with me?"

"No!"

"Good. I promise not to give them pennies and set them in front of light sockets."

"I said I'm not worried."

Turning a page with a flourish, he looks down his nose at the words. "I should hope not."

"Why are you getting all pissy and sniffy with *me*? I defended you! After calling you spoiled, she accused you of not appreciating me, of being Mr. Good-Time Charlie but not doing any of the heavy lifting around here, because you don't clean toilets."

Yeah, yeah. That big ka-thump was Mary's body underneath the bus tires. But I can't have him upset with *me*.

His book smacks against his leg, and he squeaks, "What? I cleaned three toilets yesterday!"

"Because she made you."

He shakes his head and returns his attention to his book. "Whatever. This is a stupid discussion. And if this is the way it's going to be when she moves here, then maybe it's not going to be as great as I thought."

"Whoa, whoa, whoa! What do you mean, 'when she moves here'? Where's here? *Here*-here or Springfield-here?"

He snorts. "Yeah, hon. *Here*-here. You were gone for two days, and I invited my mom to live with us. Where would we put her? In the crawlspace? No, not *here*-here. Springfield-here." He puts his book face down in his lap and removes his glasses.

My heart lifts. "Really? Th-that's fantastic!"

Cleaning his lenses on the edge of the bed sheet, he grumbles, "For you. Since she thinks *you're* so wonderful."

"Now, now. She was only trying to make a point. She's

proud of you. She thinks you're a wonderful father. When you put your phone away."

I don't tell him that she was appalled when I admitted that he probably hadn't cleaned a toilet since we'd been married.

"Does he think it happens magically?" she sniped.

"It happens rarely," I muttered under my breath, but she has remarkable hearing for someone her age.

She clicked her tongue, if I'd described a backyard meth-making hobby, and said, "I raised him better than that."

"He puts the seat down," I said, bolstering his campaign for Most Tolerable Husband of the Year award. "And he *usually* keeps his aim on target."

She gave a disgusted double-wave of her hands. "Good heavens. Is that what constitutes 'above and beyond' anymore? You need to make that boy pull more of his weight around here. He's not just a playmate."

Then she explained, "I loved Brice's father, but he was useless around the house. He thought taking out the trash was a huge favor to me. But as soon as Brice was old enough to do it—probably about first grade—he even stopped doing that. He couldn't cook, never held a toilet brush, and thought all the laundry was washed together in one load. Frankly, my husband was a male chauvinist. But he was a product of his upbringing. Which is why I was determined that Brice would be a more enlightened product of *his* upbringing. Obviously, I failed."

I laughed at her harsh critique of her parenting skills and of Brice's role in our family. "He's a great husband and father."

"The thing is, there's less pressure on dads, even today. And it's not fair."

"He does as much as—if not more than—I do."

"Even *if* that's the case, it's considered voluntary. He's applauded and admired for being 'so good' with the kids or for 'babysitting' when you're at work or at the store."

"He *never* calls it that."

"No, but other people do."

"Well, that's not his fault." I sighed. "C'mon. He'd be crushed if he heard you say this. He'd be hurt that you think he's not making you proud, and he'd be upset that you somehow thought you'd failed in raising a good man."

She smiled. "I guess we're both our harshest critics, then, eh?"

That's when I realized I'd been played. I narrowed my eyes at her. "Point taken," I said, draining the last of the tea in my mug.

Now, determined not to tell him any of the details of that conversation, I cuddle up to Brice's arm. "Seriously, though, this is great. So, what's the plan? Is she going to buy a house here or live in an apartment or…?"

"An apartment. She has a place picked out nearby. A senior community."

"Nice!"

He smiles. "You're right. This will be good. I do miss her and regret not being able to see her more. And I hate that, living in St. Louis, she doesn't get to spend more time with the kids. It's bad enough that Dad never got to meet them. Or get to know you better. I don't want any more regrets like that."

"Exactly." Not liking the depressing direction in which this conversation is heading, I briskly say, "Now, let's talk about something else. Like how much I missed you, and I'm glad to be back here, in our bed, as opposed to sleeping next to someone who quite obviously has an entire king-sized bed to herself most nights and doesn't understand the concept of staying on her side of the mattress or sharing the covers."

His eyes sparkle. "You slept with Mitzi, huh?. Well, she and Jared shared a bed at least once."

Going along with his joke, I add, "It's hard to believe. She still can't say the word 'penis' without blushing."

"It's a ridiculous word."

I pick up his book and place it on his nightstand. His glasses, I pluck from his hands and set on the bridge of his nose.

"What are you doing?" he asks.

"I'm about to put the moves on you." I peel my shirt up and pull it over my head. "And I want to make sure you're wearing the proper eye protection."

He throws his head back so hard to laugh that he bumps it on the headboard.

"You need a helmet now, too?"

Reverend Risk Taker pushes his glasses onto his forehead so he can get a better look at me. "Wow, hon. They're huge."

"They hurt like hell." I cradle one in each hand and heft them like cantaloupes in the produce department. "And they're liable to explode at the slightest touch, so proceed at your own risk."

Experimentally, he pokes at my left one with his index finger. "They're so hard!"

I look down at them. "They're absurd. And they'll probably never be the same when they finally deflate."

He tilts his head. "I'll still like them." He grabs my wrist and pushes me onto my back while pulling his glasses from his forehead and tossing them in the general direction of his nightstand. "I'm going to steer clear of 'the ladies' tonight, though, if that's okay with you."

"Preferred, as a matter of fact. Like I said, they're tender."

He grins down at me. "I missed you. I didn't cry for you for fifteen minutes at bedtime, like *some* people." From the corner of his mouth, he mutters, "*Mom…*"

I crack up at the idea.

"But I did stay on my side of the bed, and it was lonely. And I kept waking myself up with my snoring, because you weren't here to nudge me to roll over. And when Aidan woke up, there was no use pretending I couldn't hear him, because there was no one with me to witness my act."

"I knew it! 'I'm a heavy sleeper,' my ass!"

He laughs sheepishly and presses his nose to mine. "I know I'm not fooling anyone, but it still works half the time."

I push at the waistband of his pajama pants. "Well, the couple in the room next door to us woke me up with their loud sex, and it made me horny. If I'd been alone, I would have done something about it, but..."

I feel him harden against my leg, and his breathing quickens. "Yeah?"

"Yeah. Instead, I took a shower and…"

He yanks his pants down and kicks them clear of his feet.

"…did some things in there instead."

Of course, I conveniently don't tell him that those "things" weren't at all sexual but involved pointing the shower head straight at my chest and letting milk pour from my nipples. Then again, the word *nipples* might be sexy enough—we're not as picky as we used to be about the dirty talk.

I figure less is more, though, and leave it at that. Some mystique is good.

I tug at my panties while he kisses my lips, then my neck, but honors his promise not to stray farther south.

"I love you so much," he says on a sigh when we join.

All silliness having flown from my mind, I reply emotionally, "I love you, too. I'd do anything for you."

"I know you would. And I would, too, for you. Anything."

Time doesn't stop with those dramatic declarations. There's no meaningful, soul-searching eye contact. But the words ring in my ears long after our lovemaking is over, and we're dozing chest-to-back, spent and content.

7

JEN'S BOMBSHELLS

ary waves to me from the packed sanctuary, where she's sitting next to Jen. I've just dropped off Aidan and the twins in the nursery, and as I make my way toward my seat, I'm surprised that Jen got here earlier than we did. Good thing, too, or we'd be stuck sitting in the second row (gasp!), as the church is full-to-bursting for Palm Sunday.

Max is hanging out in the back of the sanctuary with Brice and Wes, who are handing out palms for the children to carry while processing into the church. It's Max's first time participating in Peace's Palm Sunday tradition.

"Where are Mitzi and Jared?" I inquire, not sure we'll be able to save them seats for much longer.

Jen murmurs, "Mitzi wasn't feeling good this morning. Hard time breathing. They sent me ahead without them and told me not to worry about saving their seats."

"Oh."

"I'm sure she'll be fine," Mary says, taking in my worried expression. "You know how it is the first time that baby robs you of oxygen. It's scary, but you get used to it."

I nod, remembering all too well. I almost passed out a few times with the twins.

Turning my attention to Jen, I ask, "Did you and Wes get to hang out last night at all after you got into town?"

She cranes her neck to look back and smile at the organized chaos surrounding my husband and her boyfriend.

Finally, she answers, rather coldly, "Yep. And we didn't even need chaperones to make sure we were following 'The Rules.'" She makes exaggerated air quotes as she turns to face forward again and leafs through the bulletin, as if she cares about the announcements and prayer requests for people she doesn't know.

Mary does a halfway decent job of pretending she's not listening to us.

"What's your deal?" I hiss.

"Nothing. I'd rather not talk about what Wes and I do in private."

"Since when? Do you have something to hide?"

"No. It would be nice for some things to be private, though. That's all." She sighs. "If you must know, we ran into some people from church—of course—while we were out last night."

"So? It happens." Actually, it happens a lot. This town isn't that big. I couldn't tell you the last time Brice and I were out that we *didn't* run into someone from Peace. Or my work. But I guess I remember a time when I wasn't as accustomed to it.

Jen explains with forced patience, "So, first of all, it's annoying that we can't go anywhere without running into someone from here. It's like we're being followed, or something."

"Don't be silly." I don't tell her I've often felt the same

way, because I know it's irrational, and it would be wrong to feed each other's paranoia.

"And for another thing, they always act like they can't believe Wes is out in public, like a normal guy with a normal life. Or maybe they just can't believe he's out with *me*."

The organist pauses between pre-service songs, so I wait until the silence ends and music fills the sanctuary once more before continuing. "Listen. You, Mitzi, and I, we're around pastors all the time, so we know they're just guys. Clueless, human, weird, dumb guys. And it's easy to forget that other people don't see them that way. They're better than that to other people."

"That's wrong, though. We should educate people—"

"No. It doesn't work that way. They *need* to see them as someone more... *holy*. Or something. I don't know. I can't explain it. It's been so long since I've been a normal person—"

"When have you ever been a normal person?"

"A regular church member," I clarify. "Who looks up to and respects the pastor, because I think he's better than I am."

"You still think that, so you're a bad example."

"You know what I mean."

"Well, it's dumb. Anyway, Wes isn't my pastor; he's my fiancé."

I bite back my original retort (it's quickly forgotten, anyway) and say, "What? Since when?"

Suddenly, she desperately needs something at the bottom of her purse. "Since... a while."

"Oh." I feel like someone's punched me in the gut.

"Congratulations!" Mary offers, squeezing Jen's hand, then going back to reading the insert in the bulletin about Peace's seniors' social club.

I blink. "Yeah. Congratulations. Um, wow. Holy——" At the last second, I remember where I am and stifle the profanity. Then I blurt, "Have you guys had…?"

"No!"

Not even the Bach cantata streaming from the organ drowns out her vehement denial. She looks over her shoulder and smiles nervously at the couple behind us. Then she turns back to me and says much more softly, "No. Not even close, okay, Mother Superior?"

I can't help giggling at that characterization. Me, Mother Superior? How far we've come in so little time!

She nudges me with her shoulder. "Shut up."

"Sorry."

I think we're finished talking, because the service should be starting any minute, anyway, but she mutters a few seconds later, "I thought you'd be happy for us."

"I am," I say, a tad too quickly and emotionlessly.

More truthfully, I'm trying to process the information and not think too much about the guy in this situation being Pastor Anthony, AKA "Lurch," AKA "Reverend Intense," AKA "The Starer."

The increased volume of the organ interrupts my thoughts, as the organist transitions into the opening hymn. We begin singing as we stand and turn to watch the children parade in with the palms.

Earnest Max is following an older child and watching his every move. I can almost hear Brice telling him, "Do whatever Garen does, okay, Stinky?" and Max taking those instructions to heart. He looks so grown-up, though——and so Brice-like——as he arrives at the front of the sanctuary.

I can't even sing the hymn, because watching him lodges a boulder in my throat. For the time being, I forget everything else. I only have eyes for two people right now. One of them (the taller, handsome one) is leaning down to whisper in the shorter one's ear. The tall one is apparently trying to convince the shorter (adorable, serious) one to lay down his palm, like the other children have done. The shorter one's having none of it.

Finally, as the other children have returned to their parents, Brice gives up and points toward me, pushing gently on Max's shoulders to send him my direction, still clutching the palm branch.

I motion for him to come sit between Jen and me, and he comes running, stage-whispering, "Look, Mommy! I keept the leaf!"

The hymn ends, and Brice stands before us.

"Well!" he says. "There's always one who doesn't want to give it up. Who does that kid belong to, anyway?"

Everyone laughs. Max flutters the palm under my nose. I swat it away.

Jen leans down and whispers, "Keep it still, cutie."

Brice continues with the welcome and some announcements, mostly about Holy Week activities and events. While fending off the fern, I feel as if someone's looking at me. Sure enough, Wes is watching us from his chair closer to the altar. Jen gives him a tiny finger wave that makes me cringe. He smiles shyly before looking down at his hands in his lap.

For the rest of the service, the two lovebirds behave themselves, keeping their eyes on Jesus... or whatever. At least, Wes does. And Jen seems to be trying harder to follow along with the service than she usually does when visiting our church, so I take that as a good sign.

But— But why?! That's what I think through most of the service.

Why, Lord? How can this end well? They're in love? They're engaged? For real? Does he know about everything? *I mean, every-*

thing-everything? Things that Brice doesn't even know? And what does he know about me? *Has Jen told him about Secret? Oh, gosh. She probably has, hasn't she? Never mind that, though.*

Jen. And Wes. I thought he was just a phase she was going through. Something to check off her list. After all, she's dated a cop, a few lawyers, a doctor, and an architect—now, he was dishy. Some English guy. Only one date, though. She said he was new to the States, and she couldn't understand half the terms he used.

Anyway, it stood to reason that she'd want to sample what the clergy had to offer. And I was sorry, Lord, that it would likely end with Wes getting hurt, but that's how I figured it had to end. It had to end. Why isn't it ending, Lord? If nothing else, the long-distance aspect of their relationship should have killed it.

But now they're engaged, and... what? Wes Anthony? My quasi-brother-in-law? It's one thing to see him around now and again; he's an okay guy in small doses. But to be exposed to his intensity in close, extended social situations? Lord, why must You insist on challenging me in these ways?

Okay, fine. It's about her happiness, not mine. I get it. I don't think she's going to be all that happy with him, that's all. Remember the exhibitionist? Way more Jen's speed. Or what about that freaky-deaky guy who was a CPA by day and a DJ by night? He was all tatted up but only in places that a dress shirt and suit would cover. Even in the summer, he wore long sleeves. His co-workers and family members had no clue. Definitely Jen's type.

What do she and Wes even talk about? Luther's Small Catechism? Luther's Large *Catechism? Okay, sorry. That was crude. You get where I'm going with this, though, right? After the novelty of dating a pastor—or being married to one, if it goes that far, You forbid—wears off, then what? She has a short attention span, God. I'm warning You.*

Suddenly, the sermon is over, and it's time for Communion. Jen confuses me by getting up with Mary, Max, and me to go to Communion, instead of staying in the pew like she normally does. I shoot her a look, but she avoids eye contact with me as she placidly takes her place behind me in line.

Okay, this is new. And weird. But I guess she's going up for a blessing?

When we arrive at the rail and kneel, I see Brice hesitate. Thankfully, Wes notices, too. He steps up to Brice and whispers something in his ear.

Brice nods solemnly, steps forward, and sets a wafer in my hand. "Take eat. This is the body of Christ..." Then he gives one to Jen, who's holding her hands cupped before her. "...given for you..." He moves to his mom. "Take eat. This is the body of Christ..." And the next person. "...given for you."

Wes, having already given Max his blessing, nudges me with the cup. I flinch but give him my attention. "Take drink, the blood of Christ, shed for you for the forgiveness of your sins."

I quickly chew my wafer, swallow, and accept the cup against my lips. Then I watch, dumbfounded, as he repeats the process for Jen. After he moves down the line, she closes her eyes, bows her head, and appears to be praying. I realize I'm supposed to be doing the same thing, but all I can think is, *What's happening?*

After we've been back at our seats long enough for me to offer the lamest post-Communion private prayer ever (and an apology for such), I stare at Jen's profile until she finally looks at me.

"What? Stop staring at me!" she hisses.

"What's going on?" I say.

Feigning confusion, she looks around us and whispers, "We're in church. Communion is ending. Umm..."

"You took Communion!"

"Yeah."

"Since when do you take Communion?"

She shrugs and examines her fingernails. "Since I became a Lutheran. Wes gave me adult instruction."

"Is that what you're calling it now?"

She tilts her head and narrows her eyes. "Grow up, Peyton."

"Sorry," I mumble. "But really?"

Puffing out her chest, she looks toward the front of the sanctuary again and juts out her jaw. After a few seconds, during which her nostrils flare and her eyes blink rapidly, she says, "I take it you don't think I'm worthy enough, or something."

Before I can vociferously deny that accusation, Communion ends, and so does our whispered conversation.

Church also concludes shortly thereafter, but before I can address what my best friend has said, she starts a conversation with Jared and Mitzi, who found seats near the back when they slipped into the sanctuary after the first hymn.

As the three of them chuckle and joke about first-time pregnancy paranoia, it occurs to me that nobody else is asking Jen about her sudden conversion to Lutheranism.

Then Marianne wends her way over to us and confirms my growing suspicions that I'm—again—the last one to know something when she wraps Jen in a huge hug and says, "Hey, there. Congratulations! You're one of us now. No turning back."

Jen grins and thanks Marianne for her warm welcome "into the fold," and I know she's sending me a message as much as she's thanking our friend.

Well, screw that.

I scramble to gather my purse and Max, who's still

flicking me in the face with the palm branch every chance he gets, and exit the pew, taking a spot in Brice's "reception" line, focusing on holding it together. I vaguely notice Mary talking to a group of ladies her age, who are setting off car alarms in the parking lot with their high-pitched cooing about Max and Brice's interaction at the beginning of the service.

"Peyton?" I hear Mitzi call after me.

Then Jen says, "Let her go." I don't hear the rest of what she mumbles, but I can imagine the gist of it.

I simply need to make it to my car. Oh, shit. The other boys. Okay, I need to make it to the nursery, then get out to the car.

I swallow repeatedly, concentrating on the buckle on my Mary Janes as the line inches forward. I'm so Lutheran (unlike *some* people) that it doesn't even occur to me to skip the pastor greeting and high-tail it to the nursery. And I should rebel more often, because as soon as I make eye contact with Brice, all efforts at keeping it together dissolve.

He distractedly ends his short chat with the person in front of me and tilts his head. I merely shake my own head and bite my lip to let him know talking about it isn't going to happen, especially not here, not now.

"Just shake my hand," I say through tight lips.

He does. "Okay. What's going on?" Lifting Max, who's begging to be picked up, he blinks as he gets his turn at being slapped in the face with greenery.

What would normally make me laugh doesn't even get a second of my attention. "Later. Do you mind getting the boys for me and telling your mom to meet me at the car?" Before I even get a response from him (I know he'll do it), I hurry away.

Let him—and everyone else—think what they want or

need to think. I don't have anyone but myself to blame for their assumptions, anyway.

Brice was okay having a conversation with himself in the church parking lot as he got all the kids buckled into their seats.

"What's wrong? You don't want to talk about it? Okay. Does it have something to do with Jen going to Communion? Because I didn't know about that, either. I guess Wes forgot to mention it to me. But why would that upset you?

"Did my mom say something weird? Because you know she loves you. She's just outspoken this weekend. Right. You don't want to talk about it.

"Are you going to be okay? Because I have some stuff I have to do around here, but if you need me to come home… Okay. You're shaking your head, but now you're starting to cry. Am I being too nice to you? I know that's sometimes an issue when you're upset. Yes. Okay.

"I'm going to let you go home, then. Mom's on her way. I flagged her down when she was talking to Mrs. Whitney. But call me if you need anything or want me to come home. I have some meetings this afternoon, but I can probably rearrange a few thin— All right. Closing the door now and stepping away. I love you!"

But I don't think I'm going to get out of talking to him about it now that he's home, and the kids have been relatively cooperative about going to bed (although I can still hear them chattering up there every once in a while), and Mary's upstairs packing to drive back to St. Louis tomorrow.

Still not sure I'm ready for this conversation, I've turned on a loud, distracting movie, one of my favorites, even though I was not at all the intended audience for it. A Gerard Butler with washboard abs (maybe I *was* part of the intended audience, after all) has sent a man to his death with a swift kick to his chest and is bellowing about Sparta when Brice comes to a stop behind the couch, places his hands on my shoulders, and says, "This may be more dire than I thought."

I ignore his discussion prompt and continue watching the film, tilting my head to try to see up Mr. Butler's "skirt."

He tries again. "Mitzi's worried about you. She says she's been trying to call you all day, but you won't answer your phone."

Keeping my eyes on the television screen, I say, "Why? Did she want to tell me something that everyone else already knows?"

He squeezes my trapezius muscles, where they join with my neck. "Oh. Is that what this is about?"

"What? My watching this movie? No. I enjoy fine cine-matography, special effects, and first-class acting. You gonna watch this?" I pat the sofa cushion next to me.

He releases a held breath, creating a clicking sound in the back of his throat. After he accepts my invitation to sit, he asks, "Will you please turn off the movie?"

I flap my lips but do as he asks.

When the TV screen goes dark, he begins, "Now. I'm sensing some resentment—"

"Please, don't pastor me, okay?" I whine.

"Hmm. The rarely used verb form of 'pastor.' Well, sorry to disappoint, but I wasn't planning to *pastor* you. Now, may I continue?"

Grudgingly, I allow it.

He sighs. "As I was saying, it's obvious you're feeling

resentful and maybe left out of the loop regarding Jen's latest big news, and—"

"Not just that. I'm out of the loop on *everything* lately."

"Okay, but—"

"And that would be hurtful enough, but Marianne's *in* the loop on everything. Before me. And she's been friends with Jen and Mitzi for all of five minutes."

He opens his mouth as if to say something but closes it again, widens his eyes, and blinks rapidly when I keep talking.

"*Plus*, it's like I'm a stranger to them. Jen said something so horrible to me after Communion—"

His eyes sparkle as he asks, "You two weren't reflecting on the Sacrament?"

"I would have been," I shamelessly lie, "if she hadn't been accusing me of acting all superior and treating her like she's not worthy to be a Lutheran. As if! Like that's even possible. We all suck and don't measure up."

"Interesting paraphrase of Romans 3:23, but… proceed."

"I was shocked that she never told me that Wes was instructing her. Or whatever. Or that she even wanted him to do that. I mean, that's a big deal! How could she not tell me? Am I *that* hard to talk to?"

Brice pinches the bridge of his nose but doesn't say anything.

"Oh, great. You think so, too? Well, that's fan-fucking-tabulous!"

"Hey, that's not—"

"You know what? Never mind. Forget it. I deserve this. I made my own bed, and all that shit." I drop my head back and stare at the ceiling. "I don't feed people a bunch of bullshit that they want to hear, so I'm not personable enough? Fine. I get it. I've been too honest."

"I don't think *that's* the issue."

I lower my head and look him in the eyes. "What is it, then, huh? Am I no longer likable? I'm not good friend material? Other people are more fun or are better listeners or seem more engaged than I am? I've acted like a lunatic in so many past situations that I'm no longer approachable? Great."

When the only response I get is a long-suffering sigh, I say, "And I'm doing it again, aren't I?"

"What?"

"Acting like a lunatic."

Instead of answering that dangerous question, he chirps, "Hey! You know what? How about I go pop some popcorn and we finish watching that movie?"

"They don't love me anymore."

"That's not true, Peyton."

I nod, tears filling my eyes. "It's okay. Well, it's *not* okay, but I get it. I understand."

"Honey, I think the fact that they love you is what makes it even harder for them to know what to do and what to say."

"Yeah. I've become *that* person. Even better."

"Forgive me for oversimplifying, but can't you stop being *that* person? If, in fact, you are? Which I'm not saying you are; I'm agreeing with you for the sake of argument."

The terrified look on his face would make me laugh if he weren't so afraid of *me.*

Instead, it makes me cry in earnest.

He pulls me into a hug. "Oh, c'mon now. Can we talk about what's really bothering you?"

"My friends hate me and don't tell me anything

anymore. *That's* what's really bothering me," I say wetly and possibly incomprehensibly.

"But that's not what upset you originally, is it? When Jen went up to Communion, you didn't know that everyone else knew she had been taking instruction from Wes. Everyone other than me, of course. I didn't know, either. But when he told me, my first reaction was joy. I was happy for her." He rubs my back. "Why do I get the feeling your first reaction wasn't happiness?"

"I'm happy for her!" I snap.

"Okay, okay."

"But for crying out loud! What's the deal with the new game in our circle of friends called, 'Shock the piss out of Peyton'?"

"It has a catchy name."

I push away from him. "Well, it's annoying. Before church, she told me she and Wes are engaged."

"Oh, my. That's news to me, too." He rubs his chin, stares into space, and smiles. "Good for them."

I snort. "Yeah. And look out, Peace."

Nodding down at his lap, he chuckles at me. "Oh. I see now."

"No, you don't."

"Yes, I do!" He hugs me again, squeezing tightly. "Are you worried that you'll no longer be the most reluctant pastor's wife in the world?"

"Worried? No. Well, maybe for everyone at Peace, yes."

The grin is strong in his voice. "My, my, my. You're about to be usurped."

"Screw you!"

"Bring it."

"No, I mean, that's *not* what I care about."

"Tell me, then."

"This could be bad," I say. "Really bad."

"How so?"

The first thing that pops to mind is one of the oldest secrets I've ever been given to keep and is something I'm not at liberty to discuss with anyone—even him. I also refuse to let myself hold that against her and use it as one of the reasons this life wouldn't be a good fit for her.

Instead, I choose to reveal something more superficial. "She thought the Apostles' Creed was a rock band."

He pinches his lips together, and his nostrils flare as he works mightily to suppress his laughter.

"She's only been in a church a handful of times, mostly for weddings and funerals."

He nods. "Okay, but that's not—"

"She says she and Wes haven't slept together, but everyone's going to think they have." I ignore the dubious expression on his face. "The 'Christian concern' will pour into your office."

Sighing, he says, "And if that's the case—which I don't think it will be—I'll remind people that Christ probably wasn't really 'concerned' with such things and that they should focus on their own lives, not petty gossip. Hon." He grabs my hands. "Don't you think it's unfair to use this information against her, to preemptively worry about it even being a factor?"

I reply hotly, "I didn't say it was fair! But I've known her forever. I know stuff. I know what I'm talking about. And she makes me look like *the* Church Lady, m'kay?"

He laughs while wrapping his arms around me. "Oh. So, she could possibly—I don't know—make a mockery of the members in Parents of Peace, insulting them and telling them she thinks their priorities are a joke? Or maybe she'll tell off the associate pastor in the middle of a potluck? Nah.

She'd never do that to Jared. I bet she *will* blurt something confidential to a group of people, though. We all do that at least once. Well, *I* never have, but, you know, it happens to *some* people."

"Point taken, Reverend Smart Ass."

"Wait. I'm not done. What if she uses the worst, dirtiest, nastiest, foulest words in the English language in front of another pastor? Oh, gosh. That would be embarrassing for Wes. But he'll get over it."

I struggle against him, but he holds me in place, so I give up and say, "What you're saying is that she couldn't *possibly* be a worse pastor's wife than I am, so I should shut up and stop worrying about it."

"The last four words only."

"But I do worry. Because I want her to be happy. The Jen I know won't like this life."

"Because *you* don't like it?"

"I like it okay," it pains me to admit.

"Oh, good."

"I like *you*. And you're part of this whole pastoral package I signed on for, so…"

"Flattered beyond words."

"Well, you're no Gerard Butler."

Putting his mouth against my ear, he breathes, "This is Springfield!" making me giggle and break out in goose-bumps from my hair follicles to my feet.

He finally loosens his grip on me and brushes my hair from my teary face. "I love you," he says seriously. "And so do your friends—our friends. A lot. And if they're anything like me, they wish you loved yourself a little more."

"I'm a horrible person," I whisper toward my lap. I don't want to see his reaction to my self-assessment. "I'm sad and angry and negative and pathetic, and I can't even be happy for other people. And every time I tell myself I'm not going to be that way anymore, I fail. Sometimes right away, sometimes hours or even days later. But always, eventually."

Quietly, he says, "You're not horrible. And you keep trying to do better, no matter how many times you fall short. That's all any of us can do. Giving up is failing. Acknowledging that you have room to grow is not failing. It's aspiring. It's inspiring."

"Please. I just stopped crying." Finally, I muster the nerve to look at him.

He smiles sadly. "I know, but it needs to be said. You're wonderful and lovely and beautiful, inside and out. And if you don't believe that because I don't say it enough, then I have a new mission in life."

"You say it too much. It's embarrassing."

"Start saying it to yourself, then. You'll be amazed at how much better you feel when you say it and believe it."

I dab at my eyes. "Damn you. Shut up."

He stands and stretches. "I'm going to see if Mom needs anything. I think you should call Jen. And that's me 'pastoring' you. Don't let her go another minute thinking she doesn't measure up in your eyes. You know firsthand how much that hurts."

With that, he makes his exit, whistling on his way up the stairs. At the top, he booms, "What's that I hear? Little boys who are supposed to be sleeping?"

Their screeches drift through the air vents in the ceiling as Brice bursts first into the twins' room, then into Max's. I smile and thank God Aidan's a heavy sleeper.

While Brice is nibbling on the boys, I guess it's time for me to eat some crow.

8

OLD SECRETS

*W*e were so young. So young and stupid. And scared. At least, I was. Scared out of my mind.

What if someone finds out? What if there are complications? What if she starts freaking out, regretting what she's done? What am I doing?

Everyone—including Mitzi—thought Jen and I were cramming for a huge art history exam. But college, exams, and everyday life were far from our minds that weekend twelve years ago. And we weren't anywhere near the campus library; we were holed up in a hotel room, like two guilty teenagers.

We had our instructions from the doctor, several bags of chips and fun-sized candy bars, and two secretive days stretching in front of us. I was there for companionship, entertainment (I owned the complete first season of *Small-ville*, one of my own dirty little secrets), and assistance, in case of a medical emergency.

But boredom and bad cramps were our greatest adversaries that first afternoon and evening. Oh, and guilt.

It felt wrong, disrespectful, to sit there, watching a super-hero show, as if nothing significant had happened. Then again, we had to pass the time somehow, and Jen was never one for histrionics. If she wanted to lose herself in Tom Welling's eyes and a few mindless action sequences in the days following her procedure, that was her choice. Who was I to judge?

After the sixth episode of the show, as we were reconsidering our dedication to the franchise and if we had it in us to watch all of the episodes, back-to-back-to-back, Jen readjusted her heating pad and said, "We can never talk about this ever again."

Thinking she was referring to our dorky series marathon, I said, "Come on. It's not *that* bad. It's not as nerdy as liking *The Lord of the Rings* films." I kept my eyes down on my nail-polishing job, hoping she couldn't tell that I was a closet fan of those, too.

She snorted at me, but there was a sadness to the half-laugh. "*This*, you dumbass. Not the show." She gestured to the room around us, then pressed her hands against her still-flat abdomen. "I don't ever want to talk about *this* again."

"Of course. I understand."

And I did. Not because I thought she was a baby killer. I didn't know what I thought, actually, except that I wanted to get through the weekend without any crises. I tried *not* to think, as a matter of fact. I was there for her. Period. My political or religious views—as fuzzy as they were at the time—didn't enter into the equation at all.

"I didn't have a choice," she said for the umpteenth time.

I wasn't so sure about that, but I was sure *she* was sure of it, and that's all that mattered, ultimately.

"I'm such an idiot," she muttered, staring into space.

We sat in silence for a few minutes. I wish I could have contradicted her self-assessment, but my words would have sounded hollow. At the time I *did* think she was an idiot. Not all-around, maybe, but definitely as it applied to her judgment regarding that asshat of a boyfriend, Neco.

Boyfriend. Ha! He used her for sex, and Jen knew it. She claimed she used him just as much, that they had an open relationship, but Neco was the only one seeing other people. Jen sat in our dorm room, staring at the phone all weekend, while Neco lived it up, building a reputation as being "such a gentleman" with the sorority girls. He'd drop off his date of the night at her door with a sweet kiss, then place his booty call with Jen, who never turned him away. It was infuriating to watch and was the topic of many arguments between Jen and me.

Our other most frequent fight centered around the fact that she was often careless about taking her birth control, despite the fact that Neco *refused* to wear condoms. I didn't understand how someone who had taught me everything I knew about my reproductive health and how to protect myself could so moronically disregard her own wisdom on such a regular basis.

All the arguments we'd had in the past, though, were already there in that room with us. I didn't need to say a word on either topic. If anything, it would have sounded like I was saying, "I told you so," and that's the last thing I wanted to say. I hated that I ended up being right on that score.

When I figured she'd had enough time to castigate herself, I tossed a candy bar across the bed at her. "I think you need another Snickers bar. And I think Clark Kent wants to help you fall asleep, so let's start the next episode. You don't want to piss off Superman."

The rest of the weekend passed without incident, and life resumed. We never spoke about it again.

It's not that we didn't appreciate the significance of what had happened; rather, it was *too* significant to dwell on it. Or mention it without reopening the messy wound. So we never did. Ever. Exactly like she wanted.

It's a mild April evening. Dusk is settling over the backyard and patio, which means it's getting chilly, but my fleece pullover and long-sleeved t-shirt will keep me cozy while I talk on the phone out here, where there's no chance of Brice overhearing me. It's all part of the promise I made to Jen more than a decade ago. I've spoken of it to no one, not even my husband.

I've never been tempted, either, because it's never come up. As a matter of fact, as crazy as it sounds, I'd almost forgotten about it. Almost. Most days, I've done a good job of forgetting, anyway.

There have been times, of course, when that's been impossible. When I found myself in a similar situation to Jen's, only as an older, ostensibly wiser adult, the memories coincided too well with my then-current reality for me to ignore them. Still, we never uttered a single word to each other about it, unless you count the times she tried to convince me to do the same thing she'd done. Even then, however, the advice was dispensed as if from someone who didn't have her own personal experience backing her up. We had become disturbingly good at pretending it had never happened.

No matter what I decided, though, I knew she'd be there for me, as I had been there for her. And just because I chose a different option didn't mean I thought of myself as better than her. I've never thought of myself as better than anyone.

And that hasn't changed, despite what she may think and how I may have acted when she told me about her engagement or her new religious status. I want her to know what she's getting into, that's all. And I want to tell her I still love her.

That is, if she answers her phone. After the fourth ring, I'm afraid it's going to go to her voicemail, but she picks up with a bored, "Hey."

"Hi!" I say, then realize my cheerful tone sounds fake and is, for the most part, inappropriate to the conversation we're about to have. I follow up with a more moderate greeting. "Hello. Uh, do you have a minute to talk?"

"Wes and I were just—"

"I really need to talk to you."

Obviously, she's with Wes. I expected that. But this is more important than dinner or watching a movie or planning a wedding (gulp) or making out (ew).

"Do you have a second, and can you find somewhere private to go?"

"Well, aren't we demanding?" she grumbles, but I can tell she's walking. Then I hear a door close. "What's up?"

"I'm sorry about this morning. And every time I've ever acted like a Mother Superior."

"It's only been recently; that's why I'm confused. You always made it seem like you were excited that Wes and I were dating. But now that it's serious, you act like you hate him, or something."

I close my eyes. "I don't hate him. He's… different. And not what I would think is your type—at all—but I don't hate him."

"Maybe my type's been all wrong in the past. Ever think of that?" she snipes.

After silently counting to three, I say, "Listen, I didn't call you to fight. I called to apologize."

"So far, this apology sucks."

"I'm sorry! I'm trying to— You've dropped a lot of information on me today, and I'm trying to wrap my head around it all."

"Can't you just be happy, Peyton? Is that too much to ask? How difficult is it to 'wrap your head around' happiness?"

I snort. "Have we just met?"

She sighs. "Well, stop thinking so much about yourself for once and focus on someone else's happiness. I'm happy. There. I said it."

"I'm happy you're happy," I say dully.

"Forget it."

"No, really! I am! That's the bottom line."

"But there are all kinds of things above the bottom line that are factoring into it?"

"Well, yeah. I'm sorry, but I think the way you told me about being engaged was crappy. I think the way you hid becoming a Lutheran was—I don't know—shady, not to mention unnecessary. And it hurts that Marianne Effing Price knows everything before I do lately!"

"Oh, come on!" Having heard her say that a million times in face-to-face conversation, I know she's wrinkling her nose like something smells rotten, and her eyes are slits as she reacts disdainfully to what she would say is a melodramatic exaggeration.

I, however, don't back down. "She knew Mitzi was pregnant; she knew you were meeting us in Kansas City; she knew you were a Lutheran. And I can only assume that she and Mitzi both knew about your engagement before I did, because that's the new pattern."

"Now you don't like Marianne, either?"

"I like everyone!" I say through clenched teeth. "That's not the point." I take a deep breath to calm myself and continue, "It's not about liking or disliking anyone. I dislike being left in the dark, being pushed out of the group. What happened to us?"

The question I've been silently asking for months—possibly years, if I'm honest with myself—brings on the tears when I say it out loud for the first time. It's not a loud, sloppy cry. It's silent; it's achy.

When she doesn't have an answer, I say with a wobbly voice and a puckered chin, "Remember when you and Mitzi could barely be in the same room without me there to moderate? But then, if Mitzi wasn't with us, it wasn't the same. The balance was off, somehow. The same was true if you weren't around, and it was Mitzi and me hanging out. Without *you*, something was missing. We worked as a group, but remove one of us, and it wasn't the same. At least, that's how I thought it was. But now I'm starting to see that when you remove me, everything still runs just fine."

"Peyton…"

I wait, hoping she'll contradict me, hoping she'll tell me that my absence from the trio has been noticed, felt.

She sighs. "You got married. And not only to—seriously —one of the greatest guys I've ever met, but you married an entire *lifestyle*. And just as we were getting used to that, to understanding that you couldn't be the same Peyton you'd always been if you wanted to succeed in your new life, you became a mom, and your priorities shifted again. And again, with the twins. And again, with Aidan. It's been less than five years since you married Brice, but it may as well be a lifetime. The changes you've undergone in that short amount of time… You've left us in the dust, P."

Around a sob, I say, "No-o, I haven't. I'm the same person on the inside."

"Oh, P. How can that even be possible? It *shouldn't* be possible."

"I didn't set out to be a baby factory, you know. I-t just happened!"

"That's not even what I'm talking about," she says. "It's a part of it, I guess, but it's not the whole thing. I just mean, you're way ahead of us when it comes to life experience. I feel like I'm still stuck back in college, or shortly after, fumbling my way through adulthood, trying to convince myself that this is my life. And you, you're way past the point of feeling like you're playing house with Brice. You're established. You're—"

"Old? Boring? Complacent?"

"No." She doesn't sound very convincing, though.

I take a deep, shuddering breath. "I'm sorry. I called to say sorry for storming from church this morning, for not answering my phone all day. I called to explain that I wasn't upset about your engagement or your Lutheranism; that I'm upset about being left out, which is a dumb, selfish reason to be upset. And I called to say that I don't think you're unworthy—at all—to be Lutheran or even to be a pastor's wife. I mean, look at me! If I can do it, anyone can. But follow Mitzi's lead, not mine. Unless you're trying to figure out what *not* to do or say."

She laughs.

Watching the lights in the neighboring houses pop on for the night, I say softly, "Tell me you love him and that you've told him everything, and I'll shut up."

She's silent, so I prod, "Well…?"

"I love him," she says emotionally. "I love him in a way I used to scoff at. I love him the way I've seen you and Mitzi love your husbands and the way I had decided in the past was for weaker people than I am. I really do love him, P."

I nod and dab at my nose with the inside of my t-shirt collar. "And you've told him everything?"

After a pause, she answers, "I've told him what he needs to know."

My heart sinks. "You don't think he needs to know about it?"

"It's a part of my life I don't talk about. You and I don't even talk about it, do we? Ever."

"No, but—"

"Why does he need to know? So he can feel as heart-broken by it as I do?"

"It's a big deal," is all I can think to say.

"Yeah, it is. A big deal *breaker*. I can't let a mistake I made all those years ago screw this up."

"So, you plan to *never* tell him? Oh, Jen."

"Please, don't sound disappointed in me. I don't need that."

"I'm not disappointed! I'm worried for you. I'm... sad."

"Well, I don't need your pity, that's for sure. But consider this: do you think Brice would have married *you* if you had followed my lead?" She sounds angry, like she's sneering.

I can't even bear to imagine what she's hypothesizing. "C'mon, that's not fair. At the time, you didn't consider it a mistake. And I don't think it makes you unworthy to marry Wes. I need you to know that, to believe that. But I think it's definitely something he *needs* to know."

"If you think he needs to know, then you obviously think it's something that could affect how he feels about me." Suddenly, her tone changes from defensive to menacing.

"You promised not to say anything to anyone about this, and I'm holding you to it. I love him, and he loves me, and something I did when I was not much more than a stupid kid doesn't have any bearing on that. I'm a different person now."

I can tell she's panicking at the thought that I'll break my promise to keep her secret. "Of course, I'm not going to say anything. It's not my place. I think it would be better if he knew, though."

Coldly, she replies, "I'll take your advice into consideration, even though it's pretty hypocritical, coming from you, the queen secret keeper."

Stung, I simply blink into the growing darkness, focusing on a broken branch teetering in the wind on the roof of Brice's wood shop.

"Now if we're finished talking, Wes and I were about to go to dinner."

I clear my throat and try to shift gears. "Oh. Right. Sorry. I didn't mean to keep you so long."

"It's fine," she says, her voice still icy. "I'm sure I'll see you again before I go home."

"Yeah! Of course."

"Good night."

"Bye. I love you."

I get the last unsatisfactory word.

9

BURNOUT

*W*hat has happened to the past two months? They've gone by in a blur, that's what. Brice has spent nearly every Friday and Saturday of that time in St. Louis, helping his mom fix up and sell her house. He took Max with him each week, which was helpful, especially considering that Mary managed to potty train our oldest angel during her two days per week with him. Since Max always asks me for candy after he uses the toilet, I think it's a safe bet what her strategy entailed.

Now that her house has sold, and she's about to close on the sale, Brice won't have to take any more trips there. He's hired a full-service moving company to pack and bring her things to Springfield two weeks from now. Then we'll be squarely into the month of July.

The summer's getting away from us, but I've still had no update on that vacation I was promised.

This week, Brice has been busy doing the things around *our* house that he had to put off for the past two months. Just as he doesn't clean bathrooms, I don't clean gutters. Or trim hedges. Or do anything that involves yard equipment. I don't even mow the lawn. He's had to do that a few times in the evening after work. I feel bad that I don't do those things, but it's better for everyone that I refrain. I know my limits.

As for the inside of the house, it's like the place is falling apart around us. Every evening this week, he's had a project to tackle, starting with the dripping faucet in the powder room. Then the dryer seemingly died, but it ended up being a worn-out switch. Or something like that. I didn't listen after I heard him say, "Simple fix," meaning, "It's not going to burn our house down with us in it." Brooks knocked a hole in the wall with the doorknob on his bedroom door. The garage door opener really did die and had to be replaced, but not until after Brice spent several hours trying to diagnose the problem.

And the garbage disposal. Well, I clogged that up with potato peels, and I wasn't strong enough to plunge the clog loose. Turns out, it had nothing to do with upper body strength, because Brice eventually ended up spending quite a while on his back under the sink, taking the disposal apart, cleaning it out, and putting it back together. Mary may have resented the sexist division of labor in her marriage, but I'm glad her male-chauvinist husband taught Brice how to do all this stuff. We'd be broke(r) if we had to call service people to the house every time something went wrong.

Tonight, nothing is broken (that I know of), but we have to deliver on the promise we made to Max that we'd convert his crib into a "big-boy" toddler bed when he used the potty and didn't wear diapers anymore. Unfortunately, this is a two-man (or one man, one woman) job.

My part of the job consists of holding parts and tools, overseeing operations, criticizing when necessary (which is often), and checking on Max to make sure he's staying in our bed, where he's temporarily "sleeping" while we perform this conversion.

Brice is providing the muscle for this job. He's also supposed to be reading the directions, but he's doing precious little of that, to my dismay.

"Is that really the next step?" I question him now as he sticks out his tongue while tightening a critical bolt without consulting the instructions. "I'd think you'd need to take care of that other doohickey first." I wave my hand in the general direction of the part to which I'm referring.

Without even looking up, he retracts his tongue into his mouth and grunts with the effort to turn the bolt. "How many cribs have I put together?" he asks in reply.

"Four. But this isn't a crib."

"I read through the directions last night before bed," he says. "I've got this. Just hold that side steady and flush with the bottom."

"I always thought you were supposed to wait until the very end to tighten everything."

He sighs. "Hold. The side. Still. Please."

"I am!"

"No, you're not. Every time you talk, you move it."

"Are you telling me to shut up?"

"Not in so many words…"

I bite the inside of my cheek and fume, but I make a more concerted effort to do what he needs me to do.

He picks up another screw and twists it into the pre-drilled hole opposite from the bolt he recently gave the Hercules treatment. After a few turns, the screw meets more resistance than it should.

"Are you holding that level?" he asks impatiently.

"Yes!" I check after the fact to make sure I'm not lying.

"I can't get this screw to go in any farther." He continues

to try, though, rising on his knees for better leverage and straining to turn the screwdriver.

"Don't strip it!"

"I'm not going to strip it." He sits back on his heels and wipes sweat from his face with the front of his t-shirt. As a last resort, he consults the printed directions, having to turn quite a few pages to catch up to the point in the process to which he's skipped. After a few seconds of reading under his breath, he returns to the tightened bolt and begins to twist it to the left, muttering, "This is too tight."

"What did I say?"

"Would you like to do this by yourself?" he snaps.

"It requires more than two hands, so no. But it would be nice if you'd read the directions. Or listen to me when I say things."

"I guess it would have made too much sense to get the model that only requires you to remove one side of the rails to convert it to the toddler bed. Noooo... we had to get *this* one. I don't know why this couldn't wait until the weekend," he grumbles, not for the first time.

For the second time of the evening, I explain, "Because we're helping Jen move this weekend."

I won't back out on that, either, because it's my first chance to prove to her that I mean it when I say I'm happy for her, and I support her decision to marry Reverend Roboto... er, Wes.

"Plus, we've been putting this off for weeks," I add.

"Another week would have been fine."

"The kid would be in high school and still climbing into his crib every night if we waited for it to be convenient."

"I hate doing stuff like this with you. We always wind up arguing." The bolt marginally loosened, he returns to the screw, which now twists into place with ease.

"Well, this isn't exactly my idea of a fun evening, either, but it has to be done. Bitching about it isn't going to make it less awful."

"Thank you, Captain Obvious."

I chuckle mirthlessly. "Wow. You are such a dick sometimes."

He has no response to that, at least not one he wishes to voice.

I roll my eyes. "Yeah, I know... 'Hold the side steady,'" I imitate him, trying to goad him into a reaction.

His jaw twitches, but he simply continues to walk around the bed, tightening bolts and screws. Finally he works his way to my side, where he jerks the frame from my grasp. We hear a sickening crack and stare, wide-eyed, at each other.

"Was that what I think it was?" I ask, unwilling to visually confirm it.

He closes his eyes and takes a deep breath before twisting his mouth to the side. Then he surveys the damage.

"Oh, Chuck Norris," he hisses.

"Did it break?"

"Yes. Of course, it did." He runs his hand along the frame, then squeezes the split leg. "Aw, man...!"

I try to see around his shoulder. "Now what do we do?"

"It's not *that* bad. I can fix it. Maybe."

"Oh, good. You know, you didn't have to pull it so roughly from me."

He ignores that observation as he goes to work once more with his screwdriver and ratchet.

"What are you doing?"

With exaggerated patience, he says, "I have to take it apart to fix the broken piece in my wood shop."

"What will that involve?"

"Gluing, filling, clamping, sanding, staining..."

"What? That's going to take forever!"

He keeps his eyes on his work. "A couple of days."

My hands on my hips, I say, "Well, where's Max going to sleep in the meantime?"

Looking up at me like I'm a simpleton, he replies, "Uh, with us, I guess."

Amazingly, what took nearly an hour to construct is disassembled in minutes. He holds the cracked leg in his hand and inspects it at closer range, under the light.

"Seriously. How fast can you fix it? How many nights will he be sleeping with us?"

"Two, maybe three. Depends on how long I have to wait between steps. And if it works. I might have to try to make a whole new one."

"What?" I stomp across the room to where he's standing. "You said it wasn't that bad!"

"It's not. But that doesn't mean I can fix it. If nothing else, I can order a new part." He snatches the instructions from the floor and turns them over, looking for a customer service phone number.

I flap my lips. "My gosh! Let's buy a new bed and call it good."

"No! This bed was expensive!"

"Yes, which is why you should have treated it more carefully."

He tucks piece of wood under his arm and storms to the door. "I messed up, okay? Sorry! I'm going to try to fix it, but I don't know if I can. It would be nice if you didn't bust my balls about it."

I pull my head back at his strong language. "Okay, fine!"

When I don't say anything else, he leaves, his feet heavy on the stairs. A few seconds later, I hear the back door slam.

"Sorry!" I mutter sarcastically while I lean the large

pieces of the toddler bed against the wall and gather the small screws, bolts, and brackets to put in a place where little hands—and mouths—can't find them.

Once everything's in order, I head for our room, where I doubt I'll be getting much sleep the next couple of nights. I'll be getting even less of anything else, which—come to think of it—is fine by me.

～

"You wanna fool around?" Brice asks me three nights later as he sets his book and glasses on his nightstand.

We've become one of *those* couples. You know, the ones who spend more time talking about having sex than actually doing it. My libido has left the building, and Brice's doesn't seem to be lurking around as much, either, lately. I blame *my* lack of interest on the high-powered birth control I begged Dr. Klein to prescribe me. I don't know what Brice's excuse is.

We've just reclaimed our room after the toddler bed debacle. Brice was able to fix the leg—what a guy!—but I'm exhausted from three nights of Hell. I'm looking forward to a solid night's sleep with no one's toes pressed into my back, so I answer his rather uninspiring question with, "Not really. Do you?"

"That's why I asked. But obviously not, if you don't want to."

"Okay. Maybe tomorrow night?"

"Vacation Bible School starts tomorrow evening. I won't be home until late, and I'm sure I'll be tired."

"Oh, yeah. But I thought Jared and Wes were taking care of that."

"They are. I have to be there for the first day, at least,

though. To make sure everything runs smoothly."

"I bet Jared doesn't schedule his sex life around VBS."

"Jared's about a decade younger than I am. He thinks Hulk Hogan is a reality TV star."

"What does that have to do with anything?"

"I'm just saying, he could organize and run VBS, stay late to write a sermon, take a five-mile jog, and still go home and have energy for sex. Because he's young."

"But what does Hulk Hogan have to do with it?"

"Nothing. I was using that example to underscore Jared's youthfulness."

"I don't get it."

"Never mind." He sighs. "All right. No sex tonight, none tomorrow. How about next weekend?"

With a shake of my head, I reluctantly give up trying to figure out the Hulk Hogan reference. "It's too depressing for words to schedule sex that far in advance. Can we play it by ear?"

"It would be nice to get a commitment. Something to look forward to."

"Let's just do it now, then," I say blandly.

"That sounds… enticing."

"I'm sorry; not in the mood, that's all."

"You're never in the mood anymore." There's a definite sulk in his voice.

"I'm tired. And I hate when you consider, 'Do you wanna fool around?' foreplay. It's not anything close to a turn-on."

"Since when do you require foreplay?"

"I guess now."

"Great."

"Well, sorry. Heaven forbid you should have to work for it."

"Oh, for the love of— You know what? I'm not in the mood anymore, either. So, thanks."

"You're welcome."

He flounces onto his side and turns off his light. I follow suit, but I wait a few seconds, because I don't want him to think I'm turning off my light just because he turned off his. Apparently, this brand of birth control brings down my mental age by about two decades, as well.

On my side of the bed, I stew. He's allowed to use VBS fatigue as an excuse, but I'm not allowed to use "I-kept-four-kids-alive-cooped-up-in-the-house-on-a-rainy-Sunday-then-cooked-dinner-and-put-four-kids-to-bed-by-myself" fatigue as an excuse? How unfair is that?

"Jerkamuffin," I mutter.

"Sorry?"

I pretend to misunderstand his meaning. "You're forgiven."

"No, I—"

"It's okay. I know *your* job and *your* needs are more important than mine."

"You're kidding me with that, right?"

"No. It's not a joke or at all funny. But it's true."

He sighs. "Unbelievable. Is this something you and my mom have been talking about behind my back?"

"What? No! I don't talk to your mom about sex. I get uncomfortable when she sees me fold your underwear."

He pulls on my shoulder to force me onto my back and looks down at me. "I'm not talking about sex. I'm talking about your thinking that I think my stuff is more important than yours."

"I don't need your mom to point out to me what's been obvious in this marriage from the onset."

He blinks rapidly, then says in a barely audible near-whine, "All I wanted was to have sex." Flopping onto his back, he crosses his arms over his chest and stares at the ceiling.

I'd feel bad for him if I weren't so angry.

"How can you say that?" he says.

"Because it's true?"

"I'm sorry you feel that way."

"No, no, no. You're not going to pull that stunt. This is not about my warped perception. I'm right about this. And most of the time, I would even agree that it's the way it should be. Only an idiot would say that my career is as important as yours. It's not. But that doesn't mean it makes me any less tired than what you do all day. So if I say I'm too tired for sex, that's as valid as your saying that *you're* too tired for it."

"I never said it wasn't valid! But you're *always* too tired lately."

"When are we going on vacation?"

"What?" He seems thrown by the rapid subject change, but he adjusts quickly. "I don't know."

"You said you'd take care of everything, but you haven't said a word about it in months."

Again, he sighs, making me worry he might hyperventilate at some point in this conversation. "I've played around with a few dates this summer, but with Mom moving and with VBS and Wes's vacation schedule and Jared needing some time off for when Sasha's born, I can't seem to string a whole week together that I can be away. Plus, you have stuff going on at the gallery, too, right?"

"I do, yes. Thanks for asking. Carrie's put me in charge of a couple of openings. *Not* any of *his*," I hasten to add when Brice nearly gives himself whiplash to shoot me an alarmed look across our pillows.

The reference to artist Matt Benson, my quasi-stalker, seems to snap Brice out of his sulk.

He grabs my hand and brings it to his lips. "Listen, I'm sorry. I'm sorry it seems like I've dropped the ball on our vacation, but I'm trying. I am."

"It's always going to be something, Brice. You have to simply block some dates out on the calendar and tell everyone you'll be gone, and they have to deal with it."

"You're right. I know." Turning toward me, he props his head in his hand. "How's this: our anniversary. Florida. Hotel on the beach. No distractions, no stress. Just you and me."

I chew my lower lip. "October seems so far away."

"I know, but it'll be perfect. Nice and quiet down there, not a lot of tourists at that time of year, but still warm most days. I'll put it on the church calendar first thing tomorrow. And you'll let Carrie know so she doesn't give you any assignments. Our anniversary falls on a Saturday this year, so we'll leave the day before. Fly down, rent a car, hole up in the hotel for our anniversary, go to Vince's church on Sunday, then spend the entire following week doing whatever we want. Or nothing at all."

I have to admit, it touches me that he knows so many months ahead of time that our anniversary falls on a Saturday. I couldn't say the same.

"I'd like that," I murmur, moving closer to his chest.

He pulls me against himself and rubs my back in a way that lets me know he has no expectations of things going further. I relax and close my eyes.

"You're important to me," he says, his voice rumbling through his chest and against my ear.

"I know."

"Just making sure you do."

10

LABOR INTENSIVE

"*H*allelu, hallelu, hallelu, hallelujah… Praise ye the Lord!"

Great. Not only did VBS wreak havoc on my home life and sex life, but nearly six weeks later, I'm still singing dorky songs, because Brice is constantly singing or whistling or humming them around the house.

These are songs I haven't thought about in probably twenty years! But in a matter of two notes, they come back so easily, like repressed memories of walking in on one's younger brother while he's "taking care of business" in the shower. (Oh, man! I'd nearly forgotten about that!)

"Praise ye the Lord! (Hallelujah!) Praaaaaaaise ye the Lord!" I punctuate this last line with a long row of raspberries.

"Inspiring," Jen says, giving me the sarcastic slow-clap.

I ignore her as I buzz around the church gymnasium, checking the food on the buffet tables, rearranging the confetti on the gift table, straightening the labels on the decaf and regular coffee urns, and counting the chairs for the umpteenth time to make sure I had Howard, one of the church's trustees, drag enough down from the racks in the cavernous storage closet.

Since we arrived at the church—late, thanks to Jen forgetting some of the stuff she was in charge of providing for this baby shower *we're* throwing Mitzi—Jen has been distracted, looking around everywhere we go, as if she's waiting for someone to walk around the corner or through the door at any second. I know she's looking for Wes, but I refuse to acknowledge her space-cadet behavior. I'm too busy doing the work of two people to talk about it, anyway.

"Are those shoes new?" she annoys me now by asking so irrelevantly.

"Yes," I answer, using some tongs to straighten the salami on the meat tray.

"They're fabulous. 'Fuck me' shoes, if I've ever seen any."

My head snaps up, and I look around to make sure we're still alone. "Jen! Language. We're in a church."

She rolls her eyes and stands. "Technically, we're in a gym. But whatever. Has Brice seen you in those shoes? You *have* to take those on vacation."

"Hurry up and help me put these chairs in a circle before people start showing up. It will be better for the games I have planned. *We* have planned, I mean."

She complies, but she remains on the topic of the shoes. "They're fierce!"

Once at home in three-inch heels like these, I now live mostly in running shoes, as if I ever run for anything but the toilet. Still, my feet aren't conditioned for this abuse anymore.

"They hurt," I say dully.

"That goes without saying."

As quickly as possible in the painful, clacky shoes, I pull

two chairs at a time until they're all arranged in a large circle in the middle of the gym. It looks as if I'm setting up for an epic game of musical chairs.

"Well, I'm not taking them on vacation," I say, acknowledging Jen's earlier advice. "I'm taking flip-flops and sneakers. Maybe some pretty sandals for church and in case Brice wants to go out to dinner somewhere nice—"

"I'm not suggesting you wear them in public, you dolt."

"Is everything about that with you?"

"It's been a long time, P. A really long time. A long, long, long—"

"Okay, I get it."

"And it's irksome that *certain* people don't appreciate their unlimited access to that activity and take more advantage of it."

I laugh. "Oh, is that how you imagine my life? Nothing better to do than seduce my husband 24/7?"

"That's how it *should* be."

Sliding chairs, their rubber-tipped legs skittering noisily across the floor, I retort, "Right. Yes. We put Aidan in his exersaucer, block the older ones in the living room with baby gates, and go at it. I like to do it in the kitchen, wearing sexy lingerie and these shoes. If the kids see us, oh well; they have to learn sometime. We're progressive that way. Of course, that's why we have so many kids. We hump morning, noon, and night."

"'Hump'? That's a word used by someone who only has sex in her bed. On a scheduled night during the week. Or month."

"I wish," I grumble, then smile tightly. "Can we please stop talking about this? My mother-in-law could walk in the door any second now."

"Oh, Mare's hip to the sex talk. At your wedding reception, after she'd had a few, you should have heard her talking about how she hoped marriage would relax Brice, 'if you know what I mean.' And she'd said that while wiggling her eyebrows at us. Mitzi and I nearly peed our pants."

"Nice. I really didn't need to know that."

"I'm only telling you so that maybe *you'll* relax a bit. When did you get so uptight, anyway? You used to be fun."

I try not to let that hit too hard on the sensitive, "bad-friend-material" nerve that seems to be hanging out, exposed for my friends to slap around at will. Instead, I keep it light by replying, "I'm pretty sure they removed all my fun when I had Aidan. They figured I wouldn't be needing it anymore."

"You need it now more than ever. Stop being such a fuddy-duddy." She sticks out her tongue at me. "If that's what being a pastor's wife is about, maybe I should reconsider."

"It *is* what it's about much of the time," I break it to her.

"That's your interpretation. I'm going to be a fun pastor's wife, I've already decided. As a matter of fact, I'm going to reinvent the role altogether. I'm going to dress stylishly, and if anyone has a problem with it, they can go to Hell."

I close my eyes and count to ten. "Great. In the meantime, can you please blow up the helium balloons and tie them to the chair backs?"

By some miracle, everything's ready by the time Mitzi waddles through the doors and puts her hands on her cheeks while she grins and takes in the scene.

In the past hour, the room has filled with an eclectic mix of church ladies, young and old. Everyone loves Mitzi. I had to extend an open invitation to the entire congregation so nobody would get upset that they weren't invited (although I let the guys off the hook by making it a traditional, ladies-only event). And it seems the majority of the female church members have taken me up on that invitation. I hope we have enough cake.

The next two hours go by in a blur as I emcee games and act as scribe for Mitzi while she opens presents. Everyone oohs and aahs and coos over the tiny apparel and soft plush toys, but I remain focused on names so my friend will be able to easily write her thank-you notes. I even make extra notes, based on the surrounding conversation, so she can include thoughtful details in the notes: *Wilma thought you'd get lots of pink things, so she chose the yellow dress.*

By the time the guests have gone, and Mitzi, Jen, and I are the only ones left, I barely have enough energy to survey the mess, much less clean it up. And before I can even think about that, we have to help Mitzi load all of her presents into her car.

Then I can take off these shoes.

As I'm fantasizing about going barefoot, two angels walk through the gym doors. Jared stops short at the sight of the gift pile in the center of the chair circle. Wes continues in, smiling shyly at Jen before putting his hands in his pockets and surveying the loot.

"Good thing you have two cars," he says quietly to Jared. Without further delay, he begins stacking the presents in his arms and carrying them to the exit.

Jen stares after him with a dopey smile on her face, as if he's striding off to battle a dragon in a full suit of armor.

Jared, recovered from the shock, follows Wes's lead, leaving the three of us alone once more.

"Such good guys," Mitzi says on a sigh, stretching her legs out in front of her and rubbing her enormous belly. "I'm not sure I could move if I wanted to."

I may not want to, but I have to. None of this cleanup is going to happen if I don't do it.

As I'm starting to despair at the overwhelming task ahead of me, Howard enters the gym. "Hi, ladies," he greets us, too shy to make eye contact but heading straight for the chairs. "Everything went okay?"

"It was great," Mitzi answers for all of us. "I bet you want this chair I'm sitting on, don't you?"

"Eventually," he says with a smile. "But you're fine for now."

"I'll get those tables cleared off, so you can fold them up," I say. "Mitzi, how much of this cake are you taking home? All of it, right?"

She laughs. "No way! I'll eat it all."

"That's the point. Anyway, there's not that much left," I fib. Relatively speaking, it's true. Only about a quarter of the giant sheet cake remains. Never mind that it could feed a moderate number of sweet tooths for about a week—or my kids for a day or two.

As if reading my mind, she says, "Take it home to your guys. They'll love it. Brice asked me to save him a piece, anyway."

"Howard, would you like to take any of this home to Melody and Gracie?" I call toward the storage closet, where he's hanging chairs on racks.

"Okay, thanks," he replies.

I cut a huge slab and divide it into portions that will fit on three large paper plates. Running into the adjoining kitchen, I hunt down some plastic wrap and package the cake for him to transport home. That leaves me with enough cake for a toddler's sugar-buzz from Hell, but it's better than it was. I can always hide most of it... and keep it for myself.

Jen snaps from her reverie when Wes and Jared return

for another trip to the cars. Suddenly, she springs into action, picking up dirty plates and cups and shoving them into an industrial-sized black garbage bag. I'd love to ask her what her deal is, but it'll have to wait until I don't have to think about all this work anymore.

"You *are* taking home these cold cuts and cheese and veggies," I inform Mitzi, "if I have to strap it to the roof of your car."

She waves dismissively at me. "Whatever. Brice would eat that, too."

"Brice isn't waiting for your baby shower leftovers to save him from starvation." We laugh at the idea of it.

My laughter dies in my throat, though, when Wes and Jared return, and Jen's eyes flick nervously in Wes's direction.

"Hey, uh, Wes and I have to go," she says, wincing when my jaw drops and I gesture at the mess around us. "Sorry. I didn't think we'd still be cleaning up at this time, and we made plans, the two of us."

"I thought you two were going to hang out with Brice and me tonight!"

She shrugs. "Something else came up. Anyway, you seem kind of tired."

Translation: *You're crabby.*

I hold back the snappy retort so I don't prove her right. "Yeah. Okay. Um, whatever."

"I'll help you," Mitzi offers, dragging herself from her chair.

I help her up but say, "No way. You're not cleaning up after your own baby shower. Go home and let Jared rub your back."

He grins at me. "That sounds like a great idea. We can watch some episodes of *Doctor Who*."

She sighs and waddles toward him. "That sounds really nice, now that you mention it."

"Go," I say to all four of them. "Howard and I have this."

Mitzi and Jared have barely cleared the door when Howard clears his throat. "Actually, as soon as I get these chairs put up, I need to go. Gracie has a tee-ball game. Sorry." He blushes. "I thought you all would be done by now."

"The shower went on forever," Jen says. "You should have had one less game, or something."

I can't stop the sarcastic bark of laughter that escapes my throat. "*I* should have had one less game? You're right, Jen. *I* should have known better. *I* should have known that every female church member between the ages of eighteen and ninety would show up today, and that the gift opening would take more than an hour. What was *I* thinking when *I* planned this party?"

Turning to Howard, I smile, mostly sincerely. "Don't worry about it, Howard. Of course, you have other things planned today. It was nice of you to take the time to help us with the tables and chairs. Tell Gracie I said 'good luck.'"

With a shy nod, he takes the chair most recently vacated by Mitzi and a few other stragglers and places them in the closet, which he then locks before giving us a quiet salute and exiting the gym.

Wes edges toward the door. "We, uh, really have to go. The jeweler will be closing soon," he says to Jen.

She doesn't hesitate to grab his hand and follow him. "Sorry about this, P. I'll make it up to you when I watch your kids for a week in October." She winks, as if she's joking, but something tells me she thinks that makes us perfectly even.

And maybe she's right. That is, if we're keeping score. Thing is, I thought we were way beyond that in our relationship.

I stare after her and Wes for a few seconds after they leave, but mostly because I can't bear to look at the room around me. When I finally get the nerve, the sight makes me want to cry. Then I remember, I can take my shoes off!

I still want to cry.

Hours later, when I finally arrive home, I kick off the torture shoes for what I hope is the last time—ever—and stuff all the leftover food that Mitzi forced on me into the fridge. Before leaving the kitchen, I cut a large piece of cake and plop it onto a plate. Then I pour a huge glass of milk and carry it and the cake into the living room, where Brice sits hunched over an assortment of books on the coffee table.

He pauses in his leafing through onion-skin pages to look up at me and smile. "Hey."

I study his face and immediately notice the dark circles under his eyes. Oh my gosh! He looks awful! Okay, not awful. But not great. He looks worn out. How have I not noticed this?

Of course, I haven't noticed because this summer has been so hectic that he probably could have walked through our living room in a spandex unitard, and I wouldn't have blinked. *That's* how unaware I've become. Unaware of him as a man. Unaware of myself as a woman. Unaware. And I can't remember the last conversation we had that didn't involve details of our schedules or the consistency of one of our children's bowel movements.

I hold out the food and drink. "Brought you something."

His dark-ringed eyes light up when they take in the size of the piece of chocolate cake I'm offering him. "My, my, my! Now, *that's* a piece of cake!"

"I know. Mitzi's orders. 'Give Brice the biggest piece of leftover cake, because he deserves it.'"

He laughs. "Oh, really? I've always liked her." Tossing his pen and glasses on top of his open Bible, he takes the plate from me and forks a huge bite into his mouth. He closes his eyes while he chews. "Mmm! If Heaven has an official food, it's gotta be cake."

I sit next to him so I can serve as his human cup holder. The cold glass numbs my hand, but I don't mind. Surveying the academic chaos in front of us, I say, "Whatcha doin' here?"

Gently taking the glass from me, so as not to slosh milk over the edge, he answers, "Research," before gulping half the contents. He wipes his upper lip with the back of his hand and expounds, "Local pastor asked me to guest post on his blog, but he's pretty conservative, so I decided to go with a topic that's difficult to politicize—forgiveness. But it's such a broad topic! So I'm narrowing it down, trying to go at it from a multi-cultural perspective—you know, how do people of other faiths view forgiveness and what can we learn from them?—and I want to make sure I have all my facts straight and that I have some illustrative stories to flesh out the preachy-preachiness."

He takes a deep breath and another bite of cake, so I use the opportunity to get a word—or two—in. "Oh. Nice. I can't wait to read it. Hey. Are you feeling okay?"

With his mouth half-full, he answers what I think is, "I'm great, now that I've had this cake."

I smile patiently but don't let him off the hook. "No,

really. Not just right now. All the time. Lately. Do you feel okay?"

He sets down his fork, drains his milk, and searches my face as if trying to figure out what I want to hear. His tongue snatches a crumb from the corner of his mouth. "Um, yeah. I think so. Why?"

I shrug. There's no way I'm going to tell him he doesn't look like he feels well. "You're not tired?" I fish.

He chuckles. "Most of the time, yes. But I attribute that to the volume of diapers I change on any given day."

Setting the empty plate on the couch's arm and the glass on the floor, he returns his spectacles to his nose and takes up his pen and legal pad.

"What's your favorite Bible verse about forgiveness?" he queries. The cutest thing about it is that he's totally serious.

Of course, I draw a complete blank. "Uh... Um... Well..."

He blinks at me, then grins. "Oh, right. I forgot. Not your area of expertise."

I slap his shoulder, and he fake-flinches.

"Ow."

"That did *not* hurt."

"It stung a little. But I *forgive* you."

"You don't feel sick, do you?" I try to return to our earlier conversation.

As if taking stock of himself, he rolls his eyes toward his forehead, pooches out his lower lip, and thinks about it before answering, "No. Why? Did you put something in that cake?"

"What? No! Are you asking me if I poisoned you?"

"No. Well, maybe. I don't know! You're the one asking me weird questions!" He picks up his Bible and seems to be reading a passage. "Listen. I have to get back to this. I told

Dan I'd email him my post by the end of the day tomorrow, and—"

"You don't look good." Immediately, I regret my choice of words.

He precisely puts down the Book and angles himself to face me more squarely.

I clarify, "You don't look *bad* or ugly or anything like that. Just worn down. Haggard."

He narrows his eyes and looks me up and down. I stiffen under his study.

"Well, you don't look all that hot, either," he finally says, lifting his chin.

My stomach drops. "I don't? I mean, I know. I never do. But do I look *sick*?"

Grabbing my hand, he says, "No. I'm sorry. You look fine. I was trying to get back at you for telling me I look like dookie, but you look good." He glances down at my feet, then over his shoulder. "Hey, where are those shoes you were wearing earlier?"

"By the garage door, waiting for me to throw them in the trash, because they're so uncomfortable."

"Nonononono. Don't do that."

I laugh at the earnest expression on his face. He relaxes and smiles.

"I like those shoes," he says quietly and shyly, like he's admitting something shameful.

"They'd look great with your vestments. Go ahead and wear them tomorrow."

He winces. "Oh, darn. We're not the same size. No, I prefer them on you."

I blush. "I'm sorry I made you think I think you look bad. I don't."

"'Haggard' is pretty specific. Not a lot of room for misinterpretation there."

"It's the first word that popped to mind. I'm sorry!"

"No, no, you're right to ask if you're worried."

"So you're just tired?" I squeeze his hand. "That's all I care about, that you don't feel sick."

He nods. "Yeah. It's been a long summer, helping Mom sell her house and helping both her and Jen move. I'm ready for some relaxation."

"I'm sure." When his attention seems to wander back to his books, I say, "Hey," to regain his eye contact.

"Hm?"

"I'm sorry—" I stop, not sure where to even begin. Finally, I summarize, "I don't want you to think I take you for granted. I know you do a lot. Especially lately. And I'm grateful."

He rolls his eyes. "Hon, it's not a big deal."

"Maybe not, but—"

"Just doin' my job, Miss. Now, about those shoes…"

Neither one of us seems to care a bit about the cake, the blog post, or looking haggard after I clack back into the room in those "fierce" high heels.

We're busy rediscovering each other when my cell phone rings from my purse in the kitchen, and Mitzi's ring tone floats into the living room. Not wanting him to stop what he's doing, I pant, "I'll call her later."

That gets no argument from Brice, who continues using his tongue for the type of oral skills he'll never need behind the pulpit. Seconds later, however, Jared's ring tone blares from Brice's pants pocket across the room.

Now he stops.

"You're not thinking of answering that," I say more as a statement than a question.

"I probably should," he says regretfully, looking up into my face with hooded eyelids.

"Let him leave a message. You can get back to him later." I pull him more level with my face and nibble at his lips, then his earlobe, as his phone goes silent. It almost immediately resumes ringing. Jared. Again.

He shivers but rolls away from me, sits up, and crawls to his pants, where he digs his phone from the pocket. "They obviously need to get in touch with us," he reasons, concern replacing the desire in his eyes. He presses the button to pick up the call before it goes to his voicemail.

"Yeah," he says, clamping his lips together and breathing through flared nostrils so it isn't obvious he's out of breath. After listening for a few seconds, his mouth drops open, and he grins. "Really? Of course, we'll be right there! I'll call Mom to stay with the kids. You need us to bring anything?… Okay. If you think of anything, give me a call back.… Yes. See you in a few."

He ends the call and smiles over his shoulder at me. "A baby's about to be born."

When he starts collecting his clothes, I know we're not going to finish what we started before moving on to the night's next activity: hanging out in a hospital waiting room, drinking crappy coffee.

*J*ared's waiting for us in the corridor when the elevator doors open. Brice had texted him from the parking lot to let him know we were on our way up, but we had expected to sit in the waiting room until Jared could find a convenient time to come out and greet us.

"Why aren't you with Mitzi?" I ask, teasing, before realizing he doesn't look well, sort of chalky and sweaty and drawn.

While cleaning his glasses on his shirt tail, he answers, "She told me to come get you and bring you to her right away."

My heartbeat quickens. "Oh. Is everything okay?"

He shrugs. "I guess so. Except I can't do or say anything without her biting my head off."

I stifle my smile and manage to ask without laughing, "Has she had her epidural yet?"

Placing his glasses on his nose with great precision, he says, "Yes. But it's weaker on one side, so they've had to move her around, and she's uncomfortable, and... Anyway!" He smiles and resumes his usual chirpy demeanor. "This is a great day, huh? I'm going to be a dad in a few hours! Or less. Or more. Or whatever. God willing, of course."

Brice claps a hand on his friend's shoulder. "That's right. It *is* a great day. One of the greatest of your life, believe it or not." He laughs.

"Not helping," I mutter toward him.

He gestures toward the waiting room and says to Jared, "Why don't you and I go in there for a while and talk, maybe pray for a few minutes, to give you a bit of a breather. Let Peyton and Mitzi privately complain about clueless guys for a while."

"I need someone to take me to the delivery suite," I say.

Jared readily complies, and as I step into the room, Brice pokes his head in and says, "Hey, Mitz. I'd ask how you're doing, but... Well, I have a feeling I already know."

"You have no idea!" she snaps. "Don't act like you do."

His hands shoved in his pockets, Jared rocks on his feet and tells his wife, "Brice and I are going to give you and Peyton some privacy—"

"Fine. Whatever." she says.

I grab her hand—the one without the IV—and give both guys a sympathetic look, effectively dismissing them.

When they're gone, I turn my full attention to her. "Hey, Sweetie. I can't believe this is happening. Were you having contractions at the shower? You didn't say anything."

"I thought they were Braxton-Hicks, still. You know, there's no way to tell the difference. I don't care what any of the books say. They feel the same. By the time we got here and checked in, I was dilated seven centimeters."

"Wow! That's great!"

She levels an un-Mitzi-like glare at me. "That was hours ago. I'm still at a seven."

I pat her hand some more. "Sorry. I know it's not 'great,' in the traditional sense of the word. I take it you've had a rough go of it since you got here?"

"I've been sitting at a seven for hours. Hours, Peyton. Do you know how frustrating that is?"

"Actually…"

"I just want her out. Why won't she come out?"

"Well, it's warm and safe and cozy in there. Plus, the epidural is probably slowing things down a little. They have you on a Pitocin drip?"

She nods pathetically while the contraction monitor jumps to life. A long, strong one builds and sustains for a good minute. Mitzi watches it, unimpressed, then sighs when it's over.

"Are you feeling that?" I ask.

She shakes her head. "No. They finally got the epidural right, so I can't feel anything. Except hungry. I'm so hungry!"

"I can find a nurse and ask for a popsicle for you."

Again, she shakes her head. "No, thanks. I've already had two." When I smile and tilt my head at her, she says, "You know what the worst part is? Jared. He's driving me crazy. And I feel terrible about it, but I can't help it. I just wish he'd stop driving me crazy."

"He can't help it, either," I say, at the risk of angering her with my defense of him.

"He almost passed out when they gave me my epidural. So not only was I in major pain because of the contractions *and* the huge needle they were sticking into my spine, but I had to worry about him." She nods toward a chair in the corner. "A nurse had to help him to that chair, where he sat with his head between his knees."

"Poor guy."

"Poor me! I'm the one having a baby. All he has to do is watch, and he can't even manage that!"

I pat her hand and push her hair behind her ear. "You look pretty," I fib, trying to calm her down.

My insincere compliment goes ignored.

"Oh, great. Another useless contraction," she observes when the monitor buzzes.

"They're not useless. Really. They're working. But it's your first baby. It takes a while for your body to figure out what needs to happen. Try to relax. Do you have some music to listen to through earbuds?"

Her mouth pinches, and she shakes her head. "No. Jared forgot my MP3 player, even though I specifically asked him if he had put it back in the hospital bag after he used it last time he went jogging. 'I thought I did!'" she mimics him. "He didn't."

I pull mine from my purse, where it's always waiting, in case I have to run into the store or anywhere else I don't want to be approached by strangers—or strange people. This town is full of friendly, talkative, often reality-challenged folks. The earbuds keep them at bay, I've found.

"Here. It may not have all of your favorite music on it, but it will block out most of his nervous talking, and you can get some rest. You won't be able to hear the contraction monitor, at least." I set it in her lap. "I'll get it back from you later."

She tears up. "Thanks, P."

"Oh, don't mention it. You know…" I pat her belly. "Soon, she *will* be here. And all of this will be a memory. You'll even convince yourself it's a happy memory."

She snorts.

"No, really," I say. "And I know it's easier said than done, but cut Jared some slack. This is an overwhelming day for him, even if he's not in any physical pain. It's hard for him to see you go through this. He loves you more than anyone else in the world. Cherish these last few hours of being the only girl in his life."

Squeezing my hand, she says, "I know you're right. I just *can't* savor this moment. It's too nerve-wracking and annoying. I want it to be over."

"I know. Listen to some music. I'll go find your husband and send him back here. I'm sure Brice is giving him some advice to be more of a silent supporter. Brice knows the drill. I'm a horrible birther. Scary."

She laughs at my admission. "Thanks."

"No problem." I kiss her forehead. "Oh, and when they tell you to push, don't screw around. Push *down there* like you're... you know..."

She wrinkles her nose. "In a room full of people?"

"Yep. But the harder you push, the quicker she'll be here. Don't try to be all dainty and delicate about it." I wink at her. "And don't let Jared look down there."

After a weak chuckle, she says, "Got it. Hey, will you call Jen for me? And Marianne? But wait until *after* the baby's here. I don't want a big crowd waiting for it to happen. Too much pressure!"

"I'll take care of everything. You worry about one thing. Well, two. Having that baby and not killing Jared. You're going to need his help in the next few years."

In the hallway, on my way to the waiting room, I pass the father-to-be on his way back to his wife's side.

He smiles wanly at me. "She hates me, doesn't she?" he asks, hardly slowing down.

I snag his arm. "She doesn't hate you. She's scared. And tired. And worried. And she wants you to shut up. And stop passing out."

He blushes. "I wish she hadn't told you about that."

Rolling my eyes, I laugh. "It's not like I'm surprised." Over his offended noises, I say, "Relax. And I don't want to see you again until you have a baby in your arms. Then I'm going to take lots of pictures, so make sure you look manly and strong and conscious." I wrap him in a hug. "Good luck."

If he and Mitzi only knew what I gave up to be here for these pep talks.

We sat in the waiting room for hours, until my stomach made such an alarming noise that Brice hopped to his feet and said, "Oh, thank goodness! I'm starving, but I didn't want to sound selfish by suggesting we go eat." He pulled on my hand. "Let's go. They can call us, text us, or whatever when she arrives."

Now, down in the cafeteria, I'm inhaling a chicken quesadilla like it's the only thing I've eaten since breakfast. Oh, wait. It *is*. I didn't have time to eat anything at the shower. At least Brice ate a few bites of cake before we got the call tonight. Last night. What time *is* it?

I glance at the clock over the cafeteria doorway and groan inwardly. It's almost one in the morning. Sunday morning.

I pause in my indelicate ingestion to say, "You're going to be so dead at church later."

He swallows a mouthful of Salisbury steak and mashed potatoes. "I texted Wes earlier and gave him the scoop. He was already scheduled to preach, so he's going to lead the liturgy, too."

My stomach clenches. "You told Wes what was happening?"

The look on his face lets me know he thinks my question is moronic. "Of course. Who knows how much longer we'll be here? I have to make sure I'm covered. Is that a problem, or something?"

I gulp and shake my head, hoping to regain some feeling in my jaw and neck with the motion. "I guess not. But he's probably going to tell Jen what's going on."

"And?"

"She may be hurt that Mitzi didn't tell her or want her at the hospital, waiting." Now it's my turn to criticize his moronic question with my facial expressions.

He goes back to eating his food, muttering into his plate, "You guys are exhausting."

"I know! But we can't help it." I don't tell him that I actually feel guilty that I'm the only one who knows and is here. That is, I've felt that way since I stopped feeling superior about it.

Brice's phone buzzes on the table between us.

She's here! pops up in a text bubble.

I'm ecstatic, but I keep eating. Brice starts gathering our trash, even though he still has a half-full plate. He stands with his tray.

When I don't move, he says, "C'mon. We need to get back up there."

"Sit."

"But—"

I point at him with a tortilla wedge. "The first time they interrupted something I was enjoying, I came running, no questions asked. This time, I'm finishing my damn quesadilla. And I suggest you finish your food, too."

He grins sheepishly while retaking his seat. "Well, I guess a few more minutes won't matter. And I *am* hungry."

"Exactly. They have lots of stuff to do before we'll be able to see her, anyway."

Forty minutes later, we're standing outside Mitzi's private room, where some nurses are getting her settled, when another nurse comes by, wheeling a clear-sided bassinet containing a tightly swaddled, red-faced, sleeping baby. Jared's right behind her.

Before she turns into the room, he stops her. "Hey. Can we— Our friends have been here all night. I'd like them to see her for a second," he tells the nurse.

She cheerfully says something about security measures and having to match the baby's anklet to Mitzi's bracelet but that she'll be right back. True to her word, she returns seconds later with the baby, compares Jared's bracelet to the newborn's anklet, and settles the baby in her father's arms before walking away.

Jared remains rooted to the floor tile he's currently occupying. "Okay. Someone come get her from me. I don't want to walk with her."

I laugh but step forward and take her from his arms. "You better get over that, Bud. You'll have to walk around with her—a lot."

Brice crosses the hallway and stands with us, pulling back the baby blanket so he can get a better look at her face. He puts one arm around Jared's shoulders.

"You did a great job, brother."

"I did, didn't I?" Jared replies. "Sasha. Isn't she great?"

"She's beautiful," Brice concurs.

I blink down at her. She's still too swollen and new to

strongly resemble either of her parents, but I can tell that she's going to have Mitzi's lips and Jared's forehead.

Three nurses emerge from the room, and one tells Jared, "All set. We're going to let her rest for about an hour, then come back and check on her, make sure she's comfortable."

Her eyes flick toward us, so Brice assures her, "We're leaving soon, Donna. I know these aren't normal visiting hours."

She flinches at his use of her name, then does a double-take of his face. "Oh, Pastor Northam! I didn't recognize you without your…" She gestures to her neck. With a gentle slap to his arm, she says, "Take your time. But she does need some sleep. The poor dear worked hard."

I slip into the room and stand next to the bed. Mitzi opens her eyes and smiles at me. "Hey," she greets us in little more than a whisper. "I see you've met my princess."

"I have," I say at the same volume. "She's amazing." I hand the infant over to her mother, who looks positively angelic as she gazes down into her daughter's face.

"Can you believe it, P?" she asks. "Sasha's here."

"It's funny how that works out."

Brice appears at the other side of the bed and plants a kiss on Mitzi's head. "Congratulations, Mom. You have a keeper."

"Thanks," she says. To me, she reports like a proud child, "I did what you said, too. I pushed so hard that they had to tell me to rest a couple of times."

"You follow directions well," I say with a smile. "Nice result."

"Yeah. I only had to push for, like, three hours," she brags.

I blanch at the statistic but shoot Brice a look that I hope conveys he needs to keep his mouth shut and now's not the time to compare war stories.

"That's great," I coo. "We're going to head home now, but we'll be back tomorrow to see you guys. Let us know if we can bring you anything. Try to get some rest."

After final hugs, Brice and I exit the room. He says goodbye to the nurses on our way to the elevator and thanks them for bending the rules for us. We say nothing until we're alone in the elevator, riding down to the lobby.

That's when Brice breathes, "Three hours?"

"*Only* three hours," I quote more accurately. "Which, to be fair, isn't the longest I've ever heard, but it's still a long time."

He puts his arm around me and pulls me closer to his side as we exit the elevator, cross the lobby, and walk outside, where it's humid and warm, but not sweltering like it has been during the daytime. "Obviously, I have no concept of what that's like for the woman giving birth, but from an expectant father's perspective, that had to have been the longest three hours of Jared's life. I can't even imagine."

"Yeah, it goes pretty fast when you're the one pushing, as long as you're not feeling it. At least, the first hour does. I don't know. I think three hours is a long-ass time, no matter what."

"Three hours is a long time, even when you're doing something *fun*. Much less *that*." As we approach my car, he unlocks it and shivers. "Three hours. Holy Chicago." He opens and holds the door for me while I climb in.

I wait until he comes around to the driver's side and gets in behind the wheel before saying, "Well, she's proud of it, so let's give her that victory. The next one will slide out a lot easier, and she'll have a moment of clarity when she'll realize, 'Good God! Three hours was *not* quick.' She doesn't need some know-it-all veterans like us to rub it in."

He laughs while he turns the key in the ignition. "Is that what we are? 'Know-it-all veterans'?"

I keep a straight face while I say, "Yes. I bet I can birth our next one in three *pushes*."

"You're on."

"That kid'll go flying, if the doctor's not careful."

"Who needs doctors? Let's have the next one at home," he suggests while maneuvering from the parking lot. "That way, we won't need to get a babysitter. And you can get right back to cooking my meals and cleaning my toilets, with no interruption of service."

"Right. And I'll study up on vasectomies. I'm sure I can find a tutorial on YouTube, or something. There's no reason I shouldn't be able to give you one of those myself. I have steady hands. You'll be back behind the pulpit in no time."

"Think of all the money we'll save!"

"Enough to easily pay for our vacation in October."

While we drive through the sleepy streets and normally busy intersections with flashing yellow lights, he glances over at me and grasps my hand. "By the way, how excited are you about our trip? Because I can hardly contain myself when I think too much about it."

"I've had the countdown going for months," I admit. "It can't get here soon enough."

"It's going to be great."

And I don't doubt him for a second.

DESTINY

Our next one.

Yes, I actually said that. And Brice didn't even blink when I did. It was like we'd already had the agonizing discussion. But we haven't. I'm still religiously taking my birth control, as a matter of fact. Of course, I am. Aidan's only six months old! If I had it my way, my husband would be physically incapable of providing a "next one." And yet...

When I looked into Sasha's face, I felt something scary stirring in my chest. Then lower. It's not that she's the most beautiful baby I've ever seen. I think she's cute because she comes from two people I love very much, but she's a fairly ordinary baby. No, it didn't have much to do with her looks at all. It was something more, something instinctual, something visceral and biological.

And every time I think of Brice saying the words, "our next one," I feel a tingling and tickling that originates in my uterus and spreads throughout my abdomen. My brain tells that region of my body it's crazy, but since when has the rest of my body listened to my brain? Even my heart is joining the contagious rabble-rousing of my reproductive organs.

"Just try one more time," they're all saying. *"That secret smile on Brice's face sometimes? That's the daughter he sees in your future. You know it is, even if you're afraid to ask him. And you want to believe it's true."*

My smug brain assures me, though, that if I ride out the feeling, it will eventually go away, and everything will be okay. *"Nothing good comes from listening to your nether regions. They've been trouble since puberty. Do I need to name names?"*

No. Absolutely not. I remember them all, thank you very much.

However, what I remember the most, unfortunately, is that lifeless, tiny baby girl who wasn't meant to be a lasting, physical part of my life. More than any feeling, her memory keeps the whispering *What if?* from silencing. She's the dream I can't give up.

Tonight, after all the boys are in bed, as I try to put the living area into some semblance of order for the evening, my brain crows, *"See? Madness to even think of introducing another child into the mix. Oh, and when Brice says, 'What's one more?' remember how it felt the last time you birthed a baby. Think about poor Vagina. She almost turned inside out. At least, that's how it felt, remember?"*

"Shut up!" my tingly uterus demands. *"Vag and I have discussed this, and we can take it. The Boobsie Twins are on board, too. Why should Mitzi have all the baby-girl fun?"*

"Because that's the way the chromosome cookie crumbles! It's not meant to be. Anyway, you can barely afford the ones you have. What if this hypothetical next one is a girl? You won't even be able to use the boys' hand-me-down clothes. Cha-ching!"

"Ask Brice exactly what he saw on that operating table. Don't be

afraid of it. One more baby isn't going to make a difference around here. Just look at this place!"

I do, noticing there are new crayon marks on the white fireplace fascia. Baby socks and blocks lay scattered on the floor, and a folded-up wet diaper rests on the corner of the coffee table. I don't remember setting it there, so who knows how long it's been there? Animal cracker crumbs litter the couch cushions. Someone's been pulling on the reading lamp's shade behind Brice's chair… again. It sits at a jaunty angle, looking resigned to its rakish look.

The tingling intensifies. *"How could it get much worse? Plus, this is home. Who wants to live in a photo spread from* Better Homes and Gardens? *You don't. You never have. At least this way, you have an excuse to live in a messy house. 'Oh, it's the kids.' They're the perfect foils for any number of things. 'Can't volunteer at that rummage/bake sale. Gotta stay home with the kids. Oh, darn.' 'Would love to help with the spaghetti dinner fundraiser, but not many babysitters out there are willing or able to handle such a large, young brood. Sorry.' 'Can't work late; gotta get home to help Brice put the kids to bed.'"*

"You're despicable," my brain accuses my uterus before imploring me, *"Don't listen to that ridiculous organ. She spends her days drunk on hormones and pheromones."*

"I do not! And just think, the sooner the better. You pop out a baby girl by this time next year, and you're golden. Done. Brice has that little procedure, and instead of sitting on pins and needles for three years, you're breathing a sigh of relief in a matter of months. It's brilliant."

Now *that's* something that speaks to me. No more pesky birth control chemicals and their obnoxious side effects, no more waiting, and no more worrying.

My brain heaves an exasperated sigh. *"Why do I even bother?"*

∽

I'm waiting at the kitchen door with a beer when Brice arrives home a couple of hours later.

He smiles wearily at me. "Aw, thanks, hon." After hanging his keys on their peg next to the door, he takes the proffered bottle and gulps lustily. Then, tasting like yeast and hops, he kisses my upturned, expectant lips.

"How'd it go?" I ask of his semi-secret meeting with Bill Gregory, the church's treasurer.

Stifling a burp, he replies, "Fine. Neither of us likes being less-than-honest, but we feel it's for the best. Plus, Vivian wrote us a check for nearly three times the amount Pastor Long 'borrowed' from the church last year before he died. It seems petty to expose him."

"So, we're going to have to pretend the Longs are a couple of selfless philanthropists?"

"Holding grudges against dead people now, too? That's an all-time low."

Fortunately, he says it lightly enough that it doesn't sound like a serious rebuke, so I merely stick out my tongue at him like the mature adult I am.

Then he reminds me, "Vivian's doing me a huge favor by conveniently forgetting that I slugged her husband. Twice."

I sigh. *Oh, yeah. That.*

He takes another drink and moves around me to the fridge. "What's for dinner? I'm starving."

"Sit down. I'll heat something up for you."

Without a breath of an argument, he finds a chair at the kitchen table that doesn't contain a booster seat, sits, and kicks off his shoes.

"You ready for another beer?" I ask after I put his plate

of beef stroganoff and broccoli into the microwave and set the timer.

"One's enough. But thanks."

I grab a glass from the cupboard and fill it with milk for him to drink with his dinner. When I place it in front of him, I remove his empty beer bottle and throw it into the glass recyclables.

"This place has great service," he says. "And a pretty waitress."

I smile ruefully over my shoulder at him on my way back to the microwave. Judging by his popping food and the expiring timer, his dinner's hot enough. "Thanks. Customer service is our top priority."

"I like the sound of that."

After setting the plate in front of him, I walk behind him and rub his shoulders. He takes a few bites, finishes chewing and swallowing, then tilts his head back and looks up at me.

"Seriously. What's going on? I thought you might already be in bed."

I shrug and kiss the top of his head. "I haven't seen you all day. I wanted to wait up for you."

"Okay. Did something happen today that you're working up the nerve to tell me? One of the boys peed on my laptop? Max colored all my collars with pink highlighter? My mom was over and noticed a bunch of things not up to snuff?" His shoulders tense beneath my hands.

I rub harder. "Nothing like that, no. Although, the flickering light in the boys' bathroom is getting worse. I sense a trip to Home Depot in your future."

He sighs but returns to eating. After a few more bites, he says, "Nothing like that, but something?"

"You need to relax. I'm not allowed to spoil you without there being some ulterior motive?"

He thinks about it for a few seconds, then answers, "No."

Letting go of his shoulders, I back away. "Fine. I'll leave you alone, then. I'm obviously stressing you out by being nice to you."

He half-turns in his chair, draping his right arm over the seat back. "I'm sorry. I guess being braced for trouble at the church for the past few months is starting to get to me."

"Now that Vivian's paid up, and she's gone to live in Iowa near her son, you won't have to worry anymore, right?"

He wipes the corners of his mouth with his napkin. "I suppose. It'll probably always be in the back of my mind. I'm still not sure I'm doing the right thing. It seems self-serving."

"Bill thinks it's the right thing to do, too."

"He doesn't know the whole story. He only thinks he's protecting a dead man's memory, not a hot-head's reputation."

I can't resist laughing at that inaccurate self-appraisal. "You're not a hot-head." I clear his dishes from the table and carry them to the dishwasher.

Before he can dwell on his guilt and steer the conversation too far away from my intended purpose, I say, "It'll never happen again. And now you have more compassion for people who aren't as good as you are at keeping their tempers in check. You know exactly what can drive good people to do uncharacteristic things."

"Mm," he grunts.

Unfortunately, he knows precisely what drives *me* to do uncharacteristic things, too, so he knows something's afoot, and I'm about to prove his suspicions correct.

None of the boys peed on his laptop or colored his

collars. All the appliances are working. My car's running fine. But my organs are talking to each other—and me. Maybe I'll leave that part out.

Closing the dishwasher, I turn to him and brace my lower back on the counter. "Change of subject. Um, what, exactly, did you see at the urologist's office that day?" When he simply stares at me, I clarify, "You know, your... vision." I didn't mean for the last word to sound ironic, but it does anyway. It's kind of my default tone.

He pauses, tensing, then says, "It's been a long day. Can we talk about this some other time?"

"Why?"

"I'm not in the mood for a fight."

I laugh nervously, not sure it's true when I say, "It's not going to lead to a fight. I'm curious, that's all." I cross the room and sit sideways in his lap. "C'mon."

"I don't know if you're ready." His forehead wrinkles, his mouth pinches, and his eyes turn downward.

I try not to take offense or show I'm irked by his assessment. Instead, I say as lightly as possible, "I'm ready. Really. Try me."

Now I can tell he's debating whether thwarting me would cause a bigger fuss than telling me. He's the picture of a man in the midst of a no-win situation. On his left, a rock; on his right, a hard place.

Finally, he sighs and closes his eyes, and I know I'm about to get my way. For better or worse. My tummy flutters while I wait for him to begin.

He seems to be having a hard time knowing where to begin, so I kick things off with a direct question. "Did you see our daughter?"

His eyes fly open. After a beat, he nods solemnly, looking

like Max when he's admitting he's done something wrong, like pooped his pants.

I'm still not sure I believe what he saw was anything more than a dream brought on by the Valium, but I want so much to believe God was trying to tell him something.

My eyes fill, and I whisper, "Yeah?"

He nods once more. "Yeah."

"Tell me everything."

Motioning to the table, he says, as if describing a painting he's studied every day for the past eight months, "They were all here. Max, Harris, Brooks, another boy that I now know was Aidan. And a baby girl. In a high chair. Blonde. Happy. Beautiful."

My intestines jerk. "Maybe it was Sasha."

So far, Sasha has no hair, but when it comes in, it may be fair. Mitzi was blonde when she was younger.

"I've thought about that," he admits with a head-shake. "But she looked like *you*."

I swallow past the lump in my throat. "Oh."

He grins when it's clear I'm not going to flip out and rant about "no more babies."

"She's gorgeous," he adds.

I bury my face in his neck, inexplicably afraid again.

Rubbing my back, he checks, "So, what do you think?"

Unable to speak, I simply shake my head.

"It was such a quick flash that I couldn't tell how old the boys were in the vision, or if that even matters. It's also hard for me to distinguish between what I saw and what I've filled in since then. I've thought about it a lot."

When I still don't say anything, he laughs nervously. "I know Lutherans aren't supposed to see stuff like that. We don't speak in tongues, we don't have visions, and we don't prophesy, but it wasn't just a mental picture. It was a conviction. It was an absolute certainty right away that what I was seeing was true, was real." He pulls me away from his neck and looks in my eyes. "Don't tell anyone, okay? You haven't told anyone, have you?"

I shake my head.

He exhales hard enough to move my hair. "Good. I mean, I don't know. It sounds crazy. *I* believe it. I hope you do, too. But I don't expect anyone else to believe it, and it makes me sound like the pressure from the past year has driven me off the deep end. Do you think I've lost it?"

"I want to have that baby girl," I say surely, instead of allaying his concerns about his sanity.

"Me, too."

I press the tip of my nose to his. "I think that answers your question, then. We've both definitely lost it."

BIG VACATION

*W*aiting at the gate in the airport terminal, Brice and I look like dorks in our shorts and flip flops, considering a cold fall rain is pelting the tarmac on the other side of the windows, but we're dressed for our destination, sunny Florida. Either nobody else's eventual landing spot is Florida or they're jealous that they didn't think ahead to the warm temperatures awaiting them, because we're getting a lot of funny looks from the people around us.

But that's not my biggest concern. Right now, I'm wracking my brain, trying to think of anything and everything we could have possibly forgotten to do, instruct, or explain before we left the house when it was still dark outside this morning.

That makes it sound like we snuck away in the night, abandoning our children. And while it still feels that way to me (I hope that rock in the pit of my stomach goes away soon), we really didn't. Jen and Mary are there with the boys, probably getting them up right now. Which reminds me...

"Did I remember to mention to Jen that Brooks hates bananas?" I ask Brice, who's playing Angry Birds on his phone while we wait for our boarding call, which should be any minute now.

"I'm sure Brooks will let her know as soon as she tries to give him one. And Mom knows."

"Oh, that's right."

I slump in my chair once more, going through the mental checklist of house-related to-dos. Changed bedding, check. Washed all towels, check. Stocked fridge, check. Tested smoke detectors, check.

Brice sighs and thrusts his phone under my nose. "You need to relax. Here. I can't get past this level."

"I just want to make sure I'm not forgetting anything before we take off."

"Our phones will still work in Florida. They can call *us* if they have questions." He nudges my chin with his phone. "Help me with Angry Birds."

I take the device so he'll stop abusing me with it, but I don't look at its screen. I keep my eyes on his when I say, "I don't want them to have any questions. You know they won't call. They'll try to figure it out, because they don't want to bother us."

"Yes. Isn't that nice?" He palms my chin and squishes my face in his hand. "Beat that level for me, woman."

"You know, Max is the one who can really play this game," I say proudly, finally complying with my husband's request and focusing on the phone. "He's beaten a few levels that I couldn't figure out."

"That's just sad."

"Well, you're asking for help from someone who needs help from a three-year-old, so who's sad?"

He snorts. "I don't *really* need help. What I need is for

you to stop thinking about the kids and start enjoying our vacation."

"I'm sorry. I *am* excited— Yes! Done." I return his phone to him. "I can't wait to get to Florida, where it's sunny and warm—and not Missouri."

Laughing, he pockets his cell and puts an arm around my shoulders. "You know, they actually have that in their tourism literature. 'Florida: It's not Missouri.'"

"People would flock."

He nods politely at a woman who says hello as she sits down in one of the seats across from us. Her rolling suitcase bumps to a stop next to her. She's dressed like there's a raging blizzard outside.

Relevant to our original conversation, Brice says to me as he rubs his thumb along my shoulder, "I'm excited to get there, too, but part of the fun of a trip is the trip itself."

"Are you being a philosophical smart ass?" I ask mildly.

"No! I'm serious. I like traveling. I would have loved to drive, if we'd had more time. But flying is fun, too."

As if on cue, they announce that, due to the weather, our flight has been delayed ninety minutes. I stare at his profile while he bites his bottom lip, then releases it from between his teeth with a funny squeaking sound.

"Who's up for some more Angry Birds?" he asks, reaching into his pocket.

I laugh and push on his shoulder. "Dork. Are we going to miss our connecting flight now?"

"Considering we only had a forty-minute layover in Atlanta? Yes."

"Oh, great."

Keeping his eyes on his phone screen, he blindly pets my head, mussing my hair in the process. "Shhh… It's going to be okay. We'll figure it out when we get to Atlanta."

"But—" I pull my head away and try to settle my hair.

"Relax, my bride."

Resigned, I put my chin on his shoulder and watch him flick birds around for a while.

The woman across the way from us smiles when I glance up after feeling her stare on us. I smile back.

"Are y'all honeymooners?" she asks.

Before I can answer negatively, Brice says, "Yes," and places his hand on my bare knee.

I'm careful not to look over at him, not even in my peripheral vision, because I know I'll start laughing.

"Y'all are cute as can be," she says.

"Thanks!" he replies, his grin louder than the word.

She volunteers, "I'm goin' back to Atlanta after visitin' my daughter and son-in-law here for a week. They had a baby a couple of weeks ago. I think they were ready for me to go home."

I tilt my head and make sympathetic noises, but Brice gets into the conversation, his video game forgotten. "That's probably not true at all! New parents need all the help they can get. I'm sure you were a blessing."

"Oh, you're a sweetheart to say that," she says with a blush and a wave. "It's their first baby, so they have certain ways they want to do things. Things sure have changed since I had babies!"

"There's a lot to be said for wisdom and experience, though," Brice says. "I bet you showed them plenty of things that will make their jobs easier. Maybe they don't want to admit it, because they'd rather think all the books they've read were worth the time, but trust me. Right now they're saying, 'How did Mom do that one thing again?'" He winks.

"I don't know," she says, but it's obvious she wants to

believe him. "You'll be good parents someday, if that's somethin' that's in your future. Don't rush it, whatever you do. Take time to enjoy each other!"

"Oh, we plan to," he says in a way that somehow doesn't sound perverted. How does he do that? It must be that innocent Boy Scout look.

She rocks her way to the front edge of her chair. Brice hops up to help her to her feet.

"Thank you! You're the nicest person I've met in a dog's age!" she gushes. "I just thought, if we're gonna be here a while longer, I'll use the restroom and grab a cup of coffee. Can I get you newlyweds anything?"

We politely decline her offer, but as soon as she's out of earshot, I hiss at Brice, "What are you doing?"

He bites back his grin. "What? Nothing."

"Why did you lie to her?"

Looking shocked and offended, he says, "I did no such thing!"

"She asked if we were honeymooners, and you said yes."

"We are. I didn't say it was our *first* honeymoon." He wiggles his eyebrows at me.

"And you conveniently didn't tell her that we have four kids already, and you're not some wise-beyond-your-years, kidless parenting guru?"

He shrugs. "We were talking about *her*, not us." When all I do is stare skeptically at him, his smile finally slips frontward, and he says, "Okay, fine. I'm trying to get in the spirit of things here. For the next week, we're honeymooners with no children. Remember how good that felt?"

I nod, a tiny shiver running up my spine, then back down again, landing in my belly.

Pulling his head back, he asks, "What was that? Did you just... *you know*... right here, all by yourself?"

My blush goes as deep as my roots. "No!"

He kisses my nose. "Good. There'll be none of that without me."

Damn that delayed flight!

The rain followed us to Florida, but according to Brice's phone, the weather will be sunny and mild as soon as this system moves into the Atlantic between tomorrow night and Sunday morning. Anyway, we're not in a rush to go anywhere, now that we've finally made it here after a long day of traveling that included a rescheduled—yet much later—flight in Atlanta. No, staying in our hotel room for the entire rainy day tomorrow—our anniversary—sounds quite lovely indeed, although…

"Man, this place is a lot cheesier than it looked on the website," Brice laments as he drops our luggage inside the door of our suite.

The hotel didn't have much curb appeal from the street side, but I don't admit that I was disappointed when we first pulled into the parking lot. What's the point in hurting Brice's feelings or making him feel self-conscious about the choice he made?

Plus, it's what's inside that counts, right?

Looking around the room, I say, "This is nice."

And it is. It's obviously been redecorated recently. Everything looks modern, from the monochrome bedspread to the large, flat-screen TV on the teak dresser. I walk to the sliding door leading to the balcony, pull aside the curtain, and look out at the lightning over the ocean. My shoulders relax.

"See?" I tell him, like I knew it all along. "The view is gorgeous. That's all that matters."

He comes up and hugs me from behind. "Oh, wow… It'll be even better when the weather clears. You're right. I'm sorry. I shouldn't have complained." He turns to survey the room. "It *is* nice in here."

"Spending the day in airports will test even the sunniest personality," I excuse his uncharacteristic griping.

Funny enough, I feel fantastic, despite the less-than-ideal start to our getaway.

Throughout the day, during the travel hubbub, we remained relaxed and kept our senses of humor about the situation. At one point in Atlanta, we had just arrived at a newly assigned gate when the sign by the door informed us that not only was our flight now leaving from a different gate, but that gate was in a completely different concourse, back the way we came. It was leaving at the same time as originally scheduled, but that only gave us fifteen minutes to get there.

When we got to the new gate (which ended up being the real deal), we had five minutes to catch our breath before they started boarding. Flip-flops are not good marathon shoes.

Both of us napped on the short hop from Atlanta to Jacksonville, where we were miraculously reunited with our checked bag and where our rental car awaited.

Once buckled in and pointed in the direction of St. Augustine Beach, an hour away, I complimented Brice on his choice of car, a snappy German import with a microscopic backseat that wouldn't fit one child safety seat, much less four.

His eyes twinkled. "I got a deal with our credit card's reward points. I *almost* chose a minivan, just to mess with you, but I thought this would be more fun."

"I would have punched you," I said. "So, you chose wisely."

Now, exhausted, we collapse onto the king-sized bed, which has to be the most comfortable thing I've ever had the privilege of sprawling across.

On his stomach, Brice muffles into the crook of his elbow, "This bed reminds me of the one you used to have in your apartment."

"The one you made me get rid of when we got married?" I clarify in a teasing tone.

Looking sheepish, he says, "It had too many memories. But that was a shame, because it was comfortable."

"This one will have some memories of its own, by the time we're through with it."

"I'm sure it already does."

"Oh, ew! I don't want to think about that."

He pulls me closer to him and nuzzles my neck. "I've been thinking about *this* all day."

"Liar. I know there were a few times you were thinking about catching a plane. And finding food."

"I can multi-think," he says, moving his lips from my neck to my mouth.

After several deep kisses, he tugs my t-shirt over my head. I kick my flip-flops across the room and yank off his shirt while he unfastens my bra. We both wiggle from our shorts and underwear but promptly return to kissing. I shift more fully under him and pull my lips from his so I can better look into his eyes.

"You ready to make a baby?" I ask softly.

Pupils widening, he replies with a half-smile, "Wow. You don't waste time."

"I'm excited," I say, suddenly bashful, feeling like I said something wrong.

His expression softens. "Me, too." He kisses my fore-head. "We make wonderful babies."

I close my eyes, lost to the sensations magnified by fatigue and a day of building desire and well-controlled stress.

*I*t's early on Sunday morning, but we're both well-rested after spending our anniversary doing not much more than lounging around in bed. I'm glad the sun has decided to make an appearance, and we have a day planned away from the hotel room. Don't get me wrong. It's been wonderful inside the room, but this will be a good change of pace.

As we zoom down the highway before 8:00 a.m., fueled by coffee and a night of (mostly) uninterrupted sleep, I ask, "Are we going to make it on time?"

Brice glances at the clock on the dash. "Plenty of time. It takes a little less than two hours to get there, so we'll be fine."

Although I'm sure there are some lovely Lutheran churches in the St. Augustine area, we're headed to Zion Lutheran in Gainesville, where Vince Whitaker, Brice's best friend, serves.

Zion is small and only has one service, at 10:00. Its membership, consisting mostly of elderly folks, is shrinking, but the intimate numbers seem to suit Vince's personality. He's happy there, and he loves his church family.

A decade ago, that family included Brice, a fresh-from-Seminary, wet-behind-the-ears prison chaplain who considerably lowered the average age of the congregation. He used to drive nearly an hour each way every Sunday to attend services at Zion, when it wasn't his turn to conduct Sunday chapel services at the prison. At the time, Vince had only been a pastor for about five years, so he and Brice became fast friends.

Brice has lived in three other states since then, while Vince has stayed put, but the guys have kept in close contact. And as I've gotten to know Vince, he's become one of my favorite people and like a member of our family. Since he officiated at our wedding, it's only fitting that we should spend some time with him while we're celebrating five years of marriage. I'm excited to see him.

I'm also eager to get some insight into Brice's past. It's already been interesting, and we've hardly left the hotel room. The way he gazes out at the ocean when he thinks I'm not watching him, though, tells me he's remembering a lot about the time in his life when he called this area "home."

I'm hoping that being back here will get him to open up a bit more about it, because it's not something he talks about at home—ever. Even when Vince visits us, the two of them tend to discuss the things happening in their lives at present (at least, they do when I'm in the room), so other than the ultra-basic things Brice has told me, usually in passing, before we were even married, this part of his life is a blank to me. I'm dying to fill in some of the details.

So far, I've had no luck. The inside of our hotel room has been stirring up a lot of things, but if enlightening memories are included in the stirrings, Brice hasn't informed me. Then again, we've both been preoccupied with things not requiring much conversation.

Now, I'm ready to do some probing of my own.

"Are we still going out to brunch with Vince after church?" I check.

"As far as I know, yes." He grins indulgently at me. "You should have eaten a piece of pizza before we left, like I did."

"That's gross. Ladies don't eat day-old pizza."

It's probably true, but since I don't know much about being a lady, I'm wildly speculating. Plus, I *did* covertly eat a cold slice (leftover from one of our fancy anniversary meals) while he was in the shower.

But my question about brunch has less to do with the fact that I'm still hungry and more to do with looking forward to hearing the guys reminisce about "the good old days" and satisfy a hunger of a different sort, my suddenly insatiable curiosity about Chaplain Brice.

"How does it feel to be back in the Sunshine State? Have you missed it? Does it feel like home?" I fire these questions at him like an intense tabloid journalist, hoping my silliness will trick him into giving me a serious answer.

He leans forward and squints through the windshield, then looks out his window at the passing marshes, as if studying the landscape for familiar features.

Finally, he replies, "Not really. It feels weird to be back, honestly. The thing I remembered the most? The smell." He rolls down his window and inhales deeply. The surprisingly pleasant scent of salt, sulfur, fish, and road tar swirls around the car's interior. "Yep. It's Florida."

The window goes back up, and he finger combs his hair into place. "But no, it doesn't feel like home. It *never* felt like home, even when I lived here. It was always a temporary landing spot for me, a place for me to use what I'd learned at Sem, get my bearings, do something worthwhile and unique, and explore myself, so I'd have a better idea of when to take the next step God wanted me to take."

"Which was Kansas, right?"

"Ah, yes. Kansas." He rubs his temple with his knuckle.

"Why do you say it like that?" I ask, smiling at his wryness.

He shrugs and assumes a more innocent expression. "Huh? Oh, nothing. I just— I had a hard time in Kansas."

"You did? You've never told me that!"

Chuckling at my incredulousness, he says, "Yeah. I wouldn't say it was *horrible*, but I... I didn't fit in very well there. Culture shock, or something."

"I'd think it would be more similar to where you grew up than here, though."

He shakes his head and wrinkles his nose. "Kansas? No! I was a city boy. And maybe I *expected* Florida to be different, so the differences weren't as shocking to me. Plus, I had the ocean and... stuff to keep me occupied down here."

He clears his throat, squirming in his seat. Then, as if we'd left the topic and he's redirecting us, he says firmly, "Kansas. That place was rural in a way that I didn't even think existed anymore in this country. At least, the part where I lived was. Lots of ghost towns and fading towns and farm after farm after farm..." He trails off, as if remembering. "I drove *a lot* there, in my little Nissan that I bought after Sem." He pauses, then laughs. "I wore that car *out*. Anyway, you know how it is when you drive a lot; you think a lot. And I thought a lot about being anywhere else but Kansas."

I grab his right hand. "Oh, hon. That's awful! And here

I thought the first two years of your life as a pastor were the hardest, what with working in a prison."

Chewing his bottom lip, he grunts, then says, "The irony is, I accepted the call in Kansas to get away from *here*. But anyway!" He takes a deep breath and smiles. "All in the past, right?"

"I guess. But——"

"I don't want to dwell on any of that. I'm not even that same guy anymore." Gesturing through the windshield, he says with a grin, "Look out there! It's a beautiful day. I'm with the person I love the most in the world, on my way to see one of my very best friends. I'm blessed." He squeezes my hand and turns on the radio.

I can tell he thinks he's putting that topic to rest, but I'm more intrigued than ever.

∿

By the time we get to Zion, the mood has lightened, thanks to Brice's singing along—incorrectly, in many cases—to every song on the radio between Palatka and Gainesville (that's about an hour, in case you're wondering). The singing effectively pushed away the subject of his life B.C. (before Chicago), at least for now. It's probably not the best time to get too far into it, anyway.

At our destination, he holds the heavy, wooden church door open for me, looking over my head into the building, searching for Vince. We made it with a few minutes to spare, but nobody's milling around the small fellowship area between the outer door and the open entryway leading to the sanctuary. The only person in the narthex is an old, tan guy in khakis and a golf shirt. We each take a worship bulletin from him, but before we can advance farther into the sanctuary, he stops us.

"Hey, I know you!" he says to Brice. "You're that young pastor fella who used to come here all the time. Where've you been, young man? Not skipping church, I hope."

I laugh at the concept, and so does Brice. "No, sir. I'm the senior pastor at a church in Springfield, Missouri. This is my wife, Peyton." As he shakes the man's hand, he cringes apologetically. "Sorry, but you'll have to remind me of your name."

That cracks up the old guy, for some reason. "You probably never knew it! The name's Pete." He turns to me to shake my hand. "Oh, but this isn't the same young lady you used to bring with you."

My eyes widen, and I bite my lip to stifle a laugh as I look at Brice. His mouth is still smiling; his eyes, however, are not.

"No, not the same person," he says dully, nodding and muttering a lackluster, "Good to see you again," before leading me away.

I shoot Pete a bemused smile on my past as I follow my husband into a room about a third the size of Peace's sanctuary. It's actually closer in square footage to Peace's chapel, which we use for small funerals and private baptisms. What Zion lacks in space it makes up for in architectural drama, though. Floor-to-ceiling windows with sun-dappled, wooded views line the walls behind the altar and to our right, providing the illusion of worshiping outdoors.

I catch up to a speed-walking Brice as he stops by some chairs three rows closer to the front than any of the regulars are sitting. It's way out of my comfort zone, but I try not to care that everyone will be staring at the backs of our heads and wondering who we are.

Instead of pews, Zion uses metal-and-plastic chairs with cloth, pocketed covers draped on each chair's back. In the pockets of each of the covers are hymnals for the people in the following row to use. I guess the people in the front row have to— Oh, wait. This is a Lutheran church; never mind.

This observation makes me giggle, but when I lean over to share it with Brice, I notice he's looking stonily ahead. I follow his eyeline, but I can't imagine why the eternity candle would be pissing him off. It's lit, after all.

I tap his knee, and he flinches, as if I've punched him. It seems like it requires major effort for him to focus his eyes on my face. He gives me a weak smile.

"You okay?" I check, playing dumb about the rhino in the sanctuary.

He nods and grabs my hand, squeezing it. "Of course."

Risking the rhino's wrath, I smile and say, "You know, Pete didn't spill the beans. I assumed you dated *some* women before you met me. It's not a huge revelation."

His ears redden. "Oh. Well. Yeah. But—" He takes a deep, shaky breath. "You're right."

"You *did* tell me you wished you had someone like me to talk to down here, which made it sound like you lived quite the lonely bachelor life, but I guess that was to garner sympathy." I nudge him. "It worked, by the way. Nice line."

He drops my hand and looks away from me, unamused by my ribbing.

I reclaim his hand. "Honey! What's going on? I'm only kidding!"

He pretends to laugh it off, but his jaw is still tight when he says, "It wasn't a line."

"Okay. Never mind. Forget I said anything."

"I'm sorry. I—"

Before he can finish, Vince, having snuck up on us,

grasps Brice's shoulders from the row behind us and gives him a gentle, playful shake.

"When did you riffraff creep in?" he asks as he sits down, his voice's volume a hair quieter than the organ music.

The two of us turn in our seats to face him. He and Brice hug like brothers who have been separated for years; I wait my turn and receive a less intense squeeze.

"I've been waiting for you bums in my office," he says. "Then I give up, thinking you've stood me up, only to come in here and see you sitting in the Lutherans' version of the front row, like royalty, waiting for *me* to come to *you*."

Brice laughs, all previous signs of consternation eradicated from his features. "It isn't like that! We didn't realize you wanted us to check in with you first. Figured you were busy with all your pre-service checks. Practicing that sermon one last time."

"That's true; I have one chance to get it right, ya know? Unlike *some* bozos." He jabs a thumb in Brice's direction.

As usual, Brice plays along. "Yeah, yeah. Those poor early service folks at Peace..."

Vince shakes his head. "It's a shame. Well, I better get dressed. You know how upset some people get when church doesn't start on time. They dock me minutes from my sermon." He gives us a wink as he rises and exits through a door that I assume leads to the vestry.

Seconds later, a teenaged acolyte in ill-fitting robes emerges from a different door near the altar. As soon as she's finished lighting the candles, Vince, straightening his vestments, enters from the same door she used, waits for the organist at the back of the sanctuary to play the last note of the prelude, and welcomes all of us.

To my chagrin, he gestures to Brice and me and says,

"We have some very special guests this morning, Pastor Brice Northam and his wife, Peyton, all the way from Missouri. Pastor Northam actually hails originally from the Lutheran Holy Land, St. Louis." His reverent tone receives a modest laugh. "So, we all need to be on our best behavior, right? Make sure you say hi to them after the service. And with that, let's sing our first hymn."

Zion uses an order of service that I've never heard, but Brice seems familiar with it, so I assume it's one of the things that hasn't changed since he was a member. I follow his lead through the minimalist liturgy and manage not to goof up, but I have to concentrate, which means my mind can't wander without it being obvious that I'm not participating or paying attention.

Soon, it's sermon time. I've never heard Vince give a full-length sermon. He delivered the message at our wedding, but that was about five minutes long. I have to say, I have high expectations. And since when did I become *that* person?

I settle in, prepared to be impressed.

He starts with an attention-getting story that begins seriously but ends with a punchline that relaxes everyone. He looks pleased with the result but doesn't belabor it. Instead, he moves on to the crux of his message:

"Transparency. We don't have much choice about it when it comes to our relationship with God, right? Whether we want Him to know how we're feeling or what we're thinking or what we've said, done, or contemplated, He's all over it. Still, we confess our sins. Or we should. Or we try to. Confession and absolution. Give and take.

"But what about those *little* things? You know, the gossiping, the not-so-nice thoughts about one of the other members of the flock, the anger and irritability at everyday inconveniences? Is it really worth our time to pray about those? God already knows we struggle with them, so what's the point in bringing them to Him?"

He rubs his chin, as if thinking about it, and it strikes me —not for the first time—that pastors, my husband included, are truly just frustrated thespians. They love to act like they don't have any more of a clue than the rest of us plebeians. Ha!

Holding his forefinger up in the universal gesture that signifies having an idea, Vince says in answer to his own question, "Repentance. That's the point. We have to be receptive to His help; we have to acknowledge that we know those thoughts and feelings and actions are wrong. Not for *His* benefit, but for our own.

"And maybe there are some not-so-little things that we push to the back of our minds. Perhaps being dishonest for the supposed sake of peace? Or withholding information? Do you struggle with that?"

He looks out over the entire group, but his eyes come to a rest on *our* row, so I feel like he's staring straight into my soul and answering his own question with a *"Yes, Peyton, you do."*

I try not to read anything into it when Brice chooses that precise moment to grab my hand, which is now tellingly clammy.

My defensiveness with this topic immediately leads me to look outside myself for an example of what he's talking about. Judging by his reaction to Pete's harmless attempts at conversation and some of the gems he dropped in the car this morning, Brice has conveniently forgotten to tell *me* a few things. And they're things that are apparently important to him, or at least things that make him look like someone made him sniff a paper bag full of assholes.

Or what about Jen? She's making a huge mistake by not telling Wes about *it*. How will she be able to sleep at night, knowing that secret is between them? I guess exhaustion and biology will eventually take over, but until then, she'll be wracked with guilt. Right? It's one thing to withhold information from someone you're dating, but once you take that next step... You can't *not* tell your spouse things like that. You have to tell your spouse everything. I've learned that the hard way.

Which brings me back to me. As usual. Sure, Jen's asked me to keep her confidence, and I've readily agreed on more than one occasion now, but were those promises made too hastily? Were they made as much to save myself the discomfort of having some difficult conversations, or is keeping quiet the right thing to do? Do I have a responsibility to speak up? Holy matrimony is sacred. Am I undermining its sanctity by allowing Wes and Jen's marriage to begin under such an ominous cloud?

I decide to tune back in to Vince's sermon to see if he has any advice on the topic, but it's over. I missed the part where he delivered the call to action that made it seem easy to be more honest and open in all relationships. I missed the comforting words I'm sure he gave at the end, the part about being forgiven when we fail.

I'm stuck with all the usual questions and ethical dilemmas and no answers.

VINCE'S INTEL

"*I* thought we'd never get out of there," Vince says with a chuckle as he settles into his side of the booth. "I shouldn't have mentioned St. Louis. Elevated you to rock star status."

It's impossible to mope in our friend's presence. Brice and I, both contemplative and quiet in the car, have perked up since reconvening with Vince at the chain restaurant he led us to after church. While we waited for a table, we chatted about our hectic travel experience and the surprisingly hot and steamy weather, which Vince admits is unseasonable but not unheard of. Now that we're seated, and we've dispatched our server with our drink orders, we move into more personal territory.

Vince folds his hands on the table in front of him and leans forward. "All right, 'fess up. How many times have you called home to check on the kids?"

Brice and I look at each other and say together, "None."

Brice wrinkles his nose at me. "That's bad, isn't it?"

I pull my mouth to the side and shrug. "Maybe. But we've only been gone two days. Three, including today."

Vince laughs. "I love you guys! I think it's great that you're getting away. The kids will benefit from it, too."

"None of them are old enough to miss us *that* much, right?" I verify with both guys. "We'd really just be calling to check on Jen and Mom, and they'd probably be offended that we questioned their ability to handle things."

"Well said," Vince says. "So, without too many crazy details to make this pathetic bachelor jealous, are you guys enjoying yourselves so far?"

Again we answer simultaneously, "Yes," but Brice quickly buries his nose in his water glass. He sucks a couple of ice cubes into his mouth and crunches on them.

I roll my eyes at his prudishness and rub his back. Then I ask Vince what I've often wondered but have never had the guts to ask him, until now. "Why *are* you still a bachelor, anyway? Besides the obvious reasons, of course…"

He doesn't seem bothered by the question, but he does close one eye and query, "First, what are the 'obvious' reasons?"

Brice, having recovered from his bashfulness, offers, "You're ugly as sin, to begin with. And old."

"Don't listen to him!" I cry, slapping my hand over my husband's mouth. "He's full of crap. Forty-two isn't old. And you're a good-looking guy. You still have all your own teeth."

"I'm no Beautiful Brice, but if it's not my age or my looks, what're the 'obvious' reasons?"

Now it's my turn to blush. "I only meant you haven't met the right person. That's all."

"You said 'reasons,' plural."

"You did," Brice says, pushing my hand away from his mouth.

I kick him under the table. "Well, you're a pastor, and it's hard for pastors to find wives, right?"

He twists his mouth and rolls his eyes toward his forehead. "The evidence would contradict that, since most of the pastors I know are married, but I'll agree it's not easy for us to *date*."

"That's what I meant. Isn't that how you find a wife?"

With a twinkle in his eye, he replies, "I don't know. I'm thinking about sending away for one at this point. Some poor girl in a desperate situation might find hooking up with me to be the lesser of two evils and worth a ticket to the good ol' U.S. of A."

"Will you be serious for one minute?" I plead.

He fingers the tiny plastic box of sugar and sweetener packets, staring at it when he says, "Oh, I don't know... I'm pretty set in my ways at this point in my life. And where would I meet this mystical woman? The median age in my congregation is about 92—not that I'm ageist! But a woman that, ahem, mature would also be set in *her* ways. We'd kill each other over the television remote."

I cover my mouth with my hand to keep from giggling out loud at the image of him and an older woman wrestling with the remote in side-by-side recliners. Just when Imaginary Vince has picked up his geriatric wife's walker to knock the remote from her hand, Real Vince sighs.

"I'm not saying it can't happen. But it's not a huge concern of mine right now," he says.

"Fair enough," I say, letting him off the hook.

Brice puts his arm around my shoulders and pulls me to him. "If you change your mind, though, Peyton's good at matching her friends to pastors."

"Sorry. Fresh out of friends," I say, with a moue. "You snooze, you lose!"

"So I hear," he says with a laugh. "I kind of had my eye on that cute little blonde. Jen, is it? Damn that young upstart, Wes Anthony! What happened to the ladies looking for sugar daddies? Now, they all want to be cougars."

"Unless you're printing your own money at the parsonage, you're in no position to be anyone's sugar daddy, anyway," Brice points out.

"Hey, my modest existence has allowed me to build up a fine nest egg, sir, so stop making assumptions. I've invested well."

"In what?" Brice demands to know, sounding incredulous.

Vince looks down his nose at his friend and flutters his eyelids. "Let's say that some of my stock transactions in the last decade have ensured that if my entire church membership dies all at once—which is entirely possible. I've been to some wild Bingo nights with those folks—I'll be okay."

"You sly dog!"

With a feigned air of self-satisfaction, Vince adds, "Plus, you'd be amazed at how much money you have when you don't have kids."

"Oh. Well, that ship has sailed. Four, maybe five, times," Brice mutters.

Vince raises one eyebrow. "Have you started losing count? Let's see… Max, Brooks, Harris, Aidan…" He ticks them off on his fingers. "Nope, that's still four. Wait a minute. Are you two trying to tell me something? Am I gonna be an uncle again?"

I pinch Brice's side.

"Ow! Sorry!" He looks at me. "It's Vince, though. *He* can know, right?"

"There's nothing to know!" I say. To Vince, I explain, "We're trying for another one, hoping for a girl."

He laughs and puts his hand to his forehead. "Oh, no! I've seen the ending to this movie, and it's a heartbreaker."

"Not always!" Brice says.

"Okay, if you say so."

"If we have another boy, we're giving him to you," I say.

"Can I have the potty-trained one, instead?"

"No, we're already attached to him," Brice says. "Plus, we've put a lot of work into that one. Anyway, you want one fresh out of the box."

"Brice!"

"What? Oh!" He covers his mouth with his hand, but the top half of his face turns beet red, and his eyes widen with horror. "I didn't mean it like that!" he hisses from behind his hand.

"Yeah, but that's what you said!"

Vince falls sideways and lies in his half of the booth, breathless with laughter. People at the tables around us start to stare.

"You two are mortifying," I say, shielding my face with my hand and sipping my water.

Brice, recovered from his embarrassing slip, laughs at his friend's reaction. "Oops. I just meant—"

"Yeah, we know. Let's move on. Anyway, Brice is *sure* we're going to have a girl."

This statement has Vince popping vertical again. "Interesting. Last time I checked, there's no way to be sure."

Now it's Brice's turn to kick *me* under the table. I almost throw the *"Oh, it's only Vince; he can know, right?"* back in his face, but I promised I wouldn't tell anyone, so I bite my lip and rub my calf with my other foot.

"All things are possible with God," Brice says with a pompous expression.

"Indeed," Vince demurs. "Which is why I'm still hopeful that someone under the age of fifty will stumble into my humble church one Sunday and fall madly in love with me, charmed by my incredible oratorical skills."

"Is that what all the young people are calling it nowadays?" Brice wonders under his breath.

"Pastor Northam! Consider yourself censored, sir. Your classy, polite wife and I will continue this conversation without you."

Now, *there's* a first.

~

After a brunch that settled down significantly once our food arrived and all three of us were more focused on putting things other than our feet into our mouths, Brice and I firm up plans to spend Wednesday with Vince on his boat and say goodbye to him in the restaurant parking lot.

Alone with me once more in the rental car, Brice places his sunglasses on his nose and asks, ultra-seriously, "Where to, ma'am?"

I laugh. "I thought you had everything planned out. Why are you asking me?"

He seems surprised by my assumption. "What? No. I have a few ideas of things we can do or places we can go, but there's no plan, per—"

"Don't."

"Say! You want to see the prison where I used to work?"

Giggling at his word play and thrilled that he's willing to share something of his past with me without my begging him, I say, "Yes! I would. That would be fascinating. It's near here, right?"

"About forty-five minutes away. Then I can take you back to the beach the way I used to take all the time when I'd go for drives."

"Alone, or with your girlfriends?"

"Alone. Usually."

The way he sniffs and puts the car in gear lets me know that line of conversation is a no-go. I can't help thinking, though, *WTF?!*

How come I've never heard Word One about this woman—or women? And exactly how many were there? Pete made it sound like there was only one, but maybe she was the only one willing to come to church with him.

I guess I've been an idiot all these years, assuming his silence on the topic of his former relationships meant there were none. Well, I knew there were *some*, because he's alluded to "girlfriends," and I know he wasn't a virgin when we got married...

Hang on a second! Did he learn some of my favorite moves of his with that—that girl he brought to church for Pete to peer at like an old perv?

No, no, no. I need to cool my beans. He's specifically told me he was *not* sexually active between the time he was ordained and when we were married.

Yeah, but what does that really mean? I know what it meant for *us* when *we* were dating, but did Little Miss Florida get to bend The Rules more than I did?

I know one thing. She must have looked a *lot* different than me, because rheumy-eyed Pete knew right away that I wasn't her, not even a version of her that was ten years older and "filled out" by marriage and babies. Yes, Pete definitely seemed disappointed when he compared the "other girl" Brice used to bring to church to the one who was on his arm today.

Well, excuse the hell outta me, Pete! I live in a land-locked state. I have four babies. I don't tan.

I cross my arms over my chest and sigh, turning more

toward the window and gazing at the passing scenery. But this stretch of road is about as nondescript as my mood has suddenly turned.

"You okay over there?" Brice asks.

"*I'm* fine," I say with more attitude than I intended.

"Okay." He turns on the radio and mutters something about finding the station that he used to listen to the most. "They played the craziest mix of songs," he tells me now, as if I care. "Like, oldies and contemporary and hard rock and —and everything. I used to love it. What was the number again…?"

"I wouldn't know," I say.

Maybe he's confusing me with someone *else* who used to make this trip with him on Sundays.

Oh, my gosh. I need to get a grip. With everything he knows about *my* sexual history, the worst he's ever said or done is to make me get rid of my comfy bed with the shady past. Since we've been a couple, he's never thrown any of my former partners in my face and has never forced me to talk about them if I didn't want to—and I haven't wanted to. It's been our unspoken agreement. We know the most important things, but we've decided it's awkward and uncomfortable to talk about past relationships. Because it is.

Am I going to let Stinky Pete ruin my day? Hell no! Who's in this car now? Me! Not Everglades Barbie.

So, ha!

"What was that?" Brice asks, turning down the radio with the controls on the steering wheel.

Oh, did I say that out loud?

"Um, nothing. I… burped. Excuse me."

He stretches as much as he can behind the wheel while still holding on. "Man, I ate too much, too. Maybe after I give you the nickel tour of the State Pen, we can take a walk at this park I know about back in St. Augustine."

"That sounds nice," I say.

"We can take off our shoes and walk along the beach. You're going to love it there. It's beautiful and peaceful. And not at all touristy. This time of year, we might be the only ones there."

"You think so?"

"Yeah! It's great. Now, *there's* a place I've missed. I wish I could bring it back with us."

"I don't think our suitcase is big enough."

He snaps his fingers. "Darn."

The next several minutes pass with the radio providing the only sound in the car. Brice managed to find the station he remembered. Billy Idol's singing about a white wedding when I feel myself dozing in the warm sun coming through the window, the combination of my full belly and the smooth ride of the car lulling me to sleep.

When Brice nudges me awake, he's accompanying a rapper, who's "singing" about a girl gettin' down on the dance floor.

I smile around a yawn. "You weren't kidding about this station. It's almost as weird as you are."

"I love it. Oh, there it is!" He points past my nose, through my window, at a complex of buildings in the distance. "Obviously, we can't go on the grounds—"

"I don't want to," I quickly assure him, alarmed that it might have been a possibility.

"Oh. Well, good. Because we can't. I mean, I guess if I'd thought of this in advance, I could have arranged something."

"No, thanks. This is good. I just wanted to see it. Not *experience* it."

He drives through a series of streets that take us ever closer to the prison. Eventually, we drive past the entrance, past the landscape-fringed sign that says, "Union Correctional Institution." The spritely palm trees that line the streets stand in stark contrast to the setting's somberness.

"Everything looks nicer with palm trees, right?" I say nervously, staring out my window and trying to imagine Brice coming here every day. Driving past the guard shack, showing his credentials, walking through several levels of security, praying with men in jumpsuits.

He lets the car coast to a stop on a side street and puts it in park.

"Huh," he grunts after several minutes of staring at the only building of which we have a full, unobstructed view. "The place hasn't changed."

"Well, it hasn't been *that* long."

"Seems like a completely different life. I was so green…"

"I bet! Were you scared to come here every day?" I ask, feeling intimidated, even from this distance.

He smiles. "Nah. They're just guys."

"Uh, guys who raped and murdered people and dealt drugs and did other bad things to get there."

He raises his eyebrows at me. "The bad things you choose to do don't land you in the State Pen. Good for you."

I laugh at his oversimplification, so he allows, "Fine. Many of them, if released today, would go back to doing the same bad things they did to land them there, but as far as the murderers were concerned, most of them were remarkably normal guys whose lives are now defined by a single act in their otherwise ordinary lives."

"Really." It's not a question, but more of a plea for him to be real.

"Really." He cocks his head to the side, his gaze unfocused, while he remembers. "Of course, on the other hand, you have the guy who poisoned his father over a two-hundred-dollar debt he didn't want to pay back, and the man—a former pastor, in fact—who hired a hitman to kill his wife when she found out about an affair he was having. Those acts required more than one moment of bad judgment. Premeditation. But I was still never afraid around those people. Life on the inside is incredibly structured and bland and... boring."

"Until everyone's lulled into that false sense of security, and a bunch of 'harmless, ordinary guys' take the opportunity to riot," I say.

Laughing, he says, "I never said they were harmless. But during my chaplaincy, nothing like that ever happened. And there were only two inmates put to death. The first was, like, my second week on the job. Kid you not. Talk about baptism by fire!" He shakes his head. "Couldn't tell you much about that day. I hardly knew the guy, but I was expected to be there for him, which wasn't a problem, of course. But it was... surreal."

"You got to know the other guy who was executed, though, right?"

He nods. "Yeah. Greg. I still keep in touch with his folks, although not as much as I used to. I need to do a better job of that."

"You two were close?"

With a sigh, he rubs the back of his neck. "Ah, 'close'? I don't know if that's the right word. I knew him well. He didn't know much about me. That's how it works in there. I was a fixture of the institution. I was there for them. It wasn't reciprocal. Most of them didn't want to know more about me—or any of the other chaplains—as a person, anyway. But even when they did, I was trained not to divulge personal information."

"Because they could find ways to hurt you or your loved ones?"

He makes a face. "You've been watching too much *American Justice*."

I release a self-deprecating chuckle. "Then why not tell them about yourself, if they ask?"

He puffs out his cheeks as he thinks about it, then releases his held breath. "It was better that way. My ministry was about *them*. It was about their personal relationship with Christ. I didn't go there every day to make friends or socialize."

"That's what Vince—and others—were for, right?" I offer, trying to give him an opening to talk about *her* while letting him know that I understand he would need to be around someone beautiful after being stuck inside *there* all day.

"Yeah. Not that it was easy to meet people. Or that I wanted to. Most days, I'd leave here, and I didn't want to see or talk to a single person. More accurately, I didn't want anyone to talk to *me*. No more revelations, confessions, or admissions. I learned not to let anything shock me, but it's still wearing sometimes to be told things, even when you're unable to be shocked by them."

Hmmm… As my family's former official secret keeper, I know exactly what he means. And he knows I know, which is why it's surprising he's never pointed out the connection and confided in me about this.

Before I can ask him why he hasn't, though, he says, "Some nights, I didn't even want to go through a fast food drive-through on my way home, because that would mean talking to someone. I was always poised to have people tell me the things weighing on their hearts. Like the person at the window would hand me my change and say, 'Oh, by the way, I killed my younger brother.'"

I cringe. "Yikes."

It would be difficult to date someone like that. I wonder how he even met What's-Her-Gut. Nope. Not going to obsess about it.

He laughs. "Yeah, but then on the other hand, sometimes I needed to talk to someone after a particularly trying day. And in those cases, I wished that I had made more of an effort to make friends. But I didn't. I didn't even let Vince introduce me around the church. I came to services, I worshiped, I left."

"Which is why you didn't know Pete's name. I thought that was odd, given how good you normally are with names." I push on his shoulder. "Especially a character like Pete. You love guys like that."

"I do now. Not so much back then."

"Were you really all that different?" I ask, searching his face for any clues.

"Yep," he simply answers with a sad smile.

"Tell me," I urge quietly.

He opens his mouth as if he's going to comply, but after a few false starts, he says in a surprised tone, "You know what? I can't even put it into words. I know I'm different. I know I've changed, but to tell you the truth, it's hard to remember much about that guy. He's a mystery to me."

I smile encouragingly at him, but for some reason, his declaration turns my insides to ice and scares me more than the thought of what goes on inside the walls of that prison beyond our car windows.

Like he downplayed the scariness of life on the inside, though, Brice acts as if the changes he's undergone in the past ten years are no big deal. With a shrug, he says, "The old me seems like just another person I used to know and have lost touch with. But he's someone I don't even miss. So he must not have been that great." He punctuates this with a grin and looks away, toward the complex of buildings. Softly, he declares, "I miss some of the guys I met in there a lot more than I miss him."

A selfish part of me wants him to try harder to remember that guy, if only for a while. Then I realize how hard it might be for him to think about that time in his life—or the two years in Kansas, which sound equally bleak—and I resist the compulsion to ask him again to tell me more. It's not worth his psychological discomfort to satisfy my curiosity. I guess it's enough to know that he's happier now than he was then. I just hate knowing he was ever unhappy. And I don't ever want him to be unhappy again.

It's obvious that he's thinking about it, though, even if he's not talking about it. We've been walking along the beach at Anastasia State Park for nearly fifteen minutes without either of us saying a word. He pays close attention to his feet as they cut through the foamy surf. I feel like he may have forgotten I'm here, despite my fingers woven against his.

To regain his attention, I yank on his hand and pull him away from the water. "Let's sit for a while," I say when he raises his head.

He follows me to a clump of picnic tables. I climb on one table and sit with my damp, sandy feet resting on the bench below. He takes up a position next to me, dropping his shoes on the table behind us.

We don't have the place entirely to ourselves, but it's still quiet. We've encountered some other couples out for afternoon strolls and a father and son flying a kite, but we've effectively ignored the strangers, and they've returned the favor, as if we're all in silent agreement to pretend we're alone.

"Her name was Erin," he says, out-of-the-blue.

My confusion clears as soon as he takes off his sunglasses and clarifies, "The woman Pete was referring to, the one I brought with me to church."

"Ah. Erin."

He nods. And right when I'm expecting him to smile or joke or make a remark about their relationship being casual or no big deal or a distraction, he stuns me with, "We were engaged."

"To be married?" I nearly whisper, but not quietly enough for the stupid question to go unheard.

Nice guy that he is, Brice doesn't call me out on being a moron. Instead, he nods earnestly again and swallows. "Yes. And I should have told you. A long time ago. But as long as I never talk about it, it never happened. In my mind, at least."

All I can do is stare numbly at him.

"Say something," he begs.

"Uh…" is the most that escapes. The movie in my head of him down on one knee, offering a ring to a stunning specimen—in a bikini, oddly enough—is too distracting to allow me to talk. Or even form thoughts that could eventually translate into spoken words.

"We weren't engaged long, anyway," he continues after I fail to speak on command. "She said she didn't want to be a pastor's wife."

I gasp at that information, tears immediately stinging my eyes when I remember saying the same thing to him during one particularly bad fight while we were dating.

He chuckles, obviously remembering that same fight. "I know, right? But it was different when she said it. She meant it. And when she said it, I was so relieved." He scoots closer to me on the table and nudges my toes with his. "Proposing to her was a desperate attempt to make the personal side of my life as meaningful as my calling."

"But you must have loved her to ask her to marry you."

Watching a pelican dip and dive over the water, he replies, "Oh, I think I loved the idea of her and me together. I loved the idea of being married and having someone to come home to every night. I loved thinking that I could live some semblance of a normal, happy life outside of those prison walls. But..." He sighs. "It was all a fantasy."

"What happened?"

Turning his head to look me in the eyes, he says, "It's kind of a deal breaker when someone says she doesn't want to be the spouse you need her to be."

"*I* said that, too." I slide my arm between his side and his elbow and clasp his hand in mine.

He threads our fingers together and stares at them. "Big difference. When she said it, I thought, 'Oh, well. I guess that's that'; when you said it, I knew I had to figure out a way to change your mind."

"Actually, you said the offer wasn't on the table," I say lightly.

He laughs. "I did, didn't I?"

"Yes. And that's when I realized I wanted it to be. On the table, that is."

"You're contrary that way."

"You know it, too. You knew it even then."

"Perhaps I had an inkling. But trust me, I had no idea the magnitude of your contrariness."

I nudge him with my shoulder. "Shut up."

He clears his throat. "When I said that to you, I wasn't calling your bluff or using reverse psychology or the Vulcan mind meld on you."

"Nerd."

Ignoring my jab, he says seriously, "I was devastated when you told me that. And I thought it was happening all over again. But when I had a chance to think more about it, I realized there was a critical difference between what she said and what you said, even though you used nearly the exact same words. Your statement was the result of a lack of confidence. Hers was a lack of willingness."

"I'm glad you could see that, because I felt confidently unwilling at the time."

Looking down his nose at me, he says with a wink, "I guess it's a good thing I'm such a master interpreter of human motivation, then."

I roll my eyes at him, but my words are more indicative of my feelings on the topic than my actions. "Absolutely. It's definitely worked to my advantage."

He squeezes my hand, almost to the point of pain and looks down at his lap. "Oh, and it probably helps that I was so in love with you that nothing short of a restraining order was going to make me leave you alone."

I stare at his profile until he looks up at me again. Then I ask a little too hopefully, "But you weren't in love with her?"

His sheepish grin is baffling until he replies, "Well, I thought I was, and I even fancied myself heartbroken when she admitted her reservations and broke up with me—and, incidentally, asked to keep the ring."

"That little tramp!"

Cracking up at my fierce loyalty, he says, "Bah! I didn't want it back, anyway. The point is…" He unlinks our arms and holds my face in his hands. "I never felt for her the whole time I knew her as much as I felt for you the first time I saw you."

"Whatever."

"I'm serious."

"Well, it sounds good."

He brushes his mouth against mine. "It's not lip service, Missy. I'm telling you the God's honest truth."

I kiss him back, wanting to believe him. "You're a lot more mysterious than I ever gave you credit for," I say when we part.

Leaning forward, he laughs against my lips. "That's it for me. I'm all out of secrets. You know everything now."

"We both know that's not true. But we can save the other revelations for another time. Right now, I think you and I need to find our way back to the hotel."

"My finely honed intuition is telling me something quite basic is motivating you right now."

"You'd be right again," I say through my laughter.

"Right then. Let's go."

He springs from the table and jogs in the direction from which we came, backtracking after a few steps to return to the table to get his shoes—and me.

〜

We devoted the next two days to lazing on the beach. We had planned to see some of the sights in St. Augustine, but it was so sunny, hot, and humid that we decided to hang out by the water in as few clothes as possible and save our inland excursions for the upcoming cooler days promised to us by local meteorologists.

In the evenings, we explored some interesting-looking restaurants. The one we found last night was little more than a shack on a dock but served the best seafood I've ever eaten. Of course, after a day in and by the water, we were starving, and anything would have tasted world-class.

I'm also going to cite that as my excuse for getting carried away with the buckets of beer bottles that kept arriving at our table. I was downright silly by the time we returned to the hotel room. I vaguely remember twirling pieces of my clothing over my head and prancing around the room in nothing but those cursed stilettos that I caved and packed in response to Brice's special request.

This morning, I'm delaying any movement other than breathing for as long as possible. I feel fine right now, but I'm sure that won't last as soon as I open my eyes or move my head. I felt Brice stirring a few seconds ago, but he's still again. Good. Just a few more minutes…

That's when I remember we're supposed to meet Vince for a day on his boat.

Not wanting to wake up Brice, I suppress a groan and breathe deeply through my nostrils. Boats and I don't get along on the best of days. A hangover is not going to fit well into the equation. Nor are most of my usual hangover remedies. I can't very well have a heavy, fried breakfast or indulge in some "hair of the dog" right before going on a boat. Tylenol and lots of water, it is, then. Plus, Dramamine.

Now that I have a plan of action, I'm brave enough to

crack an eyelid to test the effect of light on my head. And I'm confronted by something I've never witnessed: Brice is lying on his belly, propped on his elbows, watching me while I sleep. Or maybe making sure I'm still breathing. Or not choking on my own vomit, since I'm on my back. Whatever the reason for his careful observation, he looks quite serious.

My surprise at what he's doing makes me open my eyes wider without considering the consequences. Surprisingly, it doesn't hurt. I chance a smile/grimace, but before I can say anything to acknowledge the situation (or my behavior last night), he edges closer to me, grabs my face, and puts his mouth on mine, opening my lips with his tongue.

Oh, gosh. Morning breath is one thing, but hangover breath is the worst! I—

Before I can think more about that, though, he's doing things to me under the covers that make all other thinking impossible.

Plus, oddly enough, I don't feel hungover. I feel pretty damn great, especially right this second. And this is no marathon, languid, take-your-time session. Someone's in a hurry. My body's extremely cooperative.

After we've both recovered, I roll toward him and say, "What was *that* about?"

"I love you very much," he answers with a grin that saves his earnest statement from sentimentality.

I cuddle up to his chest. "I love you, too. When I stare at *you* in your sleep, though, you get annoyed. I never thought you'd do it to me."

He rubs my shoulder blades with his thumbs. "I do it all the time."

"What?" I try to look up at his face, but I'm smooshed against his body. All I can see is his Adam's apple, which bobs twice now.

"You just caught me this time."

"Creepy!"

"I know."

"You're such a hypocrite!"

He laughs at that. "I suppose I am."

"When do you do this sleep-watching?"

He thinks about it. "Depends. Most of the time when I wake up before the alarm but sometimes when I come to bed later than you, and you're dead to the world."

"Great. I'm sure I've looked awesome."

"You're always very peaceful. And quiet."

That makes me laugh. "Oh, I'm starting to see the draw, now."

"It's not like that. But if I were to watch you or look at you during the day, you'd ask me what was wrong. 'Do I have a booger on my face? Is there food in my teeth? Is that zit on my chin getting bigger?' So, I study you while you sleep. Because I can't get enough of you."

My heart rate quickens. After a few seconds of silence, I say, "I have a zit on my chin?"

He sighs. "No. You never do."

"It's so sweet of you to pretend not to notice."

I listen to his breathing for a while, then say, "Considering I don't remember much of last night—except for a few embarrassing snippets—I feel great."

"That was my plan," he replies.

I giggle. "I mean, I don't feel hungover. Although what you just did *was* extremely nice."

"Why, thank you. But I was referring to the glasses of water I made you drink before you fell into bed."

"Oh. I don't remember that."

"Apparently."

"I *do* remember some naked prancing."

"That was after the water."

"And for some reason, I have the theme song to *Beaches* in my head."

"Maybe because you were singing about me being your hero at the top of your lungs."

"While naked?"

"You were wearing shoes."

"Nuh-uh."

"Yes-huh." He laughs. "It was adorable. Then you passed out."

"I— Wait a minute. I passed out?"

With a kiss to the top of my head, he rolls onto his back, then sits on the edge of the bed. "Yep. Hey, we have to get moving. I told Vince we'd meet him at the marina at 10:00, and it's a good thirty-minute drive from here. I'm assuming you want to shower?"

"Uh, yes. That would be a correct assumption."

"Hop on in there, Bette." He pulls on some clothes and slips his bare feet into his flip-flops. "I'll run down to the continental breakfast buffet before they shut it down. You want a muffin, or what?"

I straddle the shower door's threshold while considering my options. "Blueberry, please. And a carton of orange juice. And a coffee. Are you going to be able to carry all that?"

"I'll manage. Be right back."

He truly *is* my hero. And there go those damn lyrics through my head again.

17

SAILING

*W*hen a pastor tells me, "Hey, I have a boat! Let's go out on the water when you come down to visit," I picture something slightly more dignified than a dinghy but nothing fancy. I also imagine being forced to learn things I don't want to learn, like which side is "leeward" and which is "aft" and what happens when you untie *that* rope. Oh, and knots. Lots of knots, both the ones you tie and the ones that measure speed.

Therefore, when we get to the marina, the slips of which are crammed with huge, gorgeous, shiny *yachts*, with names like "Liquid Courage" and "Miss E" and "Lookin' Shipper," I think, *We're either in the wrong place, or we're about to get into a boat that's hidden between two of these massive watercraft.*

Wrong on both counts. As I stare up at one called "Redeemed," Vince appears at the shiny metal rail and calls down to us, "Hey, guys! Climb aboard!"

"Climb" is right.

"Good grief, brother. You weren't kidding about those stocks, were you?" Brice says when we're on deck and looking around at our luxurious surroundings.

Vince grins proudly. "No. Would I lie? But it's not just my boat. I'm part-owner with three other guys. We take turns with it and pay equally for all maintenance and repairs." Now he says sheepishly, "We use it for poker night more than anything else."

"Do you know how to drive this thing?" I ask, trying not to sound as apprehensive as I feel.

He laughs. "Yes! I'm certified."

"I think the word you're thinking of is 'certifiable,'" Brice corrects his friend.

"You two are quite the comedy duo this morning. Maybe I'll practice my man-overboard rescue techniques using one or both of you later," Vince says.

"Bring it. I'm an excellent swimmer."

"I'd like a life jacket, please," I request immediately.

"I was only kidding!"

"No, really. I took some Dramamine on the way here, and I'm ready to be strapped in."

Vince shoots Brice a look.

Brice explains, "Boats aren't Peyton's favorite things."

"Why didn't you say something? I assumed— You guys went on a cruise for your honeymoon!"

I say, "I'll be fine. Once I'm wearing a life jacket."

Brice pats my head. "The cruise was… interesting. She and I perfected simultaneous—"

Vince holds up his hand. "I don't need to know this!"

"Puking," Brice finishes with a dirty look aimed at his friend.

Pretending to wipe sweat from his brow, Vince says, "Whew! I thought you were going somewhere else with that. Well, we'll have calm waters today, I think, but I admire a woman who puts safety first. And that also sounded wrong, so I'm going to lead you on a tour of this vessel. That way, we can end this awkward conversation."

"Good idea," Brice says as we follow the captain.

Below deck, there are two small bedrooms, a galley kitchen, a table that can seat up to eight people, and a living area, complete with a huge, flat-screen TV.

"You still have your house?" Brice checks. "Because if I had a boat like this, I'd want to live on it."

"You'd be living alone," I remind him. "Of course, that may be the whole point."

"I meant *him*," he nods toward Vince. "The single guy."

"I would, but I'd be homeless whenever one of the other guys wanted to take it out."

"Oh, yeah. That's right. Too bad." Suddenly, Brice shudders. "Oh, man. I just imagined living on this thing with our four boys."

I rub his back. "Deep breaths. It was all a bad dream."

Vince opens a cabinet and pulls out a puffy, orange vest. "Here ya go, Peyton. Now, let's get this show on the seas."

Twenty minutes later, we drop anchor in gentle waters, the depth of which I try not to fathom while I congratulate myself on maintaining possession of my blueberry muffin. The Dramamine must be working. And Vince appears to know what he's doing, so as he bustles around the deck, sometimes calling out simple instructions to Brice, I shed the life jacket and stow it under one of the boat's padded bench seats, within easy reach.

Once Vince has performed all his sailor duties, he disappears below deck but returns in a few minutes with beers and a platter of cheese, crackers, and fruit.

I politely decline the refreshments but my husband digs in after popping the cap off a bottle and taking a swig. Vince sits on the bench opposite us and opens a beer of his own. Brice asks his buddy about his new sailing hobby, which is the start of a long, nearly incomprehensible conversation between the two of them. Something about Coast Guard regulations and certifications. Certain I'm not going to miss anything exciting, I excuse myself to go below deck and use the bathroom.

When I return, the guys are standing at the helm of the ship, their backs to me. I'm about to compliment Vince on his—or his friends'—hand soap and lotion selection— anything to change the subject to something more inter- esting—when I hear *her* name. From Vince.

"But— Oh, you know Erin."

"Well, I *did*. Don't think I can claim to know her anymore," Brice replies, sounding regretful. Or am I being paranoid? Maybe he's more nostalgic. Is that any better, though? Not in my book.

It's obvious they have no idea I'm back. I make an impulsive decision to let that continue to be the case. Crouching behind a cabinet marked with a sticker shaped like a fire extinguisher, I settle in to listen.

"She hasn't changed much at all," Vince says. "Still working for the state as a social worker, though."

Lah-dee-dah. A do-gooder, too? Damn. I was hoping she was a shallow bitch, working at a clothing store that sells sizes zero to three, mainly so she can get a discount on all the latest styles.

"She looks pretty much the same, too."

That's not fair, either. Ten years older but still looks like she's in her twenties?

"She has a little girl named Yulia and a boy named Bryce—with a 'y.'"

That revelation makes Brice-with-an-"i" choke on his beer.

While he sputters, Vince continues, "She's divorced, though. Recently."

Hmm… not so perfect, after all.

After a few more throat-clearings, Brice has recovered. There's a slight edge to his otherwise light tone when he says, "How did you get all this information, Whitaker? You guys go on a date, or something?"

For once, Vince doesn't laugh. "No. I told you, she came to see me a couple of months ago. At the church. In my office. She, uh, wanted to know if I still kept in touch with you."

That little ring-hawking hussy!

Brice sucks in a huge breath and seems to be holding it when he says in a choked voice, "Oh."

"I told her what you've been up to. Married. Four kids. Living in Missouri. Nothing she couldn't find out by looking you up on Facebook. I hope that's okay."

"Of course. We were still friends when I left here."

"You were? Didn't seem like it to me."

"Well, we weren't enemies. I wished her well. I'm sorry to hear her marriage didn't work out."

"But not surprised?"

"I wouldn't say that."

"She was always a bit high maintenance."

"Aren't we all, in our own ways?"

"No. You're not. I'm not. She was. Is. Like I said, she hasn't changed a bit."

And there it is again. I thought I had imagined the disapproving tone in Vince's voice earlier, but nope… it's definitely there. He doesn't like this Erin chick. Maybe he never did. I can't help but smile at his fierce loyalty.

Then it hits me he didn't include me in his list of "low maintenance" people, but I can hardly object without blowing my cover. Plus, I don't have much justification for objecting.

Holding onto the top of the acrylic casing in front of me, I shift uncomfortably on my creaky knees and strain to hear Brice, whose voice has dipped to almost inaudible levels.

"How old are the kids?" he asks.

"Yulia's five; Bryce is two. She showed me pictures. Beautiful children."

"Ah. Yes. I'm sure."

This wistful statement stirs up some raging jealousy—and more curiosity, which battles with a desire to stop my husband talking about this wretched divorcée and remembering her with any fondness. Nosiness wins.

"Anyway, I discouraged her from contacting you," Vince says now, "but she can obviously do whatever she wants. It's not like it's difficult to find you. I'm surprised she went to the trouble to ask me about you when she has the Internet at her disposal. Getting in touch with you is as easy as sending you a friend request or a private message on Facebook."

"She hasn't."

"Good."

Brice laughs. "It's not a big deal if she does."

Like hell! I wonder if he'd think it was a big deal if Drex became my new online pen pal. Or Matt. Or Chad. Or…

Brice sighs before I can get too much further in my romantic roll call (thankfully). "I'd prefer she didn't contact me, though, if I'm honest."

"I could see where it might make for some awkward dinner conversation," Vince says.

"I just told Peyton about Erin the other day. Sunday. Your sermon really got to me."

"Yes!" Vince hisses. "At least one person was awake and

listening. Anyway, I've been preaching that sermon to you for six years now. It's about time you told her. How'd she take it?"

"I'm not saying; you'll just say 'I told you so.'"

That gets the biggest laugh of all.

"Yeah, yeah, yeah. You're so wise," Brice says over his best friend's wheezing. "I wasn't hiding it from her because I thought she'd be angry or upset."

"Liar."

"Okay, a little of those things, maybe, especially since I waited so long to say anything. But like I told her, it was mostly about trying to forget it ever happened."

"What's the point in regretting it?"

"I was an idiot. I was a sad, depressed, pathetic, lonely, horny idiot."

With a choked laugh, Vince says, "That's quite a list of transgressions. But like I've said a hundred times in the past, isn't it better that it all *didn't* work out?"

"Of course!" Brice cries, then says more quietly, "Absolutely. I haven't doubted that for a second. Not since meeting Peyton, anyway. But proposing to Erin was ill-conceived."

"If that's the worst it was, then consider yourself lucky."

"I do. Every day."

"Good. Because the only thing worse than a lucky bastard is a lucky bastard who doesn't appreciate how lucky he is."

"Nice."

Now that their conversation is winding down, I figure they're going to miss me, so I duck-walk toward the stairs, stand, and make a noisy show of "returning" to the deck.

Brice half-turns and smiles at me while lowering his beer bottle from his mouth. "I was starting to wonder if I needed to make sure you were okay down there."

I squint into the sun. "You two are so boring," I say. "I decided to do some snooping, poke around in the night stands to see if I could find anything interesting." I wink at Vince, but he's so visibly relieved that I'm kidding that I make a note to check for real later.

More immediately, though, the color of Brice's face catches my attention. "Oh, hon. You're getting pink already. You'd better go reapply some sunscreen. It's in my bag downstairs."

He presses his fingertips to his cheeks. "I gotta hit the head, anyway." Without any further conversation, he trots down the stairs and disappears below.

As soon as he's gone, I turn back to Vince and say without preamble, "I heard everything you two just said about *her*."

He narrows his eyes at me. "Oh, so you *were* poking around, just not in my cabin?" When I maintain confident eye contact with him, refusing to let him turn this around on me, he sighs. "It was hard for him to admit that part of his life to you."

"I know. We all have sh—tuff like that in our pasts, though, don't we?"

With a shrug, he replies, "Most people do, yes. We learn by making mistakes. We learn better if we own up to those mistakes."

"Some of us do," I mutter.

He raises an eyebrow at me.

I try to wave off his interest. "Sorry. I'm preoccupied by a secret I know about someone that she refuses to tell to her fiancé. And not just an 'I-was-engaged-for-five-minutes-to-someone-else-once' kind of secret. A *huge* one. A potentially deal-breaking one."

"You'd be surprised what constitutes 'deal-breaking' nowadays," he says.

"An abortion? Is that serious enough?"

He winces. "Oh. That's a biggie."

Now that I've told someone else, I can't stop talking. I tell myself it's okay because I'm not naming names, and I'm saying this to Vince, a pastor who's far-removed from the principal players. But I know I'm breaking my promise to Jen, and I feel awful about it. I can't hold onto her secret anymore, though. I can't bear its weight.

Miserably, I reply, "Yeah. And this person's fiancé would care. A lot. At least, I hope he would."

"Care, yes. But stop loving her?"

"I hope not, but… maybe. He should at least have all the information."

"And you're wondering if it's right for you to provide him with that information?"

I think about it for a few seconds. "No. I know it's not my place. But I'm also not sure if it's right to keep quiet. I can't win."

"It's difficult, but it's not about winning. It's about supporting people, even when you feel they're making a mistake. You have to prepare yourself to be there if that mistake's consequences come to fruition." He walks to the bow and grasps the rail; I follow him. "I'm assuming we're talking about Jen and Wes?"

I stiffen. "I didn't say that."

He nods. "I see. Okay. Whatever. I'm not going to tell anyone, of course."

"I know you won't."

"And you won't, either."

"Well, I told *you*, didn't I? I'm a horrible friend."

He laughs. "Is that all it takes to be horrible? To confide in a pastor about something on your heart? Something that involves someone you love? Listen." He grabs my hand in one of his and pats it with the other. "You've been there for this person for a long time. And vice versa. You know a lot about each other, maybe more than is comfortable sometimes. Tough it out, though. It's worth it. Don't give up on her."

Brice pops his head around the corner, startling me. I yank my hand away from Vince. Fortunately, my husband doesn't seem to notice my guilty reaction to his reappearance but inquires, "Either of you want another beer?"

I shake my head no while Vince accepts the offer. As soon as he's sure Brice is gone, he continues our conversation. "I knew he'd eventually tell you about Erin. Not because of any nagging from me about it but because he knew it was the right thing to do. And I also made sure that no matter how *you* reacted, he knew I'd be here to get him through whatever the aftermath would be. That's what you need to be for your friend. A soft place to land if and when she finally gets the courage to tell her fiancé—or husband, if it takes that long—about this painful thing in her past."

At the sound of whistling and Brice's light footsteps behind us, Vince maintains the same tone of voice but increases his volume, and says, "And that's the story of how I beat your husband at every single one of fifty rounds of miniature golf at fifty different courses in this great state of Florida over the course of eighteen months. True story."

Brice presses a bottle of beer into Vince's free hand and stands next to me, smelling of sunscreen and hand soap. "You are pathetically proud of that," he says, effectively confirming Vince's claim.

"It's a stunning statistic, when you think about it. You never managed to beat me, not even once. Not even the time we played when I had that awful sinus infection, and it nearly killed me every time I had to bend over to get my ball from the cup. As a matter of fact, I think I clobbered you by an even bigger margin than usual that day."

"I felt sorry for you, so I didn't even try."

"What about the other forty-nine times?"

"I knew how much winning meant to you. You do unappealing—oftentimes humiliating—things for your friends when you know something's important to them."

Vince raises his eyebrows and shoots me a knowing look. "Indeed, you do."

Half-kidding, I grumble, "How do you guys turn everything into a mini-sermon? It's unbelievable."

Vince cracks up at my disdain, but Brice smirks with his beer bottle up to his lips and says, "Just one of our many talents."

"You're upset about Erin."

It's the first thing Brice says when we get in the car after saying a lighthearted goodbye to Vince at the marina. We've had such a fun, enjoyable afternoon that I'm taken aback by such a direct, serious statement the minute we're alone.

When I realize what he's accusing me of, I'm quick to say, "I'm really not. What makes you think that?"

"It's okay to admit it. You've been quiet today ever since you talked to Vince."

Agh! How do I explain *that* without telling him what Vince and I were *really* discussing?

Before I can decide between the truth and a half-truth, much less devise something to say, he rushes ahead. "I feel like such a jerk for not telling you before we came down here. I don't know what I was thinking, like it wouldn't come up. I shouldn't have risked wasting a single second of our vacation on such a dreary topic." He presses his thumb against his red knee and watches the spot turn white, then return to its sunburned state.

"Look at me," I demand.

He does, but he looks miserable. Or scared. Or something.

Laughing makes me feel mean, but I can't help it! He's so... pathetic. Time to 'fess up. "You were—what was it again?—'lonely and depressed and pathetic and horny.'"

He blinks at my paraphrase of what he told Vince.

"Yeah. I heard you."

"But you were—"

"Hiding behind the fire extinguisher's cabinet."

"Oh."

"I figured listening to you guys was the only way to hear you talk about her, though. Not that I blame you. It would be weird if you and I sat around discussing it. I get it."

He nods. "I hate that there's anything to discuss at all."

"There's not. Unless she tries to get in touch with you. Then we have some talking to do."

"Yeah. I know."

"Do you? Because I would *not* be okay with that."

I can see him swallow, so I hurry to backtrack and put him at ease again. "What you told me Sunday afternoon... It was surprising, and I'll admit I've thought a bit about it since, wondering what she was like, wondering what you two were like together. But it was a long time ago, and you haven't been in contact with her at all since you left here ten years ago, so—" I stop, thinking it might be a good idea to check the accuracy of that statement. "Right?"

He nods.

"Then it would be silly for me to feel threatened by her or your relationship with her. It has nothing to do with us."

He rests his warm hand on my knee. "It doesn't. You're so right about that. And I think that's part of why I didn't say anything before now. It seems so irrelevant!"

"It's not *entirely* irrelevant, since it's a part of your life, and I feel wrong-footed that I've been in the dark about that —and who knows what else—but the details are irrelevant, yes."

He's back to looking ashamed.

"Please, stop looking at me like that!"

"Like what?"

"Like one of the boys after they've colored on the walls... in their feces."

"I *do* feel like I've done a crappy job of making this vacation relaxing, thanks to this stupid confession."

I groan at his pun, but I cradle his face in my hands. "Hon, I'm wet-noodle relaxed. *You* need to relax."

"You're happy? You're having a good time?"

Letting go of his face, I return more fully to my side of the front seat. "How can you even question it? Other than that seriously unfunny prank Vince pulled today, when he yelled, 'Shark!' while I was tethered to the back of the boat on that raft, I haven't had this much fun since our honeymoon. I promise."

He seems like he's starting to believe me. "Okay. I'm so worried I ruined it."

"I'm getting a kick out of being with you while you rediscover all these places and show them to me. And listening to you and Vince talk about your misadventures as young, stupid guys is endless entertainment. I wish you guys would talk more like that during his visits. Hearing you two laugh and give each other a hard time is... I don't know. I can't think of a word that doesn't sound over-the-top, but 'great' doesn't cut it, either. It brings me joy, I guess."

He smiles shyly. "I know, we're dorks."

"Adorable dorks."

Taking a deep breath and looking loath to say what's on his mind, he nevertheless returns to the original topic. "So if you're not upset about Erin, what were you and Vince talking about when I came back from the bathroom?"

Eyes wide, I open my mouth, but he cuts me off. "No, don't even try to tell me it was about the stupid mini-golf championship. Vince wouldn't have to hold your hand to break the news to you that I stink at putt-putt."

I laugh at that, but at the same time, I'm freaking out that I can't divulge the details of what I said to Vince. I can't lie, either, so I simply say, "Jen and I still aren't getting along that great."

His mouth turned down, he asks, "Why haven't you told *me*?"

"I *have* told you."

"Yeah, but that was months ago. I thought things were better."

I shake my head. "We're trying to pretend they are, but… Anyway. I needed the advice of someone further from the situation. Someone who knows what it's like to be friends with someone for a *long* time, through good times and bad times."

"Oh. Well, I know how to be a friend."

Smiling affectionately at him, I tilt my head. "You're a *great* friend. That's not what I meant. It was more about talking to someone objective. I just needed to make sure I'm doing the right thing. Or trying to." My stomach flutters as I edge close to the precipice, hoping I don't lose my balance while looking over to see how far the fall would be. "It's a sensitive issue, too. One that Jen doesn't want you to know about."

His eyebrows shoot toward his hairline. "Oh? Something to do with Wes?"

"Please, don't try to guess! If you only knew how many times I've almost broken my promise to her and told you. Please, don't tempt me. Vince helped me a lot today. In about five minutes."

"Yeah, he's smart. He always has good advice."

I stare out at the mild night. "Can we go now? I'm tired, and you're crispy. Let's get back to the hotel, take showers, and discuss what we're going to do tomorrow."

"Castillo de San Marcos?" he says, his voice full of hope as he turns the key in the ignition.

I chuckle at him. "Sure."

"And will you rub aloe on me tonight?"

"Of course. It's the least I can do after how well you took care of me last night. And this morning." I wiggle my eyebrows at him, making him laugh.

He reaches over and ruffles my hair. "You're the best."

18

HOMECOMING

Our day at Castillo de San Marco yesterday was fabulous. Like Anastasia State Park, we nearly had the place to ourselves. We enjoyed a picnic under some palm trees, and Brice got his nerdy history fix with the stone fortress's guided tour and demonstrations.

We chose a late-afternoon departure from Florida today so we'd have a half-day to do some souvenir shopping on St. George Street. Since we had to switch planes in Chicago, we decided to turn our layover into a night at my parents' house, complete with a full family dinner.

After a minor snafu involving our checked suitcase not making it onto our flight, followed by an exorbitant taxi ride, we arrive at my parents' house, about thirty minutes later than we had planned.

"Is that you guys?" Mom asks from the dining room before bustling through to see for herself.

"No, Mom, it's the Avon lady," I retort, cracking Brice and myself up. We're officially slap-happy.

She graces me with one of her double-handed waves. "Oh, you two! Drop your bags right there and come sit down to eat. We started a few minutes ago. You said not to wait," she adds, although neither of us has been able to get a word—disapproving or otherwise—in edgewise.

Brice piles the duffels one on top of the other. I set my purse on his baggage tower. Then we follow Mom into the dining room, where my entire family sits around the massive, loaded-down table.

Various greetings come at us—good-natured, jealous barbs about our tans from Nicole and Lonnie; a full-on hug from my niece, Sadie; and raised wineglasses from Jason and Dustin. Dad says, "Hi," with his mouth full, but teenagers Everett and Caleb barely lift their eyes from their plates (not that I expect teenage boys to stop eating for anything).

Brice and I sit down in the chairs we used to occupy at every Sunday night family dinner when we still lived in Chicago. Being here, just the two of us, brings on a feeling of déjà vu so strong that it makes me dizzy.

As if reading my mind, Dustin says, "It's weird to see you two without kids hanging off you! I was just thinking, 'They look different. Have they lost weight?'"

"Yeah, about seventy pounds," Brice says, loading his plate with roast beef, mashed potatoes, and green beans, his favorite meal of my mom's.

Somewhat recovered from my vertigo, I smile faintly. "Temporary weight loss. It's been nice, but I miss those stinkers."

It's the truth, too. I'm just not ready to stop missing them. I could do with missing them for another week. The thought of going right back to our usual routine fills me with dread.

Brice passes me the basket of dinner rolls. "From the sounds of things, they don't miss us at all. I have a feeling

Jen and my mom are spoiling them rotten. We'll have some major re-programming to do when we get back."

I sigh. "Oh, let's not think about that right now. I'm so tired!"

"What's the story with the luggage?" Nicole asks.

"Yeah," Lonnie says before we can answer, "the airline lost our bags on the way to Barbados, and it was a nightmare to get them back. We had to buy new stuff while we waited for ours to be delivered to our hotel."

I shake my head. "It's not lost; just delayed. They'll be sending it here sometime this evening by courier."

"How nice!" Mom gushes.

"For you," Brice says with a wink. "Otherwise, I was going to have to borrow some of your underwear. I mean, Kent's, not yours." He blushes.

I nudge his foot under the table. "Ew."

His eyebrows jammed together, he turns to me. "Right? Gosh, I'm sorry. That was… wrong."

The chagrin on his face gives me the giggles. "You must be exhausted."

"Yeah, let's go with that explanation," he mumbles, returning to his food.

"You two wanna let us in on that charming conversation you're having over there?" Jason asks.

"Not really," I reply with a cheeky smile.

"Maybe Brice shouldn't have had all that alcohol on the plane," Dustin says.

"I didn't!"

"Well, nobody's wearing my underwear but me, so I'm glad your suitcase is on its way," Dad grouses. "Otherwise, you could borrow the car and run to the store for your own damn briefs."

"This conversation is ridiculous," Mom says with pursed lips. "I mean, honestly! Brice you *must* be overtired."

Keeping his eyes on his plate, he raises his left hand while stabbing several green beans onto his fork. "Again, sorry."

"I think you're hilarious, Dude," Lonnie chimes in.

I rarely agree with Lonnie on anything, but in this case, I have to say, "Me, too."

Brice beams at me but says, "I didn't mean to make anyone uncomfortable."

I roll my eyes. That's never been a concern of anyone else's in my family, so I don't know why he should have to worry about it, but I change the subject anyway, falling into my old role of peacemaker. I can't seem to help myself under this roof.

"Speaking of our suitcase, though, when it gets here, we have presents for all of you. Nothing big," I warn when the boys and Sadie start to get excited, "but little things from the Sunshine State. Probably some sand, too. The beaches were beautiful, but we kept finding sand *everywhere*."

That makes Lonnie snicker, but I choose to ignore him.

"So, what did you guys do?" Mom asks, seeming genuinely interested and ready for a full rundown.

Since Brice is still busy eating like he didn't eat the entire week we were in Florida, I answer (or attempt to), "Well... We, uh..."

Had a lot of sex.

I gulp, my mind racing to give acceptable answers and to block out some blush-worthy images.

Mind-blowing sex.

"Huh-huh."

Now, even Brice is staring at me.

"We hung out at the beach! Yes. And we went to Vince's

church. What a cute little place! If you're ever down there, you have to visit him. He'd love to see you guys. And…"

Sex, sex, sex, sex, sex!

"Let's see… Ummm… Oh! Brice took me by the prison where he was a chaplain. Scary-looking place. But neat to see from a distance. A-and… Oh, gosh. What else? Um…"

Mmm-mmm! All night long…

Brice sets down his fork and covers my hand with his. With a bemused smile, he says, "Now *you're* the one acting tired."

"I *am* tired," I snap to hide my embarrassment. "I already admitted that."

"We went on Vince's boat, remember?" he prompts, as if he's talking to a toddler or someone with dementia.

Addressing the rest of the people at the table, he then lists, "Anastasia State Park—beautiful, quiet, great for walking. Castillo de San Marcos, an old stone fortress, which is super-cool. St. George Street, where we did some shopping before going to the airport…"

"Sounds like you crammed a lot into one week," Mom says.

Oh, there was plenty of cramming.

What the hell is wrong with me?

I clear my throat. "Yeah. Um. Excuse me. I'll, uh, be back. Just have to, uh, use the restroom."

I jump from the table, but instead of heading for the bathroom on the main floor, I jog up the stairs to Nicole's former bedroom, which now serves as the main guest room and is where we'll be sleeping.

I collapse face-down on her bed, blotting my hot, sweaty face on the eyelet comforter.

I'm losing my mind. Yep. That must be it. I had so many orgasms this week that I short-circuited something in my brain. I'm sure it's possible. Now, everything is about *that*. And I was already pretty bad before. Soon, though, I won't only be thinking those things; I'll be blurting them out. In mixed company. Or at the very least, I'll smirk and make comments under my breath, like Lecherous Lonnie. Ugh.

Oh, gosh! Maybe I'm a sex addict. That was all the rage in Hollywood a few years back. But apparently, it's a thing. A thing I might be. I wonder how I could look that up online without getting a bunch of porn spam. Because what if I am one? A sex addict, that is. I need to know. I need to get help. Anyone who nearly tells her entire family she spent her vacation having the best sex of her life has an issue. That's not normal.

I hear the bedroom door open and close, then I see Brice's legs stop next to my head. I notice right away, of course, that I'm eye-level with his junk.

"Everyone thinks you're sick," he says calmly.

"I am."

He sits next to me on the bed and rubs my back. "Oh, no! You are? I thought you were just embarrassed."

"I am."

"Okay. You mind being more descriptive so I know what to tell everyone when I go back downstairs?"

I roll onto my back and pull my legs up so my knees form a place for Brice to rest his elbow while he looks down at my flaming face.

"The whole time I was trying to tell everyone what we did on vacation, I was picturing us…"

"Yes…?"

I widen my eyes. "I was picturing *us*. You know, *us*. In our hotel room."

He licks his lips. "Ohhhh. I see. Dirty girl!"

"Stop teasing me. It's not funny."

"It sort of is, because you sounded like you had a social disorder, but now, knowing that… Yeah, that makes more sense." He laughs loudly. "Well, nobody else knows. They think you're tired. Or not feeling well."

"I'm sure Lonnie knows," I grumble. "He's a sicko."

"Who cares?" He pushes my knees down to move them out of the way and leans over to the side to lie partially on top of me. Kissing my lips, he says, "We had a wonderful time. And that obviously includes what married people do when they're still very much in love with each other. I'm not ashamed of it."

"There's a difference between being unashamed and ready to blurt it out at the dinner table."

"You want to shout it from the rooftops."

"I want to cut out my tongue."

"Oh, now. I think we're both suffering from Filteritis, that's all."

"Filteritis?"

He grins. "Yeah. Our conversational filters are shot. We've had a week of uncensored activities…" He wiggles his eyebrows. "…and private discussions. So, I'm making jokes about your parents' underwear, and you're playing pornos in your head. We need to readjust to being members of civilized society again. Your family is good practice, since they're only semi-civilized."

I laugh at this accurate analysis.

"There. See? It's okay. You're not sick."

I wrap my arms around his back and kiss his lips. "I think I am."

"No, you're not!"

"I totally want to do you right now. You taste like roast beef and yeast rolls."

His pulse quickens in his neck, but he says, "I'm not having sex with you in your dad's house. No way."

"Why not?"

"It's not happening. I don't even think it's physically possible," he asserts. "I mean, look at this room. It still looks like teenage girl territory."

"It was Nicole's room. Trust me; it's seen a *lot* of naked guys."

"Not *this* naked guy."

"You can keep most of your clothes on, then."

"Peyton, no!"

I smirk at the feeling of him pressed against my hip. "Well, I believe you're disproving your theory about it being physically impossible."

"He's a depraved thing. Don't listen to him. I'm saying no. I would be stressed out the whole time."

"I thought you weren't ashamed."

"I'm *not*, when I'm a couple thousand miles away, in a hotel *not* owned by my father-in-law."

"You're no fun."

"You're too *much* fun sometimes. And I appreciate the offer. But no. Thank you." He rolls away from me and sits on the side of the bed, his back to the door.

I sigh. "Fine. What are you going to do about *that* now?" I nod toward his crotch.

"I'm going to tell myself a Bible story."

"The one about King David and Bathsheba?"

"*Not* that one."

"How about the forbidden fruit in the Garden of Eden?"

"No!"

I cackle.

"I've changed my mind."

"Oh?" I start to get excited.

"You *are* sick."

We've hardly said a word since boarding the flight from Chicago to Springfield. The tiny plane didn't allow for much private conversation, even if we *had* been in the mood to talk. Which neither of us was. Brice said he was sore and tired from a night on the ghastly bed in Nicole's old room. I claimed I was tired, too, but my silence was mostly due to pouting.

Although he told me he was kidding when he called me sick, Brice never gave in to my seduction, and we spent the last official night of our vacation lying back-to-back like a couple of old farts.

It's not helping my mood that our vacation is truly about to be over. I'm gutted by that end-of-summer-vacation dread that used to paralyze me every year, the night before the first day of school.

But we both dozed during the flight, and we woke up in much better moods.

Now, in the car, waiting in line at the long-term parking toll booths, he shoots me a smile tinged with sadness. "Well, my bride, let's look at it this way: we have a house full of people who are going to be ecstatic to see us."

I try to be as brave as he is. "True."

"Granted, two of those people are going to be happy to see us because it means they can get back to their normal, quiet lives." He digs his wallet from his back pocket as we inch forward, one car closer to the booth. "But the majority of the people will be glad for more gratifying reasons."

I nod. My throat feels too tight to try to talk, though. I

know the boys' reactions to our homecoming are going to be sweet. And I know that by this time tomorrow, I'll be fine, back to the normal routine, focused on real life and what needs to be done day-to-day. But tonight, no matter what my face says, I'll be grieving my over-too-soon vacation.

Because I'm a brat.

A greedy, spoiled brat. I know I am. I don't need someone to tell me that. How many mothers *never* get time away from their kids? How many women sacrifice grown-up vacations and take family vacations, instead, so they can make memories as a family?

Okay, so this is the first vacation I've had in five years, and my children are too young to have appreciated a family vacation, but what about five years from *now*? I'm not going to want to take them with us then, either. Let's face it: a vacation with kids is not a vacation; it's a business trip.

It's not until we're past the booth and moving at a good clip along the road that leads from the airport to the highway that I feel confident enough to say what I'm thinking without choking up.

"Promise me we'll go on vacation every year," I say.

He rubs his forehead and chuckles. "Uh… not sure we can swing that, hon."

"Not like this one," I clarify, knowing we'll be sacrificing and scrimping and saving for months to come to pay for this past week. "But both taking time off work. Even if it's a staycation, it will be a break in our routines and will ease the burnout." When he still doesn't eagerly agree, I think out loud, "We can drive to Chicago and stay with my parents for a week."

He utters a protesting grunt, but I continue doggedly, "Or stay with Nicole or Jason and Dustin or whatever. Or drive to St. Louis and pretend to be tourists. You may have grown up there, but it's all new to the boys and me. And wouldn't it be fun to show them all those places you used to go as a kid? Catch a ball game, go up in the Arch?"

He looks a lot more amenable to that suggestion, so I keep brainstorming. "Or stay in Springfield but go to the zoo. And take a day-trip to Branson and goof off at one of the amusement parks. Stuff like that."

"I guess…"

"I can't go home right now, thinking this is it for another five years. Especially if we're going to have another baby. That's what I'm saying."

He shoots me a look. "What do you mean, you 'can't go home'? You expect me to agree to all this right now, or else, what? Keep driving?" His laugh is more nervous than amused.

"Maybe," I bluff, unable to keep a straight face.

Reaching over, he pushes my shoulder. "You're silly."

"You are!" I push back. Our vehicle swerves slightly into the passing lane, where another car doesn't appreciate our intrusion.

Brice holds up his hand in an apologetic wave to the person next to us, who's waving back with fewer fingers.

To me, he says, "Cut it out! You're going to make me wreck. Then we really won't get home."

"Oh, well."

"That's not even funny!" he admonishes while laughing.

"Promise me!"

He sighs in an exaggerated fashion. "Okay, okay… I promise."

"No, for real. Like, tomorrow after church, we're going to go into your office, and we're going to look at your calendar for next summer and pick a week. We can figure out the details later, but the dates are going to be set before you can make any excuses or before other people can steal them. You're the senior pastor. *You* get first dibs."

After cringing, he says, "I don't like throwing my weight around."

"I'll throw it around for you."

"You're serious."

"So serious."

He nods solemnly. "Okay, then. I promise. Tomorrow we'll do that."

"Thank you."

He nods toward our exit, which is fast approaching. "So, I can take you home?"

"Yes."

Veering right, we enter our last five minutes of freedom.

19

DEVASTATING HONESTY

*O*h, shit. Mary looks fine, but Jen looks like— Well, she looks like someone who's taken care of four kids under the age of four for a week. Do *I* look like that on a daily basis? No, surely not. I know I usually don't look great, but she looks worse than she ever did during our worst hangovers.

I try to pretend I don't notice. It's only fair, after all. How many times has she looked the other way when I've had poop on my t-shirt and haven't seen a hairdresser in months? Okay, never. She always points it out. Which is okay by me, actually, because I *want* to know when I have poop on my clothes. But I'll give her a break this once, considering she just did me a huge favor and all that.

"You kids look wonderful!" Mary says as soon as the excitement dies down and the children have decided they're not *that* impressed with our homecoming.

I downplay it with a humble, "Oh, come on. We're just tan." My eyes flit nervously in Jen's direction.

"No, no," Mary says. "You two look ten years younger."

At the mention of age, Brice soaks up the compliment.

"You think so?" He turns his face from one side to the other and examines himself in the mirror above the fireplace mantle. "Maybe five or seven years. Or even eight. But ten?"

I laugh at him. "Yes, you look younger than when we first met."

Puffing out his chest, he turns back to the three of us adults and grins. "Wow. It was worth every penny, then."

Quietly, Jen says, "Getting away was exactly what you needed."

"Do you need a vacation to recover from our vacation?" I ask, feeling mega-guilty about the bags under her eyes.

She looks outraged at the question. "No! We had a great time, didn't we, guys? Max, come tell your mom and dad all the fun things we did while they were away."

Max chooses not to even look up from the puzzle he's putting together on the floor when he says, "No!"

Brice's mouth falls open, and he blinks in shock toward his son.

Jen waves her hand. "Aw, don't mind him. It's his new favorite word."

"It is?" This news dismays me.

Mary sighs. "Yes. It's just a phase, though. You all go through it."

"Max Augustus!" Brice scolds. "Don't talk to Aunt Jen that way. Come over here and say you're sorry."

"No!"

Eyes wide and jaw set, Brice takes a step toward Max, but Mary stops him with a whispered, "Don't make a big deal about it."

"But it's rude!"

"So is farting, but you think it's hilarious when he does that," Jen points out.

"That's—" He halts in the middle of the room but keeps

his eyes on Max when he says, "Farts are funny. But a sassy mouth is disrespectful."

"Trust me, kid," Mary says. "Ignore him. Come into the kitchen. I'll cut you some cake, and you two can tell us all about your trip."

I exchange a nervous glance with Brice, who's still looming over Max. The three-year-old is either oblivious or indifferent to his father's displeasure.

"Honey. Leave it," I urge him, not because I think it's no big deal but because I need him to tell Jen and Mary about our vacation, since the only highlights I seem to have are X-rated.

After an hour of our recap, Mary says regretfully, "Well, kids, I should probably head home. This Gammy is worn out."

I give her a grateful hug for her help with the kids, then Brice leaves to walk her to her car and make sure she has all of her things. As soon as they're gone, I turn to Jen, feeling inexplicably awkward.

My shoulders up around my ears, I ask, "How horrible was it, really? You can tell me."

She narrows her eyes at me. "What is your deal? It wasn't horrible at all. As a matter of fact, I think you're lying about these kids, because they were perfect angels for Mary and me."

"Perfect angels? Even though Max's new favorite word is 'no'? Come on."

She nods. "For real. Half the time, he does what you ask him to do, even though he's saying no. The kid doesn't even know how to rebel properly. I blame his dad."

"And Brooks didn't try to kill Aidan? And Harris kept his diaper on?"

"They were sweeties."

"Oh." Now I'm *really* uncomfortable. Because if the kids were great—and Mary's appearance backs up that claim—then why does Jen look so terrible?

As I'm wondering if I should ask her how she's feeling or if she'll see right through that question and know I think she looks like crap, she takes a huge breath, as if she's trying to suck the room's entire air supply into her lungs. Then she says, "I told Wes about… you know… and we haven't talked to each other since."

I blink at her while I try to process what she's saying. She nods while she watches it sink into my sun-saturated brain.

"You told him *everything?*"

"Everything," she confirms, looking both proud and miserable at the same time.

I grasp her shoulder. "Oh, sweetie. What happened? Did he yell at you? What did he say?"

"Not much. And of course, he didn't yell. That's not him."

"No. I guess not."

Tears fill her purple-ringed eyes. "He just— He stared at me for a long time. It felt like an hour, but it was probably only a couple of minutes."

"Oh, gosh."

I know that stare. It's not pleasant.

"Then, I guess he realized I wasn't kidding—not that he ever thought I was—because he dropped my hands like they were dirty and stood up—we had been sitting on my couch —and he shut himself in the bathroom. For a super long time. And he wasn't doing anything bathroom-related in there. I listened." She gulps. "He just didn't want to be in the same room with me." She says this last sentence on a whisper.

As if to prove to her that her hands aren't dirty, I clutch

one of them. "I'm sure he just needed to catch his breath. What did he say when he came out of the bathroom?"

"You mean, an hour later?" she asks in a tortured voice.

I wince.

"Yeah. He grabbed his jacket and told me he needed time to think and that he'd call me."

"When was this?"

"The day you and Brice left."

"What? Why didn't you say something?"

She snorts. "Right. 'I think Wes is going to dump me, because I used to be a dirty tramp and a baby killer. Have a great trip!' Sure. No."

"And he hasn't been in touch at all this whole week?"

Shaking her head, she sniffles. "Not a single text. Nothing."

"Wait a minute. What about church that Sunday?"

Her eyes on her feet, she says, "I didn't go. I couldn't. I was too ashamed."

Now my heart races. "Sit down," I implore her as I try to moderate my anger toward Wes.

As she's pulling out a chair at the kitchen table, Brice returns to the kitchen, rubbing his arms. "My word, it's cold here!" he says with a laugh, clueless as to what's going on. "My blood has thinned out, for—" He freezes as he takes in our expressions. "Uh, what's wrong?"

Before I can look at Jen to check with her, she says brightly, "Nothing!" After clearing her throat and dragging her fingers under her eyes, she gushes, "Your mom is amazing. I'm totally gonna steal her."

Looking unsure, he nevertheless replies, "Oh. I know. Hands off!" He nods toward the living room. "I'm, uh, going to hang out with the guys for a few minutes before putting them all to bed."

I shoot him a grateful look as he glances uncertainly one more time over his shoulder on his way into the other room.

Jen collapses in the chair. "What am I going to do, Peyton?" she moans.

I pull out the chair next to her, remove the booster seat, and sit, putting my arm around her shoulders. "It's going to be okay."

"It's going to be okay, meaning he'll come around? Or it's going to be okay, meaning I'll get over him?" Her face crumples. "I don't want to have to get over him."

Grabbing a napkin from the holder in the center of the table, I draw even closer to her and hand her the square of paper. "Shhh... Please, don't think the worst. Maybe he didn't call, because he knew you were staying here with the kids, and you wouldn't have a chance to talk privately."

Again, she shakes her head. "No. We even discussed before this whole mess that I'd be free in the evenings, when the boys were in bed. We were going to watch TV and play cards with Mary. So, he knew. He knew I would be waiting for him to call."

"He's not going to dump you." Unfortunately, I sound about as sure as I feel. I have to admit, an eight-day silence isn't a good sign.

"But what if he does?" She honks into the napkin. "I left everything in Chicago to be with him. I still don't have a full-time job here. I'm barely making ends meet with my freelance web designing. But none of that mattered, because I love him!"

I don't know what to say to that. I figure now's not a good time to point out to her how she would castigate any other woman for saying something like that, something so dependent.

While the silence between us drags, the joyful sound of

Brice letting the boys climb all over him as he lies on the floor in the other room serves as an incongruous backdrop.

"Daddy! You da monster!"

"Okay! Grrr! I'm going to eat you!"

"Aggh!"

"Daddy monster!"

"Sit on his head, Bwooks!"

"Oof! Hahaha! Harris! Don't tickle my feet! I might kick you."

"Tickle him! Tickle da monster!"

"No, guys. I mean it. Stop!"

I catch myself smiling at the mental image of what's going on in there.

Then Jen releases a shaky sigh. "I should let you guys get settled. I didn't want to even tell you tonight, but…"

"It's all you can think about."

She nods pathetically.

I press my forehead to hers. "Hey. You want to stay here tonight? I'll whip up some brownies. You didn't drink all my wine, did you?"

With a sad chuckle, she says, "No. Most, but not all." Then, after a pause, she addresses my original question. "I need to go home."

"Are you sure?"

Part of her response is to rise from her chair. "Yep. I need my own bed. My own wine."

I stand and wrap her in a hug. "It's going to be fine."

"I don't know," she muffles into my shoulder.

I resist the urge to say, "I do," because something tells me she's sick of hearing about the things I know. After all, I was the one who *knew* she should tell Wes about her abortion. I was the one who knew it would be a mistake to keep it from him.

I, obviously, didn't know shit, as usual.

~

I've spent the past hour loitering downstairs—sorting laundry, picking up toys, plumping throw pillows, hand-washing Aidan's bottles—in the hopes that Brice will be asleep by the time I go to bed. But if the bright strip under our door is any indication, I couldn't outlast him. There's still hope, however, that he fell asleep with the light on, so I gently push open the door and peek through the crack.

Damn.

He's sitting up in bed, as usual, but instead of holding a book, he's gripping his phone and jabbing at the screen with his thumbs.

Normally, I hate when he answers emails in bed. Tonight, however, it may keep him occupied long enough for me to fall asleep before he can try to talk to me.

I say nothing while I go about putting on my pajamas, brushing my teeth, and using the bathroom. Even my goodnight kiss is delivered wordlessly, and I take it as good sign that he's so intent on the message he's tapping out that he barely glances at me.

"Almost done," he mutters, his thumbs a blur.

"Take your time. You're not going to keep me up. I'm bushed."

"And… send." He deposits his phone and glasses on his nightstand and checks to make sure his alarm is set for church tomorrow before pulling on the chain to turn off his light and hunkering into the covers.

"Can't get warm," he grouses, pulling me closer and burying his face in my neck.

I say nothing; I don't move.

"Mmm… You smell good," he murmurs.

I reach over my shoulder and give his head a platonic pat.

He laughs. "Oh, I see."

Forced to talk, I say, "I'm tired, that's all. It's been a long day."

"I know. I thought maybe you'd want to finish what you started last night at your parents' house, though."

"Not particularly, no."

He seems fine with that answer when he says, "Okay," so I feel it's safe to roll onto my back without it being taken as an invitation.

However, when his hand lands on my abdomen and makes its way south, I grab his wrist under the covers.

"Fine, fine," he concedes, relaxing his arm so his palm lies flat on my belly.

After a few minutes of silence, when I think he's dozing, he startles me by speaking into the dark. "Do you think she's in there?"

Since the only "she" I've been thinking about for the past several hours is Jen, I can't get his question to make sense.

"Huh?"

He sounds self-conscious when he elaborates, "You know… our daughter. Do you think she's…" He pats my tummy. "…already there?"

Not in the mood to think about being pregnant, considering everything else on my mind, I reply flatly, "I don't know."

"It's pretty likely, though, don't you think?"

"Pretty good chance," I say distractedly.

That answer obviously thrills him. He scoots even closer to me, although if someone had asked me a second ago, I would have sworn it wasn't possible. "Do you feel different?"

I sigh. "I feel different when I'm *not* pregnant. That's more unusual, anyway."

Taking his hand back, he retreats a few inches. "Sorry. You're not in the mood to talk about it, I guess." He inhales, as if to say something, but stops. Then he starts again. "It's — You haven't— Have you changed your mind? About… things?"

I turn onto my right side to face him and his trepidation. "No!" Now I'm the one who can't get close enough as I press myself against him. "Anyway, it's way too late for second thoughts, knowing us."

He relaxes and holds me to him. Our bodies mold to each other from chest to feet.

"You're probably right," he says with a proud smile in his voice. "Our… stuff… knows what to do."

I crack up at his lame statement. "Our 'stuff'?"

"You know what I mean."

"Hmm."

"We don't have to try. That's all."

"Max took a lot of tries," I remind him.

He squeezes me more tightly. "I wouldn't mind having to try a few more times."

"Just not tonight, okay?"

"Yeah, yeah. I get it."

Now I feel the need to explain myself. "I have a lot on my mind."

"You do? Is this about Jen?"

I nod against his chest.

"What's going on?"

If I'm not careful, his soothing tone and gently swirling hands on my back will hypnotize me into saying too much.

My eyes drifting shut, I say in a spacey voice, "She and Wes had a fight."

He clicks his tongue. "Ah. Is there anything I can do to help?"

That question startles me wide awake like an electric shock, as I imagine him asking Wes the same thing and Wes opening up to him.

I flip to my other side, showing him my back and trying to say as casually as possible, "No. I think we need to stay out of it."

And when I say "we," I mean him, of course, and not so much me.

2 0

BACKFIRE

*M*y stomach jerks and jumps, and my heart palpitates while I stare at the shiny, dark green door in front of me. Okay. I can do this. I need to do this. This is right. This is… shit. It's probably madness, but my advice brought them to this point, so I feel obligated to at least *try* to fix it. Or beat the living daylights out of Wes. Either one. Maybe both.

I raise a shaking hand and press the rectangular button below the peephole on the door. From inside, I can hear the soft "ding-dong" my action produces. I mug at the tiny glass circle, going for "silly" to try to hide my nerves. I know the little stinker is in there, because I saw his car in the parking lot.

After what feels like forever, the door swings open, and a decidedly dismayed Wes stands aside and gestures while saying in his usual monotone, "Come in."

I do. And look around.

The place is immaculate. Every surface gleams. The couch cushions are smooth, with no butt dents, and the plumped throw pillows rest equidistant to each other at each end of the sofa. There are no knick knacks on the bookshelf or tables. Even the fringe on the area rug under the coffee table is perfectly straight, like he combed it, or something.

The lone framed picture on one of the end tables is the only thing out-of-place. It's face down. I recognize that frame. It's the one Jen bought and had engraved with their engagement date before she put one of their engagement photos in it and gave it to him.

And that's why I'm here.

Wes mumbles something about my having a seat, but I prefer to perch at the small breakfast bar that looks into the kitchen from the dining area. I don't want to leave my big butt print in those microsuede couch cushions.

Plus, I don't have a lot of time to be lingering. I told Brice I was going to the grocery store to stock up for the week, so if I'm gone too long, he'll wonder what's going on. That also means I have to actually go grocery shopping after I leave here. I guess that's my punishment for not being honest with my husband.

"I know what you're going to say," he starts, to which I roll my eyes and snort.

"I don't think you do."

Standing in the area between the living room and the kitchen, outside of my reach, he says, "Yes. You're going to say that it was so long ago that I should forget about it and be glad she was upfront with me *before* we were married and—"

I hold up a hand to stop him. "You obviously don't need me to tell you all those things. And it's none of my business."

He cocks his head, clearly confused.

"I'm not here to beg on Jen's behalf."

"Oh. You're not." He says it with no question in his tone.

"I'm not. I know you're in a tough spot. I sort of put you there, as a matter of fact, so I'm sorry." When he looks more perplexed than ever, I admit, "I told her she needed to tell you about… it. Maybe that was crap advice. Maybe ignorance *is* bliss. Maybe knowledge is *not* power in this case, but too much information. I don't know. I mean, what right do you have *not* to forgive her? That's one question I would have, but I'm not here to ask it."

He blinks rapidly but doesn't answer the question I'm not asking. Instead, he asks one of his own. "Then why *are* you here?"

My mouth dries, and my heartbeat quickens again. "The silent treatment you're giving Jen is cruel," I say.

The fingers on his right hand knead the muscle in his left shoulder as he stares me down. "How is that any more of your business than the other… business?"

"Because I can't dictate what's right for you and what you can and can't tolerate or forgive or whatever, but I do know that leaving her hanging is wrong. And when someone mistreats someone I love, that's my business. She loves *you*—"

He moans at that.

"—and she's waiting for your decision, ready to accept it, whatever it may be. I don't think she's slept a wink since she told you. You're torturing her."

He bites his lower lip, looking like he's going to defend himself to me, but when he finally speaks, it's to say, "I'm a virgin."

Must not betray my shock at this. Oh, gosh. WWBD? He would assume the Pastor Pose and nod encouragingly, even if he's thinking,

"Holy Chicago!" That's what you do now. Only you don't have a Pastor Pose. So, just sit and nod.

I nod.

"And she's not. Which I already knew, of course. And you know, I get it. I'm a rarity, an endangered species. She's lived a more conventional life than I have. I accept that."

He studies his socked feet and pauses for so long that I think he's not going to continue. Then he says, "And I also know, logically, that fornication and… the other thing… are both simply sins. Sins for which she is repentant and forgiven. Like all my sins, for which I'm forgiven. But…" He shakes his head, still looking at his feet. "I can't reconcile it. I can't picture myself with someone for the rest of my life, someone who has something that awful in her past, as part of her history. And that's *my* failing, not hers."

Now he looks up. And I wish he'd look back down. Because Wes—Reverend Flat-Line—has tears in his eyes, and I've never seen a more agonized person. I can actually *see* the war going on behind his eyes. His mouth quivers, and his hand shakes when he lets go of his shoulder and touches his forehead.

I tilt my head sympathetically, barely holding onto my own emotions, but before I can speak, he croaks, "I love her, too. I don't want to hurt her."

"You're hurting her by not talking to her about this!"

"What's there to talk about? The only thing left to say is goodbye. And I can't make myself make that call."

"Then don't make *that* call! But you have to make *a* call. Call and ask her to see you, to talk."

"You don't understand."

"I do! I really do, Wes. I know it's not simple. I know it's a hard thing to face, and it's not something to take lightly. But you love her. And you forgive her, right?"

"It's not my place to forgive something that had nothing to do with me."

"Okay. That's a start."

"It's not even about forgiveness."

I'm less sure about that answer and what it means for Jen, but I repeat, "Okay…"

"What if, because of what she did, she can't have children?"

"I don't—"

"And that's just *one* issue; a rather practical, obvious one. There are so many others that I can hardly articulate and might not even understand or think about right now. But they'll surface years down the road, when it's too late, when we're in it. For life."

I open my mouth but remember I'm not here to lobby on Jen's behalf. Keeping my true goal in mind, I say, "Okay, but… Call her. Please. You haven't said *anything* to her. She doesn't know if that means you love her, hate her, never want to see her again, or what! It's killing her."

He sounds more like the Robo-Reverend I know when he states, "I know what I have to say the next time I talk to her. I know I have to tell her it's over. But you're right. It's not fair to make her wait and wonder. I'll, uh, call her as soon as you go."

Oh, gosh. I feel like I'm going to puke. He's going to call her. And she's going to see his name on her phone, and her heart's going to lift, even though she's also going to be afraid of what he might say.

I'm the only thing holding up that horrible call, the "We have to talk" call. At the same time, my mission was to convince him to call her. Period. To end her suffering. Mission sadly accomplished.

I stand. "Oh. In that case, I won't keep you." I walk to

the door and pull it open.

As I step into the breezeway, he stops me by saying my name. When I turn to face him, he's lifting the picture from the end table. I can tell he's forcing himself not to look at the photo before he holds it out to me.

"Take this?" he asks.

I don't want to touch it, but he's practically begging me. Biting back tears for my joyful friend in the photo, I receive the frame from him and hug it to my chest.

"Don't hate me," he pleads. "I just know myself enough to know—"

"I don't hate you," I say, shocked to realize I'm telling the truth. I don't even want to kick his ass, like I did when I first got here. "I'm sorry for you. And for Jen. Maybe you can text me after you've talked and you're back here, so I know? I don't want her to be alone, but I don't want to jump the gun, either, and show up while you're still there."

He nods. "Sure. In fact, I'd appreciate if you'd be with her. I-it's going to be... hard." His voice cracks, and he moves to shut the door. "I have to go."

I don't prolong my exit any further.

I also know I won't be going grocery shopping tonight.

When I return home, Brice meets me in the kitchen, pushing his feet into his untied running shoes by the garage door. He stops in his tracks when he sees I'm not carrying any groceries from the car. And I'm crying. Or I was recently enough that it's still obvious I'm upset.

"What's the matter? Where's the food?"

Well, I guess I should be glad he asked those questions in the proper order.

"I didn't go shopping," I say, not sure I can answer his first question.

"Wha— Where have you been?"

As if it's not an unusual answer at all, I say, "Wes's apartment. Talking to him about Jen."

He blinks and rests his hands on top of his head while he processes my response. "Wes's? I thought you said we should stay out of their fight."

Checking my phone to make sure I haven't missed Wes's text, I clarify, "Oh, I meant *you* should stay out of it."

"But you said 'we.'"

"We are one, right?" When my joke falls flat (because it doesn't make any sense), I push on. "Listen, I have to pack a bag and get ready to spend the night at Jen's—"

"Wait a minute. What?" He follows me through the living room and up the stairs. In our bedroom, while I drag a small duffel bag from our closet, he fires, "What's going on? Why have you been crying? What happened at Wes's?"

"It's too much to explain."

He grabs me by the shoulders on my way past him into the bathroom. "Give me the short version, and we'll see if I can keep up."

The concern, bordering on alarm, in his eyes makes me tear up again. "Wes is breaking up with Jen, and it's my fault."

"How? Because of something you said tonight? When you went over there without telling me? When you were supposed to be at the grocery store?"

"Forget about the groceries for a second, will you?"

He mutters, "We need food, that's all."

"I'll go tomorrow! Now, will you please let me go so I can pack? Wes should be texting me any minute, and I need to be ready to go to Jen's."

He releases me, but he follows me from the bathroom to my bag, then to our dresser, as I pack. "I think I need more information. Why is Wes breaking up with Jen?"

Pretending I'm concerned with picking out the perfect pair of fuzzy socks, I sift through my sock drawer while I frantically try to think of what to tell him. Pink? No. Gray and white striped? No. I know I'm going to take the yellow ones with pink polka dots, because they're the newest pair I have, so they're still amazingly soft, but I continue my ruse of struggling with the difficult decision, touching each pair in turn. We could be here a while, considering I own no fewer than thirty pairs.

Unfortunately, he's one of the most patient people I know, and he apparently has nothing else to do, so he stands by.

Eventually, I grab the yellow and pink ones and say, "It's complicated."

"I figured that went without saying," he says, giving up on following me step-for-step. He sits on the side of our bed. "How is it your fault?"

Still avoiding eye contact with him, I say as unemotionally as possible, "I convinced her to tell him something, in the interest of honesty and transparency, and she did, and he's dumping her because of what she told him."

"Oh."

"Yeah. Honesty and transparency suck."

"That's the take-away here?"

"Yes."

"Is that your justification for refusing to tell me the whole story?"

Now I look straight at him. "I'm not at liberty to give you the details."

"I see."

The gentle understanding in his eyes makes me cry again. I don't want to keep this secret anymore. I wish I didn't know it. I wish I never had knowledge of the things that led to its existence. I wish those things had never happened.

I cover my eyes, as if that helps me hide from his probing stare. He does nothing; he says nothing.

Finally, I say, "Just… ask Wes. I need you to know. But I can't be the one to tell you. I told her I'd never tell you."

He sighs.

I uncover my eyes, beseeching him, pleading. "I can't keep the secret anymore."

Grabbing my hands, he asks, "And you think Wes will tell me if I ask him? Hon, I don't know."

"Invite him over for a beer and a man-to-man chat."

"We don't have that kind of—"

"Please! Try."

He drops my hands and holds his palms out to me. "Okay, okay. But are you really going to spend the night at Jen's? It's a work night."

"She needs me." I level a look at him and wipe my nose on the back of my hand.

"We need you too. In the morning. When I have to leave for work."

"I'll be back by then."

Grudgingly, as if he's giving me permission, he says, "All right. I guess."

I let him believe his answer matters and continue packing.

My phone buzzes in my jacket pocket. I grasp at it like I'm a heart recipient at the top of the donor list, waiting for the call from the hospital.

Call's over. She says she wants to be left alone

I stare at the text from 'Lurch,' blinking in disbelief. "But that's dumb. She doesn't know what she wants," I mutter, as if he can hear me.

Brice, who *can* hear me, says, "What did he say?"

"Nothing."

He grabs the phone from me and reads the text. I zip the duffel and loop the strap over my shoulder.

Holding the phone up so I can see the screen, he says as if giving me new information, "She wants to be alone."

"She's just being tough for him. He dumped her over the phone? What a dumbass." I snatch the device and text back:

I'm going over there right now

Seconds later, I receive the response:

Don't

"What's going on?" Brice asks.

I'm tempted to lie, but I tell him, so he won't take the phone from me again. Then I add, "He doesn't know anything, though. Obviously. He broke off an engagement with a phone call. A-and—"

"He's not the boss of you?"

When all I do is stick out my tongue at him, he chuckles and says, "I think you should listen to him."

"You just don't want to sleep alone tonight."

He shrugs. "I don't. But that's not why I think you should stay home. If she told him she wants to be alone, then you should respect her wishes."

I drop the duffel at my feet with a thump. "She blames me, doesn't she?"

With a tiny head shake that's hardly convincing, he says, "I'm sure she doesn't."

"She does," I say more definitely. "She does. And she's right. It's my fault." I sink to the edge of the mattress next to Brice and list against him when he puts his arm around me.

"Don't be so hard on yourself. You gave her good advice with the best of intentions."

"Good intentions are for shit. If she hadn't told him, they'd still be together."

"Probably," he says. "For now. But it sounds like this— whatever it is—is something that can't stay a secret forever. And maybe if it had come out later, it would have been even more painful, more heartbreaking, would involve more people, perhaps even children. This is happening now for a reason."

Staring into space, I nod distractedly. "Now Jen will never have Little Lurches." The realization is heartbreaking.

He squeezes me. "Oh, who knows? Maybe this is only a blip."

"It's not." I blink away more tears. "You should have seen him. He was resolved. Devastated, but resolved." I take a deep, shuddering breath. "Oh, and he's a virgin, which I can't believe Jen never told me. Well, actually, yes, I can. I wish *he* hadn't told me."

"And now you told me, so… thanks."

I look into his face. "I thought nothing surprised you when it came to big confessions."

His mouth twists to the side. "Oh, I'm not surprised. But I'd rather not know *some* things. For sure. You know?"

Wistfully, I say, "Yeah. I know."

LOVE AND HATE

*I*t's weird I knew Wes was going to break up with Jen before Jen did. Oddly enough, though, that's made it easier for me to respect her reported request to be left alone. After all, until she tells me herself they broke up, my reaching out to her makes it obvious I found out from someone else—namely, the only other person who she would know for certain knows, Wes.

Sure, I can fudge the timeline. I can say that Wes told me after they broke up. I can say that he texted me to give me a heads up and to request that I get in touch with her after a day or two, to make sure she was okay. I could totally say all that. I could lie. We all know I'm capable. But I don't want to lie. I'm sick of lying.

I'm sick of keeping everyone's secrets, too, including my own. Absolutely sick of it all.

But it's been two days, and I'm also sick of waiting to hear from my friend. And worried about her. Eventually, I'm going to have to come clean about my visit to Wes, so it may as well be sooner rather than later.

Today, from work, I texted her and asked if she wanted

to meet for drinks afterward. As soon as she replied with a lukewarm, *"OK,"* I called Brice to let him know.

He was silent for about three seconds, followed by, "That's wonderful. Because I made plans to take Wes out for a beer. Or five or six. Tonight. He's a mess."

"Oh. Oops."

He sighed. "I guess I can call Mom and see if she's available to watch the boys."

"No," I vetoed, coming up with a new plan on the fly. "I'll have Jen over to our house. You take Wes wherever."

"Are you sure?"

"Yeah. I think she might actually prefer to talk to me in a more private setting."

We discussed the logistics of him getting the boys home and fed before going out, and I sent Jen another text with the new plan:

Change of plans; my place at 7:00? Brice will be out of the house

As predicted, she approved.

Even better. C U then

Now, just before 7:00, after wrestling Brooks and Harris into their pajamas and their cribs, I'm pursuing a naked Max while carrying Aidan on my hip.

"Max Augustus, come here right now!" I bark.

"No!" he replies, running through the loop that is the dining room, foyer, living room, and kitchen. "I don't yaunt to!"

Aidan, thinking this is an epic game of chase, giggles and squeals, kicking his heel into my ovary.

"Oh, my mmmph!" I grunt, coming to a breathless halt

in the foyer, where I plan to snag Max by the elbow on his next lap.

Unfortunately, Max's intelligence, usually something that makes me puff up with pride, helps him recognize my ploy, so his footfalls slow, and I hear him giggling in the kitchen.

"Max! Your dad doesn't like naked people in the kitchen!" I shout, knowing he cares much more about his father's "rules" than mine.

Jen's head pops through the front door behind me. "What's going on in here?" she asks warily before crossing the threshold. "And did I really just hear you tell Max that Brice doesn't approve of nudity in the kitchen?"

"Oh, hey!" I greet her. "Sorry. I wanted the kids to be in bed by the time you got here, but they're not cooperating. Imagine that."

She drops her purse by the front door and kicks off her shoes. Taking the pajamas and diaper from my right hand, she pads into the living room and stands, looking through the doorway into the kitchen.

"Jen!" Max greets her in a near-screech, as if she's his favorite rock star. He runs to her and wraps his arms around her legs.

"Maximus, my child," she croons, "I can see your dingle. And everyone out there…" She points through the back door into the yard and toward the neighboring houses. "…can see your dingle."

His giggling ceases.

"Remember how we talked about that? That we aren't supposed to show people our dingles?"

He nods solemnly up at her.

"All right. Let's put on these jammies, then."

"No!" he says but follows her farther into the living

room, where she sits in Brice's chair and helps Max slide on the absorbent underpants and his Iron Man pajamas.

When the bottoms are up, she snaps the elastic waistband and lightly taps his butt. "Now, you better run as fast as you can and get in bed, because if you're not asleep by the time I get up there to check on you…"

She trails off ominously, but he grins and finishes while streaking past me and up the stairs, "Da Jen Monster's gonna eat my toes! 'Night, Mom!"

"Mwahahahaha!" Jen cackles after him, then yells, "Oh, don't forget to say your prayers!" Hardly missing a beat, she stands up and says to me on her way into the kitchen, "Do you at least have my glass of wine poured and breathing?"

Speechless, I take the route through the dining room to meet up with her.

"How'd you do that?" I ask while she pours wine into the hugest glass I have.

She shrugs. "That was our bedtime routine while you were in Florida. Fear is a great motivator."

"It also tends to keep little kids up at night, so what made you decide to even try a tactic like that?"

After a perfunctory swirl, she sniffs and sips, closing her eyes as if savoring the flavor. Finally, she answers, "Do you really think he's afraid of people seeing his dingle? Or of the 'Jen Monster' eating his toes?"

"If not, then how does it work?"

She sighs. "Oh my gosh, Peyton! He's three! I didn't run these tactics past a psychologist. I just tried them. And they worked. Mary said Brice does stuff like that, and they like it."

Chastened, I follow her back into the living room. "That's true, but… You were so smooth!"

With a self-deprecating eye roll, she takes another

healthy slug of her wine. Smacking her lips, she says, "I think you're making this parenting thing harder than it needs to be."

"I am not! It's hard!"

"Not saying it isn't. Just saying you're over-thinking it. As usual."

I grunt a concession, then lay Aidan on the couch and pluck a pair of footie pajamas from the nearby, ever-present laundry basket of clean, unfolded clothing. Jen continues to sip from her glass, watching while I dress the baby for bed.

When I pull the nine-month-old by his hands into a standing position, she says, "You and Brice do make some pretty babies."

I'm about to thank her when she makes a frightful sound that causes me to whirl and face her. Her wineglass still in her right hand, she has both of her hands near her face, which has collapsed in on itself.

Taking Aidan with me, I perch on the arm of the chair in which she's sitting and wrap her in an awkward side hug. "Oh, sweetie. I'm sorry."

Between sobs, she says, "I... just... couldn't... win. Having that baby would have ruined my life. At least, I thought so then." She gulps for air. "But not having it is ruining my life now."

I kiss her head. "I know. It sucks."

She sniffs and runs the base of her thumb under her eye. "Even if I'd had it, then what? It would be eleven years old now. And I'd be a single mom. Would *that* be acceptable to him? Would I be worthy then? Or still damaged goods?"

Aidan squirms in my arms and grabs a fistful of Jen's hair, the shiny, golden ringlets probably irresistible to him. Jen seems not to notice. I extricate her curls from his hand and place him on the floor. He drops to his hands and knees and makes a break for the couch, his favorite prop for cruising, the closest he's gotten so far to moving around like his older brothers.

Both hands free, I relieve Jen of her wineglass and set it on the table next to us. Then I kneel in front of her and pull her hands away from her face.

"You *are* worthy."

"I'm not. Obviously."

"And as for being 'damaged goods,' we all are. Even him. Maybe not in the same ways you are, but in his own ways." When she says nothing to that, I continue, "What happened twelve years ago, you're forgiven for that. By Someone a lot more important than *him*."

"I was an idiot for pinning all my hopes on him. Why did I think he'd be any different than those other guys? They always find a reason to dump me. At least Wes chose a reason that mattered." She takes a shaky breath while I glance over my shoulder to get a visual of Aidan. When I turn back to face her, she says, "Can I tell you something, and you won't get hurt or mad or whatever?"

I try to laugh away the unease her question stirs in my belly. "Now, when have I ever been able to make a promise like that?"

She smiles sadly. "I know. It's a tall order. But I need to tell you something, and I need you to listen, and I need you to hear me out and not take it the wrong way."

I gulp. "Okay…"

Pulling her hands from mine, she swipes them across her cheeks, sniffles, and rolls her eyes toward the ceiling before saying, "Sometimes I hate you."

I wait for her to continue, to explain what she means, to clarify how she can mean that in something other than the "wrong way." But she appears to be finished.

"Um, okay." I provide my own interpretation for her. "You mean, it upsets you that I'm married and have kids and that I don't seem to appreciate what I have?"

She shakes her head. "No. I just hate you." Quickly, she adds, "That other stuff doesn't help, but it's more about the fact that you act like you know everything and you give crappy advice, and when it all goes to shit, it doesn't affect your life one bit."

Still trying not to be defensive, I remain calm and say, "I'm so sorry that your telling Wes had the result it did. I didn't think he'd react that way."

"But according to you, it didn't matter how he reacted; it had to be told."

I think about it for a second. "True."

"But would you have had the guts to do what I did?"

"I *have* done what you did. I told Drex about Secret, knowing it was as much of a deal breaker for him as your thing has been with Wes."

"'My thing.' So, abortion is 'my thing' now?"

"That's not—I just didn't want to say the word."

She snorts. "Wow. You can't even bring yourself to say what I did. You Lutherans sure do talk a big game about forgiveness and grace, but when it comes right down to it, that's all it is: talk. You're as judgmental as the rest of 'em."

"You're a Lutheran now, too, you know? And who said Lutherans aren't judgmental? I don't think we ever claimed that."

"Oh, yes. Let's joke about it. That's another reason I hate you sometimes."

I sit back on my heels. "You know, 'hate' is an ugly word. And it's strong. And it means more than 'strongly dislike,' okay? You can't love someone *and* hate them, no matter how much you may dislike parts of them. And I'm getting how much you dislike parts of me. You're making that super-duper clear. So thanks for that."

"You're getting mad."

"Ya think?" I pop to my feet. "Actually, no. I'm not mad. I'm hurt."

"You promised you wouldn't be hurt."

"Well, I *lied*! Big fucking shocker. And I'm sorry, but I don't know anyone who can hear her best friend in the whole world tell her that she hates her and not get her feelings hurt. I can't do it."

I surprise Aidan by plucking him off the ground and holding him to me like a living teddy bear, but he doesn't fight my embrace. In fact, he rests his head on my shoulder and coos "Mama" next to my ear.

"We've been through *everything* together," I remind my friend. "Everything. And I can see where it may be easier to hold me responsible for what's happening right now, but I didn't tell you to have an abortion twelve years ago. I didn't judge you when that's what you decided to do. I haven't even told my husband about it, at your request. And I'm not responsible for how Wes reacted when you told him."

"You may have never judged me out loud, but your decision to keep Secret was a pretty clear message. 'See, Jen? If you're not too selfish, you can live with the consequences of your actions.' Isn't that what you meant?"

"My decision had nothing to do with you! It was my personal choice. I didn't make it with a life lesson in mind. It was the hardest decision I've ever made!"

"And a small part of you couldn't bear to stoop to my level and make the same decision I did."

"What?"

"You couldn't even bring yourself to talk to me about how similar our situations were. How do you think it felt for me to watch you go through the same thing? It brought it all back! And your refusal to even acknowledge the similarities was a message in itself."

"I didn't talk to you about it because you made me promise never to speak of it!"

"It was unnatural to not talk about it, though, when you were pregnant with Secret. It was like you were purposely ignoring my history."

I stare open-mouthed at her. After a few blinks, I say, "At that point, your situation didn't even cross my mind. I was freaking out at my own predicament."

"Well, I believe *that*, come to think of it."

Taking a deep breath and closing my eyes, I say, "You know what? You're upset. And you're saying awful things, because you're upset. And I'm going to recognize that, and I'm not going to say anything else. I'm going to put Aidan to bed."

I turn to leave the room, but she stops me by saying, "I hate you, because we made the same initial mistake, but it led you *here*. And it brought *me* to a completely different place."

My back to her, I use all my concentration for breathing and blinking. And not dropping the baby.

A sneer in her voice, she continues, "Everything worked out for you; everything fell into place. Because you made the 'right' decision. We're like a living, walking cautionary tale. You represent virtue, while I represent the evils of instant gratification. Is that it?" Fortunately, she's not expecting me to answer. "So now, in this tale, you live happily ever after, and I wander the rest of my days alone, bitterly regretting my evil, immoral decision. The end. Didacticism at its best, right?"

I still can't talk. Or walk. Or even cry. I'm frozen, paralyzed by her hurtful words. Aidan kicks me dangerously near the crotch, but not even my reflexes are working at this point, so I don't so much as flinch.

Either interpreting my silence as an invitation to keep going or unable to stop, she says, still sneering, "And you haven't slowed down since. Every time we turn around, you're knocked up again. Never mind that you're not good at being pregnant and that it makes no sense for you to continue to abuse your body that way, putting yourself and your babies at risk. For the love of God, stop having babies!"

Finally feeling like I have some control over my vocal chords, I say, "I think it would be best if you went home."

"I want my engagement picture."

Still unable to look at her, I say while staring at her hot pink shoes next to the front door, "It's on the hutch in the dining room. You can let yourself out after you get it."

I don't wait for any additional response—verbal or otherwise—from her. I'm too busy hurrying up the stairs before I fall to pieces.

Brice climbs into bed, warm and smelling of toothpaste and beer. I roll onto my back.

"Everything okay?" I check, referring to the late hour. He and Wes must have closed down the bar.

"Mm… fine," he murmurs.

"Did he tell you?" I can't wait to ask.

He pauses, probably trying to decide if it's ethical to divulge the information. Fortunately, he comes to the correct conclusion and says, "Yes."

When he stops at that, I prod, "Well? Do you agree with him?"

"How is that relevant?"

I roll my eyes and growl. "You're going to be like that? Really?"

"Like what?"

"Refusing to tell me your opinion on the whole thing."

He shifts closer to me and puts his arm around my shoulders. I allow myself to be drawn against him, and I use his chest as a pillow. While we're both still getting comfortable, he says, "I'm sure you know how I feel about... that."

"Yeah, but—"

"As far as how Wes is reacting to the news, I see where he's coming from."

"What?"

"But I think his execution leaves much to be desired. He's right to end things, though, if he feels that strongly about it."

"Oh, so forgiveness is conditional? And he doesn't have to practice what he preaches?"

"He's not debating her forgiveness."

"Bullshit."

"Here we go."

"He can split hairs and explain it however he wants, but—"

"He's not splitting hairs. Or justifying his feelings, even. He's not proud of how he feels toward her in light of this information, but he also doesn't have control over it right now. And may not ever. Why string her along? He's being as honest as he can be."

"And dumping her over the phone. When I asked him to call her, I meant to arrange a time to meet up and talk, not break up with her on the phone."

He's silent on that topic for a few seconds, then inhales as if to speak, but stops.

"What?" I implore him to continue.

With another big breath, he says thoughtfully and haltingly, "Well, as I understand it, he *was* going to go to her place, but she forced it out of him on the phone. And told him she'd rather not see him again, that she'd make sure he got his ring back through you or me or... something. Which... yikes. I don't want to be any part of that. Did she give it to you tonight?"

I know he means the ring, but I can't help but take his question figuratively, too. Addressing his true query, I say, "No. She, uh, wasn't here long."

"Oh. I almost expected her to still be here when I got home."

"It's after 1 a.m.!"

There's a shrug in his voice when he says, "So? It's not like either of you have to be up early."

"Excuse me? I do. Your children don't know what it means to 'sleep in,' since they got your damn early riser gene."

"All right. Sorry. Forget I said anything. I guess I'm surprised she wasn't here a while, that's all. I thought you guys had a lot to talk about."

"Apparently not."

He yawns loudly. "Okay. Well, night, night."

I'm not sure whether I'm relieved or disappointed he didn't pick up on my less-than-subtle prompt. I'm surprised, for sure. He's normally all over that. He must be zapped. And that's okay. He's listened to enough whining and moaning for one night. My sad story can wait until tomorrow.

GOODBYE

When I did tell Brice about Jen's declaration of hate, he treated it like one of Max's tantrums and shrugged it off. "She's hurt right now."

Relieved he had the same take on it that I did, I said, "Exactly."

I decided it wasn't important to tell him what she said about my crappy gestational skills, because I didn't want to listen to him dispute her claim. We both know she's right; we've both chosen to disregard that fact. It's none of her business. It's bad enough that her words taunt me every day. I don't want them to worry him.

As long as he's not mad at me about not telling him Jen's secret—and he insists he's not—then we have nothing left to say on the topic. I'm trying something different; I'm trying to let it go.

A month later, I haven't been able to get Jen to return my calls, texts, and emails. I guess she still hates me. Brice continues to stick with his theory that she said those things at the peak of her anger and hurt and is now too embarrassed to face me. I'm still agreeing with his theory, because

I can't face the alternative. I try to stay busy so I don't think too much about it.

Worrying about money has been keeping me plenty busy, too. I noticed our bank balance dipping dangerously low between paychecks, so I started paying more attention to how much we spend on food and incidentals and adopted some new practices, including making our own laundry detergent and cleaning supplies. Most days, I feel very Pioneer Woman (or mad scientist).

Grocery shopping has also become a major ordeal. I clip and collect coupons, search ads, and map out the most time- and fuel-efficient ways to shop at several different stores, all in the name of saving a few bucks. I miss the days when I could run to the nearest store, but the one close to our neighborhood is too expensive for most things, so those days are long gone.

Especially if there's going to be another Northam added to the family within the year.

And I think there will be.

I haven't confirmed it with a test yet (tomorrow morning, I have a date with the pee-stick), but my period is late by almost a week now. That's no fluke, right? And at the twins' birthday party a few weeks ago, I got all faint and sweaty. At the time, I explained it away with the tired old "tired" excuse. But now I'm wondering...

No. That was too soon to feel any different. I'm starting to sound fantastical, like Brice. The true explanation for my feeling worn down is that I have to go to so many stores just to get the best price on bananas.

All of my money-saving and budgeting efforts, however, aren't adding up as much as they need to add up.

So, I've crunched some other numbers. Some heartbreaking numbers. And it's time to share them with Brice.

He staggers into the kitchen as I'm finishing some coupon-clipping. With a dramatic flair, he pulls open the refrigerator and comes out with a bottle of wine, which he pretends to glug.

I laugh at his theatrics, then ask, "Tough bedtime?" as I set my stack of coupons on the counter next to the garage door so I don't forget them tomorrow when I go shopping.

Trading the wine for chocolate milk, he answers, "Yes," before drinking straight from the container. I'd chastise him, but since he's the only one who drinks the stuff, he might as well skip dirtying a glass.

"What happened this time?" I ask, mildly curious but not concerned.

He takes a few more swallows, then lowers the container and licks his lips. "It's a long story. But why didn't anyone tell us that three is so much worse than two?"

"We have four. Are you losing count again?"

"No. *Age* three." Replacing the cap on the milk, he sticks the jug on the shelf in the fridge and closes the door. "And we're going to have two of them at that age at one time! What the higgety are we going to do then?"

I shrug, leaning against the wall. "Deal with it?"

He rolls his eyes. "Obviously. But it's not gonna be pretty. Max is so angsty. I thought they didn't act like that until they were teenagers. Everything is such a big, fat, hairy deal. I asked him to put his bath toys in the basket by the tub. You'da thought I asked him to cut off one of his fingers and eat it."

My tummy lurches at the idea. I wrinkle my nose. "Ew."

"Yeah. And the whole time he's auditioning for *Les Misérables*, Brooks and Harris are his backup whiners. I don't remember Max being whiny like that when he was their age."

I giggle at the image. "And what was Aidan doing during all this?"

"Taking notes, I'm sure. 'Oh, I see… Sustained crying, supplemented by whining, usually prompts Dad to give you whatever the heck you want, as long as it shuts you up. Interesting.'" He shuffles into the living room and plops into his chair.

"You don't give them their way when they act like that."

"No, but I want to."

I perch on the arm of his chair, snake my arm around his shoulders, and lean against him. "That's different. Be strong."

"I'm weakening more each day. And the next time Max tells me 'no,' I'm going to run from the room screaming. See how he likes it."

Again, I laugh at the mental picture. "Hm. It might work." Tracing my finger along his ear, I say, "You know, we don't have it all that bad. They do some typical things, but have you spent any time at all at the daycare at Peace? Our kids are the best-behaved of the bunch."

"I'm scared for society."

We laugh together, but I flick his ear playfully. "Stop it. They're good boys. They're just testing the boundaries."

"Testing my sanity."

"That, too. Don't flunk."

"We're severely outnumbered, you know?"

"Are you just now figuring this out?"

"It didn't seem to matter, until recently. Now, they're organized. It's like we have to be ever-vigilant for an uprising."

I give his shoulders a squeeze. "They still need us for way too much."

"But do *they* realize that? I think they'll overthrow first, think about the consequences later." He cranes his neck to look up at me. "Just watch your back. Keep an eye out for strategically placed toys on the stairs. Stuff like that."

"You're crazy."

He grins. "I'm just being silly."

"I know."

"I love those boogers."

"I know."

"And I love everything about fatherhood but crying and screaming and whining."

"Then stop doing those things."

He widens his eyes, mimics a sarcastic laugh, and holds his hand in a claw shape, as if to threaten to tickle me.

"Don't. I'll pee on you."

"Gross."

"I didn't say it was sexy or awesome. But I've had a lot of babies. Sneezing is a gamble some days. If you tickle me, I can guarantee you'll get wet."

"Another fun thing dies."

"Hey, can I talk to you about something serious, for real?"

He immediately sobers. "Of course. What's up? Have you been in touch with Jen lately?"

I shake my head. "No. It's not about her."

Grabbing my hand and squeezing it, he says, "Okay. What is it?"

I swallow and take a deep breath. "I... I think I need to quit my job."

His blinks become more frequent, and his eyes darken and widen between those blinks, but otherwise his face remains passive. I can tell he's trying not to react. "Oh?"

I nod.

"Does this have something to do with a certain person?"

I tilt my head and shoot him a questioning look, so he expounds, "You know. *Him?*"

Not sure exactly what he could mean but knowing who he's talking about, I say, "No! Matt's been fine. Absent. I haven't seen him in months. No." Flustered by the mention of my admirer, I force myself to breathe more evenly and say, "I think it makes more sense, that's all. Especially if— Listen, I'm already barely breaking even with my pay and our childcare costs. With another one, it'll actually be *costing* me money to have a job. That's stupid."

"But you like your job."

"I like expensive shoes and overpriced coffee, too, but sacrifices must be made."

His eyes turn down. "Aw, hon. I'm sure we can find other places to trim the budget. You don't have to give up your job. I'll— I'll cancel my satellite radio subscription. And I'll call the phone company to see if I can bundle some of our services so—"

I shake my head. "No. Well, you're probably going to have to do all that, too. But I've been thinking about this for a while. The biggest place to cut costs is with our childcare expenses. It makes the most sense."

"I'm the one who pays the bills. Things aren't that bad."

"I saw the bank balance the other day and almost hyperventilated. Please, don't try to spare me the worry. I need to know these things, you know?"

Nodding, he gives my fingers another squeeze. "Okay, it's been tight lately. But quitting your job should be a last resort."

"I think we're there, don't you?" I search his eyes, which tell me I'm right.

He sighs. "If you're sure."

"I am. I don't have to quit right away, I guess. I have a few more months."

Staring off into space, he says, "Yeah," then blinks and focuses his eyes on my face. "Wait. Are you— Is this more than a theoretical discussion?"

I wasn't planning to tell him tonight; I wanted to wait until I took the test in the morning. But it seems silly to be coy.

I bite my lower lip and shrug. "Maybe. I think I'm pregnant."

"You do?" he nearly whispers, as if he's worried about scaring the fetus away.

For some reason, his reaction chokes me up, even though it's borderline comical. "Yes," I say through my tight throat.

"Oh, hon. That's wonderful!"

I clear my throat. "Well, I haven't taken a test yet, but I'm late. And your gooberish reaction is making me cry, so that's a good indicator."

He pulls me down into his lap. "It's happening," he murmurs near my ear. "It's really happening."

"I know. How crazy is that?"

"Crazy-good."

"I think so."

He pulls away from me so he can look at my eyes. "Yeah? Even though you're quitting your job at the gallery?"

"It'll be fine," I reassure both of us.

"And you're going to have to trade your SUV for a minivan."

Inside, that sparks the biggest reaction, but I work hard to keep a neutral expression on my face when I say, "Yeah, I know."

He grins. "That's it? No temper tantrum, no crying, no gnashing of teeth?"

"Nope. I'm a grownup now. It's only a car."

"So, you're just going to say, 'okay,' and let it go?"

"Yes! Why is that so hard to believe?"

He shrugs, obviously having an answer but not feeling safe enough to share it with me.

"I fought the good fight. No use crying about something that's now unavoidable." Pressing my lips against his, I hope to end the discussion. It's one thing to concede defeat; it's another to have my face rubbed in it.

He smiles into the kiss, pausing only long enough to concur, "True," before catching my lips between his again. When he flicks his tongue against my teeth, I almost spontaneously combust.

Oh, gosh. I'm so pregnant! No test necessary.

Taking the home pregnancy test was my body's cue to turn on the first trimester symptoms, full-force. Sunday morning at the kitchen table, both of us are groggy and not particularly communicative—or pleasant—after a long night of dealing with a round of Max's night terrors. At least Brice can drink coffee. I'm stuck being groggy and unpleasant. And nauseated.

"I'm not going to church today," I tell him, daring him with my no-nonsense tone to argue with me about it.

"That must be a nice option," he says, taking the challenge.

"I could go. And barf in the pew. Is that what you want?"

He sips his coffee and keeps his eyes on the emails on his phone. "Yes. That's exactly what I want. You know me."

"Okay, Reverend Sarcasm, then I'll stay home, like I said."

"So, the boys aren't going to church?"

"Not unless they suddenly know how to drive."

"Nice."

I put my head down on the kitchen table and muffle into my arms, "You're the one not being very nice. Or sympathetic."

My observation elicits nothing but silence at first. Then I hear his coffee mug tap against the table near my head, and his hand falls on my neck.

"I'm sorry. I'm tired. But you're right; nauseated is way worse."

I grunt an acceptance to his apology.

His warm hand leaves my neck as he stands to take his cup to the dishwasher. "I'll take the boys with me to church. They can go to Sunday school and stay in the nursery until Mom can bring them home. We'll figure out a car swap."

I pull my head up to regard him across the room. "You don't have to do that. I'll be fine with them here."

"No, you go back to bed."

"Do I look that bad?"

He cringes. "Now that you mention it, sort of. No offense. You're really green."

"Great."

"Green's a good color on you," he tries.

I laugh mirthlessly. "Fail. But thanks. You need me to help you get the boys dressed?"

"Nope. I got it. But I'd better hurry." He strides to the living room, where the post-breakfast bunch is watching some TV. "Hey, guys. Let's get dressed for church."

Max offers his usual, "No!" on his way up the stairs.

Brooks and Harris chorus, "Chutch!" while following their older brother as quickly as possible.

Aidan accepts being picked up without a sound, although Brice says to him, "Why don't you keep that drool to yourself? Aggh! Hands off my— Okay, my face is better than my clothes, I guess. Good gravy, you're a tooth factory!" He stops in the kitchen doorway before following the older boys upstairs. "Did you see this new tooth?" he asks, pushing down on Aidan's lower lip with his index finger to reveal the tiny chomper peeking through the baby's gums.

"Yep," I reply. "He has another new one coming in up top, too."

"He'll have a full set of pearly whites before too long." With that, he turns and carries his toothy youngest upstairs, delivering a mature lecture about dental hygiene.

I remain at the table for a few minutes, listening to the ruckus over my head before dragging myself up to find the diaper bag and make sure it's fully loaded and ready for service. When I'm sure it contains everything Brice (or, more accurately, Mary) will need for the next three hours, I set it on the counter next to the door leading to the garage and shuffle my way upstairs to bed.

What feels like seconds after all five guys have crashed out the door, and the garage door has buzzed and thumped to a close, the sound of the front door opening and closing startles me awake. Near tears with the frustration of my alone time ending so quickly, it hits me that whoever entered the house is too quiet to be my brood. Immediately wide awake and no longer focused on my nagging nausea, I hop from the bed and creep to the top of the stairs, looking over the banister into the foyer below.

I smell her rather than see her. It's a combination of her makeup, body lotion, hair care products, and perfume that

I'd know anywhere, combined with the leather from her jacket.

"Jen?" I call down weakly, the nausea returning full-force, taking the place of the momentary relief I felt at not being robbed in broad daylight.

There's a slight pause followed by, "Hi. Um, I thought you'd be at church."

I descend the rest of the way and meet up with her in the kitchen, where she's setting some things on the island. Looking more closely, I see the items are her house key, the modest engagement ring that she and Wes picked out together a few months ago, and a book she borrowed from me so long ago that I'd forgotten I'd lent it to her. Or that I ever owned it.

The book gets the first explanation. "I'm never going to read that. So…"

I ignore the stuff and her statement. "It's good to see you. I've missed you," I say, laying it all out there, instantly tearing up.

She rolls her eyes, but I can see they're shiny, too. "So, it's true. You're pregnant again."

I sniffle and place my hand on my flat (well, as flat as it ever is) belly. "Yeah, but—"

"Mitzi told me. And your sappiness is proof."

"I'm not being sappy. I'm telling you the truth."

She sighs. "Whatever. I, uh, was hoping to drop off these things while you were out."

"Why?" I ask. "I'm not mad at you. I've tried to tell you that a million times the past few weeks."

"What if I'm still mad at *you*?" she says. "I guess that never occurred to you, though."

My silence is admission enough.

She snorts. "Of course. You're the victim. Right."

Instead of saying something that will start another fight, I simply say, "I'm sorry. Please, don't be mad at me. I hate this."

Clearing her throat, she fingers the items on the counter and says breezily, "I hope you don't mind that I let myself in. Like I said, I thought you'd be at church——"

"I'm not feeling well."

"So I was going to leave these things here on my way out of town——"

"Where are you going?"

"And I told Wes I'd have you or Brice give him his ring." Now she falters, but she regroups and rushes on. "The house key, well, I figure someone else might need it, and I'd save you the trouble of having to make a copy."

"Where are you going?" I repeat, dread, fear, and sadness joining forces to stir up a good panic beneath my breastbone.

She shrugs. "Somewhere warm for a while. You know, Christmas is going to suck balls this year——more than usual, even——and since I'm not tied down to an office with my freelancing, I thought I'd go somewhere relaxing and... not here."

I swallow tightly. "Oh. What about your apartment?"

Looking up at me, tears balancing on her lower lids, she asks, "Does it really matter?"

"I guess not. It's just— I —" I don't know how to finish that sentence without sounding like an overbearing mother, so I stop and head down a different path. "I hope you have a good time, wherever you're going. Let us know when you get there?"

That receives another shrug. "Maybe. We'll see. I'll be in touch with Mitzi, if nothing else."

It's like a slap across the face, but it's better than nothing, so I nod and choke, "Yeah. Okay."

She takes a deep breath and abruptly speed-walks toward the dining room. I backtrack through the living room and meet her at the front door, which she roughly pulls open while saying over her shoulder, "Anyway, good luck with the new little one. See ya."

The door whooshes shut behind her, leaving a draft of cold air and perfume in her wake.

I sit on the bottom step of the staircase, cover my eyes with my hand, and weep silently.

FINALLY

I'm not going to lie; it's been rough. I've been having a hard time coming to grips with Jen's departure. If it were just a personal sabbatical of sorts for her, it would be one thing. But it feels like she's taking a break—partly—from me. From our friendship.

It's been more than three months since she left. Three months since I cried on the stairs. Three months since I tossed her house key into the junk drawer, where I'm sure it will be forgotten, buried beneath the books of matches and packages of batteries and nearly empty rolls of scotch tape. Three months since I gave Wes his ring back and had to pretend I didn't notice that he almost started crying when I plunked the jewelry into his hand.

It all seems so final. Before she walked out that door, there were no attempts to reassure that this is a temporary thing. On the contrary, it felt like she was saying, "This is it. This is our new reality. Get used to it." She just didn't have a ring to give back to me. All she had for me was a dog-eared paperback and a house key.

And life without her is like getting used to life without

the Internet. I know, that sounds callous and cold-hearted, but she'd appreciate that comparison.

Plus, hear me out. Having a friend like Jen is a luxury that I'd started to take for granted. I'll admit it. I didn't realize how much I'd come to depend on her, until she was gone. I turned to her for everything from the spontaneous quest for ridiculous information ("What is the point of 'anal bleaching?'") to the kind of critical second opinion that could mean the difference between waiting until the morning to take a kid to the doctor or rushing them to the ER. I relied on her to keep me in the loop with friends and family. I used her for entertainment.

And now that she's gone, I've found that I almost constantly need her. And it's virtually impossible to function normally without her.

Before she left, even when we weren't speaking to each other (or she wasn't speaking to me), there was a comfort in knowing that she was still around. I got used to working around her unwillingness to communicate with me, much like one would deal with a touchy Internet connection. Or dial-up, versus Wi-Fi.

Okay, fine. My analogy is breaking down. The point is, I'm lost without her. And if someone had told me this would be the case, I would have scoffed at them. Sure, I could imagine missing her. Sure, I could conceive that not having her around would be sad and dull and boring. But I never would have believed that I would have such a hard time functioning. I'm a mess.

Mitzi tells me Jen went down to Florida (score another one for "Florida: it's not Missouri"). Mitzi swears up and down she doesn't know where in Florida or even how long Jen plans to stay there or if she'll be coming back to Spring-field or going back to Chicago when she's finished there. If she'll ever be finished there. Again, Jen's been vague, when she's been in touch at all.

We're at the tail end of Lent, heading into yet another exhausting… er, I mean, *spiritually fulfilling* Holy Week and Easter. The days, weeks, months, and years that comprise my life are blurring and meshing together in a haze of church observances (I can't believe tomorrow is Palm Sunday, yet again!), children's birthdays (Aidan turned one last month; Max turned four earlier this week—how is *that* possible?), and gestational milestones (puking's out; heart-burn is in).

I'm round again, but this time, nobody seems to care or notice. Of course, I'm fine with that. I'd rather that than have them talking about us behind our backs—"Pastor's wife is pregnant again? Oh. Nice. They *do* know about over-population, right? And what causes babies?"—but I try to ignore the tight smiles and the passive-aggressive comments —"Wow. Five kids. That's a lot." Gee, I hadn't noticed. I'm glad you brought it to my attention—and focus on the people who either ignore it altogether or are happy for us.

I'm a little more than halfway through this pregnancy, which has been blessedly uneventful since the departure of the first-trimester pukies. The baby's active, keeping me awake some nights, letting me sleep others, and making sure she lets me know when I eat something that doesn't suit (she hates eggplant). But since heartburn is my biggest complaint, I'm counting myself lucky.

And now we're going for the most anti-climactic ultra-sound ever. It's time to confirm what Brice and I have been mostly sure about since before she was even conceived, which is something that still creeps me out when I think about it too much.

As far as Brice is concerned, though, it's not weird at all.

In fact, as the ultrasound technician runs his Fisher Price microphone back and forth across my belly, my husband says, "She's beautiful!"

The guy chuckles, smirks, and says, "Hold your horses, Daddy-o. We haven't even gotten a look between those legs yet."

Brice laughs it off. "Oh, right. But I just know it's a girl."

"Said fifty percent of parents to little boys," the technician quips, directing the wand lower and pressing harder against my abdomen. "Okay, here we go. I'm assuming you want to know."

We both nod enthusiastically. He makes some minor adjustments, presses a button on the keyboard to freeze the picture, and says, "Lucky guess, Dad. Say hello to your daughter, folks."

I blink at the vagina, large as life, on the screen. I've been waiting for this moment for almost seven years, if you count back to that fateful day that I originally hoped to see that image on an ultrasound monitor.

And I do count it. It counts, for sure. The difference in what I felt that day all those years ago and what I feel now is so vast, though, that I almost can't process it.

I bring my fingers up to my face and pinch at my trembling lips.

Brice is already holding my other hand, which he squeezes more tightly while he whispers, "There she is."

The technician continues with his measurements and analyses. Every once in a while, he points out features in an effort to reassure us that everything is going as expected:

"Her upper lip looks good; no cleft palate."

"She's on track as far as average weight and length."

"There are two arms, two legs, and her fingers and toes look normal."

"There's her spinal cord, fully formed and looking exactly as it should."

"And... heartbeat." He turns up the volume on the monitor so we can hear the familiar whooshing. "Right as rain."

It isn't until he gives me some tissues to clean the gel from my belly, hands Brice a folder of pictures, and leaves us with a dismissive "Congratulations" that I let myself dwell on the significance of the day.

Brice and I press our foreheads together and pray, both of us tearful and joyful, both of us remembering another baby girl who never made it this far.

I start to worry that they need this room, so I dress and lead Brice from the clinic to the parking lot, where we smile into the spring sunshine, holding hands on the way to our cars, which are parked nose-to-nose.

"Incredible," he finally stops grinning long enough to say as we stand next to my vehicle.

I can only nod. "She's real."

"Of course, she is!" He opens the folder of pictures, and we look through them again, taking turns snapping photos of the pictures with our cell phones so we can email and text them to family and friends.

Well, *some* friends.

We divide up the long list so we don't send anyone duplicate messages but also don't forget anyone. While thumbing through the images on his phone, he says, "Okay, I'll get my mom and all the church people, including Jared. You take care of your family, plus Mitzi (she'll want to hear it from you, not Jared), the Pryces, and Jen. Right? Who are we missing?"

I want to say, "Jen," even though he's mentioned her,

because it's the truth: I *am* missing her. At times like these, it's most painful.

Instead, I smile bravely and reply, "I think that's everyone. Oh! Don't forget Vince."

He laughs. "As if I would! I can't wait to rub it in his face that I was right. He may be the undisputed mini-golf champ, but—"

"You can prophesy like nobody's business?"

With a playful narrowing of his eyes, he replies, "Oh, sure. Make fun of me."

"I'm not! But since you're not willing to tell him what you 'saw'…"

"Air quotes? Really?"

"He's not going to be very impressed that you got a 50-50 guess correct."

His grin fades. "Oh. Yeah. I guess you have a point there." Just as quickly, his smile returns. "He'll still be happy for us, though."

"Of course, he will." I go up on my tiptoes to kiss his lips. "I have to get to work. And make some calls and send some texts."

He nods and returns my kiss, then pats my belly. "Be a good girl, Beatrice."

"Uh, not even close," I say, swiftly vetoing his latest name suggestion.

"Oh, come on. I like it."

"No."

"What about Bea*trix*?"

"Worse."

"You're harsh."

I open my car door and slide in. "Whatever. She's my daughter, too, and she's not going to be named Beatrix or Beatrice or Merwyn."

He gets a far-off look in his eyes. "Merwyn. Oh, I love that name!"

"I know you do. But if you love something, you should set it free. Especially that name. Let it go."

Chuckling at my tough attitude, he gives me one more kiss, and we exchange *I love you*s before he crosses in front of my car to get to the driver's side of his minivan. He opens the door and gets in, setting the folder of ultrasound pictures on the passenger seat.

While I wait for him to drive off, I focus on my phone, pretending I'm scrolling through the contacts list, when actually, I already have the number ready to go. Finally, he backs out of his space. I press the button to call Jen.

As usual, it goes straight to her voicemail. It's not as though it's unexpected, but it still brings on the tears.

At the tone, I say emotionally, "Hey. It's me. Again. We're having a girl. And you're the first person I'm telling. And I'm sorry to be bothering you, because you obviously don't want to hear from me—and maybe this news is especially difficult for you to hear from me—but you were the first person I wanted to tell. Before Mitzi, before my parents, before Nicole or Jason, before anyone. I hope you're doing well. I miss you. I hope you come home soon, wherever home happens to be for you. I love you. Bye."

Then I hit the button to cancel my message.

This has become a frequent routine of mine. I do it about twice a week. Which may explain why she's programmed her phone to send my calls straight to her voicemail. If she thinks it's odd that I never leave a message, she's never been curious enough to call me back or text an inquiry into the matter. Maybe she thinks I'm calling on the off chance she'll take my call one day.

Honestly, I don't know what I'd do if she picked up.

~

Purple threw up in here. The soft lilac paint dried darker than I would prefer, and the deep purple scroll stenciling along the chair rail in the middle of the wall is… intense. Bold, let's say. Oh, well. I'm sure I'll get used to it. I'm not going to admit in a million years that it turned out more vivid than I'd planned.

"Whoa!" Brice practically shouts in the doorway of the empty room that used to belong to Aidan, who's at a play date with Sasha at the Laszewski residence. His voice echoes off the walls and hardwood floor. "Um, what happened? Did you add another coat? Of a darker color?"

"No, this is what you painted earlier," I snap.

"Yikes."

"What's wrong with it? I like it."

"It's— Never mind." He walks farther into the room and inspects my part of the job more closely. "The stenciling looks great."

"Thanks."

His eyes stray higher, and I can see he's worried about the base color. "When there's furniture in here, I guess it won't be so… jarring."

"It's not like it's neon," I say, not sure who I'm trying to convince. "Is Aidan moved into Max's room?"

Brice nods. "I've reassembled the crib, anyway. I'm not sure how you want everything arranged. That's what I came in here to ask you."

Closing the window that was keeping the room well-ventilated, I follow him from the nursery. I close the door to prevent the older boys from running in there and putting their hands on the damp paint when they return from their ice cream run with Mary.

In Max's room, I direct while Brice provides the muscle, sliding dressers and toy boxes and the bed and crib into their new places. The changing table is in Brice's wood shop, awaiting a new paint job to transform it from its espresso wood stain to a more feminine white, which will match the crib we're receiving from the Pryces.

"There's a lot of stuff in this room," Brice remarks, his hands on his hips as he surveys the new configuration. "I think we need to consider thinning out the toy collection."

I level a bemused look at him. "Good luck with that. When, pray tell, are you going to be smuggling out the aforementioned retired toys?"

He wrinkles his nose. "They don't play with half of this junk."

"Doesn't matter. The minute you try to take anything out of this house, you'll find out it's the kids' most beloved toy of all time."

He laughs. "Whatever."

"Trust me. The other day, I tried to throw away a yo-yo that was busted into two pieces, and it almost caused a riot."

"Then let's box up some stuff now and put it in the garage, while they're out of the house," he suggests, making a move toward Max's toy box.

I rub my lower back. "I'm tired. Does this have to happen today?"

Sometimes Reverend Can-Do exhausts me.

He grins over his shoulder at me. "I'll do it myself, if you're not up for it."

Before I can declare that I don't think he realizes the magnitude of the job he's undertaking, we hear little voices and banging car doors.

"Too late," I say, smirking at his frustrated sigh. Then, to appease him, I offer, "Maybe some other time I can keep them busy downstairs while you rob them of their childhoods."

Narrowing his eyes at me, he says, "Very funny. I'm only trying to cut down the clutter."

"Nesting?"

He snorts. "Yeah. Sure."

"Mommy? Daddy?" Max's voice calls from below.

"Up here!" I yell back. "In your room. Come here and see it!"

Six feet thunder up the stairs, followed by a set of slower footsteps. Max arrives first. His initial delight ("Wow! Lookit my new bed!") is quickly replaced by wariness ("Wait a minute. Dat's not a new bed!"), which morphs into indignation ("Hey! Dere's a baby bed in my room!").

Brice eagerly explains, "Yeah! You and Aidan are gonna be roomies. How fun is that?"

I roll my eyes at his over-trying and add, "You know, your baby sister needs her own room, so she doesn't wake you guys up with her crying."

"Dis is *my* room!" Max reminds us.

Brice says through a tooth-clenching smile, "It still is. You just have to share it with Aidan."

Oh, no. Not the s-word. Why'd he have to say the s-word? Sure enough, it elicits a piercing reaction from Max.

"I don't wanna share!"

Harris buries his face in my legs at the noise and starts crying. Brooks runs up to Max and hits him on the shoulder while telling him to be quiet.

"Brooks, don't hit your brother!" Brice rebukes. "Say you're sorry."

Crushed at being chastised, Brooks whimpers, but we all know him well enough to know the whimper is a prelude to a good scream, so we tense in anticipation. Max cries harder, even though there's no way Brooks's smack was painful. In an effort to console Harris, I pat his head, since he's too heavy for me to lift and hold.

Mary tsks and says, "My, my, my! I think some boys are ready for naps," as Brooks reaches full volume.

Perhaps worried about being left out of all the fun, the baby kicks and rolls. I rest my hand on my belly and mutter, "Get used to it, Sweetie. This is your soon-to-be life."

"*J*not talking to you, Harris! I talking to Daddy!"
[Indistinct, adult male murmuring.]
"I don't want waffles! I want pancakes!"
[More murmuring, albeit louder. Still unintelligible.]
"No! Pancakes!"
"MAX, SIT DOWN!"
Okay, I heard that.
"No!"
"Sit down and eat your waffles, or I'm putting you in time out. Forever!"

I crack an eye to look at the time on the clock. And groan. It's not even eight o'clock yet. I usually get until at least 9:00 on Saturday mornings before they start raising a big enough kerfuffle down there to prompt me to get up for good.

I sit up in bed but have to lie down again when the room spins around me. Ew. I have "drunk's vertigo." And that's not fair, since I haven't had any fun like that since... Florida.

Closing my eyes makes it worse, but when I open them, the ceiling spins above me, and that makes me feel like I'm going to fall off the bed. "Ugh," I grunt. I roll onto my side, hoping that will alleviate the dizziness.

That's when I feel the wetness between my legs.

My heart races even faster while I fumble for my phone on the bedside table with one hand and explore the fluid coming from my body with the other. The liquid is clear. Clearly amniotic fluid.

"Oh, God…" I moan. "No! Nononono!" I try to send Brice a text, but my hands shake too much. Eventually, I settle for screaming his name. I hate scaring him. I hate scaring the kids. But I'm scared. And I don't know what else to do.

After screeching his name for the fourth time, I hear him say on his way up the stairs, "Stay down there, boys!"

He runs into our bedroom, his eyes wide. "What's the matter? What's—"

I gesture to the wet spot on my pajama pants. "My water broke."

"Your water…? What?" He shakes his head. "But— No. It's not—"

Three little people crowd around the bed.

"Whatsa matter, Mommy?" Max asks sweetly. "Did you peed the bed?"

"Where's Aidan?" I think to ask. My mind is pinging off in a billion directions at once. Right now, it wants to know where my youngest is.

Brice keeps his eyes pinned to my wet pajamas. "Uh, he's— He's in his high chair. He's fine." He blinks and lurches into motion, herding the boys into the twins' room. "Guys, I need you to play nicely together. In Brooks and Harris's room. All right?" His voice cracks and shakes on the last word.

"Daddy, what's wrong?" Max asks.

"Everything's fine," Brice lies. "But I need you to do what I say."

"Okay."

I hear the boys digging through their toy boxes, arguing over who gets what. Brice returns to the bedroom, pushing buttons on his phone with a shaky hand. "I'm calling Dave."

I nod pathetically, still too dizzy to do much else. Except cry. I can cry. Because I know this isn't good.

"Are you having contractions?" he asks me while he listens to the rings on the other end.

"Not bad ones," I say, sniffling, feeling a tiny scrap of hope at that realization. "They're like period cramps."

Brice audibly swallows and nods. Then he mutters, "Ding-danged voicemail," before saying in a louder voice, "Dave. Brice Northam. Sorry to bother you, but it's an emergency. We think—actually, we *know*—Peyton's water broke. I'm taking her to the hospital as soon as I can get someone here to watch the boys. Call me back at this number. Thanks."

He barely has the phone in his shorts pocket before offering me his arm. "Okay. It's okay. Everything's going to be okay. We *know* it is, right? Because… we know."

"I don't know," I choke out. "I'm so scared. It's too early. Way too early."

Sounding a lot more confident, he says, "Yeah, it is. But she's going to be fine. They'll figure out a way to stop it at the hospital. Come on. Up you go. Let's get you dressed." He pulls me to a standing position and moves to leave me, but I keep a tight grip on his arm.

"You can't let me go. I'll fall. I'm so dizzy!"

In a soothing tone, he says, "All right. I was going to get you some towels, but—"

"I need to sit."

He eases me onto the mattress again.

"I know," he mutters, as if coming up with a bright idea. "You sit, and I'll dress you."

"Forget it. I'll go in this," I say faintly, referring to the pajama pants and t-shirt I'm wearing. I can't imagine having the energy to change my clothes *and* get down the stairs *and* get into the car *and* make it into the hospital.

He seems to consider it for a second, then acquiesces. "Okay. You're right. Getting dressed is a waste of time."

I nod, but I doubt he can distinguish the movement from the fierce tremors making my head bob. "The boys. Call your mom."

"Oh, right. I'm going to go get Aidan, too. Are you okay for just a second?"

I wave him away, suddenly out of breath. My belly feels tight and heavy. There's pressure against my cervix. As he rushes down the stairs, gasping, "Mom!" into his phone, I utter a weak, "Hurry."

But I already know we're too late. It's happening again.

The past twenty-four hours have been terrifying. But at the same time, they've been miraculous.

The first miracle occurred when Mary got to our house in record time. ("I hit all green lights, kids. Now, go!") The second miracle was that we had the same luck on our way to the hospital. But the third miracle was the best one of all. Soon after we arrived at the hospital and they got me hooked up to every machine known to medicine, we heard her heartbeat.

Brice grinned at me through his tears, the color

returning to his face, and squeezed my hands in his. "See? She's okay."

The nurse with us wasn't as blindly optimistic. "That's a good sign, sure, but we need to get that labor stopped. Now." She hung a bag of something on the IV pole and pushed a bunch of buttons to get the liquid flowing into my veins. "This should stop the contractions. Dr. Klein will be in shortly to talk to you guys."

When Dave did arrive, he gave us the undiluted news: "Get comfortable, folks. This is going to be your home for the next several weeks. And that's if everything goes well."

I blinked and swallowed, desperately trying to block the memory of Secret, limp and blue, being pulled from my body seven years ago. My lips felt numb when I said, "Whatever needs to be done. Tell me what to do."

He pointed at me. "You. Stay in bed and do everything we tell you to do. No questions asked." Pointing to Brice, he said, "You. Make sure she does what we tell her to do. And both of you, pray. Pray a lot. Because if your baby's born before the next two months are up, we're going to be facing some huge challenges. And she might not make it. Two months is a long time to delay a labor that wants to happen. But we're going to do everything we can."

Then the fourth miracle happened: the contractions stopped altogether.

As soon as they stabilized me, they moved me to the maternity ward, my new home-away-from-home. Brice called his mom, then my parents, who were already booking a flight to get to us.

Exhausted from the emotional and physical stress, I fell asleep. I considered that the fifth miracle.

When I woke up on my left side, the bed rail was down, and Brice was sitting in a chair pulled up to the side of the bed. He was bent at the waist, the top of his head against my belly, his face toward me, his eyes closed. The baby kicked, and he smiled, but his eyes stayed shut.

"She's saying hi," I whispered.

His eyes flew open, but he didn't sit up or even move his head. "Hey, there," he said softly. "How are you feeling?"

"Like someone sewed my cervix shut and is pumping me full of drugs," I answered. "In other words, great."

He chuckled and stood. "Now that you're awake, I might run home and check on things there, get some stuff for you. Dave said you could have your phone and a laptop, and I'll grab your e-reader."

That should keep me busy for a day, I thought but didn't say. "Thanks. What time is it?"

He looked over my shoulder, where I presumed there was a clock, and answered, "A little before five."

I suppressed a dismayed groan at the slow passage of time. After all, I'd better get used to it, I told myself sternly. An eternity—or what feels like one—is not too long to wait for the safest time for her to be born.

He reached in his pocket for his keys, and I noticed for the first time that he was still wearing the basketball shorts and t-shirt he was mucking around in with the boys when I screamed for him this morning.

"Take your time," I urged him. "Get a shower and a nap, and spend some time with the boys and your mom and even my parents, when they get there. I'm fine. And I'm not going anywhere."

With a tired smile, he murmured a noncommittal, "We'll see."

He was gone for about two hours. Less than that. I didn't even get through the whole baseball game I was half-watching while ceaselessly praying.

After that, he was never away from my side for longer than ten minutes. He was aware of every beep and click the machines emitted. He watched the nurse's face when she came into the room to take my vitals, because he knows what they *don't say* is sometimes more important than what they do say. He asked questions and reported his own observations and lent a hand whenever necessary (helping me to the bathroom was the most strenuous of those tasks, after they removed my catheter). He kept me comfortable and entertained. He held my hand while I slept. And he prayed. We both did a tremendous amount of praying.

I spent a fitful night, interrupted every couple of hours by vitals checks, crying babies in other rooms, and my infinite supply of worries:

What if she dies?

What if she lives but is born too soon? I can scarcely parent healthy, so-called "normal" (whatever that means) kids. How am I going to cope with a child with special needs?

How is Brice going to manage at home without me?

What if Brice manages just fine without me?

How much is all this going to cost? How are we going to pay for it, even after the insurance company pays its portion?

How can I even think about money? Does that make me a bad person?

Am I going to see the boys at all during all this? Will they miss me? What if they don't miss me? Are they scared?

I'm scared. I'll likely remain scared for the next two months, or however long this goes on. Can a human sustain fear for that long without permanent psychological damage?

Aren't I already psychologically damaged enough?

Do I quit my job now, assuming this will end in my

having the baby that was going to require me to quit my job? Or do I hold out, waiting to see what happens? Is that considered hedging my bets? Does it signify a lack of faith?

Did they really sew my cervix shut? I was kidding about that, but I read about it once. I'll need to ask Dave. I should probably know something like that. Do I want to know, though?

When I wake up for good this morning, I hear Brice on his phone, behind me. From the sounds of it, he's standing by the room's window, looking down onto our scenic view of the parking lot.

"Dave says the first twenty-four hours are crucial, and we made it. Labor's stopped, she's resting as comfortably as possible, and they're pumping her full of stuff to keep her uterus relaxed and also to help the baby's lungs develop more quickly…. Yeah, I know. It was scary, especially considering…" He clears his throat. "Well, you know…. No, her parents are staying at our place for now, but I appreciate the offer. Just, uh, take care of things there at the church for me…. What's that…? Oh, you know, I'm not sure. Maybe Mitzi could give her a call? I don't think Peyton's up to it right now…. No, it's not that. It's, well, I'd like to keep the drama to a minimum, ya know? She's still upset about all that…. Exactly. Thanks. Well, I'd better let you go, then. Just wanted to give you an update so you could keep us in your prayers and maybe give us a mention in church today." He chuckles. "Yeah. We're gonna need it. Thanks. Take care."

I remain motionless on my side, facing away from him, thinking about what I've heard. I assume Jared asked if Jen knew what was happening; that must be who Brice was referring to when he suggested Mitzi give "her" a call.

"She's still upset about all that."

And here I thought I've been hiding it so well. I thought

I was being so strong and solid, a real trouper. Or maybe he just knows me that well.

I hear the bed rail click behind me, and the waterproof mattress cover under the stiff bed sheet squeaks and pops. Then solid warmth presses along the length of my spine. I relax against him.

He kisses my neck as he tucks his legs behind mine. "Good morning. How did you sleep?"

"I slept," I answer as positively as possible without lying.

"They won't have to be as vigilant every night as they were last night."

"I know. It was hard to turn off my thoughts. And I think it was hard to sleep alone in a weird place, too. This is nice. I missed you."

"I was right over there the whole time," he reminds me, referring to the cot they wheeled in for him to sleep on a few feet away.

"Not the same," I grumble. "The nurse is going to flip if she comes in and sees you up here with me."

"Nah. I asked them if this would be okay."

"You did?"

"Yeah. I didn't want to do anything wrong. I couldn't imagine this would be a problem, but what do I know? So, I went out to the nurses' station a while ago and asked permission, just in case."

I laugh at the thought.

He drapes his arm over my side and rests his hand against my belly, careful not to nudge the fetal heart monitor. "They said as long as there was no funny business…"

"No, they didn't!"

"Yes, they did," he says through his laughter. "When I was shocked that they felt the need to even mention that, they said I'd be surprised what couples tried to get up to, especially after several weeks in residence."

"People are crazy."

"I don't know… That hospital gown is pretty irresistible."

"It's easy access, too."

His tone is suddenly serious. "I'm sorry you're going to be stuck in this bed for the next two months."

"Beats the alternative."

"Good point."

"Plus, you're the one who's going to have to deal with the boys on your own while still going to work and occasionally coming by here to visit me and—" I stop before every single concern I've had for the past day comes tumbling out. If I don't voice them, they're not real, right?

"Shhh… Hey, don't worry about all that, okay? And what's this 'occasionally coming to visit' nonsense?"

My eyes fill, and my voice thickens. "How are you going to find the time? Or the energy? I'll understand if you can't make it by here."

He sits up. Left without his support, I roll onto my back. He looks down into my face and solemnly promises, "I will be here every single day."

"Brice…"

"Every. Day. You hear me?"

I nod while choking back a sob.

"I'll figure it out, okay? I don't want you worrying about it."

"Okay, but—"

"Your parents are here now, and I bet they'd stay indefinitely if I asked them."

"You and Dad would kill each other."

A corner of his mouth inches upward. "You're right; I

won't ask them. But they'll be here for a while. And after they leave, my mom can stay with the boys in the evenings, after I put them to bed."

"You'll be so tired."

"Never too tired to spend time with you."

I cry harder, the sobs making my belly quake.

"Hey… It's going to be okay."

"The boys are going to forget me."

"No, they won't! Hon, I'll bring them here all the time to see you."

"You will?"

"Of course! We're not going to leave you up here all alone." He kisses my belly. I rest my hand in his hair. Looking up at me through his lashes, he says, "We're going to miss you and want to come see you every chance we get."

"This is going to be so hard," I whisper to keep the tears under control. "And I know it's worth it. *She's* worth it. But how am I going to do this? How are *we* going to do this?" My eyes beg him to give me a comforting answer that I can truly believe.

I almost break down completely when he says, "With God's help," but he hastens to add, "and by accepting that this is the way it has to be. And keeping in mind that Hannah will be a healthy, happy baby, because you did this for her."

While I nod and swipe at my face with my hands, he retrieves a tissue from the box on the rolling table by the bed and hands it to me.

"Come on. How many times have you wished you could stay in bed all day? Now, you get to do it for the next—"

"Please, don't do the math and say the number," I mumble from behind the tissue.

He laughs. "Okay. But you have to put the best spin on

it. And you'll get into a routine here. The days won't drag so much after this becomes normal to you."

"You're right." His face brightens at that statement. After blowing my nose, I say, "Her name's not Hannah, though. So, don't get attached to that one. Although, it's the prettiest name you've come up with so far."

"I like it."

"Well, I went to elementary school with a bully named Hannah, and she ruined the name forever for me. Sorry."

He sighs dramatically. "I'll keep trying, I guess. And hey!" He grins. "You'll have lots of time to think of names, right? You can give me a list each day when I visit, and we'll slowly narrow it down. It'll be fun."

He's trying so hard. I don't have the heart to say anything other than, "You're right; it'll be fun."

THE PRODIGAL FRIEND

I'm having a bad day. And not just one of thos, "I-shit-my-pants-at-the-grocery-store" bad days. No, more like an "I-might-lose-this-baby" bad day. Again. Well into my third week in the hospital on bed rest, this is my fourth day like this. My nerves are shot.

Brice doesn't look much more composed when he enters my room and takes in the nurses bustling about. Unfortunately, he knows from past experience to stand back, that there's nowhere near the hospital bed where he can stand and hold my hand but also be out of the way. Propping his elbow in one hand and his chin in the other, he leans against the wall opposite the foot of the bed and watches with worried eyes.

I blink back tears of anger and frustration. I've been doing everything they tell me to do, when they tell me to do it, exactly the way I'm told to do it. I haven't seen my children in more than a week because they've been passing around the sniffles, and I haven't wanted to risk getting sick and giving my body any more reasons to be uncooperative.

And still… my body doesn't seem capable of holding my baby inside.

Again, I wonder, *Is this it? Is today going to be another date branded into my brain and on my heart, a date I can't see or hear without bringing me back to this moment, or even a moment worse than this, the moment I see her and know she's gone?*

I bite my lower lip, set my jaw, and tighten my nether regions like I'm holding in a fart in a wall-to-wall room of lit candles.

You can't come out, I tell her, closing my eyes and gritting my teeth. *You just can't. It's not time yet. Keep growing in there. Strengthen your lungs, develop that brain. Stay. Inside.*

Finished talking to my daughter, I turn my attention to God. *Don't do this to me twice, Lord. I can't handle it. Don't do it to Brice. He* can *handle it, but it's still not fair to make him. You and I will be in a fight like never before if You let anything happen to another one of my babies before she's even allowed to enter the world. So, pull one of those miracles You're so fond of pulling from wherever You pull miracles, and stop the contractions. Please. I'm begging You. Please.*

Several tense minutes elapse. The nurses have done all they can do, administering the drugs to relax my uterus. Now all we can do is wait. If the contractions slow and stop, we've averted yet another crisis. If they continue and strengthen, I'll be giving birth to a baby with little chance of survival. And even if she survives a birth this premature, she'll have major health problems that will impact the rest of her life. Cognitively. Physically. She'll be struggling from Day One.

At first I'm not sure if I'm imagining it through sheer hope or if the peace and calm descending on me is, in fact, real. Then I feel even more relaxed. And more relaxed. Finally, damp with sweat, I take a deep breath and open my eyes. The contraction monitor next to my bed is quiet, the green line across the screen low and flat, with only the occasional, lazy squiggle in it.

"It appears to be working," Dawn, the day shift nurse routinely assigned to me, confirms my unprofessional assessment. She pats my upper arm. "You did good, Mom. You know the drill; lie there for a while, exactly like that. Try to stay as relaxed as possible. Deep breaths. I'll get you some water."

I nod but don't say a word to acknowledge her praise. I don't deserve it. My body is betraying me; it's betraying my daughter, heartlessly trying to evict her.

Dawn nods at Brice and pauses on her way past him. "Dad, you've got two tough girls there. You and those sweet boys are in for a load of trouble."

He smiles proudly. "Bring it. But not for a few more weeks, huh?"

She laughs. "We'll see what we can do to buy you some more time to prepare yourselves."

With that, she follows the two other shift nurses who have exited the room before her.

As soon as she's gone, I say to Brice, "I'm sorry."

"Enough of that."

I stare straight ahead at the pattern on the curtain I have memorized by now, as I've lain on my left side countless hours during the past three weeks, with at least four weeks to go—if we're lucky. We're not even halfway there.

"I swear, I'm doing everything they tell me to do. I even stopped watching certain movies, the ones that make me tense, because I noticed I started having tiny contractions when I was nervous."

He sits in the chair next to the bed and leans down so he's looking into my face. "Peyton."

"What?"

"I want you to stop blaming yourself for this. For all of it. For every little thing that happens. You're not in control here. At all. Stop taking credit for everything."

"Are we fighting nature?" I ask him what I've wondered often in my loneliest hours in this bed. "Is it God's will that she not make it? Are we trying to force *our* will on the situation? Are we going to be punished for it?"

Resting his hand on the top of my head, he answers, "This *is* God's will. All of it. Do you really think we're strong enough to fight it?"

"No. That's why all the things we're doing aren't working."

"They *are* working. She's still here." He pats her, as if to prove it.

As usual after one of these episodes, she's still, as if she's hiding from the flurry of activity. But the fetal heart monitor lets us know she's still alive, no matter how quiet she is. Sometimes that whooshing is the only thing that keeps me sane. I'm not sure if I'll be able to sleep without it when this is all over.

Too tired to argue with him about it any longer, I close my eyes and reluctantly say, "You should get back to the church, now that things are okay."

He lets go of my head but his hand curls around one of mine, squeezing firmly. "I'm done for the day."

My eyes pop open. "What? It's not even noon!"

"It's a Tuesday. There's nothing going on there that's more important than what's happening here. Jared and Wes can handle it. Unless you want me to leave."

"No!"

He laughs at my insistence. "Okay, then. You're stuck with me until it's time for me to pick up the boys."

"Are they still snotty?" I ask, my heart dropping at the

regretful nod he gives in reply. Putting up a brave front, I begin lightly, as if I'm not bothered. "Oh. Okay. I just—" It's no use pretending, though. I stop, my throat tightening in a way that I wish it could teach my vagina to do. Pushing on, I choke, "I miss them, that's all."

What I don't have voice enough to say without breaking down is that I'd really like to kiss their cheeks and smell their hair and press their hands into mine.

"Maybe in a day or two," he proposes. "I'll bring them to you as soon as I can."

"I know you will." I smile weakly.

Talking in the direction of my belly, he murmurs, "Hang in there, Sweetie."

I'm not sure if he's talking to me or the baby. Or both of us.

I know most people by smell now. Yeah. Dubious talent, for sure. But helpful, too, since I spend most of the day sleeping, or resting with my eyes closed. My sense of smell helps me determine if I want to ignore or acknowledge the person entering my room. I'm a captive audience here, so I've learned to keep my eyes closed until my nose makes a ruling.

Of course, I've always been able to pick out Brice and my close friends and family in an olfactory lineup, but now I've expanded my nasal knowledge to include Wes, many of the ladies from the church, and Dr. Klein and the maternity ward nurses.

Nine times out of ten, I fake sleep when Wes comes by. It's not that I'm holding a grudge against him (for once); it's simply too awkward and stressful to make small talk with him. Half the time, I avoid the church ladies, but I realize it would seem unnatural if I were *always* sleeping, so I suck it up every other time.

And I like most of the nurses, but there are a couple that should keep all sharp objects out of my reach, including ink pens, because sometimes I want to stab them in the neck. (Cabin fever makes me hostile, in case you hadn't noticed.)

Dawn—my favorite—smells like citrus and gardenia; Winnie—also nice—smells like lavender; Nurse Ratchett... er, I mean, Pamela smells a lot nicer than she is, like milk and honey. And on and on. There are about a dozen different nurses, all women, whom I can identify with my eyes closed. I'm scarily accurate.

That's why I'm unnerved when I don't recognize the smell of the person who quietly enters my room while I'm dozing—not fully napping—waiting for Brice to return from transporting the boys from daycare and to the house, where they'll hang out with Mary for the night. It's too soon for him to be back, and anyway, it's definitely not him—or any other male, for that matter. But the scent doesn't match any of the women I know, either. It's light and clean, not perfume-y. And absolutely unfamiliar.

Stumped, I open my eyes (always a last resort) to see who's there, in case she's standing over me with a pillow, poised to put it against my face.

My brain almost can't register whom I'm seeing.

"It's amazing the lengths you'll go to in order to slack on the parenting duties. Poor Brice," she drawls.

Her hair's shorter, much shorter, the curls lying close to her scalp, like a frilly bathing cap, and giving her an elfin, tomboyish appearance. I blink once, twice, three times. She breaks eye contact first, looking down at her hands. My eyes follow, and I notice her usual French tips are no more. In their place are short, blunt, unpolished nails.

"Jen?" I whisper, wondering if someone slipped something wacky in my IV cocktail earlier today, during the preterm labor scare.

"I would have been here sooner," she says in a bored tone, "but I figured you had enough going on without me bringing my drama around." She looks up at me and gives me a self-deprecating half-smile.

"Did Brice say that to you?"

She laughs. "No! What the...? As if he would ever say something like that to anyone!"

Convinced this is happening, that she's really here, I struggle to sit up.

"Whoa, whoa. Careful now, Beluga." She offers her hand to give me some leverage.

After I've adjusted the head of the bed to support myself in a sitting position and I've caught my breath, I say in a stilted, formal, unfamiliar manner, "Thanks for coming to see me. You look different. But good! Did you just get into town?"

"A couple of days ago. We checked into the hotel late Tuesday night and slept most of the day yesterday. At least, *I* did. I don't know what Vince did. The guy can't sit still, though, so I'm sure he went hiking, or something."

Nothing she's saying is making any sense. Not a bit of it. And I'm too preoccupied with figuring it out to be as overjoyed as I should be at her sudden return.

"Vince? Whitaker? Pastor Vince? Brice's friend?" I splutter.

She nods casually. "That's the one. We drove up here togeth—"

"Wait, wait, wait. What?" I shake my head, almost sure now that I'm dreaming. I tap my IV port. "Ow," I mutter when it hurts.

She watches me with exaggerated patience.

Before she snaps at me, I say, "I don't understand. Can you start from the beginning?"

With a long-suffering sigh, she replies, speaking slowly, as if explaining to Max, "Vince and I decided to come see you guys, and we drove together, and since Vince wanted it to be a surprise, and I gave up my lease on my apartment months ago, we stayed at a hotel."

"You and Vince?"

She narrows her eyes at me. "We're friends. That's all."

"Okay…"

"I'm serious. He's been…" Obviously not sure how to finish that, she restarts, "I didn't know where else to go. I wanted beaches and warm weather and solitude, so I went to Florida, because I remembered how great you looked when you got back from there. Rested. Restored. Whatever."

I continue to stare, open-mouthed, at her, so she proceeds. "Anyway… After a couple of weeks, I got lonely. Bored. I've always enjoyed Vince's company, so I went to his church one Sunday. And we went to lunch together afterward and talked for, like, three hours. About everything. And nothing. It was nice."

"But you're just friends."

"Just friends. We have separate rooms at the hotel. Call and check, if you must, Mother Superior."

I chuckle, in spite of my shock that this is even happening. "I believe you. Sheesh."

"Vince is a good listener."

"He is."

"And he's funny."

I nod.

Her eyes light up, and she becomes more animated.

"Like, on the way here, we were driving and driving and driving. It should have felt like the longest trip ever, but it flew! And it's not like we talked the whole way. There were lots of times that we just listened to the radio, or whatever. And that's the thing. I didn't feel I *had* to be talking the whole time. He's so good at silence!"

"A dying art, for sure."

"Yeah! But then, after an hour of not talking, he'd say something related to what we'd been talking about before we stopped talking, and it was like we never stopped. Crazy."

"Hmm. Crazy."

She looks around the room, almost as if she's just realized where she is. Nodding toward the plant-laden windowsill, she says, "You starting your own greenhouse in here?"

I look over at the greenery and sigh. "That's not even half of what I've received. Brice takes one or two plants home every few days. I guess people don't know what else to do."

"At least they're not burying you in casseroles."

"Oh, they're doing that, too. It's nice, though, because that way, Brice doesn't have to spend a lot of time cooking for the boys. He heats up something in the microwave; they eat. He bathes the kids and puts them to bed. Then he comes to sit with me while Mary stays with the boys."

"Every day?"

"Pretty much. Sometimes he brings them here before taking them home for the evening. They've been fighting colds lately, though, so I haven't seen them in a while." I smile tightly.

She grabs my hand. "You don't have to be all cheerful

and brave with me, you know? I know what you're really like, so there's no use pretending."

I laugh while blinking at the tears produced by her tough declaration of understanding. "I'm going crazy here."

"It's only been, what, three weeks?"

"Almost four," I exaggerate slightly.

"No, it's been three. I remember when Vince told me what was going on. He was one of the first people Brice called."

"I thought Mitzi told you."

"I already knew from Vince by the time she called."

"I see. And where is Vince right now?"

"He went with Brice to pick up the boys and do guy stuff. I guess. I didn't ask. We got to the hospital as Brice was walking out. You should have seen his face when he recognized us. Priceless."

I grin at the movie in my head.

She laughs. "It was like he thought we were a mirage. Plus, I think my hair threw him. *And* it was probably confusing that Vince and I were walking in together. So, he smiled at us as we were walking toward him in the lobby, but I could tell he was just smiling like he does at everyone he comes across—the guy is abnormally nice, but you already know that. Then he did, like, this funny double-take when Vince said, 'Hey, brother! Where you headed?' I thought the corners of Brice's mouth were gonna get caught on his ears. Biggest smile ever. Then he noticed me, and Vince and I both got the hugs of our lives. It was really sweet."

In other words, he had the type of reaction I *should* be having but can't seem to muster. Maybe I know on some level that if I let go of my emotions, there will be no getting them back under control. I choose to focus on my husband's response.

"Aww. He got emotional, didn't he?"

She shifts in her chair and avoids eye contact. "A little. Maybe. I imagine you're both on the edge at any given moment."

I nod, then tell her, "We had another scare this morning."

"That's what Brice said. He said it had been a long day."

"They're all long. I— I'm so scared."

"All the time? That has to be exhausting!" Her tone is flippant, but I know that's her way of trying to lighten the mood.

"It is!" I say with a tiny laugh. "Look at me! I sleep all the time."

"Your hair's a mess."

"Permanent bedhead."

She goes into the small adjoining bathroom and returns with my hair brush. Standing next to the bed, she runs the brush gently through my hair, stroke after stroke after stroke. I close my eyes, letting goosebumps take over my body as I relish the feel of the bristles against my scalp.

After a few minutes, I slur, dangerously close to drooling in the process, "This is awesome."

And I'm only talking partly about the pampering.

MENDING HEARTS

By the time Brice and Vince return to the hospital, I have on a full face of makeup, and my hair's been styled like I'm poised to compete in a maternity ward beauty contest. I feel ridiculous. Ridiculously *great*.

Brice grins when he gets a full look at me. "Hey! You look nice!"

"Nice?" Jen questions, clearly offended. "She looks amazing. Like, all the other ladies on the floor would hate her if she was allowed to leave this room and be seen."

"Well, that's true all the time," Brice says.

"Nice save," I say with a laugh.

Vince steps forward and gives me a hug. "Hey, kiddo. You look great, especially considering the day you've had. How are you feeling?"

I shrug but hug him back. "Fine. Much better now that you two are here."

"Us two?" he points to himself, then Jen.

I nod. "You two."

He fans himself and rolls his eyes, as if he's flattered to the point of embarrassment. "Oh, you!" Turning to Jen, he says, "Did you hear that? She's happy to see us. I hate to say 'I told you so,' but…"

She widens her eyes at him and suppresses a smile with great effort. "Shush!"

His hands fly up in front of his chest, palms out. "I said, 'I hate to say it.' I'm not delighting in the fact that I was right."

Brice snickers at Vince's theatrics.

"Is this true?" I ask Jen. "You thought I wouldn't want to see you?"

"Well, I wasn't very nice to you last time I talked to you. The last two times, actually," she supplies, in place of a direct answer.

"So? You're still my best friend. I… I've been a complete dumbass without you!"

Now Brice and Vince look decidedly uncomfortable around us, but neither of them says anything. I appreciate their letting us have our moment without their male interference.

"I thought you hated *me*, that you never wanted to see me or talk to me again," I continue, ignoring the squirming men. "Because I'm self-centered and judgmental. I'm not, though. Judgmental, anyway. I guess I can be self-centered. I try not to be, but I always fail. Plus, trying not to be self-centered feels pretty self-involved and counterproductive. But I have to concentrate on being less inward-focused. I guess that makes me a not-so-great person and a crappy friend—"

"You're doing it again, by the way," Jen says. "Going on and on about yourself. And you're going to cry off all your makeup."

I sniffle. "The thing is, I've never judged you for

anything. None of it. But I could never convince you of it, for some reason."

"I know. I was projecting my own insecurities on the things you said to me."

"I'll take credit for that one," Vince mutters.

Jen punches his shoulder but laughs. "Be quiet!"

I disregard their antics and say earnestly, "I *did* think you might not fit in as a pastor's wife, but that's only because *I* don't fit in, and we're so much alike. And I didn't want you to be unhappy. It had nothing to do with worthiness."

"I know. I'm sorry I didn't give you more credit than that." She pushes Vince out of the way and practically throws herself on me. "I'm sorry I said I hated you. It wasn't true. I didn't. I don't. I hated myself for letting myself get hurt, for all the things I did to lead me to that point in my life. And the other thing I said." She lifts her head to look at me. "You know, about— Well, that you should stop having babies. That was out of line. And now that all this is happening…" She gestures to the room around us. "Gosh, I feel like such a jerk! I'm sorry!"

I close my eyes and weep while I pat her on her foreign-feeling, close-cropped hair. "I'm sorry, too!"

Brice clears his throat. "Um. Coffee, Vince?"

When I open my eyes, I see the guys edging toward the room's door.

"We're done," I say. "You don't have to leave."

Jen straightens and reaches for a tissue on my rolling table. After honking into the rectangle of paper, she says, "Yes. It'll be so awkward if we're alone now. Please don't go."

Neither man looks like he believes us, but they remain in the room.

I dab at my eyes so as not to ruin my makeover, then I change the subject. "How are the boys?" I ask Brice.

He perches on the foot of my bed and relaxes as he gives me the evening update. "They're fine. Aidan fell at daycare today and scraped his chin, but Brooks has inflicted worse on him, so I don't think it's going to slow him down. Max has decided he doesn't like any green foods, so that's going to be fun. Harris…"

As Brice continues his monologue, I watch Vince and Jen in my peripheral vision. He puts a comforting arm around her shoulders and murmurs something I can't hear through Brice's update. Jen smiles privately and nods, still dabbing at her eyes and nose. Vince's arm returns to his side after he gives Jen one final squeeze, and he steps a few feet away, where he seems to be admiring my budding florist business by the window. Her eyes never leave him.

"What do you think?" Brice is asking me now.

I think Jen's "just friends" claim is a load of b.s., is what I think but can't say. Whether Vince is aware of it is another issue. I have no idea what I'm supposed to be thinking about what Brice has said. The last thing I heard was that Max doesn't like green food.

"Try giving Max green M&Ms, to show him that some green things are good," I try.

He waves his hand as if to brush that suggestion aside. "No, Harris's cough. It sounds deep. Should I take him to the doctor?"

"Oh. Yes. Shoot. Does he have green snot?"

"They all do. Is that bad?"

I try to smile reassuringly as I stifle a sigh. "Yes. You might as well take them all at the same time."

He rubs his temples. "Oh, man!"

Jen pipes up, "I'll help you. Just tell me when."

"Me, too!" Vince volunteers, spinning to face all of us. "We'll triple-team 'em. Those kids won't know what hit 'em."

"Thanks, guys, but…" With a weak smile, he finishes, "Thanks. That'll be nice."

He exchanges a wan look with me. I know he's not worried about handling four boys by himself—he does it all the time, especially lately. He's worried more about the expenses: the doctor's office visit, the insurance co-pay, the inevitable prescriptions… It's a lot with one child. Multiply it by four, and you have a budgeting brain-buster.

But this is the life we've chosen, mostly. There are some major components of it that weren't our choice, but even those are things we wouldn't change for anything. And others? Well, given the option between an expensive, long-term stay in the hospital and a short-term stay with a tragic ending, we'd take the former over the latter any day.

I try to let him know with a look that I understand his worries and that I share them. I don't want him to feel alone in all this. I might be stuck in this bed, but my head and my heart are often with him, in our house, with our children, puzzling through the challenges of maintaining a semi-normal routine and existence for our whole family.

I can only hope he gets the message, though, because soon after promising he'll call the pediatrician first thing in the morning, he squeezes my foot through the blanket and says, "It's been a long, tiring day. I think we should leave you to get some rest."

It's obvious he's tired, so I don't object, fearing he'll feel guilty for wanting to go home. I smile and say easily, "I could sleep. And I'll see you tomorrow."

"Definitely." He rises and waits for Jen and Vince to say their goodbyes and step into the hallway to wait for him.

After he leans down to give me a gentle peck on the lips, I say, "Have some fun with those two."

"Won't be the same without you," he claims, and by the look on his face, he means it. As quickly, though, he pushes his moroseness aside and says brightly, "I'm glad you and Jen patched things up."

"Me, too. I've missed her."

"And she missed you. *I* miss you," he says with a wry twist to his mouth.

My heart drops. "I know. I'm sor—"

Putting his finger against my lips, he says, "Don't you dare."

I kiss his finger, then command, "C'mere," puckering my lips.

He lowers his head, relaxing into a kiss that conveys our love and longing and promise to each other that none of that will change, no matter what happens today, tomorrow, or in the upcoming weeks.

Finally, he groans into my mouth and pulls away, backing toward the door. "Gotta go, before I break my promise to those nurses about keeping things under control in here."

I laugh and wave him out. Perhaps worried I'll try to change his mind, he's gone before I can say anything else.

"Bethany. Grace. Sophie. Are you even listening to me?"

I focus my blank stare on Brice's face, tilt my head, and smile. "Sorry. I was thinking about"—at the last second, I decide not to be specific—"something else."

"Obviously. Did you hear any of the name suggestions I just gave you?" He thrusts the piece of paper in his hands toward me before I answer. "Never mind. Here they are. You can read them and put big X's through them later."

I take the paper and peruse his list. "No, no. These are good. You're finally suggesting names that don't make me cringe."

"Big improvement."

"Yeah, I know."

He studies my face for a few seconds, until I squirm and say, "What?"

"Are you okay? I mean, do you feel okay?"

"Why? Do I look bad? You got used to seeing me with all that makeup on."

"No! You look…" His expression softens. Gone is the concern of a few seconds ago. In its place is affection and bemusement. "Why do you always assume you look bad?"

"Because I usually look bad? And I'm in a hospital bed. And I haven't showered in… I don't even know. The days blur together." I concentrate on trying to remember my last shower. Dawn helped me, so it had to have been a weekday. "What day is it?" I ask.

"Friday. You showered yesterday."

Wow. It seems so much longer ago than yesterday.

"How do *you* remember these things?"

He shrugs. "I just do." Scooting closer to me and moving the tray table out of the way, he plucks my hand from on top of the covers and seems to be examining the IV bruise across the back of it. "I'm not asking because you look sick; I'm asking because you look distracted. What's up? Stomping on my name suggestions is usually the highlight of your day and gets every ounce of your attention."

I debate giving him a blow-off answer and keeping my thoughts to myself, but instead I ask a question of my own. "Has Vince said anything to you about Jen?"

Brice stiffens. "You'll have to be more specific."

I knew it! I purse my lips and narrow my eyes, studying his face for clues about how best to proceed. Finally, I decide he's holding back, because Vince must have told him something pastor-to-pastor that's confidential. Or something silly like that.

In case we're not dealing with pesky pastor privilege, I say, "I think they've gotten close."

"I think you're right."

"I am?" When he seems guarded about my enthusiastic request for confirmation, I tone it down and clear my throat. "Uh, yeah. I know. And she says they're just friends, but—"

"Maybe you should leave it alone." He squeezes my hand, and I wince, so he lightens his grip. "Oh, sorry." He kisses the bruise. "Forgot for a second."

I ignore his apology. "I'm not going to get in the middle of anything, but I wondered if you think—or know—if Vince feels more than... friendly... toward Jen. You know, are they on the same page? Because the other day, when they were visiting together—"

Brice sighs. "Hon, this is something that's none of our concern. We have so many other things to think about right now. If they have feelings for each other, that's their business. I can't deal with anyone else's feelings right now. I'm emotionally maxed out."

Feeling foolish for having brought it up, I look away from him. "Oh. Okay. It's just kind of soon for her, don't you think? I don't want her to get hurt again, and—"

"Do you really think Vince is going to hurt her?"

"Well, not on purpose! I didn't think Wes would hurt her, either, but he did. Bad."

"They're grownups. And it's their lives, not ours."

"I don't have a life right now," I snap. "I sit here in this bed, and I drive myself crazy worrying about you and the boys, so I think about other things. And I've noticed they're kind of handsy. And they watch each other when they think nobody's looking. And— And—"

"Peyton." He makes sure I'm looking him in the eyes when he says, "Like I told Vince, it's none of my business."

"Why'd you tell Vince that? He asked your advice about it? Is he worried about Jen's…" I swallow loudly. "…past?"

His shoulders slouch, and he stands, pacing at the foot of my bed. "I think he's more worried about her future."

I stare at him while I process this riddle.

Finally, he says, "Can we *please* stop talking about this? It feels like gossiping. And I hate gossiping."

He's acting as if I'm torturing him.

"Fine, fine! You don't have to be all dramatic about it," I grumble.

I have all the information I need, for now, anyway. His reaction speaks volumes. Vince *has* talked to him about Jen. A lot. And not just about pastor-y things, either.

Switching gears, I pluck the list of names from the tray table. "Now, about this," I say, re-scanning the list. "I actually like a couple of these names."

He hurries back to the bed and sits on the side, craning his neck to look at the paper. "Yeah? Which ones?"

I point to one, then another. He grins. "I like those, too."

"I like them so much that I think… I think that's it."

"For real?" Practically bouncing on the bed, he verifies, "But what about the others on the finalists' list?"

I shake my head, staring down at the two names that have jumped out at me. "Nope. These are the ones. First and middle name." I rub my belly. "She's going to be gorgeous, and those are going to fit perfectly."

He rests his hands on top of mine. "They do fit."

"You have an advantage, you know. Because you already know what she's going to look like, after she doesn't look all Winston Churchill-y anymore."

Laugh-sniffling, he rubs at his eyes. "Yeah, but I've kept that in mind with all the names I've given you, and you've hated ninety percent of them."

"There's no way our baby looks like a Millicent."

"Okay, I threw that one in there for fun. Although 'Millie' is cute."

I push on his shoulder. "You're cute," I say, making it sound like an insult.

"You are!" he replies with a poke to my cheek.

"Stop it!"

"You started it."

Slapping footsteps and loud voices and giggles alert us to the impending arrival of our children. Brice hops from the bed and strides to the door. He steps into the hallway and implores in hushed tones, "Shhh... Guys. Babies and mommies are sleeping." At a more normal volume, he says, "Hi, Mom. These guys wearing you out? Where's Vince?"

"He's parking the van," she answers, lifting her cheek to her son on her way past him into the room. "Hey, kid," she greets me faintly while patting flat her windblown, white hair. Her cheeks are flushed; her eyes are dull.

"Hey, Ma," I return her greeting while the boys rush my bed.

"Look out for Mommy's cord!" Max bosses his younger brothers. "If you unplug the baby, its batteries will go out."

"Babies don't have batteries, you knucklehead," Brice says, laughing, as he picks up Aidan and sets him on the bed with me. Without any assistance, my monkey twins climb up, each one trying to get closer to me than the other.

"Then why's Mommy plugged in?" Max asks, pointing to my IV.

"That's special medicine to make the baby grow faster," I say. "In case she wants to come out early."

Mary plops into one of the chairs by the window. "Boys, stop crawling around on your mother," she tells the twins.

"It's okay. I missed them."

"They miss you, too. Trust me."

Brice and I exchange glances before he chuckles and asks, "Mom, is everything okay?"

She waves away his concern and snaps, "It's fine. I'm just tired is all! These boys are running me ragged."

After making sure I have a grip on Aidan, Brice moves away from the bed, sits on the arm of the chair next to his mom, and massages her shoulders. "I'm sorry. Why didn't you say something? I would have stayed home with them today."

"It's only been today!" she cries, shrugging his hands from her shoulders. "Stop treating me like an old lady!"

He puts his hands up and stands. "Okay. Um. What do you want me to do?"

She shoos him. "Maybe you can take them for a walk, or something. I'll be fine in a minute. I just need some quiet."

He plucks children from the bed like flowers from a garden and sets them on the floor, except for Aidan, who he flings onto his shoulder like a sack of mulch. "Let's go, guys. I think they have ice cream down in the cafeteria. I'll race you to the elevator!"

As soon as he clears the door, Mary says, "Oh, great. Ice cream. Like that's gonna help."

I stare into my lap. "I'm sorry they're wearing you out. We ask too much from you."

She sighs and closes her eyes. "The last thing I wanted to do was to make you feel bad, kid."

"I know!"

"I lost my temper. I'm sorry."

"Please, don't apologize." Mortified that our family has pushed her to this point, I say, "Listen. When you're ready to go home, Brice will take you. And he'll handle the boys the rest of the weekend. And next week, too."

"How's he going to do that?"

"Well, he'll bring them here with him when he comes to visit. Or not come to visit."

"No. Out of the question."

"You need a rest."

"We all need a rest, kid."

"Not me. I'm rested. All I do is rest. I'm useless."

She heaves herself from her chair and comes to stand next to me, combing her fingers through her hair. "Now, that's enough of that. You have the most important job of all of us."

"And I'm doing a shitty job of it."

"Shush, now!"

"I can't carry this baby to term. And I can't be a mom to the ones I already have. And I'm hardly a functional wife…" I bite my lip, then try to laugh off my self-pity. "It's stupid. Never mind me. You're the one who's tired and stressed out. Because of me. And I turn it around and make it about me. My gosh! I'm a piece of work."

She laughs. "You *are* a piece of work. But not in the way you mean."

I scoff.

"Brice is so proud of you."

I blink away tears. "Yes. Nobody holds down a bed like I do."

"I'm serious. He comes home in the evening and talks about how good you look and how patient you're being and how well the baby is growing, thanks to you." She tucks my hair behind my ear. "We're all trying to do our part to help *you* out in all this. We *want* to work hard for you, so you have nothing to worry about. All you need to think about is growing that baby. And here I've gone and blown it. Me! I thought for sure it would be someone else who cracked first. I'd blame old age, but I'm not *that* old."

We laugh together.

"Forgive me, kid?"

"There's nothing to forgive," I say, sniffing. "Forgive *us* for leaning so hard on you. You came here to live to enjoy life and spend quality time with us, not be a nanny."

"I happen to like being a nanny, thank you very much. Most days. The boys have just been especially ornery today."

"Oh, one of *those* days."

She nods. "Yes. If I say, 'black,' they say, 'white.' In four-part harmony."

"Sounds like they need to spend some time with their dad. Outdoors."

"Maybe you're right."

"And you need to spend some time in your own apartment, with your feet up. Enjoying the silence."

She smiles. "That sounds nice, kid."

"Then it's settled." I refuse to let my problems—or my problem-children—become someone else's burden. And it feels good to make a helpful decision.

"*W*ho's taking care of your church while you're up here, freewheeling in Missouri?" I ask Vince during our now-daily visit. He must have pulled the short straw, because he got the early morning shift.

Jen usually arrives sometime around 11:00. She stays with me and monitors the flow of church visitors throughout the afternoon, keeping people moving. "If someone's staying longer than 20 minutes, they're staying too long. And need to get a life."

Everyone clears out around dinnertime, when I generally eat alone. Sometimes Brice joins me, but more and more often, he spends the evening with the boys and doesn't come to visit until they're in bed. He sits with me for a couple of hours, but I typically wind up telling him to go home when he falls asleep in the chair next to my bed.

Vince rubs his jaw and considers my question about his abandoned congregation. "Oh, people love to retire in Florida, you know, so several of Zion's members are retired pastors. They step up when I'm away, like when I go to conferences or guest preach at other churches. I never actually take any vacation. But this is a special situation. I'm not really on vacation, anyway."

"Do you consider this to be business?"

He laughs. "No. Well, personal business, maybe." I've never seen Vince look shy—until now.

"Ah. I see."

And I do. It's obvious now that my suspicions about Vince and Jen are correct, but I'm past obsessing about it. Whatever happens will happen without my interference or knowledge. It will probably happen better without my involvement, as a matter of fact.

"Oh, do you?" he questions.

"I think so."

He leans forward in the chair. "Brice needs me right now. He's the closest thing I've ever had to a brother."

"The feeling's mutual."

"Yeah, I know. That's why being here right now is a no-brainer. He can focus on his responsibilities at the church and at home a lot easier when he knows you're not here alone with your thoughts and worries and fears."

I wince. "He told you that?"

"He doesn't have to tell me." He grasps my hand. "Strong people won't tell someone that, anyway. I'm here so he can—I don't know—let go a little. Without admitting that he's letting go."

I smile quietly. "Right. Because he can do anything. He can do it all."

"That's what he likes to think."

"So… what? You're going to stay here until the baby's born?"

He pulls his mouth sideways. "Well, depends on how much longer she hangs in there. I think it's already getting to the point that Brice isn't as anxious anymore. You've made it six whole weeks longer than your doctor thought you would. That's pretty miraculous."

I nod. "I know."

"Almost as miraculous as Brice delegating some of his duties to Jared and Wes."

We laugh at that, then I ask seriously, "Like what?"

Vince thinks about it for a minute. "Um… Well, he and the other guys have redistributed some things so that he can stick close to the church and the hospital. Like, he does all the hospital rounds now."

I already knew that. On his hospital rounds days, he pops in to say hi, see how everything's going, and to let me know when he'll be back in the evening.

"But Jared officiates opening prayers at weekday activities, and Wes visits all the shut-ins. Wes and Jared trade off on funerals and weddings. You know, stuff like that. Brice handles more of the administrative, day-to-day stuff. From his desk. He likes staying close to the boys. He walks down to the pre-school several times a day to peek in at them. Most of the time, he doesn't let them know he's there; he observes from a distance. But sometimes, he grabs a quick hug from Aidan or sits with the twins during story time or asks Max about his art projects."

My throat tightens, so all I can do is whisper, "Really?"

Vince's eyes crinkle at the corners. "Really. He has his priorities in order. And if he could check in on you with a simple walk down the hall from his office, he'd do it for you, too. A lot of guys would be scattered or rattled by this situation, but not him. He's focused. Nothing—*nothing*—is going to distract him from what's most important here. I'm just glad to be here to shoulder some of the load. I'm an excellent grocery shopper. I don't know if you knew that about me."

I press a tissue against my eyes and chuckle. "That's great to know."

"Years of practice." He lets go of my hand so I have two of them to dab at my drippy nose.

"Sorry. I don't mean to cry all the time. It's uncontrollable."

"I'm used to it. I make the ladies cry all the time. Mostly with my bad jokes."

I laugh while marveling, "He's so good, Vince!"

"Yeah, I know, right? Annoying, isn't it? He makes it so difficult for the rest of us mere mortals."

I slap at his knee. "I'm serious! And you'd be exactly the same if you were in his place. But I—" I stop and think about how I was during the only comparable situation in our lives. "When Brice was hit by that car, normal life came to a stand-still. I had to have people come live with us to take care of the kids. I took time off work. My only concern was him. And still, my sanity was constantly hanging by a thread."

"Maybe you felt that way on the inside, but once the initial danger was past, you adjusted and worked within the bounds of your new reality. That's all he's doing."

"But we had fewer kids then. And still, I was always overwhelmed. He's just amazing."

"Well, don't tell *him* that. Gosh, he'll be impossible to live with."

He pats my shoulder and doesn't stop until I look over at him. "Hey," he says seriously. "In times like these, people do what they have to do. They don't analyze it or calculate what the bare minimum effort is to keep the machine moving. They don't do it to be praised and admired. They do what feels natural and right. He's doing what feels natural and right. For him. And if you asked him—which I have—he'd admit to feeling guilty and selfish at times."

"What? Why?"

Vince shrugs. "Because he's allowed to walk around and play with the kids, and you're not. Because he can go outside, in the fresh air, and you can't. You know, being able to walk down the hall at church to check on the boys, he recognizes that's a luxury you don't have right now."

"Meanwhile, I lie here like a beached whale, while people wait on me hand and foot all day."

"That wouldn't be enjoyable to him, so he doesn't see that as pampering or a perk. He pities you."

I sniffle. "Great."

"Okay, not the right word. He sympathizes with you. And he knows this is a tiny bump, and the result will be worth it."

I nod. "Yeah. He tells me that all the time."

"You agree with him, right?"

"Of course!"

"Then let's praise God that he's well-equipped for this. And that you guys have a brilliant support team—including yours truly—to lend a hand when needed."

After a watery smile, I say, "I *am* thankful. You and everyone else have been so great."

"Oh, c'mon." After a pause, he rolls his hand toward him. "Keep going."

I blow my nose. "Thank you for telling me more about how Brice has been doing. I can't get him to talk about himself when he's here. He only wants to talk about me. And the baby. And the boys. He would never even think to let me know what you've told me today, because he doesn't think it's remarkable. But it is. And I'm glad I know."

"Keep all that in mind next time he leaves the toilet seat up. Or whatever." He hops to his feet. "I'm going to run to the hospitality room to get some coffee, then swing by the nurses' station to flirt for a while. Can I get you anything while I'm up?"

I check the level of ice water in my giant cup and nod toward it. "I guess I should refill that so I can enjoy an afternoon of being helped to the toilet. Do you mind?"

"Helping you to the toilet? I think I'll leave that to the nurses. I'll be glad to get you some more water, though." He grabs the plastic mug and pops off the top, which he sets on my table. "Be right back."

And with a wink, he disappears around the curtain.

Vince is gone for a while—a long while—but I don't think much of it. He *does* like to talk to the nurses, although I wouldn't call it flirting. As usual, he'll say anything to get a reaction, especially if that reaction is a laugh. It's also not uncommon that the coffee pot in the hospitality room is empty, so maybe he had to make more. Whatever the reason, I'm certainly not impatient—time flies when you're playing Candy Crush—or concerned—until he returns, and I glance up at him. I do a double-take at his suddenly chalky pallor.

His usually tan face is a few shades lighter than it was when he left the room. The corners of his perpetually smiling mouth point toward the floor. His eyes, normally twinkling with glee regarding some sort of mischief he's perpetuated or is about to unleash, are dull, sad, wary, and full of pity. Dangling from his right hand, near his thigh, is my plastic water mug. It's still empty.

"What's wrong? What's happened?" I immediately ask him, my heart racing.

He shakes his head almost imperceptibly, as if he's having an internal debate with himself. I can tell he doesn't want to tell me. He doesn't want to say whatever it is out loud. Full-blown panic grips me by the shoulders and shakes me.

"Tell me what's going on. What's the matter? Oh, my gosh. It's one of my kids, isn't it?" My voice takes on a whining, pleading tone. "Please, tell me it's not one of my kids. Or Brice. Just tell me!"

Again, he shakes his head, tossing the empty plastic mug on the foot of the bed and rushing to my bedside. He grabs my hand. "It's not Brice or one of the boys. Shhh./" He exchanges my hand for my head, which he pulls to his chest. Rubbing my hair, he says, "I need you to calm down."

I struggle against him "Tell me! It's Mary, isn't it? Oh, gosh. My kids killed her. They wore out her heart, and she—"

"Mary's fine. Please."

"It's bad. I know it's bad by the way you look."

"Oh, man. I have the worst poker face ever. I told him I wouldn't be able to act normal. Listen—" He lets go of me. "Brice is on his way up right now. He called me to make sure you weren't alone, in case you got a call before he could get here, but he wants to be the one to tell you. Well, I'm sure he doesn't *want* to, but he knows he needs to."

"Tell me what?" I stuff my fist against my mouth.

"I should have waited in the hall," he mutters to himself.

Brice appears in the doorway, rescuing his friend from my continued interrogation.

"What's happening?" I grill my husband, bypassing a greeting.

In two long strides, he's next to the head of my bed, taking Vince's place. He pulls up the chair next to me and sighs deeply, fingering the white square in his collar. His eyes are dry. I'm not sure what to make of that. I reach for his hand, which he readily provides.

Squeezing my fingers, he clears his throat and says, "I'm so sorry to have to tell you this, but... It's about your dad."

"No, it's not."

My irrational response seems not to surprise him or deter him. "Yes, it is."

"No."

He holds eye contact with me. "Your mom called me a while ago, and—"

"Why'd she call *you*? If something was wrong, she would have called *me*," I point out stubbornly, wrapping myself in warm, sticky denial.

He sighs. "She was worried about telling you over the phone. She was worried about, you know, a lot of things." He places a damp palm on my belly. "C'mon. Let me finish, okay? This isn't easy to say."

"Just tell me already! That's what I've been begging you to do!"

"I'm trying!" He takes a quivering breath and lets go of my hand to run his fingers through his hair. I notice his hand is shaking. Quickly, as if he's removing a verbal bandage, he says, "Your dad passed away."

I gasp.

"Early this morning. It looks like he had a stroke, but they won't know for sure until—"

I dissolve and bury my face in my hands.

"Oh, hon. I'm so, so sorry."

"I just talked to him!" I say into my palms. "He was fine!"

"That's why they suspect a stroke. No warning."

I choke off the tears and remove my hands from my face. When I do, it registers that Vince is no longer in the room. I don't really care, though.

"Oh, gosh. My mom! And Jason and Nicole. Are they okay?"

Brice tightens his lips as if he's considering how much to tell me, then says, "They're dealing. Everyone's still in shock. And I didn't get to talk to your mom long, because she had to take care of some things."

I can't even let myself ponder what "some things" encompasses.

Again, Brice clears his throat. "Um, another reason your mom called me and not you, directly, is… She, uh, wasn't sure about—" After a pause that seems to drag on forever, he blurts, "Dave says you can't travel."

As I let that reality—and all of its horrible implications —sink in, he continues, "But I'm sure we can figure something out. We have the technology to—"

"What? We're going to Skype my dad's funeral?" I can hardly say the last word, and as soon as it's out, I break down again. Loudly. This time, I mean business.

My crying and moaning bring Dawn running. After consulting with Brice in hushed tones, she bustles to the head of my bed and smooths my hair.

"Sweetie, I'm so sorry to hear about your dad."

I nod up at her, seeing her eyes fill with tears.

She sniffs and swallows. "I know your heart's breaking, but I need you to calm down, okay? Baby needs you to calm down."

I try to swallow my grief, but it can't be suppressed. As I continue to keen, she glances at Brice, then back to me and says, "Take some deep breaths for me, all right?"

I attempt to do as I'm told, but each breath catches on a sob. Brice watches helplessly from the foot of the bed.

"I'm… trying…" I gasp, not sure if I'm telling this to Dawn or Brice or myself.

Dawn soothes, "It's okay. As a daughter, you need to cry. But as a mama, you need to calm yourself. And it's not fair. We get that." Brice nods and squeezes my foot through the thin blanket.

Finally, when it's clear I have no control over myself, she murmurs, "I'll be right back."

Before Brice can return to the head of the bed to try to comfort me, she returns with a syringe, which she pokes into a port in my IV.

"This'll help you rest," she says.

I shoot into a more upright position. Through my sobs, I yell, "No! No! I n-need to talk to my m-mom!" I turn my head and look down the length of the bed, beseeching Brice, "I n-need to talk to N-Nicole and J-Jason. I c-can't sleep right n-now!"

He covers his eyes with his trembling left hand, his wedding ring glinting in the late-morning light streaming through the window.

"I'll stop c-crying!" I hiccup. "Please. Don't m-make me sleep!"

My limbs suddenly feel like they're made of wet sand. I try to kick my foot, but the most I can manage is to scoot it slowly from the middle of the bed toward the edge of the mattress.

Brice drops his hand from his face and whispers, "It's okay. I love you."

My eyelids droop. He blurs and doubles and disappears. I hear the plastic mug hit the floor. Then… nothing.

I'm not even fully awake when I remember what's happened and resume crying, but this time, I do a better job of controlling my distress. The tears leak from my still-closed eyes and drip over my nose, down my face, and onto the pillow, where they join the others already there, dampening the fabric under my cheek.

My throat aches from my efforts to stifle the noise. I can't be sedated again. I understand why they did it; I'm not mad that they did it. But I can't let that happen again. I have to stay present, no matter how painful it is. It's the least I can do for my family.

Why should they have to face this horror, while I'm allowed to sleep through the nightmare, as if it's not happening? They don't have that luxury. They have to hold it together and get through this. I can do it, too.

Even if I can't be there.

That heartbreaking detail produces a whimper I can't suppress. When I feel someone press a tissue against the wet tracks on my face, my eyes fly open.

Brice smiles gently at me in the softly lit room. "Hey," he whispers.

"Don't call the nurses in here. I promise not to get too upset," I say, feeling and sounding frantic.

"Shh… It's okay. I'm not getting anyone. And I'm sorry about earlier."

Around my crying, I say, "She was only doing what she thought was right. And you have to defer to her."

He nods. "I thought it was best for you not to think about it for a while, too."

I struggle to sit up, so he helps me. After the bed buzzes to an upright position, I glance out the window and see it's dark.

"Oh, gosh. It's night." I seek out the clock and confirm it's late; much later than Brice normally stays. "I slept so long! My family—"

"Knows you're thinking about them and that you wish you could be there with them. They also know you can't, and you don't have a choice."

"Maybe I do," I wheedle. "Surely riding in a car or on a plane can't be that bad. I'll let you push me around in a wheelchair. I'll—"

He shakes his head. "I already proposed those things to Dave. He says you have to be under constant medical supervision. Especially now. We've held off labor longer than he thought we would. I think he's worried that the next time will be the real thing, no matter what we do. Plus…" He scratches his ear. "I don't think he's going to try to stop it next time."

"When did he tell you this?" I ask, annoyed I'm hearing it secondhand.

"While you were sleeping. I talked to him again, trying to figure out how to get you to Chicago." While I picture that conversation, no longer miffed but grateful that he tried, he continues, "Dave's observed some things that make him think she might be better off out here than in there, at this point. He can't be sure, so he's not going to induce, but…"

"If I start having contractions right now, and I start to dilate further?"

"We'll be having a baby." Quickly, he amends, "*You'll* be having a baby. I'll be doing what I always do. Getting on your nerves. Observing in amazement." He lets a tentative, crooked smile break through.

I'd laugh, but I'm too busy trying to process everything. All of it. My brain feels like it's about to burst. Too much information. Too many emotions. Too much.

I close my eyes and bracket my belly with my hands.

"You okay?" he asks, gripping my fingers.

I nod. "Overwhelmed. What am I supposed to be feeling right now?"

Keeping my head pressed into my pillow, I look over at him. I detach as much as possible when I say, "My dad is dead. My baby is alive, by some miracle, and she could be born at any minute, but that means I can't be with my family. My family has one another to lean on. I'm stuck in this bed."

"You always have me."

My lips quiver, and my chin tightens. "I know. Otherwise, I'd fly apart."

He half-stands so he can kiss my forehead. "Oh, hon. I hate this. I… I wish I could fix it."

"You can't, though."

"I know. I feel so helpless." Standing fully, he rests his cheek against the top of my head. "That's what I told your mom when I last talked to her. She asked me to do the funeral, and I had to tell her no. She understood, but she was disappointed."

"You should go."

"No! I'm not leaving you here!"

"Really. My family needs you more than I do." I'm not sure that's true, but it sounds good. And it's a sacrifice I'm willing to make to try to make up for my own absence.

"Peyton. I'm not telling you this so we can discuss it. I'm not going."

A part of me is relieved, but I feel bad that I'm thwarting my mom's funeral planning.

"This is a mess," I stare into space, letting the tears stream unchecked down my face.

"Your dad wouldn't want you to be upset."

I snort. "Yes, he would! He'd be pissed if we weren't despondent enough.

"'What the hell?'" I say, imitating him. "'I don't deserve more than a few sniffles? Someone better be throwin' themselves on my casket. And don't get me one of those flimsy, cheap coffins, either. Steel-lined. Mahogany. I'm worth it, damn it.'"

Brice chuckles against my hair.

"He's not really gone," I say, hoping that by saying it out loud, it will make it true.

After a pause, Brice replies, "No. He's not. He's just not *here* anymore."

"I'm never going to believe it." It's more of a prediction than a defiant statement. When my husband doesn't seem to know what to say to that, I explain, "Because I won't *see* him dead. Because I won't get to say goodbye. It will never be real."

Silence meets that hopeless declaration. For once, I want him to give me a pastor answer to refute my despair. For once, he doesn't have one.

≈

Pity, not resentment, is the general sentiment from my immediate family regarding my predicament and my inability to travel to Dad's funeral. Every time I talk to Nicole, she winds up breaking down and saying, "Oh, this must be terrible for you! I can't even imagine!"

While I'm glad she understands it's not my choice and she's not upset with me, her sympathetic statements are a constant reminder that it *is* terrible. I'm trying to be a good sport about it, because acting like a brat and crying and pouting will only make things worse, but if I thought it would bring my dad back, I'd throw the biggest temper tantrum this hospital has ever seen. Sedatives be damned!

It won't bring him back, though. And plans are moving forward just fine without me.

My mom's coping mechanism is to go into realtor "open house" mode, staging everything to look just right and go just so, according to schedule. I can tell when I talk to her on the phone that she's still in shock. I bet if I pretended nothing unusual was going on, she'd follow my lead and be glad to talk about the boys and the baby and the latest goings on at our respective churches.

As for the funeral plans, she's arranged for her pastor— Brice's successor, Pastor Westerman—to perform the service, but Vince is going to deliver the eulogy, which Brice wrote.

Jen and Vince have semi-kiddingly offered to play the parts of Peyton and Brice at the funeral. They even took Max with them, because he's old enough to know some-thing's happened and remember his Grandpa. I thought it was important that he got a chance to say goodbye, but the other boys are blissfully oblivious and are in daycare, as usual. Mary, Brice, and I plan to listen in from my hospital room, through Jason's phone. It's all highly irregular, and it feels wrong, but these are the concessions we're making due to the extenuating circumstances.

None of it is helping to convince me this is happening.

My dad, dead? No way. Kent Stratford is too ornery to die. And to have a blood clot take him down in his sleep? That's even more preposterous.

Now we're moments away from the service. Brice's phone rests on the rolling tray table in front of me. Jason already has us on the line and has even provided some preliminary commentary.

"Holy crap! There are a lot of people here. Dustin, record some of this stuff on your phone for Peyton. If nothing else, she has to see what Mrs. Hanson is wearing."

Mary chuckles from her chair across the room.

"No, I don't want video," I say weakly, even though I know it's no use, considering my brother doesn't have his phone to his ear.

Then I hear him hand off the phone to Sadie before he has to take his position as one of the pall bearers. "Here. Hold this for Aunt Peyton. Be careful not to hang up on her."

"Hi, Aunt Peyton; hi, Uncle Brice," the teenager whispers into the phone.

Like a dumbass, I wave at the phone, then roll my eyes at myself.

Brice smiles at me and grabs my hand, as if to keep it from doing anything else stupid.

I'm nervous, like I'm waiting to watch one of my children perform in front of a large crowd. I can't figure out why I'm feeling anxious, either. But my stomach is unsteady, and my mouth is dry. My muscles are tense, like I'm bracing for disaster. Disaster? At a funeral? The worst has already happened, hasn't it?

Tinny organ music blares through the phone's speaker, making me flinch. The baby flinches, too. After a flurry of kicks, she settles once more, and I try to follow her example. I take a deep breath in through my nose and release it slowly.

That's when I feel the first hard contraction.

I freeze.

The music stops. General coughing and sniffing comes from the congregation. I imagine Jason and the other pall bearers are setting down the casket at the front of the church.

Pastor Westerman greets the gathered assembly. My uterus relaxes—and contracts again.

I close my eyes. *Really, Lord? What are You doing? This is all I have. This is the only way I can say goodbye to my dad, and it's a shitty excuse for a farewell to begin with. Don't do this to me. I'm just nervous and tense, right? These aren't really—*

Another one hits me.

"Contractions," I whisper to Brice when the congregation starts singing the first hymn.

Mary scoots to the front edge of her chair. Brice doesn't move. As a matter of fact, he does a great impersonation of a ventriloquist with no dummy when he says, "For real?"

I nod, my eyes filling with tears. "Sonofabitch!" I hiss, more in response to the situation than because I'm in any pain.

Brice fumbles with his phone, hastening to mute it before I let loose with any louder swear words.

"How many? How fast?" he asks at a normal volume as soon as the he hits the "mute" button.

"Three, right on top of each other. But they're short. And they don't hurt."

In other words, I plead with my eyes, *Don't tell anyone yet.*

He shakes his head at me. "Uh-uh. The normal rules don't apply, and you know it." Reaching over the bedrail, he stabs at the nurse's call button.

I swat at his hand, but I'm too late. He shoots me a warning look and sets his jaw.

"But your eulogy!" I protest. "I didn't read it before Vince and Jen left, because I wanted to hear it with everyone else."

"Maybe Dustin will record it" is his lame consolation.

"I hope not! How tacky!"

"You can read it later. It's on my computer at home. I'll print out a copy for you."

Before I can tell him it's not the same, Dawn steps into the room. "What's up?" she asks, then winces toward the phone. "Oops. Sorry," she whispers.

Brice waves away her concern about the phone. "It's muted. Someone's having contractions."

Dawn's left eyebrow rises. "Oh? Like the kind that mean business?"

Reluctantly and honestly, I nod. "Yes."

She presses the call button on my bed. A disembodied voice issues from the speaker on the bedrail. "Yes?"

"Sherry, call Dr. Klein and let him know Peyton Northam's contracting." She presses her hands against a place that only a few months ago I still considered moderately private. "Ask him if he wants us to take her to a delivery suite or straight to the operating room."

During the last conversation I had with Dr. Klein, he

was still on the fence about whether to attempt a vaginal birth or go straight to C-section. At the time, my vote—not that it matters—was on the operation, but only because I could go the rest of my life without feeling another contraction and be okay with that. But now that we're getting down to the actual decision, the thought of being cut open—and recovering from a major surgical procedure—is less appealing.

While we wait for word from Dr. Klein, Dawn preps me for transport.

"What do you need me to do?" Brice asks, shifting from foot to foot like he needs to use the bathroom.

"Not a thing, Dad," Dawn says with a wink. "After your sweet baby girl is born, you guys'll come right back here to this room, so you don't even have to take anything with you." She nods toward the tray table and Brice's phone, through which Pastor Westerman is saying glowing, mostly true things about my Dad. "You may want to hang that up, though."

Disappointment and pain from my latest contraction tag team to bring on the tears. "But it's my dad's funeral!" I whine. "I… I… Just a few more minutes," I bargain, widening my eyes and flaring my nostrils in an attempt to rein in my emotions. Acting hysterical isn't going to help my cause.

"No cell phones in the delivery room or operating room, Sweetie," Dawn says with a firm head shake. "Sorry. No exceptions."

I can tell I'll only humiliate myself if I belabor the issue, so I simply nod and look away when Brice taps the screen to wake it up, then disconnect from the call. The ensuing silence is heavy and sickening.

Mary, who I'd almost forgotten was still in the room,

steps up next to my bed and pats my shoulder. "I'll text Vince to see if he can record things for you, even if it's just the audio."

Minutes ago, I would have been against this plan, but now that I have no other choice, I smile bravely and say, "Thanks, Ma."

She rewards me with a smile of her own. "Of course, kid. And think, you're about to finally have this baby. It's a happy day!"

When I have a hard time shifting gears from "This is the day of my dad's funeral" to "This is my baby's birthday," she excuses herself from the room—"So you kids can have some privacy."

She crosses paths with Sherry, who strides into the room and takes up a position opposite Dawn across my bed. "Off to the OR," she chirps. "Dr. Klein will meet us there in twenty minutes."

I wipe the tears from my face, preparing myself for my parade through the hospital halls. Brice shoots me a know-ing, sympathetic half-smile.

Before the nurses get the bed rolling, he leans down and brushes his lips against mine. Then he whispers, "You look beautiful. Now, let's go have a baby."

29

LIGHTNESS AND DARKNESS

I wake up on the ceiling. At least, according to my vantage point, that's where it appears I am. Of course, that's highly improbable, illogical, and... impossible. I'm not clinging to the ceiling, like a spider. I'm not bobbing around up here, hitting my head, either. I'm just... here. But I'm also down there, lying on the operating table.

It's a mess down there, too, I note with strange detachment. Blood everywhere. My gosh! Is all that blood normally inside me? Wow. That's incredible. Those scrubs and surgical gowns are toast. Into the incinerator!

Where's Brice?

Oh, cool! In addition to being above everything, I can also see through walls. There he is, a few rooms away, huddled around a bassinet with two other nurses. As of this moment, he seems not to have a clue what's happening in the OR. He's absorbed in his new daughter, Addison.

Perhaps because something similar to this situation happened when Max was born, he doesn't appear anxious or worried that I'm still in the other room and nobody's come to give him an update on me yet. I'm the emergency C-section who cried, "Wolf!"

I see a tiny foot, which Brice reaches out to stroke. He holds up his phone and takes a picture, then reviews the result and takes another. His eyes sparkle as he returns his phone to his pocket and his gaze to his daughter. I can imagine him saying—as he's done all the other times —"She's beautiful, hon. Just beautiful."

One of the nurses with him is monitoring the baby's heart and lungs with a stethoscope while another tackles the more mundane task of filling out forms and making the baby's ID anklet. Nurse #2 says something to Brice. He smiles and holds out his arm, accepting the matching security bracelet that proves the newborn belongs to him, and vice versa.

Suddenly, his eyebrows pinch closer together. Nurse #1, who was listening to Addison's breathing, has said something to him. He says something back, his eyebrows pushing up on his forehead so that it resembles a crinkly washboard. She smiles reassuringly and pats his upper arm as she pushes the bassinet from the room and walks in the direction of the nursery.

Brice follows their progress until the door closes and obscures his view. Then his shoulders drop, and he hooks his thumbs in his trouser pockets. He's been through this before, too. Harris had a slight heart murmur when he was born and had to be taken to the nursery for the pediatrician on call to observe him for a while. Brice knows better than to waste energy on worrying until they tell him something definitive. He crosses to a window and pulls his phone from his pocket, his thumbs racing across the screen.

I resume watching the rolling baby bed, not wanting to lose sight of my daughter. She's little, but her color looks good, and she seems to be breathing just fine on her own. Those extra weeks in the womb, plus the drug they gave me intravenously to encourage lung development, seem to have done what Dr. Klein intended. She's still technically premature, so I'm sure there are precautions the medical staff will be taking as a result, but from where I sit (wherever that is), she seems miraculously normal.

Although I can see through walls, I can't see through clothing (maybe that's for the best). But I somehow know she has blonde hair under that knit hospital cap. A tow-head. Wow. I didn't think Brice and I had one of those in us. He said she was blonde when he "saw" her, but all of our babies have had thick, dark hair. Like their dad. It's odd to have produced a fair-headed one.

"Hey." A familiar voice to my left interrupts my ruminations as the nurse punches a code into a keypad on the wall, and two large doors swing open to allow her entry into the nursery.

Reluctantly, I look away and turn my head to face the voice. There sits my father.

I hug him, as if I've been expecting his arrival, but I still can't help asking, "What are you doing here?", if only to maintain some sense of normalcy.

He shrugs. "I'm dead, like you."

Almost as soon as I let him go, a sleeping baby appears in his arms. He holds her out to me. "I thought you'd want to see Secret."

"Oh." I receive her and see that she's not sleeping, as I originally thought. She's wide awake, looking up at me with more wisdom in her eyes than some of the oldest, wisest people I've met.

Physically, she doesn't look anything like the baby I gave birth to all those years ago and the one I see when I close my eyes and recall that day. I objectively study her pink, serene face. In it, I see traces of Stefan, but she looks much like all the other babies I've had, even my newest one. Only less Brice-y.

"She's different," I say.

He cranes his neck to watch the action below. "Yeah, well, she was 'brought to completion' and all that. Made whole."

I kiss her forehead. She blinks at me. A strange yet pleasant warmth suffuses my chest.

Dad says, "I was watching my funeral, but it's hit a lull. Your husband wrote a nice eulogy. I guess. He didn't have to do that, considering…"

"Considering you were always a jerk to him?"

He laughs. "Maybe I was, but I was just trying to keep it real for him. Everyone else treats him like the second coming of Christ."

"No, they don't!"

"Close enough. He needed someone like me to remind him that he's just another guy."

"He has plenty of people like that."

He harrumphs. "Well, anyway. I heard things were getting hairy here and that you were watching the show, so I thought I'd join you. It's not going to get interesting at the funeral again until people have had a couple of drinks at the luncheon, so we have a few minutes. They're throwing dirt on me now."

"Does anyone there know what's happening to me?"

He shakes his head, then nods toward Brice, who's still typing away on his phone. "Looks like most of the people *here* don't know what's happening to you."

I nod. "Yeah. He has no clue, does he?"

We both watch the subject of our discussion for a while.

He stops typing and folds himself into a chair, but that doesn't last long. Soon, he's up again, checking the time on his phone, then pacing.

"There's no point upsetting the poor guy," Dad says, agreeing with the doctors' decisions to keep my husband in the dark about my bloody, dead condition.

"Well, he's going to have to know eventually! Why aren't they telling him?"

Dad levels me with his most serious look, the look he gave me when, as a teenager, I once asked him to pick up some feminine hygiene products for me at the store. Now, instead of saying, "Have you been smokin' something?" like he did that day, he says, "You can't stay up here. You know that, right?"

I hold Secret more tightly. "What do you mean? I'm *here*. With *you*. And you're not just a little dead. You're dead-dead!"

"Yeah? So what? You're 'dead-dead,' too. There's no such thing as a little dead."

Laughing, I say, "All right. But where *am* I? What's happening?"

He shrugs. "Heck if I know what's happening. You learn early on around here to go with the flow. And 'here' is Heaven, of course. Although this is sort of like a holding area."

"Purgatory?"

The afterlife veteran sighs. "Does this look like Purgatory? Never mind." He waves away my ignorance. "No, it's not Purgatory."

In life, I would have been embarrassed to be so utterly stupid, but all I feel at this moment is curiosity. *Okay, so I was wrong. Big deal.*

"Why can't I hear what's going on down there?" I inquire.

"You don't need to be able to hear them."

"Can *you* hear them?"

He nods. "But that's not important. The most important thing for you to know is that you're not here to stay."

"How do you know that?"

Again, he shakes his head, but this time he looks as mystified as I am. "I'm not sure. It's weird. I just know."

Since I've had the same experience while here, I know exactly what he means. He knows; like I know my new baby has blonde hair. Like I know her heart and lungs are fine.

One thing I'm oddly unsure about, though, prompts my next question. "Is this real?"

His cryptic "I guess" doesn't clear up anything for me, so I elaborate, "Because… we're Lutherans."

"And?"

"Well, we don't believe in stuff like this. You know, near-death experiences."

"We don't believe in Purgatory, either, but you were quick to assume that's where you were. And I told you, there isn't anything 'near-death' about this."

"You know what I mean. I guess what I'm trying to say is that I'm willing to accept that Heaven may hold some surprises for me, some things I've never been taught to expect. I'm trying to figure out if this is a dream. When I get back down there"— I nod to the mess below—"am I going to remember this?"

He shakes his head. "Probably not. It's not a matter of memory, though. It's a matter of capacity to understand. Down there, you believe what you're able to believe."

"What about faith? Faith is believing what you can't understand, right?"

"In a way, yes. But there are some things we don't know, some things we're *unable* to know."

"That doesn't sound Lutheran at all," I mutter.

"When you're finally here to stay, you'll figure out that labels like 'Lutheran' and 'Catholic' and 'Baptist' don't mean a hill of beans."

I stare at him. He *looks* like my dad. He *sounds* like my dad. But that would never have come from my dad's mouth. I must be in Heaven.

"What?" he asks after several seconds under my scrutiny.

"You mean, Lutherans aren't the only ones up here?" I tease.

He narrows his eyes at me. "Never claimed that would be the case, did I? No."

"I guess not, but—"

"You're stalling," he accuses. "But the fact is, you have to get back down there."

"It's so nice up here, though. I miss you." Again, I notice I don't feel sad when I say it. Just matter-of-fact. I cuddle Secret some more. "And this. This is nice. I never got this with her."

He gently removes her from my arms. "Yeah, well, Secret and I are getting to know each other, and you'll have your turn someday, too. But not today. You have another baby girl down there to meet. Addison Grace, huh?"

I nod.

"Nice name."

"Thanks."

As mysteriously as she appeared, Secret disappears. Neither Dad nor I question it, and I don't feel the despair or disappointment at her exit that I'd expect to feel. I simply accept it.

Nudging his head in the direction of my husband, Dad says, "Brice would be a basket case without you."

"No, he wouldn't. He'd be fine." As if to prove my point, Brice sits once more and braces his elbows on his knees, folding his hands and bowing his head.

"I think you'd be shocked," Dad says. "If you could feel shock up here. Which you can't. But you'd definitely see a side of him you've never seen before. As a matter of fact, you should get back down there before you see something classified."

I raise an eyebrow and wait for him to explain.

"It happens. It's not a biggie, if you're here to stay. But if you have to go back down there and live, it can be hard, after you've returned to your emotional, Earthly self, to reconcile some of the things you might witness up here."

"Like what? I thought I wouldn't remember, anyway."

"Subconsciously, you might."

"Maybe that's why I can't hear anything."

Tapping his temple, he says, "See? God knows."

"Why am I here at all, then?"

Dad wraps one arm around my shoulders. "You're here to say goodbye to me. You know, since you were too *busy* to come to my funeral." He nudges me so I know he's kidding.

I let this possibility register. It makes just enough sense in this nonsensical scenario. However, I can't feel the kind of grief I'd normally be feeling at such a final goodbye, so I don't know if it's going to "count."

In response to my unspoken concern, Dad says, "It's not final. When you reawaken down there, you'll feel a sense of peace, a sense of closure. You'll know that I'm up here, keeping tabs on things—in a general way. I don't normally watch life on Earth as if it's a movie. I do watch a lot of sports, but I was told in orientation that I can't do anything to change the outcome of the games. If I could feel disappointment, that would have been a bummer."

We laugh together for a few seconds, then he says, "Well, Princess P, you're about to be missed."

The activity in the OR becomes more frantic. Nurses and doctors fly around the room. A crash cart makes an appearance.

"You don't want them to use that thing," Dad says, pointing to the defibrillator. "Plus any minute now, they're going to think it's their duty to tell Brice what's happening. You don't want to do that to the poor guy."

Speaking of, a quick check reveals that Brice has gone from praying to staring intensely at the door to the room where he's waiting for an update from the doctors.

I sigh. "All right, then." We hug one more time. "Take care of Secret for me. I guess I'll see you, uh, in a few decades?"

He chuckles. "Nice try. You'll see me *when you're ready*. I'll see you whenever I want. Although, don't worry about me seeing anything personal or private. Not interested."

I blink at him. "I hadn't even thought of that, but good to know."

He winks. "Do I know you, or do I know you?"

And with that, he's gone. I fall into blackness, knowing for the first time ever what that "peace that passes all understanding" is all about.

For a while now, I've been in and out of awareness, but no matter how hard I try, I can't seem to swim to the surface of this drowning sleepiness. Trying to wake up has proven so exhausting that I eventually give up and sink to the bottom of the crushing darkness, marshaling my energy for the next attempt at wakefulness.

I don't know how long I've been fighting this, time-wise, but I get closer to the surface with each try. I can even hear what's going on around me. Maybe that's what's motivating me to wake up. After all, the last time, I could clearly hear Mary trying to convince Brice to get some fresh air. I also heard him reject her suggestion.

"I want to be here when she wakes up."

Mary's voice hovered just above a whisper, as if she was trying *not* to wake me. "The chances of her waking up in the next five minutes—"

"Are good. I know it'll be soon."

Her voice softened. "Of course, it will be, sweetheart. Of course."

"Is everyone holding up okay at the house?" he asked.

I felt his fingers weave through mine, and I wanted so badly to press my knuckles against his, to let him know I was listening, that I appreciated his strength and refusal to leave me alone. But I couldn't move a muscle. Not an eyelid twitch, nothing.

Meanwhile, Mary replied, "Everyone is fine. Considering. The place looks like a youth hostel, with all those air mattresses."

"Someone can sleep in our bed."

"*You* should come home and sleep in your bed."

"No."

"Fine. I'm not going to nag you."

"Thank you."

The heavy blackness pulled at the edges of my consciousness. The harder I resisted it, the faster it yanked me down.

"You look so tired."

"I thought you said you weren't going to nag me."

"I'm not! I'm worried about you, that's all."

"Why worry when you can pray, right?"

His familiar motto said in such a borderline-bitter tone made me sob inside. Of course, I made no sound.

Oblivious to my distress—or even to my comprehension of the conversation—he went on to make Mary promise that she wouldn't bring the boys to see me, "not like this." I faded and faded, until finally, their voices were gone, and the stifling velvet of unconsciousness wrapped around me once more.

It was the longest I'd remained aware of my surroundings, though. And it gave me the most clues as to what was happening. Unfortunately, I couldn't process those clues while comatose. And during my next periods of awareness —much shorter, although more frequent, they seemed—I was too busy trying to figure out what was going on to think back to what Brice and Mary had said.

The voices—both familiar (Jason, Dustin, Mom, Nicole, Jen) and strange (nurses, I assumed)—cycled through my semi-wakefulness. Most of the time, things were serious, bordering on somber. Other times, there was laughter. Quiet, subdued laughter, but laughter nonetheless. That's when I came closest to making my mental presence known. When people were laughing, or I could hear smiles in their voices, that's when I most desperately wanted to be included.

But it's been no use. Nothing, not even the sound and smell of my newborn daughter next to me on the pillow, has succeeded in stirring me.

I fear I'll be trapped here forever.

∼

It's becoming routine now, this gradual fading up of sound and smell and touch, so I know not to get too hopeful, that I'll arrive at a certain level of awareness and stop, as if I'm trapped under the ice of a frozen lake. I can swim parallel to the ice for miles and never find an opening. It's best to focus on listening and experiencing as much as I can. Fighting to break through only tires me more quickly and sends me back to deeper sleep before I'm ready.

In this particular instance, the silence around me suggests I'm alone. Nobody's holding my hand or talking. The TV is off. The blood pressure cuff around my upper arm buzzes to life, squeezes to the point of pain, then whooshes and clicks until it slackens again.

As I'm lamenting a wasted trip to the surface, rustling to my left alerts me to someone's presence. When the air moves close to my face, I concentrate all my attention to isolate my sense of smell, identifying my companion as Brice.

A sense of resigned contentment blankets me. As long as he's here, I'm okay. I know it's selfish. I know I should want him to be with our children and our family, living life more fully. But I don't want to be alone.

He sighs. My hand rises in his warm, dry grip. My elbow bends and straightens, bends and straightens. My shoulder pops as it rotates so that my straightened arm becomes level with my ear, my hand over my head. This motion repeats several times on the left side, then the same happens to my right arm. My limbs tingle and warm as blood flows more freely through them.

A few minutes later, cool air hits my legs, and the right one begins pumping, as if I'm riding a one-pedaled bicycle in slow motion. My leg fully extended, my right ankle rotates slowly and gently. The toes on my right foot curl and crack.

Soon, the same treatment begins on my lower left extremities.

In the middle of these involuntary calisthenics, an unfamiliar woman's voice says, "Oh. You're way ahead of us, I see."

Brice grunts an affirmative reply, then says, "I saw it was time and thought I'd go ahead."

"You're doing great." The female voice advances closer. "I'll help you sit her up."

I bend at the waist. Hands support me from the front, preventing me from flopping too far forward. Brice's fingers knead my neck and shoulders, then work their way to my lower back and hips.

If only this stranger would leave us alone.

I crave his touch and wish I could be more participatory.

Too soon, they're easing me against my pillows once more, my upper body at a sixty-degree angle to my lower body. Brice's lips press against my forehead.

His helper asks if he needs anything. He pauses, then replies, "No. Nothing you can get me." His tone contains a mixture of sheepishness and self-pity.

She shuffles away after doing some uncomfortable things that I've come to realize have to do with a catheter, and he traces his finger down my nose.

The air next to my face becomes cooler. I hear the chair creak next to my bed. The vinyl squeaks against his legs and bottom. Warmth envelopes my left hand. My wedding ring slides up and down my finger, from my second knuckle to the base of the digit, and back again several times. Lips land on my palm.

With my hand still curled against his mouth and nose, he murmurs, his breath warm against my fingers, "Please, wake up."

My heart rate speeds up, but since the volume on the machines has been turned down (at his request, I heard during one of my forays to the surface), he's oblivious to this physiological response.

"We said we'd do anything for each other. You said you'd do anything for *me*. I haven't forgotten that. And I'll do anything for you. Just wake up. Please."

I wish I could swallow the lump in my throat. But considering I can't even control whether my mouth gapes open or remains shut while in this state, the lump is likely there to stay.

"I can't do this without you. Just being around the kids…" His breath catches on a sob. When he resumes talking, his voice comes from a higher position. I can tell he's standing next to the head of my bed, looming over me.

"Being around the kids reminds me that you're not with us. And if I develop new routines that don't involve you, it's like I'm giving up. Like I'm giving you permission to keep sleeping. Or for you to leave forever. And you can't. I'm collecting on your promise. You said you'd do anything for me. This is it. Stay with me. Wake up. Please. Please!"

He breaks down, burying his face in my neck. For once, I pray to fall back into deeper sleep, to spare me this torture. But I remain helplessly aware.

After several heartbreaking minutes, he straightens and wipes his tears from my neck.

"Oh, gosh. I'm sorry." I hear the rasp of a tissue being pulled from a nearby box. The soft paper rubs against my skin. He misses a spot close to my ear; the air takes its time drying the rogue tear.

"I'm so sorry," he whispers again. "This is not for you or me to decide. It's not fair for me to put it on you. I'm so weak. So weak."

The bedside chair wheezes as he plops into it. I listen to him cry for what feels like an eternity. Then I hear indistinct noises, sibilant esses and plosive tees suggesting a near-silent prayer. Is he pleading with God? Asking for forgiveness? For what? For being human?

I have a short conversation of my own with God as I feel myself slipping under once more. *Why did You send me back here to listen to my husband's misery? Why? Please, let me return to You or wake me up. I'm leaving it in Your hands, letting go of the decision. But make a decision. End this uncertainty.*

30

WAKING UP

*W*ithout my even trying, my eyes pop open. They open to a wideness that borders on painful. At first, I don't see much of interest. Someone must have removed my contact lenses (poor, unlucky person who got *that* job deserves something a little extra in their Christmas stocking this year), because anything farther than ten feet away is blurry, like it's behind a window coated in Vaseline.

Ah, yes. I knew I would regret not taking up that eye surgeon, a member at Peace, on his offer of a free Lasik procedure. At the time, it seemed creepy, like he was trying to buy his salvation by giving the pastor's wife something that expensive for nothing. I politely turned him down, acting like I enjoy those first few minutes of every day when the world is a blur, like I enjoy the time I spend each night removing my lenses, like I enjoy the eye infections I get without fail each allergy season when I rub too hard and scratch my cornea with my contact.

But I clearly neglected to plan ahead to the "waking-up-from-a-coma-and-being-able-to-see" benefit. Should have overcome that creep factor.

Fortunately, Brice is sitting close enough and at an angle that not only is he clear to me, but I don't have to move my head. That's a good thing, because apparently, I can't do that very well right now, either. Or talk. I think that's because my throat is so dry, though. Here's hoping.

Well, I guess I don't have to say anything. He'll notice eventually that I'm awake. That is, if I can stay this way long enough for him to notice. I wish I could shout at him, "I'm awake! I didn't leave you! I *would* do anything for you! Look at me!"

But I can't. I'm mute until I can remember how to make spit.

In the meantime, I take in my surroundings. Or at least the area within a ten-foot radius of my head. This is definitely a different room than the one I inhabited for nearly nine long weeks, waiting for Addison to be ready to be born. I don't have the best sense of direction, but something about the angle of the sun through the windows tells a primitive, instinctual—usually ignored—part of my brain that this room is oriented differently than that one was.

This room is also brighter. For some reason, the lights in my old room never got brighter than the "dark, dingy castle" setting, but this room is glowing, mostly with natural light from an entire wall of windows. Maybe their theory is that the bright sun alone will be enough to wake someone from a coma.

The size of this room is another indicator that I've been transferred. This one is much smaller. Based on my few moments of lucidity and clarity over the past few days—weeks? *Months?* Oh, dear God, please not months. My neck is telling me it might have been months—I suspect only one or two people at a time, in addition to Brice, have been allowed to visit me. Whereas the rooms on the maternity ward are designed for large, happy gatherings of friends and family meeting new siblings and grandchildren and nieces and nephews for the first time, this one seems to have intimacy and peace in mind.

I can't see the hands on the clock or the text on the page-a-day calendar across the room on the wall, so I have no idea how long I've been "asleep." A lot longer than usual, I take it. Even on my laziest Saturday morning.

I turn my attention back to my husband. Wow. He looks tired. He almost looks his age. As long as I've been asleep, he looks like he *hasn't* slept. At all.

Earbuds jammed into his ears, he focuses on the book in his hands while I stare at him in silence, wishing I could ask him a few of the hundreds of questions I have. Starting with, "What day is it?" "Where's Addison?" "Why did your mom say our house looks like a youth hostel?" "Why do I keep getting weird flashes of you in a room, touching a newborn Addison, then waiting to hear from the doctors about me?" "Have I been using a bedpan?"

You know, the really important things.

He's focused on that book, though. It's probably about transcendentalism or something equally cerebral that would put me back into a coma—from boredom.

Eventually, he glances up at me, then back at his book, then quickly at me again.

All the color drains from his face as he moves closer to me. "Oh, no. Oh! Oh, dear God. No!" He drops his book and lurches forward, choking on his spit. His glasses slide from his nose and clatter to the floor.

"What?" I finally manage to croak, my mouth feeling as if it's full of paste and marbles. It kind of tastes like it, too.

He freezes, then nearly collapses, grabbing the bed rail for support as he gasps for air. "Oh, my— Sweet Lord. Praise God," he mumbles with his forehead pressed against his knuckles. Finally, he rises on shaky legs, his trembling fingers tapping against my face.

"You're awake. Not dead."

"Uh…"

"It's just… you weren't blinking. I looked up. And you weren't blinking. And I thought… I… I couldn't see you breathing." He coughs out a quick laugh that almost immediately morphs into a sob. His face collapses. "I thought—" He covers his face with both hands, muffling into them, "I'm sorry. I'm just so—"

I want to do something, anything but lie here, staring at him, crying, but I'm unable to speak, too weak to lift my arm to reach out to him or to hit the nurse's call button. I'm as physically helpless as the baby I gave birth to, however many days ago that was.

While I pray that it's indeed only been days, not weeks or months, and add a small request for the ability to use my voluntary muscles (I hope God doesn't think I'm greedy), Brice takes a mighty breath and wipes his face on the shoulder of his t-shirt. Red-eyed, but no longer openly weeping, he attempts a wobbly smile.

"Is Addison…" I begin.

His whole demeanor changes. Eyes brightening, he replies, "She's perfect. Just beautiful."

I somehow already know this, but his declaration makes my eyes fill, anyway. "Is she still… here?" The question comes out like a squeak, as I picture her hooked up to tubes and wires, needing a machine to help her with every breath. Before Brice can answer, though, I seem to know that's not the case.

She's healthy and growing stronger by the day. How I know this is a mystery to me. Maybe I've heard and retained more information in my unconscious state than I even realized?

Shaking his head, he says, "No! Oh, Chicago. I'm sorry. I know you want to know everything, but I can't... I can't think fast enough." He takes a deep breath and closes his eyes, as if organizing all the information in his head. "Let's start over." He sits on the edge of the bed and pulls my hand into his lap. "Hey. I'm so glad you're awake. We've missed you."

His emotions threaten again, but he holds it together long enough to say, "Addison is doing fine. She went home"—he bites his lip and closes one eye, remembering —"the day before yesterday. Your mom and sister and brother are at the house, taking care of the kids. My mom, too, of course. The doctor wants to keep a close eye on Addison, and we're not supposed to take her out in public much for a few weeks—you know, germs and stuff—but she's breathing on her own and getting used to life on the outside."

I'd laugh at his prison-speak, but I'm still having a hard time producing enough saliva to prevent my lips from adhering to my teeth. I swallow painfully and swivel my eyes in their sockets, searching the immediate area for the ubiqui-tous hospital Big Gulp water mug.

Thankfully, my extremities are starting to wake up, so I'm able to lift my hand and point to my mouth. Unfortu-nately, my muscles are stiff, some of them painfully so. I cringe and close my eyes.

"Are you hurting?" he asks. "Oh, wait. I was supposed to buzz the nurse as soon as you woke up."

He hits the button on my bed with still-shaky fingers.

When someone answers, he says in a voice overflowing with glee, "She's awake!"

Within seconds, a sunny, solid woman in bright blue scrubs bustles into the room. "Well, you're right!" she says to Brice, and I recognize her voice as the one who helped him with my 'exercises.' "She *is* awake. We knew it was only a matter of time, right?"

Without waiting for him to answer, she fusses with the machines around me and pretends she doesn't notice that Brice is still just this side of blubbering while she asks me, "How much would you give for a drink of water right now? I bet a lot."

The mug comes into focus, but before she holds the straw to my mouth, she says, "Slowly. Only enough to get your mouth and throat working again. We're keeping you hydrated with your IV. And gulping will upset your stomach. So, little sips."

I diligently follow her commands, but too soon, she pulls the straw away.

"Now. Pain level."

I shake my head, which causes my neck to creak. "Oh," I moan. "Neck hurts, and my arms and legs are sore."

She laughs. "Yeah, you're going to be a bit stiff. We've tried to move you around a little each day, but still..." She shoots a cheeky grin at Brice. "Actually, your hubby's been quite the helper with your physical therapy. He's sometimes already halfway through your exercises by the time one of us gets a minute to come in here. Twice a day, without fail."

"Maybe I didn't do them right," he says uncertainly.

"You did fine," she reassures him, then asks me, "How about that C-section incision? Pinchy?"

I nod, noticing it for the first time, now that she's mentioned it.

"I'll order some ibuprofen for you. I'm Debbie, by the way." On her way out the door, she adds, "Oh, and I'll call Dr. Klein and let him know you're awake."

After she leaves, I try to swivel my head in a full range of motion but tense at the tightness in my neck.

Brice wraps his hand around the base of my skull and massages. My eyes flutter at the hurts-so-good sensation.

"Is that better?" he asks.

I moan what I hope he knows is a "yes." He continues, so I assume we've become successful at communicating nonverbally during the past few...

"What day is it?" I mumble.

"Wednesday," he answers, then says, "Oh. Right. Um, you've been out of it for six days."

"Is that all?" I ask. It feels like six months, according to my body.

He chuckles. "I know. It's felt like forever."

He rubs for a while more, until I say, "Psst... Hand me that water. Just a tiny sip."

Without arguing, he complies. I don't abuse my power over him but take just enough to wet my whistle, swishing it around my mouth before swallowing. "Thanks."

"You're welcome." Perching on the edge of my bed, he studies my face.

"How bad do I look?" I rasp, trying to feel the state of things by patting my hair with my hands and palpating my face with my fingertips. My hair feels clean, albeit lank. My face feels... like my face.

"You're breathtaking." Again, his eyes fill.

A rusty wheeze that I think is supposed to be a laugh escapes from me. "I'm sure."

"I'm serious. Can I kiss you?"

"When was the last time I brushed my teeth?"

"*You* haven't done it for almost a week. But I brush your teeth for you every morning and every night."

"Not anymore, you don't."

The left corner of his mouth rises. "I don't know. It's kind of a sweet routine that I was hoping to continue."

"I don't think so. But I guess the least I can do is let you kiss me."

I involuntarily stiffen as he leans in.

He stops. "You want to brush your teeth first?"

I lift my hand to my mouth and cover it. "Do you mind?"

He laughs. "No. Hang on."

After disappearing into the adjoining bathroom, he returns with a toothbrush pre-loaded with toothpaste, a cup of water, and kidney-shaped plastic dish. He holds the dish while I brush. But when the brush falls from my weak hand for the third time, he plucks it from the bed, where it's fallen, and takes over the job.

Too tired to object, I hold my mouth open while he efficiently runs the bristles against my teeth. "Eeee," he says to get me to pull my lips back and, "Aaah," when he needs to reach my molars. It's a routine I've seen him go through countless times with the boys. After cleaning every tooth, he holds the plastic dish under my chin. "There you go."

I spit, then rinse and spit again.

When he settles on my bed after taking the oral hygiene supplies back to the bathroom, I lift my lips to his.

His kiss is tentative to begin with, but it deepens when he realizes I'm not going to break—or pass out. Although I do worry I might swoon. His hand cradles the back of my head to hold my face against his as he barely separates from me, enough to say, "I love you."

"I love you, too."

"Don't ever do this to me again."

"I don't plan to."

"No more babies."

I smile against his lips. "No more babies."

He kisses me again, but this time I'm the one to pull away.

"I'd like to see the babies we already have, though. Especially that baby girl."

"As soon as we talk to Dave, I'll call everyone to come see you."

"Everyone?"

"Family."

"And Vince and Jen."

He smiles. "Like I said: family."

31

ONWARD, CHRISTIAN SOLDIERS

I drop the bag of frozen peas into Brice's lap, feeling guilty at his resultant flinch but not necessarily guilty enough to apologize. I'm too exhausted to apologize.

"I know today's about you…" I begin.

"Darn tootin' it's about me," he interjects playfully.

I plop onto the couch next to him, eliciting a grunt from him. "Do you mind? Things are a little tender over here."

I'd roll my eyes if that wouldn't be inexcusably insensitive, but, "I'm zapped," I admit.

It's something I've said too much lately, but I've also been strictly informed since coming home from the hospital three weeks ago that it's my duty to make it known. Every time.

Brice settles the frozen veggies against his crotch and drapes his arm around my shoulders. "I know. Watching me say goodbye to my virility must have been an emotional experience for you. But don't worry; your best friend in the whole wide world will be better in no time. He's resilient."

"I know you are."

"I wasn't talking about me."

My head flops back onto his arm as I chuckle weakly. "Good one."

He laughs too for a second, then says, "Seriously, though. Are you okay?"

I sigh. "Yes. I shouldn't have said anything. I was mostly preparing you for the news that I'm too tired to make dinner."

"That's hardly earth-shattering. Just relax. Take a nap. And I'll try to help as much as I can when Mitzi, Jen, and Mom bring their respective charges home."

I snuggle against his shoulder. "No, you won't. You're supposed to take it easy. And it's my job to make sure you're following the urologist's orders. Paybacks are hell, by the way."

There's a grin in his voice when he replies, "Fine, fine. I'll get caught up on ESPN, or something."

We're quiet for a few minutes while he surfs around on his phone, and I think about the short list of care instructions we brought home with us from Brice's procedure.

"Speaking of doctor's orders," I say, breaking the silence, "is it mean of me that I'm gleefully anticipating when you'll have to provide a sample to the urologist to make sure everything worked the way it was supposed to work?"

"It better have worked," he says, shifting gingerly in his seat, adding, "And yes, that's mean-spirited. Although, the joke's on you, because I've become highly skilled and efficient at that task recently."

I push away from his shoulder and stare at him with my mouth open. He continues to show me his profile, not pausing in the typing he's doing on his phone.

"Brice!"

He glances at me but returns his eyes to his phone. His tongue pokes from the corner of his mouth while he tries to suppress a grin. "What? You were in the hospital for more than ten weeks! And we still have two weeks before your postpartum visit with Dave. So, yeah. I've been using the self-service pumps."

All I can do is laugh, which encourages him to continue. "I think I've been a good sport about it, too. I've been a good sport about a lot of things. Like, 'What'd you get for your birthday, Pastor?' 'Oh, you know, the usual: a card and a vasectomy.'"

"That's not the only thing you're getting! Anyway, it's not your birthday until the day after tomorrow."

He laughs at my defensiveness. "Oh, in that case, the treadmill is still the worst birthday gift you ever gave me, pending what happens on Sunday."

"Screw you!" I manage to say through my giggles and while slapping repeatedly at his shoulder.

He shields himself with one hand while still holding his phone in the other and reading something on the screen. "Oh, I wish! I've forgotten what that's like."

"You're on the verge of never experiencing it again."

"What a waste of money today has been, if that's the case. Abstinence is so much cheaper."

"Yeah, and if I had died, this whole conversation would be moot."

Suddenly, all playfulness ceases. He lifts his eyes from his phone and sets the device on the couch arm next to him.

"I'm sorry," I say meekly before he can scold me for making light of something so serious. I haven't gotten around to telling him about hearing him break down, begging me to wake up, while I was semi-conscious—and maybe I never will tell him—but I'll never forget it. "I kid because it's scary."

"I know," he says, his jaw relaxing. "But I'm not kidding when I say I'd gladly trade sex for the rest of my life\ as long as you're still around."

I know it's true, but I play dumb. "Really?"

He reconsiders for a second. "Okay, maybe not 'gladly,' but 'willingly.' Absolutely."

"That sounds like a miserable existence. I think I'd rather be dead," I state.

"Wow."

Laughing once more, I defend myself, "C'mon. We all know my priorities are out of whack—pun intended—when it comes to the wild monkey dance."

He snorts his agreement.

After several minutes of contemplative silence, I say, "I wonder how close I got to seeing my dad again. Something tells me he's a downright pleasant guy in Heaven." I clear my throat. "As a matter of fact, I'm sure of it."

And I am, too. I'm just not sure *how* I've come to be so sure of it, other than the obvious conclusion that everyone's nice in Heaven.

Brice kisses the tip of my nose. "I'm sure of it, too. Like I wrote in his eulogy: in Heaven, your dad can finally admit that he likes me."

I smile at the memory of the line that got the biggest laugh when Vince read Brice's words: *"The Lord says, 'In my house, there are many mansions. And there, Kent Stratford will readily admit he was wrong—about some things.'"*

At the time I listened to the eulogy, the day after I woke up, I'd assumed Brice was speaking in generalities, but now I wonder aloud, "Do you think *you* were one of the things Dad was wrong about?"

He shrugs and twists his mouth to the side. The tips of his ears redden. "I dunno. I'd like to think I deserved his love and respect, as a son-in-law and the father of his grand-children, if nothing else. And that maybe he was too proud to show it."

My throat clamps shut, but I eventually manage to say, "I think he was in absolute awe of you."

"Nah…"

"Yes. And it scared him. And he worried that his Princess P loved you more than him. Which I did. I do. In a different way, of course. But still…" I pick at the couch cushion. "He had hurt me in a way that he suspected I'd never have to worry about with you. And he regretted that he *had* hurt me."

"When did he tell you this?"

I think about it for a second, trying to remember a specific conversation. Did he ever actually say it to me? No. I guess not. But I know it. Just like I know I'd hate fried bulls' testicles without ever tasting them.

I opt for the less colorful, more eloquent, "Not in so many words, I guess. I feel like he did, though. Maybe you're not the only one in this family having visions and otherworldly experiences." I nudge him with my shoulder.

He smiles gamely. "Did you take a detour to Heaven the last time you were on the operating table?"

I laugh at the idea of my being allowed anywhere near Heaven but say haughtily, "Maybe I did, Reverend Smart Ass."

"Did you play a harp? Get an angel's autograph? Ooh… did you have wings?"

"I was only visiting," I supply automatically, playing along. "For some reason, I had to come back here. My job's not done, or something."

He clicks his tongue and chucks me under the chin. "Ah, I see. You got rejected. Well, better luck next time."

"You are such a dick."

He roars before catching himself, then winces. "Agh! Figgity! Hurts to laugh too hard!"

"Serves you right."

I can tell by the gleam in his eyes that he's about to tickle me, not realizing it probably won't end well for him, but before he can do more than hold up his hands and curl his fingers toward me, the front door opens. Judging by the newcomers' quiet entrance, it's Jen and Addi. Seconds later, Jen confirms my suspicions when a muttered curse follows a slight clatter and thump.

"You okay in there?" I call, not really concerned enough to get up.

She lurches through the arch from the entryway to the living room, the large lavender diaper bag dangling from the crook of her right elbow, the infant car seat/carrier containing Addi hanging on the opposite arm.

"Don't mind me, you two. Don't get up."

"I'm under strict orders to stay right here," Brice defends himself.

"I don't feel like getting up," I declare.

She hoists the car seat onto Brice's chair and drops the diaper bag onto the floor. "Why do such little people need such heavy supplies?" she grumbles.

I ignore my friend's griping while I stare at my infant daughter.

Brice and I are so done with having babies. So done. Obviously. After all, he's made the ultimate move to make that true. But if there was any baby whose face could launch a thousand eggs, it's the one in the room with us right now.

My eyes travel from her clear, smooth skin to her

rosebud lips to her dainty nose to her perfect ears to her blonde, silky hair. I'm still as amazed by her as I was the first time I held her, the day I woke up.

That day, I worried that we had missed out on some important bonding time. While I slept, my milk dried up, so I never nursed her at my breast. Which was fine by me, physically. But I did wonder about the emotional effects.

Of course, I didn't need to fret. The minute they placed her in my arms for the first time, we fell mutually in love. She locked eyes with me, and what she conveyed in that single look took my breath away. *I'm yours.*

Since coming home from the hospital, I've been relieved to discover that Addi is my easiest baby by far. It's not that she doesn't act like a newborn; no, she wakes up at least twice each night for feeding, and she soils plenty of diapers, and she fusses when she's gassy or hungry or wet or bored or for any other number of reasons. But she and I seem to be on the same wavelength. I don't usually have to guess what's wrong with her; I simply know. And once I take care of her immediate need, she rewards me with coos and smiles and silence. Most of the time, I can even anticipate her wants before she resorts to the fussing.

Brice claims we're simply getting better at parenting, and I pretend to agree with him, because I don't want to point out something that would hurt his feelings: he doesn't have the same touch with her that I do. Sure, she loves her dad. She smiles and coos for him, like she does for everyone else. But with me, she's at peace. And I feel the same sense of calm when I'm with her. We're *simpatico.*

Now Jen extricates a sleeping Addi from her car seat, laughing when the baby arches her back and sticks out her butt in a mighty stretch. "The princes aren't back yet?"

I say around a yawn, "Nope. Max and the twins are still

at the pool with Jared and Mitzi; Aidan's with Mary, holding court at the retirement center."

"Playing Bingo for Ben Gay?"

Brice laughs then hisses, "Oh, don't make me laugh."

Jen smirks. "Oops. Sorry."

"Anyway, it's still just the king and me here, so pull up a seat and enjoy the silence."

With a raised eyebrow, Jen says, "Uh, you and Brice are *not* the king and queen. You're a handmaiden, and…" She nods toward Brice. "You're the court jester."

"Gee, thanks," he mutters, going back to looking at his phone.

I can tell Addi's working her magic on her Aunt Jen, so I feel it's safe to ask, "Did Vince make it back to Florida without any hitches?"

Keeping her eyes on Addi's face, she answers, "Yes. He had a smooth trip this time. I got a text from him about an hour ago."

Vince has had to return to his own congregation and normal life, but during the past few weeks, he's made several visits back here. Jen's sticking to the "just friends" story, but we all know Vince isn't wearing out the road and sky between here and Florida because he wants to support his best friend, Brice. He definitely wants to be more than "just friends" with Jen.

I think the feeling is mutual, but Jen is cautious. So far, Vince has shown remarkable understanding and patience.

"I… I'm going to move to Florida permanently," Jen announces, still focusing on Addi, as if she's telling the baby this news.

My heart and brain race in tandem. While I struggle to find a coherent thought to grasp and verbalize, she looks expectantly at me.

Brice, as usual, is able to respond first, but he must be off his game, because all he utters is, "Oh, boy."

"And before you say anything, I'm not moving there to be with Vince."

That statement doesn't help me in my quest for something to say. As a matter of fact, it confuses me.

"Okay." Well, it's not the most eloquent thing I've ever said, but it's a start.

"I really loved it down there. The weather, the ocean, the... weather."

"You said that twice."

She shrugs. "I like it. There was stuff to do there."

"You don't have to justify it to me. If you like it there, and you want to live there, and you'll be happy there, I think you should go for it. Right, hon?" I consult Brice, who's conspicuously quiet next to me.

He flops his head to the side and drops his phone in his lap, feigning sleep, complete with fake snores.

I roll my eyes at him, but Jen laughs and moves on. "I don't want you thinking I'm going down there for a guy, that's all." She blushes. "I'm not."

I try not to let my smile take on the knowing tint that will surely make her more defensive when I say, "I believe you. Of course, Vince isn't just any guy."

"You're right..." she says, like someone who knows she's walking into a trap but can't do anything about it.

"So, even if he *is* one of the reasons that make you like Florida and want to live there, what's so wrong with that?" I say.

"I know you think I always make bad choices based on men, but this isn't one of them. I'm not being impulsive. I'm not letting lust get the best of me. You always say—"

I laugh nervously. "Yikes. Maybe I should shut up more often."

With a sheepish grin, she says, "You've been right a lot of the time."

"Being right doesn't give anyone the right to be a judgmental know-it-all." I move from the couch to the arm of the rocker, where she's sitting.

She fingers Addi's silky hair. "I know it's really soon after the whole thing with Wes, but that's just it. It was so nice down there in Florida, far away from him. It's— I can't even go to church here. Because he's *there*."

At this admission, Brice "wakes up" and opens his mouth to say something, but Jen cuts him off. "I know there are other churches in town, but I like Peace. I don't want to go to any other church here. In Florida, I never have to worry about running into Wes."

"Hey." I put my arm around her shoulders and tug her closer to me. "I get it, okay? Please, stop trying to convince me this is the right thing for you to do. My biggest worry about this has nothing to do with your motivations."

She swallows. "What are you worried about? What am I forgetting?"

I sigh. "The only thing wrong with your plan is that you'll be so far away. I'll miss you."

She grins. "Yeah. I won't be available to babysit at a moment's notice, that's for sure."

Not too long ago, I would have been hurt she'd even joke that I'd miss her for that reason. Now, I take her teasing at face value and laugh with her. "Exactly. You're deserting us. Should Brice and I take this personally?"

"You definitely should. Your kids are hideous and bratty, and you and Brice aren't any fun to be around. Duds, every single one of the Northams." She nuzzles Addi. "Except this one. She's sweet. There's still hope for her."

"Maybe you should take her with you to Florida, save her from the fate of being part of this family."

"Hey!" Brice objects.

"I'd buy her the cutest little bikinis and sun hats."

"Make sure you post pictures on Facebook."

Instantly serious, she grasps my hand. "You'll come visit me, right? You and Brice? Or even the whole family? The kids would love the ocean."

Before either my husband or I can answer, we experience a large, loud influx of testosterone. Jen stands and transfers Addi to my arms.

"Mitzi and I will take care of the boys. You three relax for a few more minutes."

I sink into the recently vacated rocker. "Thanks!"

"Aunt Jen!" the three oldest boys chorus as they run past us on their way to the kitchen, with Mitzi and Sasha hot on their heels. Mitzi says "hi" on her way through without pausing, then sing-songs, "Boys! Everyone sit down at the table, please."

Jared, looking sweaty and dazed, enters the room and stands behind Brice, resting his hands on his friend's shoulders. "Dude. I need to thank you for something."

Brice twists before thinking, cringing in pain. "Thank *me*?"

Checking over his shoulder, ostensibly to make sure his wife's still in the kitchen, helping Jen feed the kids a post-swim snack, he says, "I've been trying to convince Mitz for months that Sasha should be an only child. I think hanging out today with your kids sealed the deal."

At Brice's offended expression, I cough to hide my laugh.

"Uh, thanks?" Brice replies. "They're not that bad!"

Quickly, Jared qualifies, "No, no! It's not that they're bad at all. They're just numerous. Having one is so much easier."

"I'll grant you that," Brice says. "And I guess, anything I can do to help a brother."

Jared nods toward his friend's lap. "That hurt pretty bad?"

"Not too bad," he answers, then after glancing at me, amends, "I mean, it doesn't tickle. It's a huge sacrifice. But, you know, I'm tough." He winks at me.

For once, I let it go.

ACKNOWLEDGMENTS

As usual, I have so many people to thank that there's no possible way for me to mention them all here. I am an incredibly blessed person. My life is enriched by the people I come in contact with every single day, whether it be in person or in a virtual sense. I may not have a lot of readers, but the readers I have are the most loyal, encouraging, caring, genuine readers out there. You'd think my family and my pathetic bank account would be motivation enough to keep writing and publishing books, but without readers to read the books, it's all meaningless. I could find other, much more effective ways to make a little extra money every month. I definitely don't do it for the money.

So instead of listing individuals' names (I'm terrified of inadvertently snubbing someone with my sieve-like memory and horrible head for names), let me just say a heartfelt thank you to every single person who's "liked" my Facebook page and put up with my often inane posts. Also, thanks to my Twitter followers who get absolutely nothing from our Twitter relationship, since I'm such a deadbeat tweeter who never actually goes on Twitter to retweet or tag or hashtag or followback any of that other business. It's a wonder I even know the terms. And thanks to my blog followers and subscribers and occasional readers. Your encouragement on the blog front has turned something that used to be a chore (hence my title, *The Reluctant Blogger*) into a viable outlet for personal essays and other writing that doesn't have a place in my fiction but that seems to think it deserves its own venue.

I must give a special shout-out to Pastor Jeff Sippy for answering my questions about prison chaplaincy and for providing me with some excellent insight into that world. I hope it's not creepy hearing a fictional character repeat, word-for-word in some cases, your answers to my questions. They were just such good answers! Thanks for taking that walk down Memory Lane with me.

Facebook groups. I've mentioned you before, and I'll keep mentioning you, because the sense of community and camaraderie that exists in "places" like The Official Chick Lit Group, Chick Lit Goddesses, WIP Support Group, BluePointPress, and The Joy Jar Project is invaluable, especially on those days when I start to believe I'm kidding myself with this whole racket. To experience the kind of support I have experienced from people I've never even met face-to-face is amazing, to say the least. But I wouldn't want to be accused of gushing or being melodramatic, so I'll leave it at that. Love you guys!

Beta readers, you guys outdid yourselves once again and gave me some fantastic feedback. I especially appreciate how willing you were to pitch in during a time of year that is extremely busy. You guys had a *ton* of stuff going on in your personal and professional lives, yet you took the time to read through my *long*, rough manuscript and give me useful suggestions. You also caught the myriad boo-boos that always slip through my bleary-eyed proofreading efforts. Thanks to you, the final product is a much tighter, cleaner book than it was at the beginning of its life. Thank you so, so, so much!

Normally, I mention friends and family first, and I generally gloss over the personal stuff, because it's… well, personal. And while I promise not to say anything here that's too squirm-worthy or TMI, I do feel like you—and you know who you are—deserve a more explicit thank you than I usually give. Thank you to those who have been with me since writing was just a means of escaping a reality that I didn't want to face. Thanks for sticking with me. Thanks for putting up with my distracted moods and my narcissism and my obsession with imaginary people and situations and my all-around weirdness. Thank you for indulging my strange, philosophical, abstract queries and for not sighing or rolling your eyes (too often) when it inevitably came down to, "Because one of my characters…" Thanks for not making me feel like a freak. Thanks for accepting that this is who I am. Thanks for loving me because of it, not in spite of it.

And thank you *all* for reading.

—Brea Brown, 2019

ALSO BY BREA BROWN

The *Secret Keeper* series:

- *The Secret Keeper* (Book 1)
- *The Secret Keeper Confined* (Book 2)
- *The Secret Keeper Up All Night* (Book 3)
- *The Secret Keeper Holds On* (Book 4)
- *The Secret Keeper Lets Go* (Book 5)
- *The Secret Keeper Fulfilled* (Book 6)

The *Underdog* series:

- *Out of My League* (Book 1)
- *Rookie of the Year* (Book 2)
- *Opportunity Knox* (Book 3)

The *Nurse Nate* series:

- *Let's Be Frank* (Book 1)
- *Let's Be Real* (Book 2)
- *Let's Be Friends* (Book 3)

Stand-alone novels:

- *Daydreamer*
- *The Family Plot*
- *Plain Jayne*
- *Quiet, Please!*

www.ingramcontent.com/pod-product-compliance
Lightning Source LLC
Chambersburg PA
CBHW020519260626
47156CB00006B/2063